Late Postmodernism

LATE POSTMODERNISM

AMERICAN FICTION AT
THE MILLENNIUM

JEREMY GREEN

LATE POSTMODERNISM
© Jeremy Green, 2005.

First published in 2005 by
PALGRAVE MACMILLAN™
175 Fifth Avenue, New York, N.Y. 10010 and
Houndmills, Basingstoke, Hampshire, England RG21 6XS
Companies and representatives throughout the world.

PALGRAVE MACMILLAN is the global academic imprint of the Palgrave Macmillan division of St. Martin's Press, LLC and of Palgrave Macmillan Ltd. Macmillan® is a registered trademark in the United States, United Kingdom and other countries. Palgrave is a registered trademark in the European Union and other countries.

ISBN 1–4039–6632–X

Library of Congress Cataloging-in-Publication Data

Green, Jeremy.
    Late postmodernism : American fiction at the millennium / Jeremy Green.
        p. cm.
    Includes bibliographical references (p.) and index.
    ISBN 1–4039–6632–X (alk. paper)
        1. American fiction—20th century—History and criticism.
    2. American fiction—21st century—History and criticism.
    3. Postmodernism (Literature)—United States. I. Title.

PS374.P64G74 2005
813′.5409113—dc22   2004059991

A catalogue record for this book is available from the British Library.

Design by Newgen Imaging Systems (P) Ltd., Chennai, India.

First edition: May 2005

10 9 8 7 6 5 4 3 2 1

Printed in the United States of America.

Contents

Preface and Acknowledgments

During the 1990s, the years of the Gulf War, O.J. Simpson, Monica Lewinsky, the dot.com boom and bust, commentary on the state of letters in the United States might have given the casual reader the impression that literature had never been in a more dismal state. The culture wars of the previous decade, with all the familiar charges of vandalism to the canon and theory-driven destruction of the mission of the humanities, continued on various fronts, while a number of critics and novelists made lugubrious noises about the death of the novel. Arguably, the novel has received such notices from the outset, and certainly in the twentieth century apocalyptic pronouncements have often signaled the introduction of one aesthetic revolution or another—the (old) novel died, so that the (new) novel might live. But the prophecies of the 1990s had a darker cast. Now the novel is dying because literature in general is in terminal decline. Already reading, particularly the kind of concentrated, thoughtful reading that literature demands, is on the wane, undermined by a culture of distraction—TV, movies, videogames, the Internet. Furthermore, the extraordinary success of the printed book, from Gutenberg to airport paperbacks, might finally have reached its limits, as digital technology proves a more efficient and capacious means of storing information.

Or so the prophets claimed. My reaction to this rhetoric was mixed. The anguish seemed pointedly to ignore the diversity and richness of contemporary fiction, which presented the best evidence that the novel is in fact thriving. Admittedly, the old labels—realism, experimentalism, multiculturalism—are now less useful than ever, but the 1990s saw the emergence of a generation of novelists who took their postmodern inheritance in new directions. However, the literary world in which these writers have launched their careers has undoubtedly been affected by changes in the consumption and dissemination of cultural goods. The network of journals, popular and academic reviews, publishing houses, and even bookstores, along with sustaining ideas about the value and importance of literature, have changed, often in ways that have been deleterious for innovative writing. But nostalgia for the novelist's erstwhile authority and for the old print venues is of little use, and often takes a decidedly conservative and technophobic turn. To make sense of fiction in the last years of the twentieth century—and the first years of the twenty-first—entails coming to terms with these altered cultural conditions, the challenges and opportunities they present, while also attending to the distinctive newness of the writing at issue.

I have tried in this work to follow a piece of advice once given me by the late Tony Tanner: write about fiction that really *is* contemporary. This book has grown from an attempt to understand what contemporary literature, particularly postmodern fiction, means at the millennium. It has also been provoked by enthusiasm for the writers I address—which should go without saying, but in these postliterary times, in the academy at least, perhaps does not.

During the writing of this book, I have received help and support from several people, and I would like to take this opportunity to thank them. Several of the chapters began life as conference presentations, and I profited greatly from questions and comments that followed, often addressed to me by people whose names I never caught. However, I would like to single out Jackie Zubeck, who organized the first conference devoted to Don DeLillo; her hard work provided an exceptionally valuable occasion for intellectual exchange. A longer version of the paper I delivered there was subsequently published in *Modern Fiction Studies*; somewhat modified, it now appears as chapter 5.

Anna Brickhouse, Jill Heydt-Stevenson, and Valerie Forman, astute readers all, gave me invaluable help with chapter 3. Conversations with Karen Jacobs, Joseph Conte, Kathleen Fitzpatrick, Mark Osteen, and Marni Gauthier proved very helpful. My greatest debt, however, is to Charlotte Sussman, who offered essential feedback and unstinting support; her faith in the project never wavered. I dedicate the book to her.

INTRODUCTION

Late postmodernism? Isn't such a coinage patently absurd? After all, postmodernism is by definition a term of belatedness: whatever else it signifies, the word refers primarily to the cultural moment or movement that comes after modernism, either succeeding or superseding the earlier formation. To add the modifier "late" suggests that postmodernism, which sprang out of modernism or wiped it from the map, has now entered a phase of decadence and decline, a state that foreshadows, in its turn, a new condition of belatedness. What comes after postmodernism? *Post*-postmodernism? At this point the preposterous and dizzying prospect of an infinite series opens up before the theorist, and all descriptions of the contemporary cultural moment can be considered as measures of a greater or lesser degree of belatedness. Nonetheless, the gesture is useful if it signals that we are no longer postmodern in quite the same way as when the concept was first set loose. Declarations of independence from modernism no longer seem bold or interesting, and we have surely grown entitled to our skepticism about the concept of postmodernism, after so many years, so much labor of definition and disavowal.

Dissatisfaction with the idea of postmodernism has been present from its inception. The word is at once hyperbolic and conceptually fuzzy: the "post" of postmodernism asserts an epochal change without providing any indication of what characterizes the new era. For many, postmodernism seems to be a quality—a deficiency, perhaps—that one attributes to the other: it is that which one denounces, finds at fault, declares oneself against.[1] How then can we begin to agree that existing definitions of postmodernism are in need of modification, when the definitions are at war with each other and might best be disavowed in the first place? As John Frow has suggested, descriptions of postmodernism form a discursive field, a terrain of competing positions, rather than a coherent concept.[2]

The bewildering variety of meanings attached to postmodernism is a measure of the term's success: the word has operated like a virus, crossing disciplinary borders and infecting seemingly discrete bodies of thought. But this is also the reason the term is such a source of frustration and confusion: architectural historians and Heideggerian philosophers mean something quite different when they speak of postmodernism. Following the sociologist Craig Calhoun, four basic ways of using the concept of postmodernism may be discerned.[3] First, postmodernism applies to a stylistic trend in art, architecture, and literature, typified by allusiveness, play, loose or arbitrary structures, fragmentation, willful superficiality, and the collision or commingling of high and low registers. Even a list as cursory as this is vulnerable to the charge that modernism pioneered many, if not all, of these things long before any putative postmodern break, particularly if we enlarge our understanding of modernism to include surrealism, Dada, and other avant-garde movements usually excluded from the Anglo-American canon of literature. Further, accounts of postmodernism across the broad range of the arts have not offered up anything like a conceptually forceful or even unified description of the brave new style. Describing how the artistic practices of the last three decades have differed from, reacted against, and revisited modernism has not led to a coherent model that might be applied across the arts and literature, but such efforts at description have grappled usefully with the distinctiveness, the *difference*, of contemporary culture.

Second, postmodernism has been used as a general term for continental theory, now firmly ensconced in the Anglophone academy. Used thus, the term applies to thinkers as various as Jean Baudrillard, Jacques Derrida, Jean-François Lyotard, Gilles Deleuze, Michel Foucault, and Jacques Lacan. All of these theorists—even Lyotard, who is most closely associated with the concept—have, at one time or another, distanced themselves from the term postmodernism.[4] It is also misleading to group them together, since their differences are very marked and their antagonisms often apparent, even to those at a remove from the French intellectual scene. Nonetheless, as Terry Eagleton has argued, the introduction of post-structuralist ideas into the Anglophone academy has produced a certain orthodoxy in ways of thinking about history, language, desire, and difference that might be described as an ideology of postmodernism.[5] Debates around the stylistic meaning of postmodernism, and the broader import of cultural change, have for better or worse been intertwined with the introduction and reception of post-structuralist ideas.

A third, somewhat different sense of the word emerges from "anti-foundationalist" thinking in philosophy. Influenced by continental thought once again, but looking further back to Heidegger and Nietzsche, this approach, associated in the United States with the work of Richard Rorty, questions the basis of metaphysical certainty and challenges many of the presuppositions of Anglo-American analytical philosophy. Though anti-foundationalist thinking sometimes overlaps with pragmatism, and thus can claim an American ancestry, it frequently avails itself of post-structuralism as well.

A fourth cluster of meanings stems from the use of the word postmodernism in social theory. The claim that we are now living in a postmodern society goes back to arguments about postindustrialism first broached in the 1960s and 1970s.[6] Such approaches emphasize the fundamental role played by new communications media in the formation of society and argue that modern social theory, tied to the thought of Max Weber and Karl Marx, must now be seen as obsolete. As Fredric Jameson has argued, this kind of postindustrial theory is frequently the subtext of other claims made in the name of postmodernism: the "post" declares a conceptual and historical break from modernity and from Marxism.[7]

Late Postmodernism intervenes in the debate around the first of these meanings. It addresses the ways in which literature, particularly the American novel, has been described under the rubric of postmodernism and asks how these accounts should be modified in the light of recent literary activity. How has postmodernism in literature developed in the years since the idea was first launched? Have the tendencies noted in early accounts grown more entrenched, or have the concerns of writers in a second postmodern generation shifted? *Late Postmodernism* is less a typology by which new writing might be categorized, than an attempt to comprehend the conditions under which literary novels are now written and understood. These conditions shape the readership, the literary and political ideologies, the self-understanding, and the aesthetic choices available to writers. To make sense of them is to try to present a snapshot of the *literary field* in advanced capitalism. By literary field I mean that ensemble of interlocking practices and institutions, including the publishing industry, the media, and the university, that constitutes, often in unexamined or unconscious ways, the environment for the practice and understanding of literature.[8] Social, cultural, and political changes are refracted through the literary field and face the writer as a set of problems to be addressed at the level of aesthetic strategy.

My title *Late Postmodernism* refers, in the first place, to the writing of the 1990s, a body of work that has yet to receive significant critical attention. A number of major figures from the first generation of postmodernists produced important work during this decade: Thomas Pynchon, for example, broke a long silence to publish *Vineland* (1990) and *Mason & Dixon* (1995); William Gaddis, who died in 1998, completed another voluminous comic novel, *A Frolic of His Own* (1994), and left behind an intriguing manuscript distilled from a career-long fascination with the mechanization of art, an essay-cum-novel published as *Agape Agape* (2002); John Barth and Robert Coover continued to produce strong work at a steady rate; and William Gass, one of the key proselytizers for experiment and metafiction in the 1960s and 1970s, finally published his monumental novel *The Tunnel* in 1995. Yet with the exception of Pynchon's two works, which were quickly incorporated into the Pynchon critical industry, this body of writing attracted little attention.[9] One novelist of Pynchon's generation did, however, attain critical prominence during the decade. During the 1990s, Don DeLillo, whose works bridge the two generations of postmodern fiction, published *Mao II* (1991), a grim diagnosis of mass media culture and the fate of the novel that anticipated the preoccupations of many late postmodern writers, and *Underworld* (1997), a vast excavation of the second half of the American century. These works, building on the major fiction he published in the 1980s, established DeLillo as the representative postmodern novelist for the end of the century.

DeLillo has been an exemplary figure for the generation of postmodernist writers who began to establish careers during the 1980s and 1990s.[10] His attention to the information overload of contemporary culture, to the morbid allure of spectacles of disaster and violence, and to pervasive feelings of anomie and free-floating anxiety are all aspects of a sensibility that has spoken with particular force to writers and critics during the past decade. In addition, DeLillo's stylistic range—his use, for example, of a variegated palette of reality-effects, from the lapidary precision with which he describes the Bronx neighborhoods of *Underworld* to the eerie, tabloid surrealism of *White Noise*—offered a model for younger writers of ways to present the cultural density of contemporary experience. DeLillo's example is, above all, one of ambition. From his earliest fiction, he has taken on the breadth of American culture, finding strategies to encompass and distill its strange and myriad forms.

The emerging voices of late postmodernism have been no less ambitious. Richard Powers, David Foster Wallace, Joanna Scott, Donald Antrim, Evan Dara, Stephen Wright, Carter Scholz, and Richard Grossman have pursued highly various but equally bold fictional projects shaped by the pressures of American history and culture. The 1990s witnessed the return, after the comparatively conservative 1980s, of highly intelligent and focused literary experimentation, including remarkable work by Carole Maso, David Markson, Rikki Ducornet, Laird Hunt, Dodie Bellamy, Dennis Cooper, and Percival Everett. *Late Postmodernism* is written in the conviction that the last years of the twentieth century saw the publication of a rich body of fiction highly deserving of critical scrutiny. But this book is neither a survey of new writing nor a conspectus of new trends. It is, instead, an examination of the generative pressures on contemporary writing, a study of how the various cultural and economic forces that now impinge on writers condition the relationship between literary strategy and literary field.

One of the curious features of the literary production of the 1990s, an era of notable productivity and ample achievement, was a widespread dismay over the current conditions and future prospects of the novel. This dismay has been shared by critics, essayists, and novelists, and has taken several different forms. A number of novelists have expressed concern over the decline of the readership for serious fiction, often making the point with a simple equation: in the words of Jonathan Franzen, "For every reader who dies today, a viewer is born, and we seem to be witnessing, here in the anxious mid-nineties, the final tipping of a balance."[11] The book and the screen are pitted against each other in a zero-sum game. As the screen—television, film, computers—comes to dominate, so the book recedes or is pushed to the margins. According to this argument, the reading of novels, literary novels in particular, will soon become a specialized or fringe activity, and any remaining notion of literature's cultural authority will be abandoned. In the long term, the book itself, as Sven Birkerts and others have argued, may be destined for extinction as all its functions are taken over by more advanced data storage and retrieval devices.[12] Some of the technologies introduced and developed in the 1990s—the Internet, handheld computers, e-books, hypertext fiction— seemed to give a foretaste of a future without books.

Arguments that see the page and the screen as antagonists locked in a death-struggle are in essence diatribes against mass culture. By these lights, the novel demands the exercise of an informed and critical mind, actively engaged in the production of meaning, while the screen breeds a passive consciousness, and submerges individuality and rationality beneath a welter of images. Such well-worn claims have appeared in various more or less sophisticated guises, even as the academic study of popular culture has raised vigorous challenges to such assumptions, rooting out the elitism of intellectuals, discerning the sophistication of audiences, and analyzing the complexity of mass cultural forms. Yet these oppositions— page versus screen, literary versus popular, elites versus masses—appear to be ineradicable, and for good reason: they express the ambiguous position of culture within Western societies. Culture, particularly academically sanctioned or canonized culture, has long served a dual purpose: on the one hand, it serves to legitimate social difference—the divisions of class, discourse, race, gender, social function—by offering an ostensibly shared terrain of image, language, and practice; and on the other, it supplies a privileged medium in which to express social distinction, a means to mark precisely those differences that culture claims to alleviate. The division between literary and popular culture cannot be entirely overcome, because knowledge and access to the literary field are not evenly distributed; they reflect, however obliquely and elusively, the stratification of an unequal society. At the same time, the opposition between the literary and the popular is far from static; it is constantly constructed, displaced, and reconstituted, more so than ever in recent decades.

Questions of cultural hierarchy predominate in the arguments of the "elegists of the book," as Richard Lanham usefully terms them.[13] Competition from electronic media, with all the resources, rapidity, and reach that advertising revenue can buy, threatens the public for serious reading, and provokes in the elegists dark visions of a post-Gutenberg subject, for whom the traditional concerns of modern literature—interiority, ethical choice, social vision—hold no interest whatsoever. This phantasmagoric being has a family resemblance to the deconstructed or schizophrenic subjects of postmodern theory; but it also has affinities with the degraded illiterates of conservative laments about cultural decline. Anxieties over the future of the book are, by definition, *culturally* conservative, but are not necessarily of a *politically* conservative character, any more than enthusiasm about the latest technology automatically signals political radicalism. Yet the arguments of the elegists do occasionally converge with neoconservative positions in the "culture wars" of the 1980s and 1990s. Where neoconservative commentators deplored the turn within English departments to theory, multiculturalism, and an expanded canon, all—it was claimed—at the expense of the study of great literature, the elegists worry about the turn from reading of all kinds, especially serious literary reading, in favor of the consumption of technologically mediated images. What these pessimistic projections share is a sense of crisis surrounding the public for literature, the authority of literary and critical activity, and the ways in which value is attributed to cultural practices.

At issue in these debates about cultural value and technology is an apprehension of change within the literary field. Such change undoubtedly has to do with the way in which books now compete with several other kinds of media, most notably television, computers, and the Internet. But more importantly, the various roles into which literature has been cast in the modern era, inside and outside the academy—offering an idealized realm of beauty, a critical vantage, a repository of humane values, and the like—have been compromised by a mutation in the attribution of value. What kind of value does literature possess? Why is it worthy of the expenditure of time, money, and effort? The elegists pose these questions with the uneasy awareness that the only answers they can supply belong to an earlier era, one whose last vestiges are vanishing away. In the past two decades, the commodification of culture has proceeded apace, to the point where the cultural realm cannot claim any distinctness from the realm of production and consumption, which in advanced capitalism increasingly entails the manipulation of symbol and information. Arguably, the autonomy of culture was always a delusion; but if so, it was a useful delusion, one that served to justify the prevailing unfreedom of society.[14] Yet the uses of literature that depend on its putative difference from other forms of cultural activity have begun to lose credibility. With the reshaping of audiences in the media age, the growth of knowledge and information processing as an integral part of advanced capitalism, and the redistribution of symbolic forms of value, literature's place has become increasingly uncertain. New discourses within the academy, including multiculturalism and literary theory, as well as late postmodern fiction itself, have engaged in various ways with this reconfiguration of literature's place and meaning.

The novelist's sense of impending obsolescence is bound up with a perceived loss of cultural authority. Although the backward glance that imagines better times for the novel earlier in the century—with the novelist at the center of a de facto coalition of high, low, and middlebrow cultural interests—is fanciful and nostalgic, the anxiety over present conditions remains powerful and indicative of genuine change. If images of cultural authority in earlier times depict an active, informed readership, a large and comparatively homogeneous group of "common readers," the present, consternating picture is one of fragmented attention and subcultural pockets of interest. From the perspective of cultural studies, the image of a mosaic of subcultures can be celebrated in terms of diversity, popular agency, and democracy, but for the novelist lamenting a loss of cultural authority, the predominant impression will be one of heterogeneity and the divergence of fragments of cultural activity. If there remains a common language, a shared set of references points, and widely available narratives, it belongs to the mass-market entertainment industry.

These discussions have an affinity with the continuing debate about the concept of the public sphere. The German philosopher Jürgen Habermas remains the key figure in this debate, even if his theory of the public sphere, propounded as long ago as 1962, has been subject to a number of well-founded criticisms.[15] Habermas bases his argument on an idealized conception of the public sphere in the eighteenth century, a period in which debate conducted through circulated essays, criticism, and commentary, conjoined with conversation in coffeehouses and salons, constituted a space within civil society where rational discussion could generate ideas of an aesthetic, moral, and above all political kind. Critics have noted, and Habermas to some extent has acknowledged, that this account overlooks the extent to which access to the public sphere was founded not just on reason, but on property rights, as well as exclusions of gender, class, and race. But for Habermas the public sphere, in spite of these limitations, retains the kernel of an ideal—the ideal of rational discussion leading to consensus—that must be lamented as the space of discussion within civil society comes to be colonized increasingly by private media interests, by advertising, entertainment, and publicity. As the public sphere gives way to the realm of mass culture, so the citizen gives way to the consumer.

The elegists of the book draw similarly pessimistic conclusions, anchoring their defense of literature in the ideal of a vital civil society. A putative decline of literacy corresponds in their view to a weakening of citizenship, of informed reflection and active participation on the part of individuals within democratic society. Literature plays a crucial role here: fiction illuminates other lives, to be sure, and makes possible cross-cultural recognition. But equally, the novel symbolizes the contention of voices in an active public sphere, and shapes a citizen-subject who is responsive to cultural and political discussion. In this respect, the solitary reader of novels, immersed for hours at a time in imaginary worlds, contrasts with the individual hooked up to various technological devices, everything from phones, fax machines, televisions, and personal CD players, to computer monitors and the Internet.[16] This fusion of culture and technology—*technoculture*—embodies the superficiality, passivity, and information overload that undermine the reflective capacities of the citizen-subject. The subject of consumption, of technoculture, is therefore condemned, either as the dupe of mass culture or as the fragmented psyche of postmodern schizophrenia. Naturally, the corollary to these apprehensive figurations is the idea that the self is crystallized in the writing and reading of literature. But this, as I will try to demonstrate, is a self notable less for its sharpened political consciousness than for its relation to property; it is, in short, a possessive individual, yet another version of the autonomous liberal subject.[17]

Such at least are some of the negative images that haunt the debate about the current status of literature. For the novelist, the problem is one of working from a position of perceived marginality. Various ways of negotiating the margin can be discerned. There are, for example, writers who proceed from a self-consciously oppositional stance, adopting an idiom of stoic isolation and stubborn resistance as a token of their integrity; their writing sets itself against the dominant force of the culture, which they seek to define in terms of mass mediation and generalized falsehood. DeLillo is the most prominent example, particularly as he has begun to craft a position in and around his dealings with the mainstream organs of publicity, an engagement he eschewed for much of his career. It is an attractive stance for other writers, insofar as it implies that writing itself can be understood as a form of resistance. In DeLillo's words, "[w]riting is a form of personal freedom. It frees us from the mass identity we see in the making all around us."[18]

Equally, the writer's marginal position can be treated as a token of minority identity, one that may be redeemed as a position of resistance to a hegemonic structure of power. Thus, Carole Maso, for example, conceives of her own boldly experimental fiction, situated within an avant-garde tradition, as implicitly antagonistic to the dominant (and for her exhausted) realism that is sanctioned in the mainstream press. Realism and the domination of women and minorities become secret sharers, elements of the exercise of cultural power and privilege, which the experimental writer can resist at the level of form and language.[19] The margin can be seen as a place of transgression, a vantage from which the writer works to dismantle dominant languages. Or it can be seen, paradoxically, as a typical position, insofar as the general social condition is one of isolation and comparative powerlessness. The margin is everywhere, the center nowhere: this is the contention implicit in Evan Dara's remarkable novel *The Lost Scrapbook*, though Dara gains particular force as a writer from his attempt to imagine the sundered voices, the atomized pieces of contemporary social life, as convergent, speaking together in some barely imaginable collective protest.[20]

Dara's radicalism stands in contrast to the attempts of certain writers to renegotiate a position of cultural authority in relation to other literary voices, notably those of the minority writers who have come to prominence in the last two or three decades. For the white male writer, in particular, the problem is one of finding a place and stance from which to speak and be heard in a competitive arena of other voices, given that his own identity, formerly naturalized by the prevailing climate of the literary world, is now exposed as a particularly privileged subject position. Equally, the white male middle-class, heterosexual viewpoint cannot be reclaimed as a subject worthy of close examination, without such an effort seeming like an assertion of privilege, a backlash against the great wealth and variety of fiction by minority writers. The open acknowledgment of the associated cluster of uncertainties and anxieties seems largely inadmissible, though projection onto academia, doubly condemned for failing to safeguard the literary tradition and for promoting multiculturalism, seems a regrettably common compromise solution. Thus, in *The Human Stain*, Philip Roth uses the setting of a New England college to examine the politics of identity, mounting an assault on what he perceives to be the blindness and dogmatism of contemporary academia. Jonathan Franzen also reserves scorn for the putative delusions and absurdities of higher education, but takes up the task of grounding a reconciliation with realism—a qualified retreat from the postmodernist literary tradition with which he tried to align himself early in his career—in the exploration of an identity position, that of white, middle-class Midwesterners.

All these writers attempt to negotiate a tension within the literary field. On the one hand, there is an acute uncertainty about the reading public—whether it can still be taken for granted, what levels of knowledge and persistence can be assumed, what kinds of contract must be established with the reader. On the other, there is a no less acute uncertainty about literary value—what it might consist in, how it relates to cultural agency, what criteria can be articulated and shared. Critics who attempt to circumvent or dismiss postmodernism have assumed that the relationship between the public and evaluative criteria is transparent. Either the public should understand, with the help of informed critics and teachers, what value inheres in literature, and learn to recognize it—this is essentially the conservative position; or the inherited criteria, which still reflect the assumptions of modernism, should be discarded, and popular taste treated as a better system of value attribution—this is the populist position. The conservative position assumes that literary value, sometimes bound up with ideas of social or ethical improvement, sometimes in scrupulous avoidance of them, remains fundamentally intact and legible. Competing varieties of popular culture are little better than a distraction—mindless entertainment, glittering trash. By contrast, the populists castigate those who would presume to legislate literary value, applying the epithet "elitist" to critical positions and literary works that impose barriers to comprehension. Here the assumption is that works of wide appeal have a democratic inclusiveness that should be celebrated. This argument has difficulty with the notion of value, not least because the marketplace steps in as an arbitrator. The association between democracy and the marketplace is, after all, a shibboleth of those neoconservative cultural warriors who have been very energetic over the past two decades. *Late Postmodernism* does not defend either position, but examines instead the way a number of novelists have tried to respond to this situation, taking up the problems of cultural memory, the public sphere, and the political vocation of the novel, all of which become urgent in the face of anxieties about the irrelevance of literature.

Late postmodernists have often crystallized these anxieties in the figure of the blocked writer. The struggle to bring work to fruition symbolizes a cultural impasse in which shifts within the literary field impede the creative process itself. Writing comes under such conditions to seem a quixotic or absurd activity, an anachronistic enterprise, thwarted before even fully begun or prolonged past the fit moment for completion. The impediment to writing can make itself felt as a problem internal to the strategies of the work, in which case the block has affinities with the "felt ultimacies" of an exhausted mode of writing, as John Barth put it at an earlier moment in the evolution of postmodernism.[21] Alternatively, the writer's difficulties may relate to the context of publication and reception. Why labor on a piece of literature that will go unread or misread? The writer's faith in her vocation collapses in the face of a general indifference to literature.

The extreme version of this incomprehension between writer and reader (or non-reader) finds expression in the trope of solipsism. In this scenario, explored with particular acuity in the work of Richard Powers, Kathryn Davis, and David Markson, writing becomes a supremely isolated activity, the product of a mind cut off from other minds. Writing stripped of its communicative function is a limit-case of literature's autonomy, its legislation of its own evaluative criteria. In a qualified and highly self-conscious return to a modernist problem, the literary work scrupulously divorces itself from commercial, utilitarian, or ideological functions. Yet in this case, the work of literature does not thereby achieve a purity and aesthetic rigor that compensates for its intransigent refusal to have any use whatsoever, but rather stumbles up against its own incapacity and inertia, and is marked by lack and melancholy. As such, writing confirms solipsism, and despairs of communication, not to mention cultural influence.

There are a number of ways to make sense of these motifs of incommunicability. The problems and paradoxes of the literary work's autonomy, hitherto felt more strongly perhaps in poetry than in the novel, can be construed in terms of the austere logic of modernism, and this approach certainly allows one to grasp the untimely modernist practice of David Markson. But at the same time, figures of solipsism, incommunicability, and failure are closely connected to an uncertainty about the status of cultural memory. For a number of late postmodernist writers, a concern with tradition—with a shared memory of literature's past—constitutes both a rejoinder to notions of postmodern amnesia and a fretful confirmation of them. The problem of memory comes to the fore inasmuch as literary activity depends upon and incites acts of remembering. But in the absence of a serious readership, the appeal to the memory embodied in texts, particularly the texts of the canon, has no resonance. It would be too hasty to assume that the appeal to the literary canon, even as a lamentable absence, automatically aligns late postmodernism with cultural conservatism, although the rhetoric of pessimism is often a mark of conservative discourse. The issue, rather, is of finding a means—a form of interrogation or reconstruction—to think about how things came to be the way they are now.

In this respect, a more instructive comparison is with Fredric Jameson's paradoxical description of the postmodern as "an attempt to think the present historically in an age that has forgotten how to think historically in the first place."[22] A number of the writers I address in this study imagine a break between the way things were and the way they are now, though the precise nature of this break and the causes that led up to it remain obscure indeed. To imagine a lacuna in the emergence of the contemporary situation from history means to imagine an irreducible difference between the present and the past. As an aesthetic choice and a heuristic tool, this strategy's force depends on the break being difficult to pinpoint or explain away. In this respect, late postmodernist fiction resembles postmodernist theory, for which the postmodern present appears utterly unlike the past—much more skeptical, suspicious, ironic—even though the causes of this transfiguration remain elusive for many theorists.

For the contemporary novelist changes in the nature of the public sphere, particularly as a consequence of technological innovation, are an ineluctable feature of the present. Print venues for publication, criticism, and general discussion, all of which contribute to the formation of the literary field, do still exist of course, but they offer a public forum that differs qualitatively from the ubiquitous television and computer outlets of publicity and debate. The writer's sense of incommunicability—of solipsism and amnesia—presents itself in this context as a problem of cultural politics, a struggle for resources, prestige, and authority. Even though new media technologies seem to offer new spaces for the reception and discussion of literature, including Internet bulletin boards, webzines, and e-mail lists, as well televised book clubs, print culture tends nonetheless to be tied to an older and increasingly unworkable model of the public sphere. As a result, the mass-mediated publics of postmodernity can appear threatening and ominous, alien agglomerations that colonize all cultural and psychic space, supplanting the book, even to the extent of wiping it out altogether. The struggle to occupy positions within the literary field is played out across a public/private divide that continually mutates in surprising ways.

It is inevitable, perhaps, that the adjective "late" should suggest decadence and decline. Certainly, the recent dissatisfaction with postmodernism, on the part of critics, commentators, and some writers, indicates that the great promises that came with the introduction of the concept—promises often couched in the rhetoric of "inverted millenarianism," as Fredric Jameson has observed, announcements of the end of this or that, of ideology, metaphysics, the great divide between high and low culture, and the like—have ceased to be compelling.[23] Yet postmodernism cannot simply be written off as a *fin-de-siécle* trend. The problems the term attempts to name—problems in late postmodernism of cultural hierarchy and cultural change, of politics and the public/private divide, of memory and tradition—are bound up with the survival of literature. They cannot be disintricated from the concerns of modernism; indeed, if anything, late postmodernism returns with urgency to those concerns, and thereby rejects, or at least revises, some of the bold pronouncements of the first generation of postmodernism, notably claims of annealing the divisions of the cultural terrain. *Late Postmodernism* argues that imaginative engagement with this fissured terrain has produced a significant body of contemporary writing, one that will repay further study.

The present book undertakes a series of case studies of recent postmodern fiction, both mainstream and experimental, to assess the widespread pessimism over the future of literature, and to argue that the novel is not exhausted or doomed, but continues to transform itself in unexpected and compelling ways. The opening chapters move from the pessimism of Barth and Roth, writers late in their careers who have made powerful fiction out of a sense of despondency over the future of American letter, to the strategies of accommodation to a new literary field hazarded by Jonathan Franzen. The threat to cultural memory, broached in the work of Roth, Barth, and Franzen, takes center stage in the ambitious and innovative writing of Richard Powers, Kathryn Davis, and David Markson. Novels by Don DeLillo and the little-known Evan Dara address the question of how literature might imagine and confront the bewildering public spheres of the postmodern era. All of the novelists I address, celebrated and obscure, have in their own particular fashion made the novel's status as a form of inquiry, representation, cognition, and critique integral to their projects, and have done so with a perspicacity and force that undercuts the fatalism that they occasionally express.

Perry Anderson has suggested that postmodern works might be divided into two broad camps according to their aesthetic conservatism or radicalism. Anderson makes use of Robespierre's distinction between the "citra-revolutionary," those moderates of the French Revolution who wished "to draw the Republic back from the resolute measures necessary to save it," and the "ultra-revolutionary," fanatics who were determined to push forward into further extreme and excessive acts.[24] Postmodern art, architecture, and literature can by analogy be described as "citra" and "ultra": the citra-postmodern would be that artistic practice that returns from the radicalism of the high modernist moment to offer "the ornamental and more readily available"; the ultra-postmodern, on the other hand, would be a variety of practice that radicalizes modernism, often to the point of refusing "immediate intelligibility or sensuous gratification" (102). *Late Postmodernism* traces an arc from the citra-, particularly the fiction of Roth and Franzen, to the ultra-postmodern, best represented by Evan Dara's challenging novel. The range of literary strategies for the majority of the writers falls somewhere along this arc. By the same token, the texts make a variety of different claims on the print and media publics. It is a telling irony that Roth and Franzen, among the most pessimistic of the authors I address, have achieved recognition beyond the usual print-based venues of the literary public sphere. Roth's novel was treated to a film adaptation, while Franzen's was snapped up by both Hollywood and Oprah Winfrey. In contrast, Dara's novel was published by a small press, and has received little recognition in any media, yet it remains an optimistic, even utopian work, because of its thoroughgoing commitment to critique and to innovation. For the late postmodern novel, the issue of establishing a partial reading public across the heterogeneous mediascapes must be solved at the level of aesthetic strategy as well as that of marketing images.

In my opening chapter, I examine the place of literary fiction in accounts of postmodernism and explore the ways in which the changing status of the novel reflects mutations within the literary field. In particular, I am concerned with theoretical and critical claims that postmodernism has come to an end, that it can be jettisoned as a category of understanding, or simply rewritten as a term denoting a historical period. Such obituaries and renovations are efforts to foreclose the problems of the contemporary that the term postmodernism, however imperfectly, tries to articulate. These problems have to do in particular with the uncertain status of cultural value. I argue that the developments of recent decades within capitalism—the shift toward an information and service economy—have dissolved the ways in which inherited ideas of value, ideas bound up with the legitimation of an exploitative and oppressive social order, function in the literary field. As writers have become aware of these shifts, they have tried to make sense of the new pressures and difficulties of an altered cultural landscape through their writing, through essays and statements, but above all within novels themselves.

The second chapter of the study looks at cultural pessimism among writers and critics, and focuses in detail on the work of two eminent novelists—John Barth and Philip Roth—who have, in distinct and divergent ways, written in response to the mutations of cultural value examined in the introduction. In the last decade proclamations of the death of the novel and the book, previously aired during the heyday of Marshall McLuhan, have returned to the conversation about literature and the contemporary moment. For many cultural conservatives the blame for these developments lies with university literature departments, and the fall-out from the culture wars has been an attempt to justify and celebrate the reading of literature outside the poisoned environment of academe. These pronouncements and projects provide the context in which I read the work of Barth and Roth, novelists who have remained active through the course of profound changes in the status of and critical discourse surrounding literature.

Barth's essays over the course of three decades chart the course of the concept of postmodern fiction, from early formulations, through intense debates of definition in the 1970s and early 1980s, to the melancholy assumption of obsolescence in the near future. Read as a narrative, these essays pursue the promise and dissolution of postmodern fiction as a symbol of cultural consensus. In discussing Barth's most recent novel, *Coming Soon!!!*, a self-conscious intermingling of the novelist's own body of work with the fortunes of the Chesapeake showboat (an anachronistic form of entertainment that undergoes innumerable nostalgic revivals), I argue that the text tries to construct a model of tradition and reference, an inscribed cultural memory, so that the showboat—of entertainment, of fiction—can be seen as a parodic but essential ark, a figure for survival and continuity.

Although Philip Roth is not usually grouped with the postmodernists, his work fits into an examination of the contemporary literary field, not least because he is an acutely observant and argumentative writer, as well as a cultural pessimist.[25] In *The Human Stain*, Philip Roth makes intertextual use of two kinds of plot, Greek tragedy and African American narratives of racial passing. The tensions and affinities Roth establishes between these scenarios allows him explore the links between cultural value, literacy, and identity in the millennial moment of theory's dominance of the humanities and scandal's dominance of the public arena, aspects of contemporary culture symbolically linked in the novel. Roth labors to salvage a rationale for the novel in an unlettered age, reclaiming for it a complexity and elusiveness he associates with the great works of modernism. For both writers, the novel is the privileged locus of the breakup of social, aesthetic, and cultural consensus, its loss of authority a token of the changes it attempts to comprehend. To throw these positions into relief, I close this chapter by looking briefly at Carole Maso's polemical rejoinder to cultural pessimism.

Chapter 3 looks at Jonathan Franzen's best-selling novel *The Corrections* in the light of Oprah Winfrey's Book Club. Winfrey's spectacularly popular Book Club appeared to discredit anxieties about the decline of reading and the end of the novel, yet close examination of the phenomenon reveals fault lines between literacy and democracy, the public sphere and the mass media, the citizen and the consumer. Franzen's notorious disinvitation from the Book Club show exposed these fault lines. Therefore, I discuss the implications of the Book Club in relation to Franzen's own attempt to craft a fusion of postmodern and realist modes. I examine the success and failure of this strategy, its attempts to elide social and cultural contradictions, through a reading of patterns of class identity and political quietism in *The Corrections* itself.

Chapter 4 brings together three remarkable projects: Richard Powers's *Galatea 2.2*, David Markson's epitaphic series (consisting of *Wittgenstein's Mistress, Reader's Block*, and *This Is Not a Novel*), and Kathryn Davis's *Walking Tour*. These works are concerned with the endangered status of cultural memory and the consequent expropriation of the author in relation to his or her texts. Each writer finds a different way to express, if not to account for, the mysterious break that separates the writer from a living tradition, a cultural memory, that might give meaning to the work over which they labor. In Powers's novel, the setting is academic, and the problem is explicitly that of the canon and its role in the formation of a writer who depends on the embedded memory of the corpus of literary works, now challenged by radical critical theory and practice. The novel turns to cognitive science, and the project of constructing an artificial intelligence, as a way of reflecting on the meaning of memory, perception, solipsism, and sentiment, simultaneously naturalizing the self-replicating cultural intelligence embodied in literature and undoing its humanist pretensions to the inculcation of moral sensibility. For Markson, by contrast, whose work self-consciously affiliates itself to modernism and reflects on the belatedness of such a desire, the break from living tradition is literalized as all tradition, conjured as citations and fragments, assumes the status of epitaph or *memento mori*. With an irony Markson savors, the assemblage of such epitaphs reprises many of the essential elements of a thoroughly modernist project, at once participating in a paradoxically recuperative break from the past, and determinedly pursuing the ideal of the work about nothing, a work of pure style, though in this case the style is in turn supremely self-effacing. In Kathryn Davis's novel, the break from tradition is associated with the expropriation of imaginative works (literary and artistic) as a special kind of intellectual property, a process associated in the novel's dystopian scenario with new forms of computer technology and the conversion of all texts to versions of "shareware." Yet the technophobic connotations are offset by Davis's subversive use of a folk tale from the medieval Welsh *Mabinogion*. This elliptical fable provides the narrative elements and much of the incidental imagery for the novel's ambivalent treatment of cultural memory as endangered and regenerative. For each of the writers addressed in this chapter, the problem of cultural memory is now central to the imaginative enterprise of writing a novel; engaging with the endangered resource of tradition involves contesting postmodern ahistoricism, while also examining the fundamental basis of categories such as the author, reader, and frame of reference.

Chapter 5 examines the notion of the public in the work of one of the leading postmodern writers of the past two decades, Don DeLillo. I argue with reference to recent work on the public sphere by Mark Seltzer and Michael Warner that DeLillo's fiction explores the role of fantasy and violence in figuring the "pathological" media public. DeLillo's work imagines—and questions—the collapse of private space and the threat to stable identities in relation to an epochal shift from word to image, from book to screen. My discussion of the public sphere in DeLillo's work opens a space for the consideration of Evan Dara's polyphonic novel *The Lost Scrapbook*. This is perhaps the most formidable political novel of the 1990s, because it imagines, through its highly disrupted form and its investigation of new kinds of connection (founded in models from particle physics, musicology, and systems theory), the basis for a politics of the counterpublic sphere, founded on a recuperation of the derelict concepts of community and utopia. This novel exemplifies one possibility for forging the link between formal and political radicalism.

The postmodern novel enters the new century amidst a portentous clatter of death notices—for postmodernism, for the reading public, and for the printed book. On a slightly different frequency, one hears complaints that the novel has abandoned all those things that are essential to its continued existence, namely psychological insight and moral observation, those qualities of the great fiction of the past that newfangled postmodernism so dismally fails to deliver. The apocalyptic and traditionalist positions are alike in their refusal to countenance change in the form and cultural situation of the novel. While the prophets of doom look apprehensively at new technologies and shifting academic priorities, the aesthetic conservatives deplore change within the novel itself. The fiction of late postmodernism embraces—with a measure of anxiety, with a modicum of hope—cultural and social change, and makes of altered conditions new kinds of fiction, writing in such a way as to grasp the contradictions and involutions of the new media environment. For the reader willing to take up the challenge of this writing, the novel continues to offer insight, inquiry, and critique in full measure.

Chapter 1

Late Postmodernism and the Literary Field

Obituaries

In recent years, a number of critics have announced the demise of postmodernism. The death notices issue from all points of the critical compass. For some on the left, postmodernism has been primarily an academic ideology that grew out of the despair of the post-1968 generation, a failure of political nerve, and an immense evasion of the continued depredations of late capitalism. News of postmodernism's expiration can therefore be taken in good spirits, since urgent political and intellectual problems might now be addressed without a detour through the latest neo-Nietzschean mills flown in from France. Everything that such a theoretical trend ruled out of court—history, capital, the subject—can now be brought back to the table, and not before time. "Postmodernism is now history," Alex Callinicos has declared with evident satisfaction.[1]

For conservative critics, on the other hand, postmodernism was never a strong temptation, and its heralded departure offers hope that the academy can be cleansed of continental nihilism. Some commentators even tried to lay the blame for the events of September 11, 2001 at postmodernism's door, as if to suggest that the trauma of the terrorist attacks on the U.S. will finally wake liberal intellectuals from their relativistic slumbers.[2] Critics of a more subtle and inquiring disposition, such as Hal Foster and John Frow, have also put temporal brackets around the concept, even if the retrospection this affords turns out to be a rather complicated matter.[3] In its more limited application to particular artistic, literary, and architectural styles, postmodernism may also be nearing the end of its usefulness as a descriptive term.

Frustration with the term is understandable: its success, as measured by the copious amounts of ink shed in efforts of definition, seems to be in direct proportion to its overuse, inflation, and sheer fuzziness. Yet obituaries for postmodernism are attempts to refuse or dismiss one or another aspect of the problems—of culture, period, and style—to which the word, however vaguely and portentously, gestures. It seems more useful to retain the allusiveness of the term, while registering its *aging*; to recognize, in other words, postmodernism*s*, distinctions of mode and moment within "full postmodernity."[4]

To speak of postmodernism as multiple is to recognize that the term is always at variance with itself, that definitions of postmodernism, whether as a new epoch or as a coherent stylistic practice, have struggled to name their object, or to match evidence to periodizing assertion. Characteristically, groundbreaking attempts to theorize postmodernism have relied on the list, the jumble of exhibits that are swept indiscriminately into a single, and therefore underdetermined, category.[5] The point of such lists, however, is in part rhetorically to mark the heterogeneous mixing of styles and modes, the confusion or cross-fertilization between media, high and low forms, and political positions that overthrow existing typologies. As a move in the language game called postmodernism, the list carries the burden of the specific, while also underscoring the break from an earlier, more composed and intelligible, era.

Here is Fredric Jameson's list:

> Andy Warhol and pop art, but also photorealism, and beyond it, the "new expressionism"; the moment, in music, of John Cage, but also the synthesis of classical and "popular" styles found in composers like Phil Glass and Terry Riley, and also punk and new wave rock (the Beatles and the Stones now standing as the high-modernist moment of that more recent and rapidly evolving tradition); in film, Godard, post-Godard, and experimental cinema and video, but also a whole new type of commercial film . . .; Burroughs, Pynchon, or Ishmael Reed, on the one hand, and the French *nouveau roman* and its succession, on the other, along with alarming new kinds of literary criticism based on some new aesthetic of textuality or *écriture* . . . The list might be extended indefinitely.[6]

If this catalog can be said to advance any definition, it involves at once a sense of historical sequence (postmodernism succeeds earlier styles, as Warhol comes after abstract expressionism), and also an immanent logic of stylistic change that does not map neatly onto historical periods (the modernist Beatles give way within a few years to postmodernist punk rock). Such a definition by example includes the claim of cultural mixing, the intermingling and revision of hierarchies of value (high composers incorporating low styles), and argues implicitly for the overthrow of the attendant kinds of understanding and organizing of cultural experience.

Postmodernism in Jameson's account also includes ostensibly experimental and abstruse kinds of work, as well as the products of the culture industries: postmodernism is a characteristic of both kinds of work, and this distinguishes it from modernism, for critics and historians are not, on the whole, given to speaking of the modernism of popular or mass cultural products from the early part of the twentieth century. Indeed, modernism is often notable for its scrupulous attempts to differentiate itself from commercial culture.[7] Postmodernism, as it emerges from Jameson's list (and indeed from his book as a whole), generates very different kinds of cultural experience, some apparently of wide popular appeal, others of a highly specialized nature, and it also makes itself felt in a variety of intellectual activities, from film and music to criticism and theory.

An epochal shift, claims Jameson, underlies all of these changes, even though it has become increasingly difficult to establish cogent historical descriptions. Jameson intends his approach to the problem of postmodernism, particularly what he sees as its disabling ahistoricism, to operate at the largest, as well as the most minute level—from the particulars of stylistic innovation to changes in the mode of production itself—and it is one of the most impressive aspects of his project that he does indeed move with dialectical facility between them. In a much more modest way, however, one might note that Jameson's cited examples no longer seem as daring or *outré* as they once did; indeed, many of them have since assumed the status of canonical works. Warhol is an institution, a museum staple, and a landmark in art history; Godard's contemporary works are largely ignored and his reputation rests on his role within the *nouvelle vague*; punk rock is the focus of nostalgia and historical accounting. Have these works ceased to be postmodern? Is the category of postmodernism tied to its illustrations, and hence something that might need to be updated or even discarded as more recent developments come into focus?

The idea of a historical break remains central to formulations of postmodernism, even as the relational and ambiguous character of the concept continues to haunt the historical accounts in which it is placed. To comprehend the meanings that postmodernism has been given involves making sense of the ways in which the rift with modernism has been understood. Should it be seen as a subtle series of variations on established themes, a devolution, an emancipation, or even a violent Nietzschean act of forgetting? As a term that encompasses the idea of a break, postmodernism takes shape uneasily between the emergence of something so new it remains unnamed and unknown, designated only by its relation to a distinct and different anterior (modernism), and a condition of historical succession, bound up with the ending of an earlier era, with decadence and decline, the aftereffects of modernism. Stylistic changes in literature, art, and architecture can be assessed as ruptures or revolutions insofar as they can claim originality and distinctiveness, in many instances through a productive antagonism to established modernist styles and forms. It is often claimed, for example, that postmodernism in literature begins with a reaction against the canonization of the great modernist writings of the earlier twentieth century—Joyce, Eliot, Pound—during the 1950s. But the epitome of this move is the impudent precision with which Charles Jencks dates the end of the International Style in architecture: "Modern Architecture died in St. Louis, Missouri on July 15, 1972 at 3:32 p.m. (or thereabouts) when the infamous Pruitt-Igoe scheme, or rather several of its slab blocks, were given the final *coup de grâce* by dynamite."[8] Jencks emphasizes the stylistic innovations that set the new architecture apart from the austerity and seriousness of the Modern, the playful historicism and depthless citation of earlier architectural styles by which postmodernism differentiates itself. The effort of differentiation, for the architect as much as the critic, depends on a partial and antagonistic view of the dominant earlier style.

In the case of literature, these splits and antagonisms have been more difficult to describe, and in the process of differentiating postmodernism from its antecedents, valuable new perceptions of modernism have emerged. The landscape of canonical Anglophone modernism, over which the impregnable fortresses of Eliot, Pound, and Joyce once brooded, now looks a good deal more variegated and complex; an awareness of modernism's internationalism has begun to offer a more nuanced understanding of the dynamics of the literary period. Genealogists of postmodernism have taken advantage of an expanded field of modernism, to find precursors in such previously marginal and idiosyncratic figures as Gertrude Stein, Raymond Roussel, and Alfred Jarry, and the recovery of neglected figures has been useful in interrogating and displacing the legacy of inherited accounts of modernism. And in many cases, postmodern writers, especially those of a radical, experimental cast, have pioneered the recovery of marginal modernists.[9] Equally, the emphasis on formal innovation and antirealism in postmodernist literature makes possible connections with earlier literary forebears, including Lautréamont, for example, or Laurence Sterne, whose *Tristram Shandy* (1759–1767) can be considered the first great antinovel, or even to Rabelais's still-astonishing *Gargantua* (1534) and *Pantagruel* (1532). But the postmodernism of Sterne or Rabelais is not *our* postmodernism: the meaning of the remarkable textual practice in these works is quite different for us than for their first readers.

In a different register, the other usages of postmodernism and postmodernity that are now inextricable from the word, notably in the areas of literary theory, philosophy, and social theory, have involved attempts to formulate a historical fracture, giving substance to the term by reference to its difference from an earlier epoch. Hence, the notion that postmodernism can be seen as a more or less intelligible break with the "grand narratives" of modernity, derived in particular from the work of Lyotard, leads to a much more complicated sense of the problems and values stemming from such temporal or epochal position-taking.[10] Postmodernism establishes itself by declaring other modes of thought and practice obsolete, while still cultivating a skeptical attitude toward the idea of historical periods and stages, tainted as they are by an insidious teleological intent. Yet as the cannier theorists recognize, the effort to forge an oppositional relationship to the past, often conceived, as John Frow has shown, in terms of binary tables of attributes, frequently compromises or even confounds itself.[11] Although the climate of postmodernism has allowed critics and writers to grasp previously neglected aspects of modernism, postmodern celebrations of pluralism and difference are often mounted on a distinctly monolithic conception of the modern. The modern becomes the antithetical category by which postmodernism defines itself. Postmodernism claims on its own behalf an enlightened, skeptical, and subversive potential, while modernism, by contrast, remains intractably caught up in its metaphysical presuppositions. In this way, postmodernism accords itself a superior wisdom, and casts modernism into the role of the comparatively primitive or benighted prior state.

Ironically, this strategy reproduces the structure of modern thought, which knows itself by placing itself in opposition to ideas about the premodern worldview. As Peter Osborne argues, this means that postmodernism tacitly continues the project of modernity even as it claims to break free from it: the postmodern knows itself through the shortcomings of the modern.[12] This is all the more evident if one emphasizes the character of the word itself: the postmodern is the state or phase that comes after the modern—but *after* in what sense? The modern might be seen as a sealed historical period, one that ended at some point during the twentieth century, perhaps World War II, or the 1960s.

But the word *modern* retains the sense of the current, the contemporary. To press the analogy with modernity a step further, one might begin to think of postmodernism as a process, a perpetual questioning, rather than a sealed historical period. Hence, for Lyotard, the postmodern can also be a moment of skepticism within the modern, or, as he provocatively observes, the modern in a nascent state.[13] For Fredric Jameson, by contrast, the modern and the postmodern are historical categories that must be understood in relation to the development of capitalism. Postmodernism comes into being when the processes of capitalist expansion across the globe and the colonization of consciousness bring about a fundamental change in the character of capitalist culture. Postmodernism for Jameson represents the cultural logic of this most recent moment, the third age of machine production, according to the schema of the Marxist economist Ernest Mandel. It is, in this sense, less a set of ideas or new styles, than a pervasive cultural process that can, indeed must, be read through the dizzying array of new styles and forms.

Postmodernism has yet to establish its own legitimacy. The "inverted millenarianism," as Fredric Jameson puts it, whereby endings are announced—the end of art, the end of history, the end of grand narratives—bespeaks the effort to formulate a radically new conscious-ness of the present, yet remains a negative gesture, a refusal of old categories rather than a construction of new ones.[14] Ends are declared but without any cogent sense of what might supersede the exhausted categories. And in this respect, one might suggest that the gesture of declaring an ending tends to freeze historical process, offering up reified categories of thought in a gesture of disavowal and repression.

Retreats

How then should we understand the desire to be done with postmod-ernism, to declare it finished and of purely historical interest, a late-twentieth-century phenomenon that can now be jettisoned? Such an impulse recognizes the success and the limits of the concept. What once seemed a new and exciting way of looking at problems has now been absorbed to a greater or lesser extent. How much really has been changed by postmodern ways of thinking—whether the influx of continental the-ory and the stylistic changes of the last three decades truly represent a paradigm shift, or whether these phenomena are comparatively superfi-cial and not of lasting interest—remains open to debate. Dissatisfaction arises once the weakness and silences of the new model theory become gradually apparent, or fail to supply adequate descriptions of the evolving situation. Furthermore, rapid turnover in artistic trends makes adequate description difficult, and postmodernism itself might well be subject to this principle of accelerated obsolescence.

So a measure of weariness and skepticism is inevitable. To say, however, that postmodernism has come to an end, or that the impulses that encouraged the formulation of the concept in the first place are now played out, entails a return to earlier modes and concerns. In this case, the way forward—beyond postmodernism—turns out to look very much like the way back—back to the less contentious issues and paradigms that postmodernism supposedly destroyed. This is not a return to modernism, but an attempt to bypass the formal challenges that link postmodernism to modernism, to return to transparency and representation, to put aside, once and for all, radical innovation and new stylistic practices.

Wendy Steiner's history of "Postmodern Fictions, 1970–1990" in the *Cambridge History of American Literature* offers a case in point.[15] Steiner, whose argument has a certain prominence given its venue, asserts that literary-historical accounts of postmodernism are tied to the critical language of the modernist era: "Applied to contemporary literature, the [modernist] approach has produced a parallel ambiguity in the term *postmodernism*: it means both the stylistically innovative writing from the 1960s to the 1990s, such as that by Pynchon or Barth, and the literature of the period as a whole. The move to equate experimental postmodernism with the overall post-1960 period is equivalent to that equating High Modernism with modernism in general: the technically self-conscious line becomes a synecdoche for the whole period" (428). Steiner denounces critical accounts, from Clement Greenberg to Jerome Klinkowitz, that equate formal innovation with artistic importance. The idea that literature and art develop in a linear fashion, one set of problems and developments superseded by the next, has an inescapably mechanistic quality that woefully underestimates the complexity of any cultural moment. One not-so-incidental effect of the privileging of the formal/experimental line, Steiner contends, is the marginalization of women and minority writers, who tend to be omitted from the honor-rolls of the pioneers. Such versions of literary history paid undue attention to the "high postmodernists" of the 1960s and 1970s, by whom Steiner means Thomas Pynchon, John Hawkes, Donald Barthelme, John Barth, and Kurt Vonnegut, at the expense of other emerging kinds of writing during the same period. Thankfully, postmodernism so defined no longer dominates the reception of contemporary literature.

According to Steiner, the literary history of the last three decades comprises the breakdown of high postmodernism, the final eradication of modernism, and the rise of a new kind of realism. The "modernist division between avant-garde and traditional fiction" (499) loses credibility during the 1970s and 1980s; experimental technique becomes available to writers not self-consciously attempting to follow and out-maneuver modernism, notably women and minority authors. Postmodernism, in Steiner's view, can be recuperated as a term once it is understood in relation to the "merging of social and aesthetic problematics" (527) in fiction written by women, fiction that engages with and contests the gendered and racialized construction of history and reality. The weakening of categorical distinctions founded on the formal qualities of fiction (experimentalism/traditionalism) allows the consideration of what Steiner calls "autobiographical factors" (528) to come to the fore. Fiction allegedly centered on the examination of form—by the close of her discussion, Steiner labels it simply "metafiction" (thus undoing the rather more subtle examination achieved in her earlier pages)—can be seen as an anachronism, a position backed up by shifts in public taste and reflected in the decisions made by prize committees. "By the mid-1990s," Steiner concludes, "metafiction had declined in favor of the dramatization of personal voices in confessional modes" (535). Writers who have inherited something from the generation of "high postmodernists" (not to mention modernists) are consigned to oblivion in their own time, and even distinguished foreign writers associated with postmodernism are brusquely cast aside: "Outside the United States, such metafictionists as Salman Rushdie, Italo Calvino, Gabriel García Márquez, and Julian Barnes are still enthusiastically received; in America, however, critical taste has moved on" (529). Steiner takes the enormous popularity of memoirs during the 1990s as evidence of a new realism, one typified by the (re)discovery of the inner life of ordinary people and the "extraordinary beauty in the unpromisingly ordinary," qualities to be found abundantly in "[p]erhaps the most powerful novel of the 1990s, Annie Proulx's *The Shipping News* (1992)" (537).

The issue here is not whether the texts Steiner champions deserve such praise—whether, for instance, *The Shipping News* really *is* the most powerful novel of the 1990s—but rather the way in which her version of literary history is written as the progressive elimination of modernism. Steiner's postmodernism, as she terms the (non-experimental) fiction of the 1980s and 1990s, overcomes the divisive esotericism of modernism and the high postmodernism that succeeded it, and achieves "an integration of style, realist depth, and the recovery of previously ignored points of view" (535). It is telling, however, that Steiner celebrates the rise of confessionalism in all media, from best sellers to daytime television, and values the weakening of the distinction between fiction and memoir. The ideal postmodern novel, it seems, aspires not to be a novel at all. Instead, it works to represent social reality, both in the sense that it offers news of the unconsidered and insignificant, lives left unexamined, and also by standing for the concerns of social groups previously marginalized. Postmodern fiction, according to Steiner, sanctifies the ordinary and celebrates "the extraordinary commonplace of love" (538), thereby gathering social diversity into the humanist universal.

In spite of her distrust of formal questions, and the embarrassment that attends her attempts to discriminate and evaluate texts—she is obliged to fall back on appeals to beauty, power, and wonder, terms that are refusals to construe, contextualize, or interpret—Steiner's history illustrates important trends in thinking about recent literature. The movement from high postmodernism, which engaged with the legacy of modernism in its own highly specialized and fetishistic way, to Steiner's postmodernism of minority social groups and popular appeal, is crafted as a narrative of progress, an overcoming of disabling cultural divisions and silences. Steiner's appeal to consensus and to literary prizes as symbols of consensus, taken up in her recent account of serving as a judge for the 1997 National Book Critics' Circle Award for Fiction, tries to inscribe literary value onto shared cultural consciousness.[16] A realism redeemed by beauties of language overcomes the taste formation of cultural elites in favor of a close relationship with a diversity of voices, writers themselves, and the subjects of their fiction. Formal difficulty, by contrast, which essentially means the disruption of realism, bears the stigma of the antidemocratic, the elitist, the privileged.

Steiner's postmodern return to realism depends on a refusal of postmodernity. By describing formal difficulty purely in terms of metafiction, a description only partially adequate even for the most relentlessly experimental of the high postmodernists, Steiner neglects to consider the ways in which a range of fictional strategies might themselves be capable of producing cognitive and affective responses touching on matters other than the meta-literary. In fact, Steiner gestures toward describing such a use of writerly strategies when discussing fiction by women, leading the reader to suspect that the term metafiction is in fact doing double duty in her account as an identity category as well as a description of a specialized literary practice. As it stands, her showcasing of Proulx's novel illustrates the restrictions necessary to present the "extraordinary commonplace" in all its redemptive immediacy.

The Shipping News concerns a beaten-down and miserably inarticulate man named Quoyle, who suffers a whole series of setbacks in his life, culminating in the death of his unfaithful wife in a car accident. With his children, Quoyle leaves his home in upstate New York and starts a new life in Newfoundland, where gradually, through his encounters with the residents of the remote maritime environment, things take a turn for the better, a turn toward the "nurturing steadfastness" (538) Steiner cherishes in the novel. Proulx's Newfoundland is a place where the old-fashioned values of community remain intact, where the obduracy of those living in a harsh landscape signifies honesty, and where contemporary social and cultural conditions can be left far behind. The imaginative space of *The Shipping News* is stripped of all traces of the contemporary social and cultural landscape, notably electronic mass media, and ethnic and racial difference.

The oppositions that undergird Steiner's tendentious narrative of literary history since the 1970s should be challenged on several counts. By sweeping the formal innovations of the high postmodernists into the single category of metafiction, she greatly simplifies the meaning of antirealism, staking out a dichotomy between metafictionists and realists, the former writing dense, hermetic, and ludic texts, and the latter producing transparent, direct expressions of experience. This opposition disregards the antirealism or postmodernism of minority authors, among them Ishmael Reed, Toni Morrison, Maxine Hong Kingston, Clarence Major, Nathaniel Mackey, Theresa Hak Kyung Cha, Jessica Hagedorn, and Cynthia Kadohata, not to mention the crucial early influence of Ellison's *Invisible Man*, a novel that belongs in the lineage of postmodern fiction as well as African American literature. It also overlooks the rhetorical framing of realism, a point post-structuralists and postmodernists have been at pains to emphasize. Steiner's conception of the literary field reduces the complexity of cultural exchanges by reifying identity categories and making them the primary determinant of literary practice.

Steiner employs postmodernism as a periodizing term: postmodernism is that era when fiction, and critical taste, leave behind the elitism of modernism to speak directly to and from the concerns of ordinary and overlooked individuals. To overcome modernism, Steiner establishes a link between formal difficulty and sociocultural divisiveness. She has hardly been alone in using the charge of "elitism" to associate ostensibly high cultural products with a hegemonic class composed predominantly of highly educated white males. The corollary is that popular culture, whether fiction, talk shows, or pathographic memoirs, is popular in the strongest sense, that is to say, pertaining to and emerging from the people. This line of argument imagines a transparent relationship between cultural consumption and political efficacy. The widespread appeal of a work of fiction is equated with its use in fostering a politics of social diversity. Consequently, those works usually designated postmodern must be rejected. Such a view is particularly anxious to consign modernism to the distant past, along with all the lessons it was once thought to teach. The novel can return to a measured, useful, and responsible existence, a realism reinvigorated and newly relevant to these confessional times.

Postmodernism and Literary Fiction

In Steiner's history, critical taste has left behind experimentalism, and has also abandoned the supporting arms of criticism that privileged textuality. This is a significant subtext of her account: New Criticism, post-structuralism, and literary theory generally are all outgrowths of modernism, and must be rejected accordingly. Oddly, the development of the concept of postmodernism in literary and cultural theory has also tended to leave postmodern fiction by the wayside. Fiction was central to early North American attempts to elaborate and define postmodernism. But with the explosion of theories of postmodernism, the influx of post-structuralism, and the pioneering work of Lyotard and Jameson, novels took up a comparatively marginal place, and studies of postmodern fiction ceased to be essential to the debate, assuming an ancillary function to one side of philosophical ruminations on the legacy of the enlightenment and failings of metaphysics.

Early definitions of postmodernism arose in the context of the literary activity of the 1960s and 1970s. Critical work published in *Boundary 2: A Journal of Postmodern Literature* (from 1972 onward) addressed the poetics of the Black Mountain school and San Francisco renaissance, as well as fiction by writers then grouped under a number of competing headings, including metafiction, surfiction, and parafiction. This critical attention coincided with and was nourished by currents of thought from the continent, particularly Heideggerian phenomenology and structuralism. At the same time, critical work by Ihab Hassan, Gerald Graff, Philip Stevick, and Jerome Klinkowitz established the case for a movement in literary fiction that represented at least a modulation of modernist impulses into something distinct and identifiable, a body of work that formed the first sketch for a canon of postmodern literature.[17] The excitement and interest generated by this work was accompanied by an unusually close relationship between fiction and critical writing on the part of several of the major practitioners. William Gass, Ishmael Reed, Raymond Federman, Ronald Sukenick, Susan Sontag, and John Barth all wrote criticism in addition to fiction, and established in their work fruitful conversations between the two.[18] Such writing, along with the professional attention of critics during the 1970s and early 1980s, including burgeoning exegetical industries around the work of Thomas Pynchon, studies of metafiction influenced by the reception of structuralism and post-structuralism, and published interviews and conversations between writers and critics, generated an intellectual climate for the understanding and cultural recognition of postmodern fiction.

A full history of these developments lies beyond the scope of the present study. It is sufficient, however, to note that academic, and to some extent popular, interest lent this body of work a short-lived cultural authority. While some of this fiction presented itself, often with pointed irony, under the banner of the end of the novel, the critical attention accorded this writing, buoyed by the reception of continental theory, was an unusual moment of generative interest in the frequently strained relations between the university and contemporary literature. In spite of—or, in a more complex fashion, because of—the prevalent appearance of motifs of endings, exhaustion, waste, entropy, and used-upness, this fiction was grasped as something new, as something different from the mainstream of more conventional, and by implication more conservative fiction. Making sense of this writing, naming it, and finding the appropriate critical terminology, contributed to the development of the concept of postmodernism.

Yet the crucial steps in the development of the concept of postmodernism, or, to put it more skeptically, the moves that expanded the field of the word's effects, represented by Fredric Jameson's first ground-breaking essays and Jean-François Lyotard's *Postmodern Condition*, pressed literature into a subordinate role.[19] Lyotard's text examined the legitimacy of knowledge in advanced or postindustrial societies in the wake of the grand narratives of modernity. To the legitimizing narratives of knowledge unfolding progressively toward eventual human emancipation, Lyotard counterposed knowledge structured as a number of incommensurable language games, and science as an avant-garde practice of invention and paradox rather than a royal road to absolute truth. Significantly, *The Postmodern Condition* relegates art and literature to an appendix, added to the English translation and aimed, presumably, at the book's audience in the humanities, for whom the discussion of scientific legitimation was primarily of interest as an intervention into the debate about modernity. Lyotard's discussion of twentieth-century artistic movements calls for an aesthetic of the sublime, an experimental avant-gardism that puts the "postmodern artist or writer in the position of a philosopher" (81), a philosopher searching for the criteria of judgment that come after the work, rather as if the work throws down the challenge of its own perplexing status and meaning.[20] Lyotard's terse proposition draws the modern/postmodern distinction between two exemplary figures, Proust and Joyce. Proust and Joyce, Lyotard claims, "both allude to something which does not allow itself to be made present." He continues: "In Proust, what is being eluded as the price to pay for this allusion is the identity of consciousness, a victim to the excess of time (*au trop de temps*). But in Joyce, it is the identity of writing which is the victim of an excess of the book (*au trop de livre*) or of literature" (80). In the modernist Proust, therefore, the great unpresentable is the unity of the self, which is displaced and deferred through the course of his immense, labyrinthine text. For the postmodernist Joyce, the unpresentable element is intrinsic to the medium itself; it belongs to the unity of the subject of writing, which is shattered by the polyphony and heterogeneity of the signifier. Lyotard's position here recalls the theories of *écriture* associated with Barthes, Kristeva, Sollers, and others within the *Tel Quel* group. Ideas of textuality entered the Anglophone academy in various guises, and were particularly important to the reception of French feminism, but they have not been especially applicable to the American fiction subsequently canonized as postmodern. Furthermore, Lyotard's aesthetics of the sublime tied postmodern literature quite closely to modernism, and appeared to call for an austere avant-gardism, as well as a return to Kant's *Critique of Judgment*.

Although Lyotard's brief essay on postmodernism in art and literature has been cited countless times, his main influence has been on the debate about the philosophical status of modernity and postmodernity. Jameson's theory of postmodernism analyzes cultural phenomena in detail, and refers to fiction on several occasions, reading Doctorow's *Ragtime*, for example, to illustrate the disablingly truncated historical sense on offer in postmodern culture. His later elaboration of the themes and concepts of his pioneering essay, the book *Postmodernism, Or the Cultural Logic of Late Capitalism*, published in 1991, discusses Claude Simon's work at some length, sets out some intriguing observations on postmodern historical fiction, and mentions cyberpunk approvingly, but otherwise has little to say about the novel or literature generally. This is in marked contradistinction to Jameson's earlier work, notably *The Political Unconscious*, in which the novel took center stage.[21] Jameson's postmodernism does not find its main expression in narrative forms. It is associated with the image, with ephemerality and fragmentation, with intense but unrelated instants of perception, and with space, albeit of a peculiar and almost inconceivable kind. The emblematic postmodern experience is that of the schizophrenic, for whom meaningful unities of perception, subtended by the continuity of conscious identity, are broken apart, splintered into fragments of heightened sensory experience. Postmodernism's paradoxical form of relation is through difference, rather than the unfolding causal patterning of narrative. Indeed, the disabling ahistoricism that Jameson sees as so intrinsic to postmodernism, militates against the narrative understanding of events. He grants the novel, no matter how marked by the superficiality and image-fixation, at best a marginal or minor status in comparison to the more interesting, because visual, spatial, and technocultural, exhibits such as film, video, or installation art. From Jameson's writing on postmodernism the reader takes away the impression that the only authentic literary narrative must be science fiction, which now, in the vertiginous environment of the postmodern, stands in for realism.

During the 1980s and 1990s, the notion of postmodernism acquired a peculiar capacity to appear everywhere even as its specific cultural objects receded. Nonetheless, important critical studies of postmodern fiction have been published in recent years. Works by Linda Hutcheon and Brian McHale have developed the formal insights of the first wave of studies, establishing powerful accounts of the postmodern novel in terms of historiographic metafiction and ontological skepticism respectively.[22] During the 1990s, attention shifted to the interrelations between postmodern fiction and emerging paradigms of systems, science, technology, and the posthuman.[23] This developing range of reference opens postmodern fiction to the contextual fabric of relations in which it is embedded, emphasizing the problematics of order, systematicity, mediation, and difference. Through these works have emerged two overlapping clusters of canonical postmodern fiction. For the commentators and critics of the 1970s and 1980s, the important figures were John Barth, John Hawkes, William Gass, Kurt Vonnegut, Thomas Pynchon, Donald Barthelme, Ishmael Reed, and Robert Coover, along with a number of less frequently celebrated writers, including Raymond Federman, Ronald Sukenick, and Steve Katz. More recent critics draw up a slightly different list: Thomas Pynchon, once again, but also Don DeLillo, Kathy Acker, Paul Auster, a few of the writers associated with cyberpunk, particularly William Gibson, and the scandalously underrated novelists William Gaddis, Joseph McElroy, and Gilbert Sorrentino, all of whom have finally attracted a modicum of critical attention.

Even though important critical work on contemporary fiction has continued to appear, the academic study of the postmodern novel has been marginalized.[24] The reasons for this are complex; they reflect much wider changes affecting the literary field. But certainly various aspects of postmodernism as it has been formulated in Anglophone literary and cultural theory have shifted critical attention away from the single author, or even cluster of authors. Ironically, this has in part to do with the rise of post-structuralist literary theory. Notions of intertextuality, for example, situate the work, the New Critical object of inquiry, among interconnected webs of significance. The older vocabulary of author, allusion, predecessor (or even progenitor), successor, and tradition emphasized the role of the author as a more or less conscious creative subject interacting with and acting upon the available literary discourses, employing, reshaping, or revolutionizing them. Intertextuality, by contrast, treats the individual work and the author's oeuvre as porous, a signifying chain that does not begin or end with the proprietary proper name, but links to, and is imbricated with other texts, both the usual literary ones (sources and analogs, to use the older terminology), and writings of a nonliterary kind—letters, diaries, manuals of conduct, legal decisions, documents of state, and so on, the kinds of material made use of most flamboyantly by New Historicism. The archive is henceforth without predetermined borders, and the work is folded back into its multiple contexts.

The related idea of the death of the author, as Roland Barthes sloganized it, became an academic commonplace with the introduction of the first wave of literary theory.[25] For Barthes, the author serves the critic as a way to contain the multiplicitous meanings generated by the codes of the text. The author functions as the source of meaning, and the agent to which interpretive conclusions must ultimately be referred. Such a conception has of course been under attack since the New Critical denunciation of the "intentional fallacy," but the post-structuralist critique of the "author function," in Foucault's phrase,[26] was more radical, having the potential to shatter the unities of textual meaning that the New Critics established through their attention to ambiguity, irony, and form. However, it is debatable just how profoundly the post-structuralist challenge to the author has been absorbed into literary study. On the one hand, suspicion has fallen on the study of single authors and on the attendant rhetoric of creativity and the imagination, a suspicion that often hardens into an outright hostility between the critical and creative wings of English departments. But on the other, the author remains a central category throughout contemporary institutions of literature, from the pedagogical selection of texts to the marketing of books. The postmodern era may be firmly established, but authors have yet to whither away. Furthermore, the author function is intricately tied to the formation of canons and the question of literary value. In this respect, the tension between cultural studies and more traditional literary criticism turns on the system of values configured around the author function, as does the related distinction between popular culture and literature.

Among all these developments, postmodern fiction finds itself in a contradictory position. On the one hand, the narrative innovation and self-consciousness of postmodern fiction makes the association with post-structuralist notions of textuality available and productive. On the other, the authority of postmodern fiction, its significance, visibility, and participation in cultural conversation, depends on the traditional patterns of literary recognition, from author profiles, interviews, and prizes, to critical studies and accession to one form of canon or another. Considered from this perspective, more than three decades on, the slogan "the death of the author" acquires a less militant, more melancholic cast. During the 1990s, a number of commentators, novelists, and essayists lamented a perceived decline in serious literary reading, and predicted the novel's incipient obsolescence, particularly as new electronic media came to dominate the cultural landscape. These laments, which revive with a negative charge Marshall McLuhan's eye-catching propositions about the dissolution of the Gutenberg Galaxy, should not simply be dismissed as conservative anxiety in the face of a changing world, though they undoubtedly have at times a conservative strain. Instead, they should be seen as a point of purchase on changes affecting the literary field, often in subtle and confusing ways, but significantly and irreversibly. The situation of postmodern fiction, as it enters obscurely into a fifth decade, sheds light on these changes.

Postmodernism and the Information Economy

A profound shift in the relations between capital and culture underlies the changes affecting the literary field. Such changes inform the ways in which literary works are produced and consumed, evaluated and comprehended. They have altered, in controversial and frequently perplexing ways, the construction and attribution of literary value, the formation and maintenance of canons, the reality and perception of reading publics, and the writer's sense of tradition. Theories of postmodern culture are attempts—albeit often oblique, partial, and mystificatory attempts—to grasp the changing relationship between culture and capital. Such changes did not occur punctually with the advent of the postmodern condition, whenever that might have occurred, but are part of a long series of shifts in the social significance of cultural activity during the capitalist mode of production.

For Terry Eagleton, these processes first become palpable in the late nineteenth century:

> From Nietzsche onwards, the "base" of capitalist society begins to enter into embarrassing contradiction with its "superstructure." The legitimating forms of high bourgeois culture, the versions and definitions of subjectivity which they have to offer, appear less and less adequate to the experience of late capitalism, but on the other hand cannot be merely abandoned. The mandarin culture of the high bourgeois epoch is progressively called into question by the later evolution of that very social system, but remains

at certain ideological levels indispensable. It is indispensable partly because the subject as unique, autonomous, self-identical and self-determining remains a political and ideological requirement of the system, but partly because the commodity is incapable of generating a sufficiently legitimating ideology of its own.[27]

Recent decades have seen these processes intensify to the point where the legitimating function of culture has been overtaken by the uses of culture as commodity. Capital has to an increasing extent penetrated the cultural realm, making it over in its own image. This is not to say that the use of culture—so-called high culture—has been stripped of all its usefulness as a means of legitimation; literature, for example, continues to be called upon to betoken subjective depth, interiority, the shared spiritual essence of humanity—indeed, popular commonplaces about fiction and poetry remain in this register. Yet the confusions over cultural hierarchies, the turbulence within the academy, and the anxieties of late postmodern writers over the future of the novel offer an indication of the ways in which the cultural realm no longer serves—or serves in a different way—the role of legitimation that Eagleton describes.

This interpenetration of the realms of culture and capital involves a number of highly complex shifts—shifts in the structure of social class, in the evolving technologies of communication and control, in the growth of the service economy, and in the increasingly informational character of late capitalism. Materialist accounts of postmodernism, particularly the work of Jameson and David Harvey, as well as ambitious attempts to describe the emergence of a new era of information economies, including many recent studies of globalization, offer a sense of where these changes come from and how they have altered contemporary financscapes, mediascapes, technoscapes, and ideoscapes (to use Arjun Appadurai's terms for new kinds of social and cultural fluidity).[28]

The transformation of the cultural realm by the economic belongs to the changes in the capitalist mode of production over the past three decades. Although debate has raged around the extent and profundity of these changes—whether, for example, a postindustrial era has truly dawned, or whether, and to what degree, capitalism has established new social, political, and economic structures, so-called regimes of accumulation[29]—the various schools of interpretation broadly speaking accept that the early 1970s crystallized the weaknesses of the existing economic order, and signaled the difficult transition to new practices of production, labor, and consumption. What began to break apart during the late 1960s and early 1970s, paving the way for the rise of neoliberalism in the 1980s, was the Keynesian consensus that sustained the economic boom in the West during the decades following World War II. This period, especially in the United States, was the golden age of twentieth-century capitalism, a period of relatively consistent growth, economic stability, and gains for both capital and labor. Unions in the industrial sphere attained limited but important bargaining rights, exercising some influence over social welfare and wages, while also collaborating with management on production techniques and increasing productivity.[30] This consensus, though certainly contested around specific issues and at particular moments, sustained the hegemony of Fordism, the system of conjoined and mutually supporting mass production and consumption pioneered by Henry Ford from the early years of the century, but only fully established after World War II.

By the end of the 1960s, however, the economic boom was faltering. As Mandel presciently observed,[31] and as Harvey accepts, the rigidities of the Fordist system, with its massive investments in machinery designed to perform specific functions within a carefully engineered system of production, its comparatively secure and protected labor force, and its increasingly saturated and stagnant consumer markets, became a hindrance to necessary growth, particularly as competitors abroad, notably Europe and Japan (now made over along Fordist lines and experiencing some of the same problems as the United States), began competing for foreign markets. A temporary fix in the form of augmented money supply led to increasing inflation and, combined with the oil crisis of 1973 (when OPEC raised prices and oil nations in the Arab world imposed an embargo on exports to the West, following the Arab–Israeli war), led to a sharp recession.[32] What followed remains open to competing interpretations and significant differences in emphasis, even among economists ostensibly working within a broadly defined Marxist tradition.[33] Suffice to say, an extensive process of restructuring has been underway since that downturn, with marked effects through the 1980s and 1990s. The keynotes of this restructuring, according to Harvey, are flexibility and mobility, as they apply to processes of labor, products, and patterns of consumption.[34] Throughout, the rapid spread of information technology enabled and amplified these changes, offering new kinds of automation on the factory floor, instantaneous feedback between the point of sale and the point of production, a rapid development in the infrastructure of communications (satellite, cable, the Internet), and the proliferation of new technology-based products and experiences to consume.

For the labor force this has entailed a shift toward temporary contracts, part-time work, a growth of "sweatshop" production, even in major Western cities, and the increasing use of cheaper labor in the less developed countries. Such changes have broken up many of the gains made under Fordism, with the closure of plants and the eradication of whole industries in some cases, with the consequent immiseration and dislocation of the communities those industries sustained. The other side of this development in the wealthiest nations is the increasing shift toward service jobs—the so-called tertiary sector of the economy—that now employ more than twice as many people as traditional industry. Central to the service economy, which covers a range of activities, from health care, education, and finance, to insurance, transportation, and advertising, is the role played by knowledge and information. The expansion of this sector has meant an increasing proportion of the workforce engaged in the handling of symbols, an "informatization" of the capitalist economy.[35]

Such developments are bound up with the information technology revolution of the 1970s. According to Manuel Castells, the elements that combined to create the technological breakthrough were put in place in the decades after World War II, in part following on from the accelerated invention of the war years.[36] Thus, the invention of the transistor (1947), the integrated circuit (1957), and the microprocessor (1971), made possible the production of computers small enough to fit on desktops and to enter the home market, as well as dramatically reducing the cost of processing information.[37] These developments have, of course, continued apace through the 1980s and 1990s, with the diffusion of microcomputers and the growth of the electronic communications network, from the U.S. Defense Department's Advanced Research Projects Agency (ARPA) in 1969 to the emergence of the Internet. With these technologies have come new uses and organizations of labor, new speeds and patterns of the flow of capital, and new production processes.

This acceleration and flexibility has had a significant effect on the expanding class of knowledge-workers (or "cultural mass," as Harvey, following Daniel Bell, terms them):[38] the marketing of symbols—of lifestyle, image, trend, and idea—has greatly expanded, while also following the speed of turnover demanded by the new capitalist economy. The promiscuous image-fixation and hybridity of postmodern culture, in the broadest sense, is directly related to these developments. According to David Harvey, such innovations and trends have "been accompanied on the consumption side . . . by a much greater attention to quick-changing fashions and the mobilization of all the artifices of need inducement and cultural transformation that this implies. The relatively stable aesthetic of Fordist modernization has given way to all the ferment, instability, and fleeting qualities of a postmodernist aesthetic that celebrates differ-ence, ephemerality, spectacle, fashion, and the commodification of cultural forms."[39] While this description of postmodern culture is hardly remarkable—it recalls Baudelaire's celebrated aphorism about modernity ("Modernity is the transient, the fleeting, the contingent")[40]—it does help to emphasize the dynamism, uncertainty, and fluidity of the new regime of accumulation, and the stamp it leaves on the cultural realm.

At the same time, it would be a mistake simply to see postmodern culture merely as the mirror of instability. What is at stake, rather, is the changing role of culture—in its traditional as well as broader, anthropological sense—within the new information economies. This is of course a tremendously large and complicated issue, one that the present discussion, and project as a whole, can only address in a very limited way. However, to begin to make sense of some of the cultural shifts in question, it is useful briefly to consider three aspects of the problem: changes in the field of publishing over recent decades; shifts in the workings and self-images of the academy; and, closely related, the attempts of postmodernist theory and cultural studies to grasp new kinds of cultural commodification.

During the last two decades, the corporate control of the communication media, including the world of publishing, has increased markedly, with a whole new set of interests spawned by the information technology industries. These trends are certainly not new, but the move toward consolidation of media resources by giant corporations proceeded apace during the 1980s and 1990s. The consequences are manifest throughout the publishing world: greater editorial control over content; fewer risks with strange or unfamiliar projects; a reluctance to keep slow-selling or backlist books in print; the intensive marketing of books through author appearances on television and radio and at bookstores; and the emergence of a market in which small, independent publishers find it increasingly hard to survive. The spread of large national book chains—Barnes & Noble, Borders, Walden Books—has frequently been at the expense of smaller, often better-informed and committed independent stores. In addition, as Herbert Schiller points out, "these big retail chains by their choice and promotions largely determine which books will become the big sellers. Their choices, in turn, are finely tuned to selecting works that have the greatest sales potential. While this criterion does not absolutely preclude material that is unfamiliar, socially critical, or seriously antiestablishment, it limits severely the likelihood of its publication—or at least publication by the main commercial houses."[41] According to the distinguished publisher André Schiffrin, the acquisition of publishing enterprises by large corporations forced on publishers a new fiscal standard. Instead of being allowed to use the revenue from best-selling books to support financially risky projects—challenging works in history, social theory, and fiction—as had been their practice, publishers under new control found themselves obliged to meet a certain standard of profitability.[42] This incorporation eroded the ambition and seriousness of publishing, even as the United States entered more conservative times during the Reagan era.

These developments damage serious writing in a number of ways. Publishers under stringent fiscal demands are much less likely to make forays into bold or experimental fiction. Such work has been obliged to seek publication through innovative (and, dare one say, heroic) nonprofit enterprises, or university presses, which in turn have come under pressure to conform to the demands of the marketplace. Furthermore, as DeLillo's beleaguered author Bill Gray points out in *Mao II*, the book itself—its intrinsic qualities—has become less important than the marketing of an image. The spectacular success of the Oprah Winfrey book club during the late 1990s heightened some of these trends, even as it produced occasionally interesting contradictions, and symbolized the fusion of different media concerns under single conglomerates (see the discussion in chapter 3). In addition, the populist rhetoric that became such a feature of nonacademic literary institutions during the 1980s and 1990s—the argument that all "difficult" books are elitist, and so on—appears from this perspective to have much less to do with the democratization of culture than with its increasing subservience to the law of the marketplace.

This law also applied effective pressure to higher education. Bill Readings has argued that the role of the university in Western societies, particularly the United States, has altered over recent decades, moving from the role of inculcating culture in citizen-subjects to a model of "excellence."[43] The role of culture, under the idea of the university that descended from German idealism and became the model for modern universities, was to unify the disciplines, overcome their divergence, and train the character of the student, thereby defusing class conflict and countering social disintegration. Fundamental to this idea was the nation-state, the culture of which formed the basis for education. The rise of global economies, however, has weakened the role of the nation-state, Readings argues, and transferred the function of legitimation away from culture. Instead, universities now promulgate an idea of excellence. By excellence, Readings means simply that which the university defines as excellent: excellence, in these terms, has no content and no agenda; it is defined according to quantifiable standards (number of articles published, number of students taught, data from student assessments, and so on), and thus is much better suited to the corporate model of production and control than insubstantial ideas about the unity of culture and its benefits to civilization.

Readings's argument is a powerful and provocative one. Even though he tends to overstate the decline of the nation as an organizational form within global capital, his contention illuminates the reconfiguration of culture—in this case, culture under shifting definitions within the academy—under late capitalism. Culture now is simply that which we decide to call culture: "Everything, given a chance, can be or become culture. Cultural Studies thus arrives on the scene along with a certain exhaustion. The very fecundity and multiplicity of work in Cultural Studies is enabled by the fact that culture no longer functions as a specific referent to any one thing or set of things—which is why Cultural Studies can be so popular while refusing general theoretical definition. . . . Everything is culturally determined, as it were, and culture ceases to mean anything *as such*."[44] Some versions of postmodernism, with their celebration of the plethora of forms taken by culture in late capitalism, emerge from the same set of coordinates; the claim that cultural hierarchies have been overthrown, whether taken up as a way to dismiss the difficulty of some postmodern fiction, or as a paean to the pleasures of consumption, suggests that culture's legitimating function is, at the very least, undergoing a significant mutation.

Theories of postmodernism, sometimes overtly, sometimes tacitly, try to make sense of this state of affairs, often through acts of disavowal or celebration. Jean-François Lyotard, for example, distinguishes between an avant-gardist postmodernism of experiment and the sublime, his own strong version of a contemporary aesthetics, and a postmodernism of consumer culture, which he associates with Jencks's theory of allusion and ornament. As to this latter, he strikes a note of disdain: "Eclecticism is the degree zero of contemporary general culture: one listens to reggae, watches a western, eats McDonald's food for lunch and local cuisine for dinner, wears Paris perfume in Tokyo and 'retro' clothes in Hong Kong; knowledge is a matter for TV games" (76). For Lyotard, this promiscuous mixing of high and low, the expensive and the cheap, the local and the global, typifies the way consumerism triumphs in the absence of clear criteria of aesthetic judgment. The only rule that can be detected in these diverse cultural instances is the rule of profit: postmodernism, in this sense, is indistinguishable from the marketplace. Yet Lyotard's list resembles those lists of heterogeneous objects that are so characteristic of definitions of postmodernism. Presented in this form, the list is more often an invitation to delight in the pleasures of variety and to celebrate the absence of strict criteria of value. Postmodernism, we are told, overthrows the hierarchies by which the experiences of high and low art are distinguished.

Certainly, postmodern claims of cultural heterogeneity, of the mixing of high and low forms, parallel the interest of cultural studies in the most inclusive understanding of culture. Postmodernism as a style has often been synonymous with difficulty, with the involutions of metafiction, for example, or the parataxis of language poetry, or more generally, with unstable tone, disjuncture, free-floating irony, formal incompletion, the aleatory and the playful, with arbitrary rules and indeterminacy, even with chaos. Yet postmodernism has also been understood in terms of the effacement of the divide between high and mass culture. Where the modernist work scrupulously purged itself of mass culture, or selectively incorporated popular forms the better to disarm them, the postmodernist text makes such profligate use of popular elements that its own high cultural status is compromised. And by the same token, many of the constitutive features of high postmodernist texts—generalized irony, self-reflexivity, intertextuality, formal play, pastiche—have become standard features of many movies and television shows. The dialectic that bound the high and low together, as rivals and antagonists, thus gives way to wholesale mixing, with a consequent unsettling of the categories by which the practices of high and low are carefully sorted, categorized, and patrolled.

Stated thus, the patterns of cultural discrimination and interaction are greatly simplified, yet this argument in favor of seismic shifts in the landscape of evaluation helps one understand a number of other important postmodernist claims. The idea that postmodernism dissolves critical distance, an important tenet of Jameson's theory, can be seen in this light as a way of recognizing the collapse of cultural distinction in the realm of theory. Postmodern eclecticism, with its disregard for time-honored boundaries and categories, resonates with the anthropological sweep of cultural studies, which, as John Frow notes, sets itself "to cover the whole range of practices through which a social group's reality (or realities) is constructed and maintained."[45] Cultural studies has been highly eclectic, notoriously finding its objects of analysis in the unlikeliest, or most mundane, of places—fanzines, soap operas, cars, shopping malls. The study of culture is no longer restricted to the sanctioned works of the literary or artistic tradition, but flourishes in its attention to all kinds of activity. This approach to the whole range of practices by which social and cultural identities are produced largely removes the critic from the business of evaluation. No longer is it necessary to argue that one kind of cultural activity is superior to another: reading Dante is no better than watching a soap opera. Culture can now be understood and enjoyed without appeal to evaluative criteria founded on aesthetic disinterestedness.

The differences between cultural studies and postmodernism are many and varied, but for the present the emphasis each places on cultural agency deserves attention. Cultural studies envisages an active subject of cultural consumption who has the capacity to subvert the dominant messages of the object of attention: texts of all kinds can be read against the grain, decoded for contingent or subversive content, or simply enjoyed for their sheer carnivalesque excess. Such arguments tend, admittedly, to be parasitical on an unacknowledged avant-garde lexicon of subversion and resistance, yet rest finally on an idiom of social recognition and democratic inclusiveness, particularly in as much as the theoretical ground-clearing of cultural studies so often—often enough that one might think of the move as a ritual of belonging—denounces the "elitist" and "mandarin" theory of earlier high cultural critics of mass culture, notably the Frankfurt School.[46]

Postmodernism, by contrast, is typically understood as dissolving or fracturing identities, social and psychic alike. Postmodern culture, in its eclecticism and relentless superficiality, might offer its consumers a serial or schizophrenic set of intensities, but it does little to cement identities or community alliances. The abstraction of such an account, which contrasts with the pleasure cultural studies takes in the specific, lends an air of the privative, of lack, loss, and absence, to the proceedings, and suggests that the dissolution in question allegorizes that of the modern agent of cultural authority. If cultural value is dispersed across a range of items, none more important than any other, then the authority of culture—the sense that reading a novel, going to the theatre, gazing at a painting, are activities with an intrinsic worth, a worth that depends on their irreducibility and uniqueness—is compromised. The choices of the cultural consumer become the index of his or her agency.

Postmodernism and cultural studies both teach that the distinction between high and mass culture needs to be abandoned, or at least reconsidered, thought through under different conditions. An elaborate language of cultural discrimination, embedded in institutions, forged, legitimized, but also contested there, evidently still exists: the cultural consumer might watch a sitcom before heading to the opera, without considering these activities to be the same kind of thing. Nonetheless, the opera or theatre, the visit to the art gallery or patient absorbed reading of a literary novel, are obliged either to mount elaborate defenses of their specialness, or must accept that they are just one more item on a full menu of consumer choices.

This point might be argued in a more unsettling way. Discussing the 1970s' work of the French novelist Claude Simon, Fredric Jameson notes that the postmodern situation has raised a new set of problems, in addition to the problems of interpretation that this difficult, experimental writing originally posed. The new problems, casting a glance backwards from the early 1990s, have to do with evaluation, with the question of whether Simon still deserves attention. This is not simply a question of fashion or the waxing and waning of a reputation, but rather an issue of the status of the high literary text in a new cultural situation: "Does not . . . the competition of the media and so-called cultural studies signal a transformation in the role and space of mass culture today which is greater than mere enlargement and which may leave no space whatsoever for literary 'classics' of this kind?"[47] If Jameson's question is answered in the affirmative, then the high literary text becomes a residual phenomenon.[48] To continue to argue in terms of the agonistic struggle for cultural authority, and the resistance to the commodification of mass culture on the part of the difficult literary text, seems increasingly quixotic.

For the late postmodernist writer, the difficulties of establishing a space for his or her own activity, not to mention attracting prestige to that position, are considerable. Can the novel retain its claim to authority if the cultural landscape is in fact dominated by electronic mass culture? What resources does fiction have available—resources that include stylistic practices, the ingenuity and patience of readers, sustaining ideas of literary value—in this emerging cultural landscape? If the legitimating function of culture, and literature in particular, has in fact been reconfigured or reduced, then the challenges of a difficult literary novel can appear arbitrary, an offensive and unwarranted appeal to specialized knowledge and expertise. Complaints about the dim future of literature and the rise of an illiterate class emerge from this situation in which cultural authority and evaluative criteria are subject to the pressures of the new consumer and information economies. My interest in the chapters that follow is in how these difficulties are negotiated within contemporary fiction. It is to this inquiry that I now turn.

CHAPTER 2

THE NOVEL AND THE DEATH
OF LITERATURE

The Ends of Literature

During the past decade, a number of critics, novelists, and essayists have announced the end of literature. For the literary theorist J. Hillis Miller, "[t]he end of literature is at hand. Literature's time is almost up"; he goes on to explain that "[t]he printed book will retain cultural force for a good while yet, but its reign is clearly ending."[1] The essayist Sven Birkerts, who has made a career out of elegizing the book, claims that "[t]he stable hierarchies of the printed page . . . are being superseded by the rush of impulses through freshly minted circuits."[2] And according to the critic Alvin Kernan, morbid symptoms of the "death of literature" can be traced throughout the institutions of publishing, the university, and the law.[3] Marshall McLuhan's flamboyant assertions about the end of the print era, elaborated in *The Gutenberg Galaxy* and a string of other volumes published in the 1960s, have acquired a new currency in the last years of the twentieth century.

These commentators find ominous signs of the end of literature and the book in the rise of new technologies, the decline of literacy, and the emergence of postliterate subjects. Such conclusions are troubling, perhaps even debilitating to the novelist: the novel's future lies at best in survival on the margins of an image-based culture. Any power to shape the larger culture is now or soon will be greatly restricted, as the larger culture turns increasingly to electronic media. Signs of such a future are evident today: visibility for the contemporary work of fiction means cinematic adaptation, while the canonical works of the past survive outside the classroom as pendants to the heritage industry. Even if complex, challenging works of fiction continue to appear, they will struggle henceforth to find readers attuned to their sophistication and daring. For the pessimist, the novel seems doomed to enjoy no more than a coterie following, its bygone authority dissipated or taken over by electronic cultural forms.

Such views express a conservative reaction against the cultural and technological changes of the final decades of the twentieth century. But they also reflect a genuine uncertainty as to the nature of literary field—the institutions and ideologies of the literary world—within the emerging media environment of the postmodern era. Arguments about the decline of literature, or even its demise, are efforts, however limited or defensive, to make sense of cultural change, to understand the place of literary reading and writing amid the turbulence of new cultural practices, markets, and technologies. As Carla Hesse has written, "what we are witnessing in the remaking of the modern literary system at the end of the twentieth century is not so much a technological revolution (which has already occurred) but the public reinvention of intellectual community in its wake."[4] Though their efforts are often couched in the accents of technophobia and apocalypse, the elegists of the book try to mount a defense of literature, and specifically literary value, in terms of the public and private significance of the novel. They try, in other words, to imagine a community of minds forged through the reading and discussion of the literary text.

In this chapter, I examine the recent work of two distinguished novelists, John Barth and Philip Roth, writers whose careers span the postmodern literary enterprise, and who have articulated their cultural pessimism in essays, interviews, and above all novels. Their remarks about the close of the literary era echo those of other elegists of the book, while their fiction pursues complicated and impassioned explorations of the place of the novel in a culture transformed by new technology, changing sensibilities, and political malaise. What place is there for the novel, for the specific form of inquiry, representation, and narration that late-twentieth-century novels, informed by the modernist and postmodernist traditions, still have the power to offer? And how indeed can this power be exercised—why *must* it be exercised—in a climate of stark political and cultural divergence? For Barth and Roth the cultural environment in the last years of the century was in various ways inimical to their literary endeavors. Though both continued to write and to add new items to their formidable oeuvres, they struggled with the perception that their moment had passed; the white male writer could no longer take for granted the undivided attention of a serious literary readership.

Both novelists thus engage with the rhetoric of anxiety that surrounds the future of literary fiction in the last years of the twentieth century. In Barth's essays particularly, the modernist theme of the death of the novel—wherein the startling innovations that have characterized fiction in the twentieth century seemed, at least for the polemicists, to put an end to nineteenth-century realism, the novel of plot, character, and milieu—mutates into the late postmodernist conception of the death of the novel as a result of changes within the wider culture. For Barth, as for Philip Roth, Sven Birkerts, and Alvin Kernan, among others examined in this study, the primary source of cultural change is technological, more particularly the ubiquitous influence of electronic mass media, which is eroding the disposition toward sustained concentration that literary reading demands. The reading of literature belongs to a kind of subjectivity now imperiled. Birkerts writes: "Reading, for me, is one activity that inscribes the limit of the old conception of the individual and his relation to the world. It is precisely where reading leaves off, where it is supplanted by other modes of processing and transmitting experience, that the new dispensation can be said to begin" (15). For the elegists of the book reading is the index of a particular social, cultural, and psychic order. As the screen evolves from film to television to computer, the kinds of attention demanded by literary fiction wither away; serious reading declines into an insignificant, specialized activity to the extent that electronic forms of data dissemination come to dominate the cultural landscape, bringing with them a new epoch in human self-understanding.

For the elegists, the symptoms of the reduced cultural authority of literature are worryingly prevalent: the readership for serious fiction is declining; universities have abandoned the task of teaching the classics of the Western literary tradition; academic and general literary culture are disablingly divorced; television and the Internet have marginalized the book as an object of cultural attention. Further, the sustaining institutions and ideologies of authorship, including expressive freedom, the proprietary claim on originality, and cultural authority, are threatened by the new economies of entertainment and information flow. The expenditure of time required to read a novel, not to mention the slow, exacting work of writing one, belongs to a bygone age, when the social organization of temporality permitted such practices, but now seems quite anachronistic in an era typified by instant information retrieval and the rapid turnover of news stories, cultural trends, and those fascinating objects called celebrities. By the same token, the kind of knowledge of texts built up over a lifetime of reading, and sometimes assumed by the authors of earlier periods, also seems destined to disappear, either because the reader has vanished or because the shared field of literature, embodied in the canon, can no longer be taken for granted. All of these threats to literature are also held to be threats to the individual and to democracy: as the defining characteristics of the individual of the print era are displaced by new kinds of experience and subjectivity, so the question of politics inescapably arises, not least because the prevailing liberal models of agency cannot be sustained in the face of radical skepticism about the individual, whether this skepticism is justified on philosophical or cultural grounds. Liberal models of democracy are thus cited as casualties of this emerging cultural landscape.

The cultural pessimism of the elegists has obvious affinities and overlaps with neoconservative positions staked out during the culture wars of the 1980s and 1990s. The death of literature, Kernan argues, can be laid at the door of new technologies, but also has a great deal to do with university English departments, which have turned away from the transmission of the humane values enshrined in the canon of Western literature in favor of various brands of militant literary theory bent on "attacking bourgeois society by undermining its ideology and exposing all authority, including all literary authority, as illegitimate and repressive."[5] According to this line of argument, pursued sometimes with spleen, sometimes with melancholy, the universities have abandoned their task of perpetuating and safeguarding the Western literary tradition. Rather than producing new readers to cherish the classics of the past and the vital works of the present, the theoretically informed textual analyst turns reading into a joyless hermeneutic labor, or into an exercise in denouncing hegemonic values. Reading in literature departments, professional reading, bears the curse either of effete super-sophistication, or ideological crudity.

Kernan makes the connection to contemporary literary practice:

> What was once called "serious literature" has by now only a coterie audience, and almost no presence in the world outside university literature departments. Within the university, literary criticism, already by the 1960s Byzantine in its complexity, mountainous in its bulk, and incredible in its totality, has turned on literature and deconstructed its basic principles, declaring literature an illusory category, the poet dead, the work of art only a floating "text," language indeterminate and incapable of meaning, interpretation a matter of personal choice. (3)

Kernan makes a number of highly tendentious characterizations here: would even the most hard-boiled deconstructionist, for example, argue that language is "incapable" of meaning, or that "interpretation is a matter of personal choice"? But leaving aside the question of whether there is any truth in these caricatures of contemporary critical practice, it is possible (and desirable) to look at Kernan's claims in the context of the anxieties over the presumed death of literature, without thereby endorsing his view of the failings of the contemporary university. The continuity of "the traditional values of literature," whatever Kernan assumes these to be, falls prey to practices of reading that are either stifled by the labors of criticism, or devalued by irresponsible relativism. For contemporary writers, such a situation must be disabling indeed: their efforts can find appreciation only in the hieratic caste of professional readers, while the criteria of appreciation are themselves in the process of disappearing, eaten away by the acids of skepticism and relativism.

Kernan's stance is a despondent one, regretful but resigned to the decline it depicts. Polemics against the teaching of English in universities have also been joined by efforts to revive the practice of literary reading outside the academy. If the future of literature is not safe in the hands of academics, as so many conservatives have come to assume, it might still be secured by the general reading population. Over the past decade, several books have appeared that set out to teach the pleasures and values embodied in the literary canon to a nonacademic readership.[6] Characteristic both in its encomia to the great literary works of the Western canon, and in its scorn at higher education and contemporary culture, Harold Bloom's succinctly titled *How to Read and Why* encourages and celebrates reading as "a solitary praxis" that affords pleasure, strengthens the self, frees the mind from cant, instructs in the knowledge of others, and teaches the reader of "the way things are."[7] The kinds of pleasurable immersion in the canon that Bloom lauds, in a book that is essentially a companion piece to *The Western Canon*, restore the reading subject and the authority of literature.[8]

What ties together the canon-defending optimism of Bloom and the somber resignation of Kernan, Birkerts, and the other elegists, is the idea of literature as the place, perhaps the very last place, where the self is insulated from and inoculated against the insidious power of contemporary culture. Such a power presents itself in the form of media spectacles, images and narratives of shame, horror, and lurid intrigue, none of which stimulate reasoned discussion or debate, but tend instead to provoke attitudes of fascination and revulsion. Against this onslaught, which in large part displaces anything resembling the traditional print-oriented public sphere, literary reading can serve, by some accounts, as a refuge and a corrective, a means to consolidate and construct the self. The time-honored notion of reading the classics to lay down the foundations of an identity serves to defend the acquisition of cultural capital.

For William Gass, a novelist and critic associated with the first generation of postmodern fiction, the benefits of reading can be bluntly stated:

> So there will be books. And if readers shut their minds down the better to stare at pictures that rarely explain themselves, and if readers abandon

reading to swivel-hip their way through the interbunk, picking up scraps of juicy data here and there and rambling on the e-mail in that new fashion of grammatical decay, the result will be to make real readers, then chief among the last who are left with an ability to reason, rulers. Books made the rich richer. Books will make the smart smarter.[9]

Gass's defense of reading as a form of power turns on the well-worn distinction between text and image, book and computer, which restates the opposition between high and low culture in the crudest fashion. Gass chooses to imagine that literary activity may be preserved from such distasteful phenomena as e-mail and the Internet, and that literacy retains a privileged connection to social authority. Even Bloom, the most ebullient of the cultural pessimists, finds the belief in literature's authority difficult to sustain. At best, literary reading holds out the promise of a different kind of power, one centered on the rarefied pleasures and existential truths of literature.

"Many of our best authors," writes Kernan, "have experienced and not recovered from a crisis of confidence in the traditional values of literature and a sense of its importance to humanity" (3). John Barth and Philip Roth, eminent writers working in different traditions of the American novel, have recently tried to make challenging fiction out of this crisis in confidence. The project of each novelist is to reclaim the vestiges of the novel's cultural authority by coming to terms with its relation to endangered consensus—the negotiation of social difference in a shared cultural field. For Barth and Roth, in spite of their very different conclusions, the displacement of the novel from its rightful place of authority signals a deep problem within the nexus of culture and politics in the United States.

In Barth's essays and fiction the postmodern novel holds out the promise that cultural and social divisions may be overcome through the exercise of literary authority, an authority vested in the memory of the great classics of the past and embodied in the formal properties of the text. The ideal reader participates in these memories through the structure of recapitulation and remaking that constitutes Barth's work, at the level of the individual novel and across his labyrinthine oeuvre. For Roth, by contrast, consensus is treated with suspicion; the novel is an inherently argumentative form, no more so than when it argues with itself, with its own perceptions and claims. Yet it is only by forcing the reader to entertain the unknowable, even the illegible—to become, in other words, a certain kind of higher illiterate—that the novel can do its work of fostering sympathetic imagination and informed skepticism.

The Novel and the Deluge: John Barth
and the End of Print Fiction

Over the course of an extraordinary career, which to date has seen the publication of ten novels, four books of short stories, and two essay collections, John Barth has played an essential role in the development of postmodernism. His fiction has often been treated as exemplary of the best and worst of that strain of writing: on the one hand, his defenders point to the dazzling complexity and narrative ingenuity of his work, its successful use of a wide range of styles and structural conceits, including the epistolary novel, the historical novel, the allegory, the romance, the tale collection, and the apocalypse; on the other, his detractors complain of the arid and solipsistic nature of his metafictional forays—fiction about fiction—and his laborious tendency to recycle characters and themes from one work to the next across the entirety of his oeuvre, a practice that reached its apogee or nadir in *LETTERS*, a novel comprising more than seven hundred pages of the correspondence of characters from previous novels by John Barth. It is beyond contention, however, that Barth's fiction has from the outset been closely associated with the emergence of postmodernism. His earliest novels, *The Floating Opera* (1956) and *The End of the Road* (1958), exemplified the black humor sensibility of the late 1950s and early 1960s, the amalgam of existentialist absurdity, slapstick comedy, and stylistic daring that marked the postwar generation of John Hawkes, Kurt Vonnegut, and, in a different register, Flannery O'Connor, as well as the early fiction of such precocious talents as Thomas Pynchon and Joyce Carol Oates.[10] In *The Sot-Weed Factor* (1960), his brilliant pastiche of the robust eighteenth-century fiction of Fielding and Smollett, Barth wrote one of the first and best examples of historiographic metafiction, a generic hybrid characteristic of postmodernism.[11] And in later works Barth pursued the metafictional strategies by which high postmodernism in the 1970s became known, and was an active and articulate defender of postmodern practice and the critique of realism, alongside William Gass, Donald Barthelme, and Robert Coover. Yet Barth's writing over the past decade, though little diminished in vigor and proficiency, has been marked by a technological fatalism that sees the demise of print fiction as inevitable.

Barth's work over four decades lets one plot the course of postmodern American fiction. In three linked essays written over the course of his career he presents a triptych on the future of literary fiction, the panels of which might be titled Decline, Recuperation, and Resignation. The best known of these pieces, "The Literature of Exhaustion," widely cited as one of inaugural performances of literary postmodernism, makes an argument in favor of experimental virtuosity, as showcased by the work of Borges, Beckett, and Nabokov, exemplars of what Barth subsequently terms late modernism.[12] Barth's especial enthusiasm for Borges is couched in a historical account of the waxing and waning of novelistic forms. The late modernism that he champions—and that provides a stimulus for his own fictional experiments—combines brilliance of invention with an acute historical sense of the unfolding development of literature. Such self-consciousness spurs the late modernists into new feats of invention characterized as "Baroque" according to Borges's definition: "that style which deliberately exhausts or (tries to exhaust) its possibilities and borders upon its own caricature" (73). Out of caricature comes new work. The novel overcomes its "felt ultimacies" (71) through parodic imitation and revision, a practice heralded by Borges and Nabokov, and pursued by Barth himself in "novels which imitate the form of the Novel, by an author who imitates the role of Author" (72). In the difference between lower- and upper-case, Barth marks his place in the unfolding dialectic of the novelistic tradition. And indeed, one of his primary concerns in the essay is to demonstrate how the work of his masters and himself proceeds through cunning raids on the corpus of literary texts stretching back to the origins of narrative itself.

Ironically, this justification of Barth's own literary project was widely received as yet another death notice for the novel. In fact the essay is at pains to establish the originality, authority, and pedigree for a new kind of fiction, thus laying to rest premature rumors of the novel's demise. In "The Literature of Exhaustion" Barth stakes out a space of literary activity unthreatened by social and cultural change, such change as imperils the novel and its tradition. He embraces the legacy of modernism, arguing that the contemporary novelist cannot ignore the great achievements of his or her forebears, while also noting the contemporary novelists' distance from high modernism, not to mention nineteenth-century realism: "Our century is more than two-thirds done; it is dismaying to see so many of our writers following Dostoevsky and Tolstoy, when the question seems to me to be how to succeed not even Joyce and Kafka, but those who succeeded Joyce and Kafka and are now in the evening of their own careers" (67).[13] The novelist must therefore engage with the great modernists and their successors in order to devise a new kind of novel, one that breaks with modernism through serious engagement with it. Yet this does not license avant-garde practice. Barth disassociates himself—and his program for the novel—from the bewildering variety of "intermedia" writing projects that emerged in the heyday of 1960s' artistic experimentalism.[14] Projects such as those he mentions—including Ray Johnson's mail art and Daniel Spoerri's *Anecdoted Typography of Chance*—aim to dismantle the authority of the artist, open the organization of the work up to chance, and embrace ephemerality. Barth, by contrast, wishes to secure cultural authority for his fiction in relation to the august tradition of the novel, and, indeed, of Western narrative in general. The authorial voice may now be a ventriloquistic performance, but it retains intact a connection, albeit an ironical one, to the conventions of the godlike narratorial voice of classic realism. Rather than overcome authorship through mechanisms of randomness and arbitrary procedures, in the fashion of the avant-garde of the 1960s and other eras, the late modernist author plays with the conventions of authorship and in so doing establishes a supple and sophisticated exchange with the historical lineage of great narrative. Thus the self-conscious masquerade of authorship offers a way to relinquish authority the better to retain it.

In "The Literature of Exhaustion" Barth tries to situate and establish the authority of his own writing in contradistinction to the practices of traditional realists and avant-garde experimentalists alike. His effort, therefore, is to establish *cultural* authority on the basis of formal innovation grounded in critically sanctioned virtuosity. Such cultural authority must be sufficient to withstand two particular threats, which Barth, based then at SUNY-Buffalo, found himself well placed to encounter—the campus revolts of the late 1960s, and the apocalyptic rhetoric of Marshall McLuhan, emanating from across the nearby border with Canada. The ructions on U.S. campuses, metonymic in Barth's account of nationwide civil unrest, threatened the university as a hospitable environment for the production and reception of fiction. But more than this, the "traces of tear gas" (64) Barth later claimed to sniff in the margins of his essay hint at the convulsions and potential dissolution of a national culture, an impression strengthened by McLuhan's announcement of the break up of the Gutenberg Galaxy. Barth's "Literature of Exhaustion" is written, therefore, with the intent of claiming credibility for the novel at a moment when its social and cultural space seemed to be under attack from all sides. By establishing a dynamic relationship with the history of narrative, avoiding the pitfalls of realism and the avant-garde, and reclaiming cultural authority, the late modernist novel becomes a symbol for embattled cultural consensus.

"The Literature of Replenishment," the 1980 follow up to "The Literature of Exhaustion," lays out a case for what Barth now calls postmodernist fiction at a moment of confidence sustained by a body of critical writing in which he seeks to intervene.[15] He opens the essay by mentioning the busy critical industry then surrounding postmodernist fiction, and in retrospect his contribution appears at a timely juncture, a moment when the vexed term "postmodernism" was debated in the context of U.S. fiction. Indeed, Barth's essay situated itself among a number of important statements about postmodernism made during the 1970s;[16] as such, it belongs to the first wave of American academic interest in postmodernism, when continental theory, especially the work of Foucault and Derrida, provided the terms of debate over stylistic practices in literature and architecture. The essay takes issue with those critics, notably Gerald Graff, Robert Alter, and Ihab Hassan, who treat postmodernism as a late, self-reflexive impulse of modernism, a logically consistent but comparatively weak continuation of the earlier movement: "postmodern fiction simply carries to its logical and questionable extremes the antirationalist, antirealist, antibourgeois program of modernism, but with neither a solid adversary (the bourgeois having now everywhere co-opted the trappings of modernism and turned its defiant principles into mass media kitsch) nor solid moorings in the quotidian realism it defines itself against" (200). To counter this judgment, Barth mounts his own defense of postmodernism as "the synthesis or transcension" (203) of modernist and traditional realist movements. "The ideal postmodernist novel," he writes, "will somehow rise above the quarrel between realism and irrealism, formalism and 'contentism,' pure and committed literature, coterie fiction and junk fiction" (203). A tall order indeed, yet one Barth feels sufficiently bold to advance on behalf of his new exemplars, Italo Calvino and Gabriel García Márquez, writers who offer in abundance narrative virtuosity and sophistication along with the traditional pleasures of the great novelists. Once again, but with greater conviction, Barth takes pains to associate his celebrated contemporaries with the supreme narrators of Western literature from Boccaccio to Mark Twain. Here, as in the earlier essay, Barth works to establish consensus. His claims on behalf of postmodernist fiction, as he now advances them, are not based so much on the formal properties of the work as on its recapitulation of the strengths of popular forms—the folk tale, myth, and the accessible narrative masterpieces of all literary periods. Often seen with some justification as the master of metafiction, the epitome of arcane literary writing, Barth here lays out his case for postmodernist fiction as the overcoming of historically entrenched cultural divisions, notably those separating elite and popular tastes, the university and the reading public. Barth enlists literary historical consciousness to argue for a postmodernist fiction that joins the middle-class origins of the Anglophone novel with the pre-bourgeois popularity of folk tales and myths, forms that preexist the great divide between high and mass culture.[17]

Such an argument presents an ideal case for Barth's own fiction, acutely and self-consciously linked as it is to the history of the novel and to the narrative dynamics of earlier collections of tales; it also expresses confidence in the capacities of the "literary" novel to cross cultural boundaries and heal cultural divisions. Where "The Literature of Exhaustion" had anxiously cleared a space for fiction to do its work, a space justified by appeals to literary history but given a curious piquancy by the threat of technology and social dissensus, "The Literature of Replenishment" presents the postmodern novel as a model and agent of cultural consensus, appealing to literary critics and general readers alike. Indeed, Barth's writing in both essays appeals to a notion of culture as consensus, as that area of activity that might speak to and perhaps even resolve divisions of class and access to knowledge.

In retrospect it is clear that 1980, the year Barth published "The Literature of Replenishment," was a high water mark for postmodern fiction. Looking back at the 1970s, one notes a string of extraordinary achievements, including Pynchon's *Gravity's Rainbow* (1973), Gaddis's *JR* (1975), McElroy's *Lookout Cartridge* (1974), and Barth's own *Chimera* (1972) and *LETTERS* (1979), books of huge ambition and formal daring, as well as a strong critical interest in the most recent innovative writing. While many writers from the first wave of postmodernism continued to produce important work in the decade that followed, the 1980s were unpropitious years for postmodernism in fiction. As I have argued in the previous chapter, the reasons for this are complicated and multiple. Clearly the position Barth articulated in "The Literature of Replenishment," wherein postmodern fiction might overcome cultural divisions, was difficult to sustain in the climate of the culture wars that emerged from the neoconservative assault on consensus, a strategy that complemented the Reaganite revolution in fiscal and social policy.

In 1990 Barth offered a pessimistic account of the novel's possibilities. "The Novel in the Next Century" despairs of the future of literature, and of the book in general.[18] Having sketched in a history of prose narrative extending in leaps of a century from 1290 (the year of the founding of the University of Macerata where the paper was first delivered) to the present, Barth goes on to imagine what the novel's status might be in 2090, and paints a picture of reading fiction as a highly specialized and arcane activity, a "more or less elite taste, akin to chess or equestrian dressage" (361). In this vision of the future of literature, the novel has the marginal status currently accorded poetry. The wide readership now enjoyed by popular fiction, and by the occasional "literary bestseller" (361), seems doomed to give way before the prodigious rise of electronic media. Here

Barth's saturnine predictions of regression toward "an oral culture deafened by high-decibel pop music more circumambient than the loud-speakered propaganda in George Orwell's *1984*" (360) resemble complaints about cultural illiteracy made by cultural conservatives in the 1980s and early 1990s, in works such as E.D. Hirsch's *Cultural Literacy* (1987) and Allan Bloom's *Closing of the American Mind* (1987). Unlike Bloom and Hirsch, Barth conveys little hope that the gloomy totalitarian future of electronic popular culture might be reversed by a program of renewed attention to the great books of Western culture; indeed, even the most optimistic of his projections presents the novel as a freak survivor in an ecology of mass-mediated entertainment.

"The Novel in the Next Century" makes an appeal for the civil and aesthetic importance of the novel that is rendered all the more poignant by the assumption of the form's imminent decline if not outright demise. To this extent, Barth underscores the role of the novel in a politics of cultural consensus, even as he despairs of any consensus whatsoever, pointing instead to a future of cultural totalitarianism, as the reference to Orwell signals. The novel's specificity as an idiosyncratic medium of individual expression, characterized by the experience of sensibility (as opposed to the senses, to which other media directly appeal), is threatened by the rise of visual media. These characteristics make fiction, by implication, a democratic medium in which the individual can express a unique vision without the compromise of collaboration, can engage with the text at her own pace, and can cherish—and perhaps even put into practice— the idea of writing a novel herself. In this respect, the novel, although brought into the world by collaborative processes of editing and book production, remains irreducibly the intellectual property of its author: "the book is much more 'mine' than any film or television play can ever be its 'author's' " (363). In addition, widespread reading, claims Barth, is part of a healthy democratic culture, in which active citizens make informed decisions about the future of the republic on the basis of absorbing a wide range of information and adjudicating among divergent views. The reading of fiction stands in a symptomatic relation to a vital print-culture that sustains democracy: "I think of the novel (and, by extension, of general literacy) as a canary in the coal mines of democratic civil society" (362).

Barth's assertions disregard the generic differences the earlier essays carefully established in favor of a sense of the novel's metonymic status. In its production and reception, the novel models participatory democracy, standing for the freedom of the author to market her intellectual property, and for the reader's ability to make informed decisions. The novel's continued vitality connotes literature's value as a supplement to the undamaged functioning of civil society. Barth's argument for the continued importance of the novel rests on the assertion of an essentially contiguous relation between fiction and democracy; it has nothing particular to say about why some novels, postmodern novels for example, might be more democratic than others. By treating the novel essentially as a unity, a metonymy for literature and general literacy, Barth insists on the beneficent role of widespread reading, thereby arguing implicitly against theoretically informed accounts of the hegemonic role of "elite" cultural practices. Barth's cultural pessimism summons up literature as a prophylactic against the passive mass consciousness of a postliterate culture: writing fiction secures the place of the individual as expressive uniqueness, a kind of intellectual property, while reading—any kind of reading—engages the reader in the active construction and consideration of meanings.

Underpinning this argument are several distinctions that operate throughout the cultural pessimists' accounts of the death of novel. Barth's defense of literature and literacy turns on the difference between two models of cultural agency: the citizen and the consumer. The citizen makes informed choices among competing viewpoints; such choices are underwritten by literacy, which affords the citizen the competence to evaluate arguments and make decisions. The consumer, by contrast, is the passive recipient of prepackaged information; in place of active discernment, the consumer forms a receptive surface for the stream of corporate messages, whether news, documentary, entertainment or advertisements. For Barth, as for a number of other elegists of the book, the citizen/consumer distinction turns around the difference between media: the citizen is a reader, the consumer a viewer. The novel's role of embodying cultural consensus appears increasingly quixotic as readers give way to viewers.

True to his original charter for fiction, Barth constructs a novel out of these "felt ultimacies"—the cultural decline of the United States and the related enervation of literary fiction. *Coming Soon!!!* makes of the endangered status of the novel, or "p-fiction" (print fiction), the occasion for a bewildering array of narrative arabesques on the theme of apocalypse, including treatment of millennial anxiety, the nervousness over the Y2K computer bug, and ecological disaster, all of which are filtered through an ostentatious grid of allusions to Biblical apocalypses, notably the deluge in the Book of Genesis and the grand finale of Revelations.[19] Although the perceived threat to p-fiction comes from a variety of sources, as Barth argues in his essays, *Coming Soon!!!* treats electronic fiction as the novel's primary rival. Electronic fiction should be read not just as a figure for media technology in general, but also as a synecdoche for cultural mixing, for the incessant newness of the subcultural field that threatens to drown the orderly, if playful, structure of literature. In an essay on hypertextual fiction, Barth quotes some fevered prose from *American Book Review*: "all kinds of viral shit festering out there, not the least of which would include dissident comix, wigged out zines, electronic journals, quicktime hypermedia CD-ROMs, a voluminous mélange of hardcore industrial grunge post-everything music, the Internet, surfpunk technical journals, interactive cable TV . . ."[20] In the face of this onslaught, Barth confesses to feeling like a dinosaur from the late age of print. His difficulty stems, as approving references to recent novels he had read clearly show (a riposte to the sense of immersion presented in the *American Book Review* passage), from the impermanence and fluidity of these cultural forms, their "viral" nature. Hypertextual fiction—e-fiction—partakes of this incessant and restless mixing, this congested sink of influence: mass culture that now takes the form of many cross-fertilizing subcultures. The "viral shit" calls the bluff of postmodern fiction: how can a novel, even one as elaborately structured and allusive as the typical Barth production, overcome the division between literary narrative and the pullulating expanse of electronic culture?

Barth's most recent novel tries to answer this question. *Coming Soon!!!* stages the rivalry between e- and p-fiction as a struggle for authority—over and within the narrative—between the Novelist Emeritus (an unnamed author closely resembling John Barth himself) and the Novelist Aspirant, an upstart graduate student who evangelizes for the new medium of electronic fiction. The more or less amiable conflict between the two, a battle for the future of novel, takes place against the backdrop of Barth's own work, with particular attention to the role of showboats in his oeuvre. Self-consciously marking the end of his career as a novelist, Barth returns to the materials of his first novel, *The Floating Opera*, and writes an elaborate set of variations on that text's own source materials, including Edna Ferber's popular novel *Show Boat* (1926), and the successful Hammerstein/ Kern/Ziegfeld musical derived from it the following year. The showboat, which appears in the novel in several different incarnations, is Barth's house of fiction, a symbol of the novel's quaint and outmoded existence, and also, in the variety performance of the floating opera, a model of post-modern fiction's mixing of registers and genres, its embrace of cultural variousness, of low- and high-brow material. Hence, the evening of skits and songs offered on the latest version of the showboat, The Original Floating Opera II (TOFO II)—Barth plays extensively with the idea of copies and travesties—has the inclusiveness and flexibility to incorporate a slew of versions, revisions, and nested narrative frames. "The New Show" presented on TOFO II incorporates foundational stories such as the Book of Genesis and the historical settling of Maryland (the subject of Barth's own *The Sot-Weed Factor*), as well as narratives of conclusion or apocalypse, including *The Tempest*, and the Revelations of St. John of Patmos. It also recapitulates John Barth's own novelistic career, from the first published novel to the text at hand.

Among these versions and variants two projects labor toward completion timed to coincide with the century's end. While the Novelist Aspirant works on an e-fiction, the Novelist Emeritus attempts to write a capstone work to conclude his career. Barth's characteristic complication comes when the two novelists meet and discuss their plans. The reader learns that the Novelist Emeritus, recently retired from teaching, plans a novel that will, granted health and inspiration, be finished by the end of 1999, five years on. For his part, the Novelist Aspirant dreams of a first effort, a hybrid of electronic and print fiction, that would tell the story of its own composition, taking for its raw materials the last days of a Chesapeake showboat and the central conceit of *The Floating Opera*: "He therefore resolves . . . to appropriate and reorchestrate, or shall we say update and improve upon, his quote–unquote mentor's first novel (published long before N[ovelist] A[spirant] himself was born), at least its central metaphor, as well as its author himself, come to think of it: a foil character whom let's call The Novelist Emeritus" (102). From this point on, the reader cannot determine for certain, at least within the terms of the novel, whether she is reading the work of the upstart e-fictionist or that of the senior writer. Who ventriloquizes whom? Is the Novelist Aspirant aping the voice of the older writer with the intent of undermining his authority, or is the Novelist Emeritus imagining a younger rival who can be overcome in a demonstration of the power of established authority and tradition? The text of *Coming Soon!!!* is divided between competing narrators. It also gestures toward competing media, since the book is punctuated by the graphic representation of computer screen icons, places where the reader of the imaginary e-text might click to make choices, or jump freely around the file that is the novel—as the nickname of the Novelist Aspirant, Hop, emphasizes—so breaking free of the putative tyranny of linear print fiction. Such icons are of course reminders that the work in the reader's hands is precisely *not* a computer file; the links, so to speak, are broken, and the novel stubbornly refuses to function as a hypertext. It proceeds in a linear, albeit dialogical fashion, moving inexorably toward the end of the century. In this sense, "p-fictive one-thing-at-a-timery" (68) mimics the irreversibility of time itself.

The bulk of the novel consists of the efforts of the Novelist Aspirant to inveigle the Novelist Emeritus into the life and activity of the showboat, and of the Novelist Emeritus to resist those efforts in favor of working on his own slowly gestating millennial novel. Thus the book moves between opposed principles of artistic production: on the one hand, the shows put together on TOFO II are characterized by improvisation and collaboration; on the other, the business of writing a novel is both solitary and unavoidably committed to the fixity of the printed word. Yet these ways of working contaminate each other. The evolving scripts of the TOFO II's repertoire take on an increasingly self-conscious and postmodern quality; their genesis provides the occasion for reflection on the nature of metafiction, pastiche, and irony. Equally, the Novelist Emeritus finds his imaginative rendering of a showboat, a fictional subject he feels entitled to revisit and reconceive in order to complete his corpus, upstaged by the real thing, not least because the real thing seems to echo and parody his own inventions. And so the proprietary grip he retains over his material seems increasingly open to question. Who owns the text at hand? Whose imagination dominates the proceedings?

It comes as little surprise that a novel so preoccupied with endings should draw to a close with a whole series. Barth is true here to a long held idea of the meanings of narrative closure, and *Coming Soon!!!* illustrates a principle of narrative construction that he has explored throughout his career. Narratives do indeed have beginnings and endings, and in this they resemble life itself. In an immediate sense, the structure of a story, a unit of meaning established over and against the contingency of time's passage, models the pattern of human life, caught always *in medias res* but fated to conclude with death. More broadly, the structure of narrative can also be plotted onto human history, which is presumed in apocalyptic thinking to have a beginning and an end, to fall within the compass and structural unity of a single, unfolding story.[21] The paradigmatic instance is the Bible, which has a narrative shape that extends from the Creation to the Second Coming. In the formation of a New Heaven and a New Earth the Biblical Apocalypse returns to the beginning of the story, the first formation of all things. Equally, the apocalyptic structure can be seen as the image of a life's literary work, in Barth's case one constantly revisited and revised over the course of more than four decades; his novels form an intertextual network of repeated characters and motifs, a literary tradition in miniature, whereby texts give birth to successors, which then rise up to revise their progenitors. *Coming Soon!!!* fits self-consciously into this textual universe. At the same time, it recalls another hallmark of narration that Barth has cherished over the course of his career. For narrative is also deferral. Scheherezade from *One Thousand and One Nights*, played in the present text by a young woman called Sherry Singer, is Barth's emblematic narrator and the muse of his dueling creators, for she is obliged to spin tales night after night to forestall her execution. In this sense, the title *Coming Soon!!!* is both a herald of apocalypse, with triple exclamation points as camp signifiers of dread, and an advertisement for future production, apocalypse deferred, because, after all, the show must go on.

The ideological lineaments of Barth's project become apparent as the narrative draws to a close. As indicated, *Coming Soon!!!* renders voice strategically uncertain: the reader cannot decide whether the split narration is indeed the product of two writers, or whether one or other of the voices is a fiction. The Novelist Emeritus may be the invention of the Novelist Aspirant, or vice versa. But in spite of this ambiguity, the novel shapes one of its endings around the idea of voice as vocation: the contest between narrators comes to an end when the Novelist Emeritus gracefully withdraws from the field, wishing his rival well. This follows the "Transfer of Authority scene" (282) previously imagined by the Novelist Aspirant, but not quite in the way the reader might expect. What follows is not the triumph of e-fiction, but the realization on the part of the younger writer that his dabbling in other forms—e-fiction, theatrical revues—has been nothing more than preparation to write p-fiction. His parasitical dependence on and oedipal aggression toward his mentor/rival give way to an epiphany of individuation, of self-ownership:

> Whatever the fate of whatever this new-found Voice of mine found to say, and in whatever medium it is said (good old-fashioned bookbound Print, my muse pretty clearly now foresaw, no doubt tricked out with souvenirs of the author's Electronic Period and calibrated echoes of his reluctant mentor), that voice was at long last not only mine but, as much as if not more than any other single attribute, me: was Who I was, really. Had GreatUnc Ennie [the Novelist Emeritus] I wondered—with whom I discovered myself now feeling an odd and gratifying atonement—experienced something similar, somewhere way back? Surely so, as must everyone have done who ever lucked beyond finding his vocation to realizing same. (372)

If it seems at this point clear, at least for a moment, that the novel at hand does indeed comprise the work announced by the Novelist-no-longer-Aspirant, complete with the relics of the e-fiction, harmless reminders of an earlier entanglement, then it is clear because the conception of authorship as self-possession has been triumphantly restored. Not only is the specter of e-fiction banished, its apparent threat—incorporated into the novel in the form of computer icons and nonfunctioning hyperlinks—turns out to be a means to restore the novel to itself and the (print) author to a position of authority. The reconciliation between Novelists

Aspirant and Emeritus that ends their rivalry signals the disappearance of the difference between the two: the apprentice writer discovering his vocation recapitulates the beginnings of the older writer. Ontological doubts, sustained throughout the text, can be put aside with the realization that the novel has reinvented itself one more time, finding its traditional work once again by turning ends—the end of a career, the end of the form—into new beginnings.

This satisfying resolution does not, however, come without cost. The grasping of a vocation and the self-possession of voice reflect authorial autonomy: the Novelist Aspirant is set free from dependence on a mentor, and works henceforth for himself, in the sense that his work embodies a singular vision that tells him who he is; it underwrites selfhood as something distinct and unique. But this self-possession depends, finally, on another kind of autonomy, a material freedom from exigencies. No sooner has the Novelist Aspirant found his calling than he loses his parents, wealthy doctors both, in a plane crash. Thus at the end of the novel he is unburdened by the market necessities that might otherwise endanger his calling. In a rather more oblique, but no less telling image, the showboat, TOFO II—threatened by a terminal and apocalyptic storm, Tropical Storm Zulu II, the twentieth century's last, and by a fire that breaks out on the vessel—is saved and promised a future as a "sort of updated 1960s mini-commune" (391). No longer struggling to keep an obsolete form of entertainment alive, the showboat will henceforth house "a little band of all-but-self-sufficient hunter/gatherers on the wind- and solar-powered New Ark, living off the marsh and what can be sustainably progged [scavenged] therefrom" (391). The novel, too, must find a way of living off the grid, or so Barth's analogy seems to suggest, a way, that is, of surviving an irreversible cultural change. It must learn to sustain itself. As such, the novel's work of forging cultural consensus must be abandoned; its isolation and removal is a symptom of its loss of cultural authority. Future readers, Barth suggests (recalling Thomas Mann), will resemble early Christians—a small, endangered but utterly dedicated sect. It is an image conjured by the monastic robes worn by the performers in the millennial revue finally put together in the latter part of the novel, and also suggested by the unlikely commune of marsh-dwellers.

Such images of autonomy, however implausible they seem, provide a measure of compensation for the novel's retreat into cultural insignificance. Barth manages to sustain an ideology of authorship as the interaction of the untrammeled creative individual, possessed of a novelistic voice, engaging with and transforming the tradition of narrative, even as all pretensions to cultural efficacy are written off. Such an ideology is sustained, precisely through the abandonment of claims to influence, engagement, and consensus. The novel must, Barth implies, embrace its irrelevance if it is to retain its essential connection to tradition. Forms of novelistic practice exhaust themselves and then provide the materials for imaginative reinvention: this is what the novel does, according to Barth, and this is what it must continue to do, electronic deluge notwithstanding.

The Fall of the House of Silk

In a *New Yorker* profile published to coincide with the appearance of *The Human Stain*, Philip Roth expressed the opinion that "the literary era has come to an end."[22] He offered the following grounds for this bleak assertion:

> The evidence is the culture, the evidence is the society, the progression from the movie screen to the television screen to the computer. There's only so much time, so much room, and there are only so many habits of mind that can determine how people use the free time they have. Literature takes a habit of mind that has disappeared. It requires silence, some form of isolation, and sustained concentration in the presence of an enigmatic thing. (86)

Roth draws a now familiar distinction between literate and postliterate generations. His own career—his own understanding of literature—was first established in the 1950s, and his terms are informed by the New Critical veneration of modernist complexity.[23] At the root of this emphasis was a pressing concern with consciousness: "To explore consciousness was the great mission of the first half of the twentieth century—whether we're talking about Freud or Joyce, whether we're talking about the Surrealists or Kafka or Marx, or Frazer or Proust or whoever. The whole effort was to expand our sense of what consciousness is and what lies behind it" (87). This mission holds no interest for the younger, postliterate generation. Roth takes pains to stress that his worries are not merely the grumblings of an older writer, swept aside by literary fashion; and, as it happens, Roth's career has undergone a remarkable resurgence in the last decade, a fact not lost on critics and prize committees.[24] Instead, his cultural pessimism rests on a larger, quasi-anthropological claim: "the American branch of the species is being retooled" (87).

Roth lays the blame for this great shift in comprehension and interest on the technological transformation of American culture. His instincts as a novelist do not, however, lead him to examine the ways in which consciousness has been shaped by the pressures and seductions of technology. Instead, his trilogy on postwar American history dramatizes the fate of a generation—his generation—subjected to social and cultural change. In *The Human Stain*, the novel that concludes the sequence, the drama takes shape as a classical tragedy complete with a noble individual brought low, secrets and ironic reversals of fortune, and transformations worthy of mythology.[25] But the novel also draws dark comedy and pathos out of the gulf between Sophoclean destinies and the absurdities of campus politics. The heroic protagonist is a vigorous but elderly classics professor, the metamorphoses have to do with that magical substance Viagra ("Thanks to Viagra I've come to understand Zeus's amorous transformations" [32]), the knives come out over a single, misunderstood word, and all the while—a lurid backdrop to the drama— the saga of President Clinton and Monica Lewinsky unfolds in the media. So tragic events unfold in banal circumstances, though as Silk tells his students at the beginning of an introductory classics class, much the same can be said of Western literature, which begins in the *Iliad* with a squabble between two men over a woman.[26] In and around these materials Roth draws a scathing picture of contemporary academia.

Roth's conservatism is evident: he portrays an academic environment that has given up on the literacy necessary for comprehension of the classics and works of fiction as challenging as his own. Athena College, the academic setting, is an institution satirically misnamed, since folly has driven out wisdom, students are idle and unlettered, and professors in thrall to the dogmatism of critical theory and political correctness. But *The Human Stain* is not simply a lament over the decline of higher education. In fact the novel engages with the politics of race, gender, and literacy in complex and contradictory ways. While certainly deploring the politics and rhetoric of the academy, Roth employs literacy as the code through which he attempts to reconstruct a concept of selfhood as mysterious, perplexing, and antinomian—the elusive heart of a literary ethos reclaimed from distinctly unpromising circumstances.

The Human Stain underscores the "retooling of the species" by contrasting two generations: men (and they are mostly men) of Roth's generation who grew up during the war or shortly after; and women and men (mostly women) in their 20s and 30s, individuals old enough to be the grown children of the 60- and 70-year-olds. The central characters in the drama embody this division: Coleman Silk, the ex-Dean of Athena College, who is in his early 70s, and Faunia Farley, his lover, a working-class woman in her mid-30s. In orbit around this pair are the narrator, Nathan Zuckerman, now in his late 60s; Faunia's former husband, Lester, a half-crazed Vietnam veteran, an anomalous figure in terms of the novel's generational scheme; and a young Professor of French, Delphine Roux, who has cast herself in the role of Silk's nemesis. Further in the background are the students at Athena College—indistinct, confused, barely educable—and the individual who seems, during a particularly misogynistic conversation, to embody all the flaws of her generation: Monica Lewinsky, a constant news presence during the summer of 1998 when the novel unfolds. The gap between the young and the old is one of power and education as much as age, though Roth proceeds to complicate such relationships through the course of the novel.

Nonetheless, the generation gap is one way of representing the question the novel asks of American history: when—and why—did everything change? For the novel leaves the reader in little doubt that everything has changed, and changed for the worse: the powerful, cultivated, intelligent, largely admirable Coleman Silk ends his career in ignominy, and can only find solace in the intensely private, erotic relationship he establishes with Faunia Farley. The disapproval that this relationship excites, once it becomes common knowledge, parallels the "enormous piety binge" with which the revelations about Monica Lewinsky and President Clinton are greeted. In both cases, the "ecstasy of sanctimony" (2) points to the public refusal to accept the flawed complexity of human beings. Other kinds of thinking that Roth considers simplistic, naive, blind to the contradictoriness and fallibility of individuals, expressive of the "tyranny of propriety" include: "civic responsibility, WASP dignity, women's rights, black pride, ethnic allegiance, [and] emotion-laden Jewish ethical sensitivity" (153). In the late 1990s of Roth's novel, these kinds of "de-virilizing" (153) propriety are everywhere—in the popular press, where Clinton is hounded, and where the right-wing columnist William F. Buckley calls for "the corrective retribution of castration" (3); in the small town where Silk resides, and where his affair with a woman half his age is a scandal; and above all in the academic world, where small-mindedness takes the form of political correctness, the ideological certitudes of which provoke Silk to resign over an absurd inquiry into a presumed racial slur.

Near the beginning of the novel, Silk receives an anonymous letter denouncing his relationship with Faunia Farley: "Everyone knows you're sexually exploiting an abused, illiterate woman half your age" (38). This "everyone knows" typifies the groupthink against which the novel battles. What everyone knows, in fact, is nothing at all: nobody understands the relationship between Coleman Silk and Faunia Farley, not even Zuckerman, who has a great deal of sympathy for them (not to mention imaginative projection onto them, since he has been "de-virilized" literally by the side-effects of an operation for prostate cancer, and detects in Coleman

Silk the potency—augmented by Viagra—that he himself lacks), and certainly not Delphine Roux, whose spite stems from her own frustrated and disavowed attraction to Silk. As if to emphasize the collective blindness, the novel is replete with secrets, is driven by secrets, chief among them the secret of Silk's identity; it emerges in the course of the book that Silk is in fact an African American who has, for more than forty years, passed as a Jew.[27] No one knows; no one can make sense of Silk. Instead, they fall back on preconceptions and platitudes, the mental habits that allow Silk to perform an ethnic identity not his own.

To prefer the collective ignorance of propriety to the struggle with the intractable contradictoriness of events and people signifies, above all, a failure of education. Silk, for example, is incensed when his son believes the rumors about Faunia and his relationship with her. He reflects, "All the reading to them. The sets of encyclopedias. The preparation before quizzes. The dialogues at dinner. The endless instruction . . . in the multiform nature of life. The scrutinization of language. All this stuff we did, and then to come back at me with this mentality?" Cultural education, it seems, cannot be converted into the durable currency of imaginative sympathy and "well-informed skepticism" (174). The most forceful expression of this failure comes from one of the professors at Athena college, who compares his students, those close in age, and alike in fatuity, to Monica Lewinsky:

> They open their mouths and they send me up the wall. Their whole language is a summation of the stupidity of the last forty years. Closure. *There's* one. My students cannot stay in that place where thinking must occur. Closure! They fix on the conventionalized narrative, with its beginning, middle, and end—every experience, no matter how ambiguous, no matter how knotty or mysterious, must lend itself to this normalizing, conventionalizing, anchorman cliché. (147)

With the last clause, the speaker—who remains unidentified, the voice of an academic saying everything he is not allowed in public to say—links together the banality of the media and the banality of the students' thinking. Roth's discontent over the retooling of the species issues forth in this scathing attack on college-age Americans, those who refuse depth, complexity, ambiguity, and even thought itself. Literature—the classics that Silk teaches, the fiction Roth writes—has nothing to say to this unlettered generation.

This, of course, is an extreme, provocative, even an aggressive position— what else would one expect from Roth? It lends itself to the perception that the novel is little more than a conservative diatribe, an attack on the state of higher education, and a disparaging commentary on the young—and not so young—people of the United States. Without going any further, *The Human Stain* might be read as a fictionalized volley from the culture wars. And, to be sure, Roth pours predictable and unstinting scorn on his representative literary theorist, Delphine Roux, who comes from Paris, like theory itself, and who wrote a Yale doctoral dissertation on Bataille. The novel, in this respect, appears to propound a view of the world that one might expect from the likes of Coleman Silk, who is passing as a very specific kind of person, a conservative academic shaped by the New York intellectuals, one who moved in the postwar years in the circles of "*Commentary, Midstream*, and the *Partisan Review*" (131).

But nothing in *The Human Stain* is quite as straightforward as it seems. Indeed, the book that Zuckerman produces, the novel that struggles to shed light on Silk's secret, on his late passion, on Faunia herself, and on the murderous rage of Lester Farley, acknowledges its incomprehension in figures of illegibility. The novel is enclosed between two Xs, and the difference between them indicates the deepening, rather than the resolution, of enigma. On the first page, amid a flurry of references to moments in American history—the Great Depression, the colonial era, the revelations about President Clinton—the reader learns of the rural post office that "flies its American flag at the junction of the two roads that mark the commercial center of this mountain town" (1). The flag flying at the crossroads presents an authoritative sign of order, of the symbolic itself, of the federal government present and legible even in this remote location. On the last page of the novel, after a tense conversation with Lester Farley on a frozen lake, Zuckerman pictures the troubled and troubling veteran in his wintry isolation: "the icy white of the lake encircling a tiny spot that was a man, the only human marker in all of nature, like the X of an illiterate's signature on a sheet of paper" (361). The illiterate's X is the mark left by one excluded from writing, from the symbolic, and from history. Yet here the X is what eludes the interpreter: it is that which cannot be parsed or elucidated, that which remains stubbornly opaque about Farley and the history that has shaped him. Between these two Xs, one legibly marked by the American flag, the other an unreadable sign, the novel elaborates a network of connections and suggestive links around literacy, legibility, and historical interpretation.

The illegible history is, above all, the history of how things reached their present state, how illiteracy, in the broad sense, overtook the desire and the capacity to profit from literature. Silk's long-estranged sister Ernestine, a retired high school teacher, poses the question most directly: "Reading the classics is too difficult, therefore it's the classics that are to blame. Today the student asserts his incapacity as a privilege. I can't learn it, so there is something wrong with it. . . . There are no more criteria, Mr. Zuckerman, only opinions. I often wrestle with this question of what everything used to be" (331). She goes on to offer a narrative of decline, an explanation that pins the blame on the destruction of community. Although contiguity rather than direct causality undergirds her account, her argument is clear enough: East Orange, New Jersey, the small city the Silk children grew up in through the depression and the war years was lively, diverse, and vital; with the planned urban renewal of postwar prosperity, the black community was wrecked, divided by new highways, and inadvertently segregated by the modernized infrastructure.[28] East Orange stands as a synecdoche for the changes in the United States as a whole: the shift away from localized communities to the commercial restructuring of urban areas, accompanied, one might add, by white flight to the suburbs, a phenomenon Ernestine neglects to mention. East Orange is left with the devastating economic consequences, in the face of which well-meaning pedagogical schemes like Black History month are a hopelessly inadequate substitute. Zuckerman makes the necessary connections:

> All of life was there in East Orange. And when? Before. Before urban renewal. Before the classics were abandoned. Before they stopped giving out the Constitution to high school graduates. Before there were remedial classes in the colleges teaching kids what they should have learned in ninth grade. Before Black History Month. Before they built the parkway and brought in 280. Before they persecuted a college professor for saying "spooks" to his class. Before she drove up the hill to West Orange to shop. Before everything changed, including Coleman Silk. That's when it all was different—before. And, she lamented, it will never be the same again, not in East Orange or anywhere else in America. (332)

This passage labors to braid together Coleman Silk's story—his extraordinary journey from the gifted East Orange boy to the disgraced ex-Dean at a New England college—with the story of national decline implied by Ernestine.

"Before" is the key signature of conservative lament, which the novel strategically places in the mouth of a dignified and intelligent African American woman. All that is visible from this vantage on history are the signs of decline, of vitality deadened, diversity defrauded, education travestied. For Ernestine, the connection between Silk's story and that of the nation lies in the ways that education, which should always be pursued under the fifth amendment of the Constitution, has been corrupted, stripped of criteria, infected with relativism. And in many ways, Silk's ascent through the ranks of academia did exemplify the close connections between the acquisition of cultural capital and elevation in social class— in short, the effective functioning of a stratified (and stratifying) educational system.[29] His fall, in turn, over the misprision of the word "spooks"—a racial slur that harks back to his beginnings, and speaks, in a sense, of everything Ernestine leaves out of her account, a history assigned to the cultural unconscious—lays bare the corruption of that system of education, its dissolution, in Ernestine's words, into "a hotbed of ignorance" (328).

Yet this understanding of Coleman's life in education is complicated by several ironies. In the first place, Silk, as the forceful Dean who modernized Athena College, has played a crucial role in establishing the institution that subsequently destroys him. He has, for example, hired the ambitious Delphine Roux, the woman who goes on to persecute him, even after his retirement. Furthermore, through his pursuit of literacy he has in effect taken the traditional route of African American emancipation. Through learning, it would appear that he has freed himself, though the price of freedom is the violent fiction he has constructed, the symbolic parricide of his passing. He can only enjoy the advantages of literacy by pretending to be white: his successes in education are achieved under the assumption of a Jewish identity.

Silk's heroic self-fashioning seems, at first sight, to illustrate the sheer power of identity available to the highly educated individual. He has, in an unusually literal fashion, made a self, fashioned a new identity out of the stuff of his education. Self-making is frequently offered as a rationale for studying the great texts of the Western literary tradition. For instance, the film critic David Denby, in his account of taking the Columbia great books course as a way to make sense of the debates raging in the culture wars, recounts how his Professor begins the semester by appealing to the power of literature to build the self.[30] In his heroic formation of a self by cunning, ingenuity, and persistence, Coleman Silk embodies the tradition he teaches: he assumes his own tragic grandeur when he falls, becomes a figure of nobility and pathos, a protagonist from Sophocles, or, in the only resonant secular comparison available, a defeated or disgraced president, "Nixon at San Clemente or . . . Jimmy Carter, down in Georgia" (18). By the same token, the power of self-fashioning remains a potent American myth: "Was [Coleman] merely being another American and, in the great frontier tradition, accepting the democratic invitation to throw your origins overboard if to do so contributes to the pursuit of happiness?" (334). His acquisition of cultural capital allows him to move from one identity to another. He thereby presses up against the limits of the idea of literacy as freedom, since literacy of the kind he seeks is socially and educationally unavailable to him as an African American in a racist society. Covertly to accept those limitations at once subverts them and demonstrates their power.

To what extent must American self-invention be restricted by ties to family, community, origins? For Walt, the oldest sibling, Coleman's fabrication of a white identity breaks his ties to the black community, and implicitly renounces the struggle for collective emancipation; in anger, he tells Coleman never to bother their mother again. For Ernestine, by contrast, the ties of family override those of racial solidarity, and Coleman should not be cut off from his mother and siblings. Coleman, she suggests, has simply taken the civil rights struggle into his own hands, and anticipated social liberation on an individual basis. The extraordinary fiction of Silk's identity, maintained over so many years, presses the notion of self-invention to a dangerously literal extreme. For Zuckerman it makes of Silk's identity something illegible. Rather like his surprising naval tattoo, Silk has an exoteric meaning: he is the disgraced classicist, the ex-Dean, and stranger still, the man brought back to life by Faunia Farley and Viagra; but he also has a hidden, secret identity, at which Zuckerman can only guess. And this is connected to the other meaning of the tattoo—that it doesn't so much mark camaraderie or a love for the navy as the moment when Silk's fiction was ruptured one traumatic night in Norfolk, Virginia, when he was identified in a brothel as black, and nearly lost his grip on the self-invention he had crafted so carefully.

The effort Zuckerman mounts in the novel is to understand the relation between the knowable Silk and his secret self, and hence to grapple with the fluidity and fixity of identity. He struggles to make sense of the ties of cultural, social, and racial identity, which can never be symmetrical in a society characterized by institutional exclusions and prejudice. More abstractly, both Zuckerman and the novel itself try to make sense of an ambiguity central to contemporary ideas about identity, and this indeed is a source of the novel's interest and power, notwithstanding its offensive caricatures and disabling limitations. On the one hand, identity is a fluid, unstable category, something that might, according to American mythology, be reshaped in the pursuit of happiness, or, from a very different perspective, that of contemporary theory, betray assertions of selfhood and assumptions of self-identity. On the other, identity is thoroughly conditioned by cultural and social forces, be they oppressive tropes of language, race, or gender. To try to make sense of Coleman Silk is to wrestle with this ambiguity, for his perplexing, unreadable identity demands that one think of both the power and the limitation of the self to make its own story.

It is this task of understanding that makes Ernestine's measured account of cultural and social decline unconvincing to Zuckerman:

> How did such a man as Coleman come to exist? What is it that he was? Was the idea he had for himself of lesser validity or of greater validity than someone else's idea of what he was supposed to be? Can such things even be known? But the concept of life as something that may not allow for thought, of society as dedicated to a picture of itself that may be badly flawed, of an individual as real apart and beyond the social determinants defining him, which may indeed be what to him seem most *unreal*—in short, every perplexity pumping the human imagination seemed to lie somewhere outside [Ernestine's] own unswerving allegiance to a canon of time-honored rules. (333)

Implicit here are questions about self-ownership and freedom—how the former relate to the latter. Coleman Silk's drama lies in the clash between the ideas he has of himself—remarkable and surprising and thoroughly constructed ideas, as it turns out, since Coleman is living inside his own fiction—and the ideas that "propriety" has of him. Yet neither side can make sense of Silk. According to the prevailing understanding, Coleman's ill-chosen word "spooks" reveals him to be an elderly, Jewish racist. His response is no less caught up in the logic of accusation and caricature: "Thrown out of Athena," he rages, "for being a white Jew of the sort those ignorant bastards call the enemy. That's who made their American misery. That's who stole them out of paradise. And that's who's been holding them back all these years" (16). It is this self-righteous rage that sets Silk to work on a manuscript that will tell his side of the story, a project of self-justification called "Spooks." Yet the manuscript proves unworkable: Silk cannot exculpate himself—he cannot, that is, narrate his own identity in any coherent, intelligible fashion.

His is a fissured identity that speaks through invective, through ambiguous, even unreadable utterances. "Spooks" wryly refers to the students who have never shown up to Silk's class, and who might as well be ghosts, yet the word is also an archaic racial slur, a term of derogation that harks back to Coleman's hidden origins. For the reader, the "spook" is Silk himself, whose race—and whose embedded memory of racial slurs speaks out like a parapraxis, a word from the cultural unconscious—is the secret, the specter, haunting his life. Thus the word reveals more than it says, and certainly more than Silk intends. Similarly, his infuriated response to the condescension of his lawyer, a man much younger than Coleman, comes in the form of another archaic term of racial hostility: Silk concludes his tirade with the surprising epithet "lily-white" (81). This intended insult comes from quite a different subject position, that of Silk the (covert) African American. Yet these phrases of abuse are ambiguous, their significance as contradictory as Silk's identity. His erstwhile friend, the black historian Herbert Keble, who sides against Silk in the "spooks" controversy, is clear about his priorities: "Representation—that was the issue" (17). By this he means the diversification of the campus community and, by extension, the ways in which public speech and action must reflect the priorities of a representative politics. But the issue is also representation in another sense. Silk's difficulty in completing his manuscript raises the question of how identity can be brought into language, particularly when the identity in question is constituted by a refusal of language, a refusal to accept the oppressive position established for a black male within the symbolic order.

From this perspective, the question of literacy links up with the larger issue of the ascription of and accession to identity positions. Silk's early refusal to accept the positions available to an African American within a racist society is achieved through a refusal to speak or write: he simply neglects to mention, or sign for the fact that he is black. The biography of Silk that the world knows, the account of a man who has risen from humble origins (he presents his father as a New Jersey bar owner) to his eminence as a highly respected and successful college Dean, is a story of success through education, through the attainment of knowledge of the great foundational texts of Western literature—the fullest possible realization of literacy. Yet this narrative, as Zuckerman eventually discovers, has as its necessary but inadmissible precondition a silence, a refusal of literacy. It is this unknowable, secret silence that finally manifests itself in the perverse language acts—racial slurs and unintelligible narrative—that attend Silk's fall from his position of eminence.

Silk's silence—and the mystery of his identity—parallels the silence of his lover, Faunia Farley. Faunia willfully refuses literacy. Her name, along with her work in the milkshed of a local organic farm and her fascination with birds, symbolizes her liminal position vis-à-vis the human/animal divide. She is illiterate like a creature of nature, no more able to read than a cow or a bird, even though she learned to read at one point, since her origins were in fact upper-middle-class, and in a final twist she turns out to have kept a diary all along. Silk, however, assumes that Faunia's illiteracy stems from her traumatic life—sexual abuse by her stepfather, several violent boyfriends, a brutal and pathologically jealous husband, the death of her children in a fire: any one of these might be sufficient cause for her resistance to the word. Yet she also prides herself on her sexual proficiency, her "spontaneous physical shrewdness" and "transgressive audacity" (31), in Silk's words, which she describes as being distinctively different from the sexuality of other, literate women. Her refusal of the law of the written word, which sets her in stark opposition to Silk, seemingly guarantees her prodigious eroticism.

The gender politics of these thematic elements and character constructions is undeniably offensive. Roth pits women's bodies and minds against each other. Faunia's erotic brilliance, her carnal self-knowledge, is in marked contradistinction to the miserable isolation and lovelessness, not to mention the glaring lack of self-knowledge, of Delphine Roux, who is, presumably, altogether too learned to prosper in love. Delphine Roux's intellectual interest in transgression, in Bataille, for example, is at odds with her real timidity, her inhibition, just as her feminism, Roth implies, is at odds with her desire to be dominated: her fevered imagination prompts her to think, on her first meeting with Silk, that he wants to tie her up; nothing, the reader is assured, could be further from his mind. In addition, her intellectual capacities are thrown into question: she is bright, certainly, yet devoid of intellectual substance; the stellar *normalienne* at once knows everything, but somehow knows nothing at all. Once again, learning has failed to translate into anything more profound. However, the savagery of the portrayal of Delphine Roux—Roth's revenge against his feminist critics—is perhaps less important to the meaning of the novel than the treatment of Faunia, an ideal of unlettered sexual prowess—woman as animal, as unthinking nature—to set beside the frustrated academic. The treatment of Faunia is split between extraordinary abjection and wholehearted celebration, and most disturbingly of all, the latter sometimes grows out of the former. Coleman confides at one point that her erotic gifts are the result of the abuse she suffered at the hands of her stepfather. There is little here to be said in Roth's defense.

Nonetheless, one must reckon with the treatment of Faunia to make sense of her role as a principle of antinomian freedom, a figure of resistance to the symbolic. In spite of the scandalous differences between Silk and Faunia—age, education, class—their relationship is founded on an obscure, clandestine parity. The novel's resistance to the voices of propriety depends on the idea of a freedom shared and expressed in carnality, in the transfigurative crossing of the human and the animal. Faunia's association with the animal world is consistent; Silk, for his part, is likened to "a snub-nosed, goat-footed Pan" (25), and Zuckerman stresses his lithe physical grace with homoerotic intensity. Stripped of his profession, his wife dead, his standing in the community degraded, Silk meets Faunia outside social determinants. Or so Zuckerman would like to believe. The erotic idyll between Silk and Faunia is constantly threatened—by the disapproval of the community, by Lester Farley, and by the acute social difference between them, which has a tendency inopportunely to erupt, at least until they are able to share their secrets.[31] Yet it is the idea—or the animating illusion—of a freedom found in carnality that the novel opposes to the deadly pieties of propriety.

In carnality, the jubilant subversion of the human/animal divide, the novel turns its sign of illiteracy, the X of the symbolic and its refusal, into a rhetorical figure, that of chiasmus. This is best illustrated through the book's title. The phrase "the human stain" acquires several meanings as the novel unfolds, including skin pigmentation (the secret of Coleman's race), and the all-too-human stain on Monica Lewinsky's infamous blue dress. As such, the stain is the mark of secrecy and shame. But it is also the trace of transgression, the mark of what really makes human beings what they are—not their conformity to civic ideals or community standards, but their animal spirits, their eroticism and will to carnal happiness. The stain is therefore a sign of resistance, a stubborn remainder or trace, a mark of that which cannot be encompassed by the rhetoric of social determinism, however well-intentioned, or by the language of collective responsibility. The stain signifies the irreducibility of the individual to the statements that might be made about him or her.

In this respect, the unfreedom of illiteracy—which, for Roth, afflicts a whole generation—crosses over with the elusive freedom of the unknowable self, that which resists the blandishments of description. Yet the X of illiteracy is precisely the opposite of the illegible X of identity. For the wager of Roth's novel, embodied in Zuckerman's narration, is that the function of literature is to probe and investigate the enigmatic nature of identity. Literacy is a precondition for the hard work of thinking about the perplexing nature of human desire, shame, secrecy, and freedom. The novel, according to Roth, works to push perception beyond the unilluminating statements of propriety, beyond the expression of solidarity (to class, race, even profession), to a place of difficult and restless thought on what must always remain elusive in language and human behavior. Roth holds back from sanctifying this function, enveloping it in a mist of ersatz religiosity; his interests are too secular, argumentative, and comic to settle for aesthetic pieties. Instead, he tries in his fiction to embody the antinomian ferocity implicit in his entanglement with the matter of American history.

Avant-Garde and Utopia

"You are afraid. You are afraid, as usual, that the novel is dying. You think you know what the novel is: it's the kind you write. You fear you are dying."[32] With these words the experimental novelist Carole Maso launches an attack on the rhetoric of the death of the novel. For Maso the death of the novel is a theme dear to the hearts of male novelists of a certain age; it is a defensive lament choked with nostalgia for the good old days when their cultural authority was undiminished. Her brilliant polemic levels a series of charges at a familiar compound ghost, the satirized "you" of her address, arguing that the novel, far from dying, is in fact opening to new influences and voices. It can profit from film, from technological innovations, including hypertext fiction (Barth's e-fiction), and from a revived attention to avant-garde practice in all the arts.

Maso challenges several of the assumptions made by the elegists of the book. She questions the rigid dichotomy between electronic and print culture, between the screen and the book, and sees in the language of competition—of internecine strife between opposed media—an assertion of privilege, a desire to look down on the fray. What the "you" of Maso's polemic fears is the loss of the power to legislate, to patrol the boundaries of literature, sanctioning approved practice—what form a novel should take, how a poem should work—throughout the literary field. She associates the assertion of privilege exercised over literature with gender relations in a patriarchal society: the authority of male critics, novelists, and publishers resembles the domination of women through conventional but violent rituals of social interaction:

> All the dark deserted roads you've led me down, grabbing at my breasts, tearing at my shirt, my waistband: first date.
> Second date: this is how to write a book.
> Third date: good girl! Let's publish it!!! (166)

Maso thus draws parallels between domination inside and outside the literary field. The oppressive but melancholic figure of the male novelist or critic—"Edmund Wilson, Alfred Kazin, Harold Bloom *et fils*"—overlaps with the political authority responsible for the disaster of the American war in Vietnam: "You who said 'hegemony' and 'domino theory' and 'peace with honor'" (165). With this gesture, Maso links her own avant-garde writing practice to an oppositional politics. Her artistic dissent is homologous with her political dissent.

Maso's refreshing counterblast to the pessimism of the elegists justifies her own fictional practice. She too looks to secure a place in the literary field, and does so by challenging the literary status quo in favor of a formally challenging, lyrical, rhapsodic fiction. Consequently, Maso gives short shrift to what she sees as the middlebrow conventions of traditional fiction.

In particular, she derogates the typical *New Yorker* story, describing it as an artifact that belongs in a museum (184), and expresses the wish that "all talk show fiction be put to bed now. Its fake psychologies, its 'realisms.' Its pathetic 2 plus 2" (168). While she invokes a "utopia of possibility" (169) as the future of avant-garde art, her account depends on a rehabilitated hierarchy of evaluation, a better critical accounting. The middlebrow realist fictions, with their mechanistic cause and effect psychologies, are overpraised in the current critical climate; they must be relegated to the museum of obsolete literary styles. Maso's utopia demands a revised conception of the excellence of literary art, one currently obscured by commercial interference in the field. She expresses a further wish that the publishing world be freed from the demands of business, and that writers resist the allure of capital as they make their way into the realm of ideas and artistic practice.

Maso avoids the pessimism of Barth, Roth, and the other elegists by imagining a new and different literary field, one that reflects the true range and excellence of contemporary writing. It is an imaginary place—a utopia proper—in which obsolete styles will be left behind, the margins brought to the center (or at least recognized and valued), and both the patriarchal and commercial dictates will be undone. Even in a polemic busy with pro- posals, denunciations, and brief, lyrical flights, Maso wishes to establish the literary and political credentials of her avant-gardism. She draws up lists of her favored progenitors and peers, notable amongst them Emily Dickinson, Gertrude Stein, and especially Virginia Woolf, the most important figure in her matrilineal descent from modernism. This mustering of authorities discreetly merges with her political position-taking in the essay. In a brief epiphanic paragraph she conjures up a scene in a train compartment, and recreates the awakening consciousness of an African American woman who sits beside her: "I recognize her delight. It is taken away, and it is given back. The miracle and mystery of this life in one middle-aged black woman on the Metro North next to me. The Hudson River widening" (172–173). This is Maso's version of Woolf's famous statement of purpose in her essay "Mr. Bennett and Mrs. Brown."[33] Woolf imagines a woman in a railway carriage taken by the major middlebrow realists of her time as the subject of fiction. She stresses the mechanical, superficial attention of Arnold Bennett, H.G. Wells, and John Galsworthy, and contrasts it to a superior method of imaginative sympathy that will summon up the active interior life of the woman, a method that she intends to make her own. Woolf's Mrs. Brown becomes Maso's black woman waking on a train beside the Hudson. The sympathetic recreation of the sensual delight in returning consciousness justifies a lyrical prose fiction, such as that Maso pursues in her finest work, notably *The American Woman in the Chinese Hat* and *AVA*. Yet this is also a scene of identification that presupposes a politics. Maso's marginal literary art occupies a place in the literary field, currently dominated by white males in positions of authority, that can be likened to the place of African American women in the social world. This implied homology licenses the identification between observer (Maso) and observed (the woman), and overcomes the differences (of race and class) that might otherwise separate them, making possible a moment of shared experience and recognition in an ambience of sensory pleasure.

Maso stakes out a position of cultural power on the margins of a stagnant literary culture, one characterized by dreary aesthetic compromise and stultifying masculine authority. She has no need to lament the threat to consensus since the present circumstances are in sore need of revision. As such, her polemic serves a reformist agenda. She envisages a literary field no longer dominated by the criteria enforced by the traditional male gatekeepers. Her explicit wishes are for an evaluative culture in which avant-garde practice, whether in literature, film, or any other art form, receives sufficient recognition. But her commitment to an avant-garde agenda leads her to imagine a future in which all will be changed, a "utopia of possibility" wherein the new world of artistic practice will also be a world of better social relations.

The tension between reformist and utopian strains in Maso's argument lets the possibility arise, between the lyric bursts of her essay, that modest literary proposals might have far-reaching consequences. Thus she circumvents the problem of linking literary agency to cultural authority. Barth wavers between seeing the postmodern novel as a model for consensus, for the negotiation if not supersession of differences between popular and high literary forms, and treating it merely as a metonymy for general literacy, a passive reflection of the state of culture. Roth envisages the novel as a weapon against the inert consciousness and collective nostrums of an age dominated by electronic mass media. The novel, for all its signal importance, is caught up in a cultural trend that it can deplore but hardly amend. Maso has, she claims, little authority to defend, since the literary culture—rather than the wider climate—is one that has failed to recognize her work. Technology is not something to fear: it offers new possibilities and new forms, as well as prompting an enlivened attention to the essence of older models. The utopian promise of modernism can be reclaimed under conditions suitably modified for its judicious reception. Thus for Maso the current circumstance is not that of the death of the novel, but of an aesthetic and political stimulus to grasp modernist innovation as the potential of fiction, now and in the future.

CHAPTER 3

JONATHAN FRANZEN, OPRAH WINFREY, AND THE FUTURE OF THE SOCIAL NOVEL

During the autumn of 2001, when the news was dominated by the horrors of terrorism and war, the falling out of Oprah Winfrey and Jonathan Franzen offered a distracting spectacle of loose talk and public embarrassment. In September, heralded by a blaze of publicity, Franzen published his third novel, *The Corrections*. Early reviews were wildly enthusiastic, lavishing particular praise on the book's treatment of character and its sheer readability. Later in the same month, Oprah Winfrey announced her selection of *The Corrections* for her television book club, thereby guaranteeing that commercial success would accompany critical esteem.[1] Trouble began, however, on Franzen's nationwide promotional tour. He expressed ambivalence about his Oprah selection, acknowledging his discomfort with the appearance of the Book Club logo on the cover of his novel, and admitting to unease over past selections: "The problem in this case is some of Oprah's picks. She's picked some good books, but she's picked enough schmaltzy, one dimensional ones that I cringe, myself, even though I think she's really smart and she's really fighting the good fight."[2] When Franzen's comments reached Winfrey, she took the unprecedented step of canceling the scheduled show devoted to *The Corrections*. Subsequent press commentary chastised Franzen for his "elitism" and "snobbery."[3] His apologies and qualifications seemed only to make matters worse, drawing further criticism of his perceived disingenuousness or, at best, his naivety.

A reader of *The Corrections* might have detected something almost Franzenesque in the comic desperation of this drama: a brilliant success gives way to disaster because of a few ill-chosen words, and the mess grows more intractable with every attempt the protagonist makes to extricate himself. The press, for its part, took delight in casting this series of events into an emblematic conflict between the popular talk show host and the highbrow author—a conflict, that is to say, between personalities representative of warring media. In what hardly amounted to a debate— a spectacle, rather, of *schadenfreude* and righteousness—Winfrey was seen as the champion of literacy and Franzen as the elitist exponent of what he was incautious enough to call "the high art literary tradition."[4] In addition, though this went unspoken, the quarrel matched an African American woman against a white male, thus raising—at least in the realm of images—the stakes on questions of hegemony, privilege, and populist struggles for recognition. The convenient opposition between democratic TV star and snobbish writer made good copy, but failed to register the complicated processes of cultural evaluation in play on both sides of the television/print divide, as well as obscuring questions of symbolic capital and social class that are essential to an understanding of both Winfrey's Book Club and Franzen's novel. It seems more useful, therefore, to ask what the controversy and the novel itself reveal about the configuration of the literary field in the age of the reading group and the television talk show.

Franzen mounted his own effort to comprehend the relationship between literary production and media culture in a 1996 *Harper's Magazine* essay.[5] Presented as a narrative of breakdown and recovery, his confession frets over the apparent irrelevance of literary fiction, and the "social novel" in particular, in a cultural climate dominated by technological consumerism, ideologies of therapy, and the omnipresence of the image. These facets of contemporary culture, Franzen claims, erode the prestige and legitimacy of the novelist; under their influence, a unified national culture, to which the writer might speak, fragments into a multiplicity of particular interest groups and specialized languages. The novelist's dilemma stems especially from the distorted relationship between private and public dimensions of experience, a concern Franzen relates in turn to competing models of identity formation. In working out a new, more productive understanding of authors, readers, and the role of the novel, Franzen distances himself from both the social vocation of fiction and from a postmodern approach to form. He seeks to secure prestige within the literary field, while also reinventing realism as social representation. His success in establishing a distinctive position for himself may be judged by reading *The Corrections*. His difficulties with Winfrey throw this position into relief, making visible its limitations as a campaign map of the literary field. To understand what is at stake in Franzen's position, this chapter will read Winfrey's Book Club, the *Harper's* essay, and *The Corrections* against each other, attending to the divergent models of literary production and social reproduction that emerge.

Oprah's Book Club

Oprah Winfrey established her television Book Club in October 1996 and drew it to a close with her forty-sixth selection, Toni Morrison's *Sula*, in May 2002.[6] During the Book Club's heyday, Winfrey chose ten novels a year for reading and discussion. Each Book Club show featured a profile of the selected author and a debate conducted among viewers who had written to the show about the novel in question. Although not successful by Winfrey's own prodigious standards—the Book Club shows typically attracted fewer viewers than her other broadcasts—the club had an enormous impact on the careers of many of the showcased writers, and on the publishing industry in general.[7] All of the Book Club selections became best sellers, some of them selling more than a million copies within a few weeks. Publishers were understandably anxious to secure a hugely profitable Oprah endorsement, and would try to influence the process by shipping likely prospects to Winfrey's staff. And, indeed, publishers readily acknowledged that the success of the Book Club influenced their decisions about the kind of fiction they wished to publish and promote.[8] The kind of novel thought most likely to attract the Oprah imprimatur was a realist work, probably written by a woman, focused on an emotional upheaval or the lingering consequences of some form of abuse, and perhaps confined to a domestic setting.[9] According to D.T. Max, writing in the *New York Times*, "Winfrey's fictional landscape is one in which people are loving, hating and thinking—but, unlike modern women, almost never working. Winfrey's choices tend to draw their themes from real life, but their locales and lifestyles come from our fantasies. In most parts of America, 'Oprah' bridges the gap between the afternoon soap operas and the early local news. The novels Winfrey chooses do much the same."[10] Yet this homogeneity should not be overemphasized. The Book Club selections certainly included domestic melodramas and paraliterary narratives of recovery, as well as children's books, but several distinguished authors also had works selected, including Toni Morrison, whose prestige tethered the series to the contemporary literary canon sanctioned by prize committees, college curricula, and academic studies.[11]

Praise and criticism of the Book Club enterprise has broken out sporadically in the press since its inception. Winfrey's champions have argued that the project worked to transform a constituency of passive viewers into an active readership, thus promoting literacy in a medium conventionally thought to be at odds with print culture.[12] The Book Club shows offered the spectacle of viewers, many of whom claimed not to be habitual readers, arguing about the meaning of books, establishing connections between fictional narratives and their own lives, and questioning authors about their novels. As such, the Book Club appeared to demystify the literary field, exposing a large daytime television audience to the discussion of texts. Winfrey's Book Club was modeled on or inspired by the relatively recent proliferation of reading groups, and in turn spawned numerous groups based around its selections.[13] Reading novels in conjunction with the Book Club is a sociable activity: solitary engagement with the text at hand leads in turn to communal and even convivial discussion. This sociability, represented on the Oprah Winfrey show by the meal shared between viewers/readers, the author and Winfrey herself, symbolized the effacement of distinctions of class and prestige.

In contrast, Winfrey's critics leveled a number of charges at the Book Club, charges that recall earlier debates about the "middlebrow" and the mass marketing of literature.[14] In the first place, hostile commentators expressed unease over the power Winfrey was exercising as a shaper of taste. She was criticized for choosing sentimental and melodramatic works of fiction, novels that turn around the kinds of problems dealt with on a regular basis in her show—spousal abuse, racism, overeating, bereavement. The narrative focus of these texts informed the content of the discussions featured on the show, wherein the sufferings of characters were likened to the sufferings of Book Club participants. In addition, Book Club selection provided an enormous boost in the sales of the chosen book, but by all accounts this seldom carried over to other works by the writer in question. It was also asserted that reading the Book Club selections represents a restricted kind of literacy; readers didn't venture to explore other significant novels, nor did they pick up volumes of poetry or serious nonfiction—they simply read Winfrey's next pick. Further, the success of the Book Club was manifested most obviously in its commercial visibility: book stores, particularly the chains, tended to give the Oprah picks their own prominent display space, and Starbucks, the ubiquitous coffee shop, signed a marketing deal with Winfrey to sell her Book Club selections in its outlets. From this perspective, an insidious metonymy was hard to ignore: the Oprah book is the literary equivalent of the universalizing corporate boom overtaking so much of the country. In general, then, the Book Club was less to be celebrated for its democratic potential, than deplored for its consumerist logic.[15]

These arguments, both celebratory and critical, share two notable assumptions. Common to both is a polarized conception of class, whereby the educated, middle, or upper-middle-class reader is pitted against the uneducated, middle, or lower-middle-class television watcher. Either Winfrey was seen to be imposing the mawkish and sensationalistic values of the television talk show on the realm of literature, or she was threatening the intellectual snobs of the world of books. For both positions, Winfrey was bringing literary fiction to television viewers envisaged by commentators as middle or lower-middle class, predominantly female and lacking in cultural capital. Depending on the animus behind the argument, habituated readers possess the education, taste, and discernment to select their own reading matter, or they can be characterized as class-conscious and antidemocratic, anxious to patrol the borders of the literary field, and to ensure that it is impregnable to incursions by the unlettered multitude. By the same token, the television watcher was conceived as passive, credulous, easily led. Arguments pro and contra Oprah's Book Club both envisaged a clear divide between the television viewer and the reader; this divide was either productively bridged or threateningly effaced by the Book Club. In this respect, the operative conception of cultural practices remained rigidly dualistic and invested in the correspondence between practice and social identity.

A second assumption, taken for granted by the Book Club's defenders and critics alike, is that reading is beneficial to the reader and to the culture in general. Reading novels, that is to say, is a better use of time than watching television. This point was even made by Winfrey herself in her frequent exhortations to switch off the TV set and pick up a book, though the exception she made for the Oprah Winfrey Show presumably went without saying. Winfrey's champions praised the Book Club for bringing the enrichment of reading to nonreaders, while her critics worried over the shortcomings of the kind of reading she encouraged (the novels weren't challenging or various enough, the discussions were inadequate), but not over the value of reading itself. To examine the social uses of reading fiction remained an inadmissible move, even though links to democratic social change, or, more precisely, to the vitality of citizenship, occasionally seem to be implicit in the arguments of critics and celebrants alike. This issue is connected to the broader cultural and social import of the genre of the television talk show itself.

Winfrey herself stated clearly and repeatedly what she thought the purpose of reading to be. Her show framed the appeal of reading as a thoroughly individual experience, at its most intense an experience of conversion. The final Book Club, broadcast on May 2, 2002, presented a series of clips from earlier shows in which the keynote was the transformative effect of reading, a point emphasized repeatedly by Winfrey herself: "Just the words themselves made me look at the world differently. . . . You heard it: A great book changes lives. . . . A great book makes us look closer in the mirror. . . . A great book tells us the truth of our own experiences. . . . Yes, that was a goose bump life-changing moment for me, too."[16] With this stress on the individualistic, life-changing nature of reading, the Book Club participated in the therapeutic and testimonial character of Winfrey's shows on other subjects. Novels are seen as occasions for identification: the situations of fictional protagonists in the chosen books typically prompted anecdotes and confessions from audience members. This kind of direct, uncomplicated identification was built into the featured readership of the show, the half dozen viewers chosen to engage and dine with the author. Typically, at least one member of the group had some biographical connection to the subject of the novel in question. So, for example, in the Book Club show focused on Andre Dubus III's *House of Sand and Fog*,[17] a novel that dwells in part on the struggles of an Iranian immigrant, one of the participants introduced herself in this way: "I'm Shahdi. I'm mother of two. I live in the Bay Area. As an Iranian woman who's lived here for the past 24 years, I could say that this book was not fiction but an autobiography of thousands and thousands of people."[18] In the ensuing discussion of *House of Sand and Fog*, the author went on to talk in some detail about the Iranian immigrant who directly inspired the writing of the character in the novel, thus reinforcing the connection between the fictional and the biographical. This insistence on the biographical and autobiographical significance of fiction, made at each level of the Book Club activities, from author interviews to audience selection and exhortation, helped emphasize that reading functions as a form of work on the self, either confirming the shape of experience ("my life is just like that") or offering a model to emulate ("my life should be more like that"). Such identificatory and reflective moments are integral to the wider appeal of the talk show itself. Oprah Winfrey presents herself as both a subject for identification—she has spoken openly of her relationship problems, her self-image and her fluctuating weight—and for emulation—she is, after all, one of the most successful, visible, and wealthy women in the United States.[19]

A number of the novels chosen for the Book Club lent themselves very readily to such practices of identification. Elizabeth Berg's doggedly unimaginative *Open House*, for example, chosen for the Book Club in August 2000, tells the story of a woman abandoned by her husband, her struggles to cope with the subsequent emotional and financial challenges, and her eventual passage to a stronger psychic state and the inevitable sympathetic new man.[20] The novel blends closely observed domestic detail, an easily digested presentation of interior states, and a strong element of wish fulfillment.[21] Discussion on Winfrey's show focused on the ways in which women cope with divorce and abandonment, with several of the participants telling how they discovered the infidelity of their husbands. The author herself spoke of her divorce and offered advice about how to cope with the aftermath of a messy separation. In this way, Berg's novel provided the occasion for a show very similar to those in which Winfrey focuses on a problem facing certain women, and calls on an expert to supplement the perspectives offered by the audience members themselves. The textual organization of the novel—its use of a realism occasionally ornamented with flights of fancy, its division into short, easily consumed sections, its relative brevity, its straightforward, almost diaristic presentation, firmly anchored in the central consciousness of the protagonist— presented very few obstacles to its treatment as nonfiction, as exemplary testimony.

Many of the Book Club selections fulfilled this demand for fictional texts that could be read as transparent commentaries on widely shared problems, yet Winfrey's show was also engaged in presenting literary icons as celebrities, figures fascinating in themselves, who conferred an aura of cultural value on the proceedings. In part, this focus on the iconic author underscored notions of creative genius, thereby propping up ideologies of the self as an autonomous source of meaning. But at the same time, it supplied a gravitas to the show itself, adding cultural respectability to a popular format often seen as degraded (and degrading), particularly in the wake of the talk show wars of the early 1990s. By the time Winfrey introduced her Book Club, she had already established a highly successful stronghold in the daytime television battlefield, and would further consolidate her media influence by diversifying with her own cable television station and magazine. The Book Club, however, helped to distinguish Winfrey's talk show from that of its rivals. The presentation of literary celebrities, particularly Toni Morrison, whose work was featured four times by the Book Club, was notable for its reverential tone; Morrison was presented as the teacher of her own texts, the source of illumination, rather than a voice participating in debate.

The show featuring Toni Morrison's *Paradise* revealed the difficulty of reconciling the incompatible demands of promoting the author as celebrity, on the one hand, and presenting the text as a record and mirror of experience, on the other. Morrison's novel was undoubtedly the most difficult to be chosen for the Book Club, and the show attracted the smallest audience of the Club's run. The Oprah Winfrey Show thematized the challenge involved in reading Morrison's novel by treating the discussion effectively as a seminar, filming it on the Princeton campus. Morrison was not, therefore, presented as a subject of identification but as an instructor, a teacher, an expert with a difficult piece of knowledge to pass on. Much of the discussion, which in this instance was conducted primarily as a dialogue between Winfrey and Morrison with comparatively few contributions made by audience members, turned around the difficulties the novel presents to the reader—difficulties of tracking chronology, adjudicating between competing versions of reality, and even establishing the racial identity of some of the characters. While this brought into play questions of history, interpretation, and literary form, matters seldom addressed in the Book Club discussions, Winfrey's own remarks, cues, and editorial decisions worked against the range and complexity of Morrison's own commentary. A discussion of the novel's nonlinear structure was prefaced by Winfrey's hortatory directive: "First of all, you have to open yourself up. You don't read this book just with your head. You have to open your whole self up. It's a whole new way of experiencing reading and life."[22] Throughout the various moments of discussion, illustration, and explanation that followed, Winfrey stressed this inchoate notion of openness. The segment concluded with questions about the enigmatic ending of Morrison's novel:

> Ms. MORRISON: You have to be open to this—yeah, it's not just black or white, living, dead, up, down, in, out. It's being open to all these paths and connections and . . . (*unintelligible*) between.
> WINFREY: And that is paradise!
> MORRISON: That is paradise.
> WINFREY: And that is paradise. Marvelous. That's great. Paradise is being open to all the places in between.[23]

Though the context makes it difficult to construe Morrison's observation, the challenge to binary ways of thinking about race, spirituality, and textuality seems very much to the point, and demands detailed elaboration. Winfrey's closing remark illustrates the problem the medium has in dealing with such intricate matters: Morrison's speculative comments are translated into a slogan, rather as if the discussion must close with a pithy formula that the viewer might take away from the show, without regard for the preceding difficulties and elaborations. Earlier in the show, Morrison spoke about the value of discussion: "Novels are for talking about and quarreling about and engaging in some powerful way. However that happens, at a reading group, a study group, a classroom or just some friends getting together, it's a delightful, desirable thing to do. And I think it helps. Reading is solitary, but that's not its only life. It should have a talking life, a discourse that follows." But the dictates of the one-hour television show, interrupted with increasing frequency by commercial breaks, restrict discussion to iterable soundbites and expressive or emotive spectacles.

Much of the academic commentary on the Oprah Winfrey Show has focused on its potential as a new form of public sphere in which important matters of race, morality, the body, and sexuality—matters often relegated to the private realm—are given public expression in the mass mediated context of the daytime television show.[24] In particular, the assumed audience of the talk show, lacking the cultural authority and prestige that would allow participation in other spaces of political discussion, such as journalism or party politics, momentarily acquires a voice to speak of matters of pressing interest and concern. Morrison's assertion of the importance of literary conversation also summons up an image of a public sphere of print culture that is in practice at variance with the format demands of television. The larger question of the significance of the talk show—and an understanding of the place of literary culture within it—turns around its possibilities as a space of quasi-political debate, albeit of a new, contradictory kind. Can a show such as Winfrey's, notwithstanding the limitations of its format, open up a productive conversation about matters usually relegated to the private realm? And, if so, can it also be said to engage literary texts in such a potentially political manner, taking the solitary act of reading into public debate, giving novels a "talking life"?

As Janice Peck has argued, current theories of popular culture tend to pit traditional literary culture against the possibilities of the newer media (230). For its critics, the new media erode the democratic potential of literacy that was once embodied in the bourgeois public sphere. Explicitly or not, this approach owes a great deal to Habermas, for whom the ideal—rather than the actuality—of the eighteenth-century bourgeois public sphere disintegrated under the pressures of commodification and the consolidation of power over the media in private hands. Habermas's account of the decline of the bourgeois public sphere in the second half of *The Structural Transformation of the Public Sphere* follows in its essentials the Frankfurt School attack on the culture industry. It is an attack taken up by recent elegists of the book, from George Steiner to Sven Birkerts, and indeed Jonathan Franzen himself, whose anxiety over the fate of print culture turns on account of the new media—television, computers, the Internet—that closely resembles, in broad thrust if not dialectical intensity, the work of the Frankfurt School, as well as homegrown defenders of high culture across the political spectrum.

Those critics, on the other hand, who see in the talk show the potential for new kinds of political speech, face the awkward fact that the Book Club returns the space of television testimony to the codes of literacy. An influential collaborative essay by Carpignano et al., for example, cherishes even such an apparently regressive phenomenon as the Morton Downey Jr. Show on the grounds that it allows a "common sense" speech to be voiced by working-class white males, and others normally unheard in the context of expert-led television discussions.[25] While the volleys and fulminations that typified such a show might seem to be nothing more than a grotesque parody of the enlightenment use of reason in the public sphere—precisely not rational-critical debate but the expression of sedimented ideology—Carpignano et al. argue that this use of speech, specific to the talk show, better illustrates the possible and latently political publicness available in contemporary culture.

Superficially, the Book Club appears to offer an updated version of the enlightenment public sphere, a space of literary discussion and debate for the age of electronic media. With the exception of Winfrey and the featured author, the participants in the discussion are not chosen according to credentials or prestige; selection, rather, has apparently to do with the preconceived notion of how the discussion will proceed, and what kinds of response the show wishes to elicit and broadcast. While it seems reasonable to suppose that certain kinds of response will thus be excluded (it's difficult, for example, to imagine an academic—a literary critic, say—being chosen to appear on the show), the show's discussions present the appearance of inclusivity. Such inclusivity might in turn be deemed democratic, in so far as it removes barriers of class and cultural capital from participation. But at the same time, the removal of these barriers reinforces the split between intellectuals and nonintellectuals, excluding certain kinds of observation and critical engagement, as Habermas warned.[26] Participation in the Book Club is also premised on the conferral of charisma through the iconic figure of Winfrey herself, who remains the visible arbiter of taste and response.

The treatment of literary significance in the Book Club remains within the talk show's therapeutic vocation. This vocation constructs subjects as "suffering and victimized," yet susceptible to the remedy of (televised) speech.[27] The talk show, with its spectacles of intimacy and pragmatic expertise, is itself a therapeutic form: the suffering self speaks of her struggles and thereby overcomes them. In its various modes, from testimonies of suffering to celebrity interviews, the talk show works by connecting private states (the shameful secrets of abuse, the intimate details of the celebrity's life) to public disclosure. In Franny Nudelman's words, "Traversing the border between private and public by introducing personal troubles into the public sphere, these disclosures initiate the process of recovery. In the context of therapy and reform, talk is taken to free women from the very trials talk describes."[28] These interactions between private and public states do not constitute a public sphere so much as "a secondary realm of intimacy."[29] "What seems to be at stake," Zygmunt Bauman suggests, "is a redefinition of the public sphere, as a scene on which private dramas are staged, put on public display and publicly watched."[30] Within this context, the reading and discussion of fiction, associated by Habermas with the traditional bourgeois public sphere, participates in the formation of therapeutic publics constituted around spectacles of private suffering. Nudelman writes: "Rather than figuring the relationship between public and private, between individual and collectivity, talk show testimony conflates private experience and public debate."[31] For Carpignano et al., it is precisely this conflation that characterizes the new political dimension of the talk show.[32] Yet, as Nudelman points out, this claim makes politics primarily an expressive phenomenon, wherein testimony is itself a kind of emancipatory action.[33] In addition, the object of political valorization, the speech of social groups excluded from professionalized canons of speech, demands a supplementary discourse of legitimation on the part of cultural critics, even though, by their own accounting, such speech presents itself as fundamentally self-legitimizing. The fact that therapeutic testimony takes place in the peculiar public space of a television talk show renders it generalizable as ideology, but not as any kind of practical, political engagement with the pressing concerns aired.[34]

The authors showcased in the Book Club segments participate in the formation of therapeutic publics in two ways: their own experience or that of the characters they write about speaks, with scant mediation, to the experiences of the Club participants. Their evident success, on the other hand, effected by the Book Club selection itself, underscores their privileged position within the show's circulation of discourse. Depending on the text in question, the emphasis falls variably on these aspects of authorial presence. Situating the chosen texts within therapeutic publics encourages reading as a process of identification, prompting readers to solicit fiction for meanings that might be publicly referred back to private concerns. The possibilities of reading novels as participants in cultural dialogue, opening onto issues of class, history, politics, and community, are thus curtailed, and the reader is encouraged to personalize the textual encounter.

Jonathan Franzen and the Crisis of Literary Culture

In a rueful *New Yorker* essay Franzen published at the end of 2001, he recounts the filming of what was to have been the biographical segment on the Oprah Winfrey show devoted to his novel.[35] Cast in the mode of desperate comedy, like much of *The Corrections* itself, Franzen's piece details his resistance to the therapeutic narrative. The ill-fated footage was to have shown him returning to his childhood home in an affluent suburb of St. Louis and reminiscing about the sources of his novel and the death of his parents, thus suggesting that *The Corrections* is essentially an autobiographical book, and that homecomings, in life as in fiction, offer reconciliation and closure. It might even be said that the act of writing the novel, and subsequently returning home on camera for Winfrey and her audience, function as forms of therapy. Franzen, however, proves a poor subject for treatment. He resists the urgings of the director to open up about his past and present emotions, and even goes so far as to decide the public/private distinction on a case by case basis, deciding for example that it's acceptable for the camera to linger on the family home, now sold, but not to take in the oak tree he planted in memory of his father. "I am failing as an Oprah author," he reflects, having finally conceded the tree, "and the team and I are finishing up some final strolling footage, well into our third hour in Webster Woods, when I complete the failure. Five words come bursting from my chest like a hideous juvenile alien. I say, 'This is so fundamentally bogus!' "[36]

Franzen's discomfort stems from his sense that the staging of intimacy is an act of expropriation. While the cameraman films the tree, Franzen acknowledges: "Part of me is imagining how this will play on TV: as schmalz [*sic*]. Rendering emotion is what I do as a writer, and this tree is my material, and now I'm helping to ruin it."[37] In constructing a senti- mental and therapeutic story using the details of Franzen's life, the TV crew takes possession of a private self that should be the writer's material; and, indeed, the *New Yorker* article is, among other things, an effort to reclaim that material. It is not that the details of the Franzen family home are to be kept from all publicity, but the negotiation of the public/ private boundary works in different ways for the writer and the TV producer. This difference implies divergent ways of conceiving of the self, as well as different conceptions of taste and entailed significations of social class. For the Oprah team, the self is constructed through a theatri- calized confession, regardless of private feelings (in Franzen's case, resentful and aggressive feelings), that effects a recovery through disclosure. For Franzen, by contrast, the self is property, intellectual and emotional property that is the private preserve of the writer. Ironically, his article about making the film for the Oprah Winfrey show, as well as his earlier essay in *Harper's* magazine, are presented as confessions. In both pieces he acknowledges uncomfortable, even shameful, feelings, but offers them as publicly significant: his sufferings, like those of his fictional characters, have symbolic resonance; they illuminate problems in the cultural realm, problems that have to do, the *Harper's* essay asserts, with the absence of a vital and informed public sphere. His confession of despair about the future of the novel is a professional complaint, a novelist's verdict on the end of the print era. His difficulty is that the accrual of symbolic significance, and hence of cultural capital, depends on the existence of a public sphere in which the novelist is granted cultural authority, and it's precisely this that he finds missing.

In the *Harper's* essay, Franzen lays the blame for the erosion of a vital public sphere on a contiguous set of social phenomena that he groups under two headings: technological consumerism and therapeutic optimism. What links these two ideologies is the belief that every problem has a solution—mental distress can be resolved by the appropriate anti-depressant drug, social conflict by social engineering, wounded narcissism by a shopping spree. The social novel, by which Franzen means the highly plotted, extensively researched, markedly political fiction that he strove for in his first two novels, tackles the unwholesome contemporary scene through satire, even as satire finds itself outstripped, as Philip Roth complained as long ago as 1961, by the sheer extravagance of American reality.[38] Franzen contrasts this kind of fictional strategy with the coolly scrupulous realism of Paula Fox's slim 1970 novel, *Desperate Characters*, a work that eventually shows him the way forward to the writing of *The Corrections*.[39] Fox's novel registers social crisis in a domestic setting, finding figurative ways of linking psychic unease and marital strife to a wider picture of class upheaval and racial antagonism. In Fox's work, Franzen finds an aesthetic model, a way to assume social significance while pursuing the novelist's traditional aims of depicting character and milieu. In other words, the link between private and public dimensions is not obtrusive, but is rather underwritten by the virtues of literary craft, of sharp perception, and of rounded character. But more than this, the example of Fox suggests that the novel can render white, middle-class experience, and particularly family life, worthy of attention.

Franzen's efforts to reclaim white, middle-class experience for the serious novel must be understood in relation to a perceived fragmentation of the literary field. One of the essay's subtexts is the way in which women and writers of color have now come to compete for prestige, offering the imaginative exploration of experiences inaccessible to the white male writer. Franzen's aim is to present the experience of white upper-middle-class Midwesterners—all those middles in an age fascinated by margins—as constituting an identity specific enough for intense fictional exploration. But at the same time, his insistence on the novelist's tragic realism, the only proper attitude, he claims, for a writer to have, proves necessary to oppose the therapeutic optimism so prevalent in contemporary culture. He wants, that is, to disengage his fiction from the burden of embattled cultural critique, and to root it firmly in his own proper milieu, the world of the Midwestern family; yet he also wants to lay claim to a conception of the autonomy of aesthetic practice that will be implicitly oppositional.

The figure of the blocked writer symbolizes the difficulty of making these negotiations. In this figure, the difficulties of making sense of the novel's purpose in a media culture—a culture that no longer reads—are visited on the writing process itself: loss of conviction, distraction, deterioration of the formal qualities driving the work, the decay of certain sustaining ideas about authorship, the bewildering nature or sheer recalcitrance of the world that the text would seek to encompass—all of these can contribute to the block, and all of them are touched on in Franzen's *Harper's* essay, a work which self-consciously employs the blocked writer—in this instance, Franzen—as a means to connote a wide range of perceived cultural dilemmas.

The essay is structured around the depression—and intermittent writer's block—that afflicted Franzen during the first half of the 1990s, from early symptoms through struggle to an eventual reconciliation and a return to work on his much-delayed novel, the book that would turn out, after many false starts and difficulties, to be *The Corrections* itself. The sources of his depression lay in the unresolved relationship between the writer and the culture. Franzen presents this relationship in terms of conflict and subversion. The serious literary writer's vocation, as imagined by the idealistic young writer, is to critique and perhaps even change the culture. From this perspective, the novel aims to encapsulate the culture and satirize its flaws, adopting a form that will reach a wide readership in order to contribute to the culture's transformation. Joseph Heller's *Catch-22* provides the model, a novel that combines critical success with popular acclaim to the degree that the book's title enters the language. Heller's novel also provides a technical example: "Heller had figured out a way of outdoing the actuality, employing the illogic of modern warfare as a metaphor for the more general denaturing of American reality" (37). Heller's approach is to push the absurdities of modern warfare—and, by extension, modern American life—to a humorous and satirical extreme, while also reaching a formidably large number of readers. There were, as Franzen explains, two problems with this approach. In the first place, American reality outstrips satirical exaggeration; and, in the second, the readership Heller attracted was apparently no longer available to the novelist. Since the publication of *Catch-22* in 1961, the place of fiction in the culture of the United States has shifted, Franzen asserts, from prominence and authority to neglect concealed behind the glittering façade of celebrity culture. A culture that eludes the critical grasp of the novelist is also, it seems, a culture uninterested in what the novelist would have to say, even if he or she found a way to say it.

Franzen's description of his malaise thus depends on an implicit notion of cultural health, in which the novelist has the capacity and opportunity to engage with the sicknesses of contemporary society, while also being able to rely on significant recognition. Cultural authority is grounded in vitality of literary activity—the viability of the novel as a form of social perception and critique—and a correspondingly serious and engaged readership. The problems Franzen faces, by his accounting, derive from the shift in cultural authority away from a system of print culture to "technological consumerism." Franzen describes his growing awareness of the nature of this increasingly dominant cultural order throughout the 1990s, beginning with the seeming evacuation of public debate and dissent during the Persian Gulf War, and continuing through the rise of Internet culture through the middle of the decade. This is a variant on familiar accounts of mass culture. "Technological consumerism" is marked by repetition, uniformity, amnesia, and superficiality; the measures of value within this system, Franzen indicates, are money and visibility. Franzen chooses concrete examples that are intended to illustrate the ways in which autonomous literary activity—literature conditioned by its own distinctive system of evaluation—could still inform heteronomous mass culture. The cover of *Time* magazine, Franzen's index of cultural visibility and significance, provides a clear instance of the shift in question: James Joyce appeared twice on the cover of the magazine, presumably as an icon of the challenge presented by literary modernism; in recent years, by contrast, the only authors to appear on the cover have been Stephen King and Scott Turow. Franzen concludes: "These are honorable writers, but no one doubts it was the size of their contracts that won them the covers. The dollar is now the yardstick of cultural authority, and an organ like *Time*, which not long ago aspired to shape the national taste, now serves mainly to reflect it" (38). This move from an active ("to shape national taste") to a passive stance ("to reflect") subtly afflicts the social novel itself, since the repetitive dynamic of "technological consumerism" informs its possibilities and aims: "The American writer today faces a totalitarianism analogous to the one with which two generations of Eastern bloc writers had to contend. To ignore it is to court nostalgia. To engage with it, however, is to risk writing fiction that makes the same point over and over: technological consumerism is an infernal machine, technological consumerism is an infernal machine . . ." (43).

Franzen's hyperbole illustrates the extent to which his essay employs a dichotomous and oppositional notion of the writer pitted against the culture in a zero–sum game. But by this logic, the writer inevitably loses, since the culture dictates the writer's material and the terms by which their confrontation might take place.

Franzen props up his insistence on the uniformity of "technological consumerism" with a series of illustrative anecdotes. He recounts, for example, his experiences dealing with Hollywood, an unsatisfactory and fruitless period during which he tried to accommodate his creativity to the demands of the movie industry. And he recalls a teaching spell at a liberal arts college, during which he encountered the insidious influence of literary theory and multiculturalism, forces that damage, he claims, the sensibilities of young readers, and so contribute to the antiliterate tendencies prevailing in the world at large. If Hollywood is governed by the iron whim of the marketplace, academia, in Franzen's scathing account, is rife with "therapeutic optimism," the ideological counterpart of "technological consumerism." "Therapeutic optimism" conceives the world in terms of soluble problems, where solutions might be as various as a technological innovation, a new drug therapy, or a set of consoling ideas.[40] Franzen detects this therapeutic mentality—its flattening of all social and psychic obstacles into (medicalized) problems and solutions— in a highly diverse set of issues and ideologies, grouping them together with breathtaking disregard for their differences: "A disease has causes: abnormal brain chemistry, childhood sexual abuse, welfare queens, the patriarchy, social dysfunction. It also has cures: Zoloft, recovered-memory therapy, the Contract with America, multiculturalism, virtual reality" (44). Literary fiction, by contrast, draws life from insoluble problems, from the "mystery"—Franzen takes the word from Flannery O'Connor—that resists the latest panacea. The prototype of this mystery is the wound inflicted on narcissism: "Imagine that human existence is defined by an Ache: the Ache of our not being, each of us, the center of the universe; of our desires forever outnumbering our means of satisfying them" (43). This "Ache" resists the emollient influences of pharmacology and politics; it remains a stubborn reminder of individuality, even though it is felt only when the individual has an experience of dismaying finitude, of impotence, and of hopeless insatiability. In his attention to the mystery of human existence, Franzen establishes the basis for the conception of "tragic realism" that he counterposes to therapeutic optimism. Tragic realism grows from the realization that life's essential problems, the problems with which great literature and art have always concerned themselves, cannot be overcome by new technologies or ideas.

Franzen's essay would scarcely merit much attention if its embrace of humanist platitudes were all it had to offer. However, the writer's anxiety in the face of competing media, and the retreat from a thwarted dynamic of public engagement, begin to suggest some of the pressures and shifts within the literary system, particularly as they are marked off against configurations of cultural value and class identity. Franzen's efforts to articulate a position in the literary field and a rationale for renewed activity aim to circumscribe and justify the writer's appropriate terrain. To achieve this he must revise the terms of his initial diagnosis, freeing the novel from the impossible burden of social satire and rediscovering the threatened reader. He manages the former by citing authorities—Flannery O'Connor, with her conception of mystery and manners, and in the last paragraphs of the essay, Don DeLillo, who supplies some resonant sentences about the writer's commitment: "Writing is a form of personal freedom. It frees us from the mass identity we see in the making all around us. In the end, writers will write not to be outlaw heroes of some underculture but mainly to save themselves, to survive as individuals" (54). Personal freedoms are born out of such necessities, and the writer's marginality becomes a marker of private authenticity. Franzen's authorities free him from the difficulty of thinking about the public effects of his fiction, even as they emphasize the inner necessity of writing.

In this respect, writing is much like reading, and Franzen rediscovers his faith in reading by turning to the work of the social anthropologist Shirley Brice Heath, who has conducted extensive research on reading practices. Heath's argument, which is based on interview findings about how, why, and where people read, translates the public domain that Franzen found so oppressive and glibly unresponsive into an imaginary community founded on the private and solitary habit of serious reading. Heath emphasizes that lifelong reading is a deeply ingrained habit formed either through emulation (parents who read seriously are quite likely to have bookish offspring) or through imaginative identification, "[c]ommunion with the virtual community of print" (51). Although, as Franzen coyly acknowledges, the findings of a social anthropologist might seem remote indeed from his own concerns as a writer, Heath's work proves strikingly easy to translate into terms better suited to the conclusions of the essay. The justifications Heath's subjects give for their love of reading turn around the word "substance": reading "substantive"—which is to say, literary—works affords a sense of ethical and intellectual integrity—in a word, "substance" (49). The circularity is fitting since it stresses that the writing and reading of literature must be understood on their own terms, according to their own customs, laws, and durable dispositions. Heath thus gives Franzen an empirical basis for the deeply traditional notion of literature as quasi-religious solace; she tells him, "reading good fiction is like reading a particularly rich section of a religious text. What religion and good fiction have in common is that the answers aren't there, there isn't closure" (49). Heath's research also allows Franzen to make a connection between his own deep-seated reasons for writing (and reading: Heath in essence tells him that the motivation for reading is the same as that for writing) and the reasons why a socially and culturally diverse aggregate of people choose to read serious literature. In this way, the awkward gulf between the solitary reader and the abstracted readership, for which the mechanisms of celebrity culture—the photo-shoots, profiles, and interviews—stand in so misleadingly, is overcome at a stroke, while questions of readership are simultaneously veiled in essential mystery. The disabling tension between a hypostatic culture and a solitary writer can thus be alleviated, though at the cost of any determinate rationale for the writing of fiction.

Franzen's position in the *Harper's* essay confirms the "civil privatism" that it would combat.[41] By returning the work of the novel to the private sphere, at the levels of both literary production and consumption, Franzen fails to engage with the absence of a political and cultural space that it is the merit and timeliness of his essay to identify. In this respect, his position deplores the therapeutic public without imagining anything but a private and spiritual satisfaction to replace it. Here, as in the case of Oprah's Book Club, the problem of agency hovers unresolved between the roles of citizen and consumer. In the Book Club, such roles are conflated, and citizenship must be reckoned with as spectacle rather than deliberative agency; in Franzen's essay, the retreat from the role of the consumer opens up the possibility only of an imaginary citizenship of privatized ideas and sensations, even as the success hankered for throughout suggests the reintroduction of a consumerist imaginary, though one dictated autonomously by the writer. The contrariety of class and taste that the quarrel with Winfrey brought up plays across the public/private divide, just as it plays, in a slightly different register, across the citizen/ consumer pairing. Such a fractured terrain of cultural authority reflects the objective status of the literary novel in the media age, while failing, as yet, to grapple with the contradictions, both disabling and potentially valuable, that such a situation generates.

As Franzen finds a solace in time-honored enigmas that is tainted with complacency, and vitiates the cultural and political critique he mounts in the first part of his essay, he cannot quite elude the social aspects of literary production that he invokes. By the same token, his essay cannot help but be a justification for a certain kind of aesthetic practice, even if the stipulations he derives from O'Connor (and indirectly from Heath)—that fiction must be comic though imbued with a sense of tragic realism—remain very general, little more than quasi-spiritual nostrums. Franzen's justification for a certain kind of practice is bound up with reflections prompted by Paula Fox's short novel *Desperate Characters*. Fox's novel, which Franzen has promoted assiduously, plays a key role in the *Harper's* essay, serving as an example of the value of fiction and an occasion to rhapsodize on the pleasures of reading. Framed by Franzen's praise, *Desperate Characters* exemplifies the kind of fiction that might, in the terms of the essay, offer a more productive path for the writer than the all-encompassing, densely plotted social novel of which he despairs. And, indeed, Fox's novel provides a structural model for *The Corrections*. But more than this, *Desperate Characters* works over a number of the issues that are central to the *Harper's* essay, casting light on several concerns that remain discreetly veiled in Franzen's presentation.

Desperate Characters both illustrates several of Franzen's most important claims, and subtly displaces them in revealing ways. Franzen's investment in Fox's novel has gone far beyond the praise with which he lavishes it in *Harper's*. Indeed, his enthusiasm seems to have played a large part in getting Fox's fiction back into print. His introduction to the paperback reissue of *Desperate Characters* proclaims the novel "inarguably great," superior to the contemporaneous fiction of Updike, Roth, and Bellow (viii). Quite how highly he esteems the novel is hinted at by his points of comparison; worrying at one point that the title is not quite strong enough, he remarks, "It's apt, certainly, and yet it's no *The Day of the Locust*, no *The Great Gatsby*, no *Absalom, Absalom!*" (xi). And further on, remarking on the formidable hermeneutical riches of the novel, he mentions the celebrated chapter on "The Whiteness of the Whale" in *Moby-Dick*. Even though he avoids making any vulgarly explicit claim, it's hard to resist the impression that Franzen thinks of *Desperate Characters* as worthy of addition to the honor rolls of the Great American Novel.

In the *Harper's* essay, *Desperate Characters* exemplifies a delicate balance between the domestic and the social novel, combining the virtues of the character-driven fiction—the darkly humorous novel of "manners"—with the stubbornly recalcitrant problem of "mystery," the sources of which may be—and the ambiguity is crucial to Franzen—social or psychological. The tension between domestic and social, private and public, is held in place by the novel's central plot device, a nasty, possibly rabid bite from a feral cat. Thus figuring exposure to the social problems that the cultured upper-middle-class protagonists have tried to ignore or retreat from, the image crystallizes anxieties about dissolving boundaries of class, race, and cultural identity. Yet Fox uses the dread that follows the possible infection to cast light on the inner lives and marriage of the central characters over a long weekend during which they oscillate between addressing their emotional and physical problems and running away from them. In sustaining the balance between internal, domestic malaise and external, social pathology, Fox combines the virtues of the traditional, domestic novel with the insinuation of social significance. This balancing act provides Franzen with an aesthetic ideal. It also symbolizes his own ambiguous cultural position: "By daring to equate a crumbling marriage with a crumbling social order, Fox goes to the heart of an ambiguity I experience almost daily: does the distress I feel derive from some internal sickness of the soul, or is it imposed on me by the sickness of society?" (36). Franzen's uncertainty is not simply a matter of aesthetic deliberation— how should a novel balance the competing claims of psychological acuity and social relevance?—but also a question of cultural authority. That Franzen finds these claims incommensurable indicates the extent to which his sense of autonomy as a writer is compromised by contradictory demands. The erosion of cultural authority stems from a problem of identity that Fox's novel delineates, without falling into the terms that a quarter-century later Franzen will find so debilitating.

Fox's central couple, Otto and Sophie Bentwood—the surname recalls Kant's remark about the "crooked timber of humanity" out of which nothing straight can ever be fashioned—have the worrying sense that the lines of property, class, and culture are being redrawn. Their house in Brooklyn, with its elegant furniture and shelves of Goethe and French poetry, lies on the fringes of slum housing. Differences of class and race confront them daily, much to the disgust of Otto in particular, who excoriates liberal guilt and refuses to conceal his hostility and revulsion. The threat of difference is figured as the threat of invasion—invasion by sound (the crying of a baby, the "locals . . . with their goddamn bongos" [4], in Otto's racist remark), by dirt, disease, and violence; and, indeed, the book is structured around invasions: the metaphoric invasion by rabies, a rock thrown through a window at a Brooklyn Heights party, a break-in at the summer house on Long Island. These incursions threaten middle-class certitudes about value and propriety even as they pose a more physical threat to the Bentwoods' well-being. Sophie's work as a translator no longer has much conviction—she can't make sense of the experimental French fiction the publishing house sends her; she cannot, in other words, pass between different languages, or different worlds: she is shut out from the youthful rebellion and new social mores she encounters, but finds herself discontented with the socially conservative ways of her husband, going so far as to seek comfort in an affair with a publisher.

Caught between her cultured, middle-class scrupulousness and her liberal guilt, Sophie occupies a position troublingly similar to that of Otto's estranged friend and law partner, Charlie Russel, who both attracts and disgusts her. The novel emphasizes this parallel in a scene where Charlie Russel, suffering from a bad conscience about his broken business and personal relations with Otto, calls on the Bentwoods in the middle of the night and takes Sophie to a bar. A symbolic seduction turns out in the novel's fine, nervous refusal of convenient symmetries to be an exchange of bad faith—Sophie longs to hear Charlie voice her own dissatisfaction with Otto, but insults him when he expresses the views she secretly harbors. Charlie, for his part, berates her for her insularity: "You are out of the world, tangled in personal life. You won't survive this . . . what's happening now. People like you . . . stubborn and stupid and drearily enslaved by introspection while the foundation of their privilege is being blasted out from under them" (39). Yet Charlie's own marriage presents a pattern no less conflictual, an inversion of that of the Bentwoods, since his wife, Ruth, has ostensibly embraced the new values: "She talks about nothing except the 'new liberation.' She's taken up Yoga and chopped off her hair. She wants to get hold of some hashish" (40). Fox is careful to emphasize, however, that this is no more than a middle-class fad: "She talks about sexual modalities, she talks about the 'wit' of pornography. She's going crazy, poor devil, and she's driving me crazy. But listen. What's strange is that we've stopped making love. All winter, a cold winter" (40). In Sophie and Otto and Charlie and Ruth, Fox presents a field of positions, all of them entrenched and unsatisfactory, in which class and cultural identities variously diverge and overlap. At one end of the spectrum, Otto fiercely resents the erosion of class identities, and the cultural flux that apparently accompanies that erosion. Sophie remarks at one point that Otto is "preoccupied with fighting off a mysterious effluvium he thinks will drown him. He thinks garbage is an insult directed against him personally" (89). At the other end of the spectrum, Ruth Russel eagerly embraces the languages and practices of a new cultural identity, but remains tied to a stubbornly invariant class identity, which gives the lie to her flamboyant gestures of social and sexual rebellion.

In *Desperate Characters*, the revision of social identity is experienced as an alarming recognition of contingency. For Sophie, the crisis lies in seeing that the pattern of her existence, its unfocused dedication to matters of high culture and civilized living, is a flimsy set of arbitrary rules: "once she had stepped outside rules, definitions, there were none. Constructions had no true life. Ticking away inside the carapace of ordinary life and its sketchy agreements was anarchy" (62). The novel extends this perception into a series of figures of order and disorder that range from the encroaching filth of the Brooklyn streets, the violence done to objects in the Bentwoods' second home, to an anecdote about an artist who reconstructs typewriters to spell out "mystic nonsense words" (123). Otto retains the hope that he might withdraw inside the social habits and beliefs, the structures and practices, of his class identity; he treats his own actions, Sophie complains at one point, "as if they stemmed from inflexible natural laws" (151). The liberal anguish of one such as Charlie Russel, who wishes to extend legal services to the poor and neglected, is tantamount in Otto's view to "the creation of disorder" (121).

Sophie, by contrast, senses that withdrawal is mere evasion (she is described at one point as "sitting in an ostrich-sized nest in bed" [115]). When she visits the hospital to have the cat bite examined, she fleetingly becomes aware that the social alterity that confronts her as chaos, and as the sheer arbitrariness of any social order, is in fact structured in ways that necessarily elude her. In the emergency room an African American attendant takes her injured hand: "She felt that old-time reassurance that she had once thought the natural property of dark people—as though they were superior caretakers of frail white flesh. Her hand arrested midway between them, she looked intently at him, perceiving for a second the existence of a world of unknown opinion about herself, her clothes, her skin and odor" (106). Her hand "arrested midway" is emblematic of the ambivalence of this moment. In one respect, her sense of the reassurance offered by "dark people" merely inverts the racist perception by which Otto sees every black male as a thief or swindler. The metonymic association of caretaking flesh and prescriptive embodiment (black bodies marked as peculiarly fleshly and material) suggests a dynamic of the master and slave. Yet Sophie's situation makes her unusually vulnerable. She is subject to medical inspection, and feels ashamed, polluted, and afraid. To this extent her hand is outstretched "like an exhibit" (107), a site of disease, and she is humbled by the ministrations of the African American attendant. At the same time, the gesture suggests recognition, a handshake, and for a moment, she glimpses him as a conscious thinking and feeling being with his own unknowable conception of her. Although this is a fleeting moment, it does suggest the ways in which Sophie becomes the bearer of a conception of limits and finitude. Implicit in this is a reversal by which those properties that support her identity—sets of ideas about value, culture, civilization, as well as the material embodiment of such values—are untethered, loosed to the turmoil of social and cultural change.

Hence, the physical invasions both prefigure and prompt a climactic reversal of the Bentwoods' cherished boundaries. In the last pages of the novel, Sophie finds herself obliged to wait for news of whether the cat that bit her was carrying rabies; Otto petulantly refuses to wait with her, setting off to work as if there were no crisis in their world: "She was indignant that he had gone. . . . He was like everyone else, witlessly inflexible, treating his own actions as if they stemmed from inexorable natural laws. Damn him! He had closed her *out* into the house!" (151). The reversal upsets the anxiously maintained boundary between home and street, lawyer's wife and slum dweller—inside becomes outside, prefiguring the violence the novel's final gesture, when Otto hurls a bottle of ink against the wall.

In Franzen's reading of the novel this closing image serves several functions: "The ink in which [Otto's] law books and Sophie's translations have been printed now forms an unreadable blot—a symbolic precursor of the blood that, a generation later, more literal-minded books and movies will freely splash" (36). The ink stain thus marks the end of a certain moment in print culture and predicts a cultural decline into genre fiction and film. Further, the moment of crisis in print culture is tied to the crisis of the novel form itself: "For centuries, ink in the form of printed novels has fixed discrete, subjective individuals within significant narratives. What Sophie and Otto were glimpsing, in the vatic black mess on their bedroom wall, was the disintegration of the very notion of a literary character" (37). Although this gives an apocalyptic fillip to Franzen's assertions about the twilight of print, the interpretation is surprising in light of both his subsequent emphasis on mystery and manners, categories emphatically grounded in literary character, and his attempt to retrieve character in *The Corrections*. What is also striking is how this strong interpretation abstracts the symbol from the figurative texture of the novel. Fox paves the way to her clinching act of violence with the following passage: "There was a siege going on: it had been going on for a long time, but the besieged themselves were the last to take it seriously. Hosing vomit off the sidewalk was only a temporary measure, like a good intention. The lines were tightening—Mike Holstein had known that, standing in his bedroom with the stone in his hand—but it was almost impossible to know where the lines were" (154). Otto's act of hurling the inkbottle recalls the stone thrown through the window of the Holstein's house in Brooklyn Heights, even as it continues the inversion of inside and outside, the figurative collapse of class distinction. The ink on the wall in the last lines of the novel literalizes the earlier image of the lines tightening yet growing more obscure: "they both turned slowly toward the wall, turned until they could both see the ink running down to the floor in black lines" (156). Class hostility and violence, both symbolic and real, inform Otto's act; they also inform the uncertainties of class identity that generate the desperation felt by all the major characters in the novel. In this respect, Franzen's remarks about the symbol of the smashed inkbottle suggest an elided connection between the loss of cultural authority commanded by the novelist, and the erosion of culture *as* authority in the shifting class structures of Fox's novel.

Indeed, it is this connection that informs one of the central conceits of Franzen's essay. Extended excerption is unavoidable:

> The institution of writing and reading serious novels is like a grand old Middle American city gutted and drained by superhighways. Ringing the depressed inner city of serious work are prosperous clonal suburbs of mass entertainments: techno and legal thrillers, novels of sex and vampires, of murder and mysticism. The last fifty years have seen a lot of white male flight to the suburbs and to the coastal power centers of television, journalism, and film. What remain, mostly, are ethnic and cultural enclaves. Much of contemporary fiction's vitality now resides in the black, Hispanic, Asian, Native American, gay and women's communities, which have moved into the structures left behind by the departing straight white male. The depressed literary inner city also remains home to solitary artists who are attracted to the diversity and grittiness that only a city can offer, and to a few still-vital cultural monuments (the opera of Toni Morrison, the orchestra of John Updike, the museum of Edith Wharton) to which suburban readers continue to pay polite Sunday visits. (39)

The literary history of the second half of the twentieth century is cast here into a schema of class and racial division. It is hard not to read Franzen's celebration of Fox's novel as both the source of and implicit commentary on this passage. Indeed, this passage invites an allegorical reading of *Desperate Characters*: the embattled Bentwoods, whose integrity derives from their refusal to quit the city, resemble the solitary artists, in whose company one must assume Franzen includes himself. Their position is increasingly precarious, but it seems to be the only position from which the connection between cultural identity and cultural capital can be defended. Franzen celebrates Sophie Bentwood's refusal to abandon the finer things—the French novels and *omelette aux fines herbes*—in favor of guilt-stricken liberalism (Charlie Russel's stance), or flight. After all, Fox appears to say, there is nowhere to which they might escape: even the rustic idyll on Long Island has been tainted.

This is perhaps a fanciful reading of the novel, but it does begin to suggest why *Desperate Characters* comes to be invested with such talismanic significance. Not only does Fox's novel provide a model for the recuperation of realism, it also represents Franzen's dilemma within the literary field. Like Otto and Sophie, he finds the lines of separation—of class, of positions within the literary field—have grown blurred. Cultural authority no longer resides in the familiar settings, the accepted modes. Franzen is caught between nostalgia for a system that would value his work without reference to its social context, and an anxious recognition of a new, emergent cultural field that leaves him in a position of marginality— insignificant and anachronistic beside the unresting machinery of mass culture, and marginal too in relation to the rise of multiculturalism. On the evidence of the *Harper's* essay, Franzen found these difficulties almost intractable. However, he did eventually complete the third novel on which he had labored for so long. *The Corrections* bears the marks of its difficult genesis, yet also represents a successful resolution: the invention of a position between class identity and cultural authority.

The Corrections

In marketing *The Corrections*, Jonathan Franzen presented a narrative of the novel's provenance and its protracted genesis. Along with vivid anecdotes about personal turmoil, writer's block, and the benefits of writing while blindfolded, Franzen supplied his interviewers with a formula: *The Corrections* combines the virtues of the social novel with those of psychological realism. The strongest and most visible expression of this idea came in a *New York Times* magazine article: "Like DeLillo and Gaddis, [Franzen] dazzles the reader with trenchant riffs on contemporary life—everything from mood-enhancing pharmaceuticals to bisexuality to cruise-ship culture. But rather than relay his thoughts about the world through chilly rhetorical pyrotechnics or plots of mind-boggling complication, Franzen embeds them in the lives of affecting human characters."[42] Franzen's novel, according to the terms set out here, might be described as androgynous, since it combines the scope and cultural insight of male authors—DeLillo's name is most often mentioned—with the psychological acuity of female novelists. By this logic, Franzen overcomes the sexual division of labor in the work of American fiction. In Emily Eakin's words: "As male novelists abandoned psychological realism for oracular pronouncements, the job of creating memorable characters became women's work—the forte of writers like Anne Tyler and Annie Proulx."[43] This is a conveniently simple selling point for Franzen's project; it stakes out a position by employing current—yet hoary—journalistic notions rather than challenging their legitimacy. The great divide summed up in the

New York Times article falls between men and women, thought and feeling, social and domestic, public and private. The formula is doubly useful in as much as it decants the uncertainties that bedevil the *Harper's* essay—uncertainties that turn on questions of class identity and cultural authority—into a successful proposal, an easily grasped diagnosis of the problems afflicting contemporary fiction and an instant solution to them.

To describe Franzen's project as a synthesis of "the intellectual heft of DeLillo and the emotional satisfactions of Alice Munro" fails to register the issues of social class and cultural value that he negotiates in essay and novel alike.[44] The *Harper's* essay tells the story of Franzen's shift from the expansive, densely plotted, political fiction of his first two novels to a scrupulously crafted realism epitomized by Paula Fox.[45] To simplify, Franzen abandons the "social novel" because its claim to cultural authority no longer seems convincing, and embraces psychological realism because it appeals to identity and the function of literature as universals. It is a shift from a model of prestige founded on the scope, omnivorousness, and satirical verve of certain first-generation postmodernists—Gaddis, Pynchon, DeLillo, though also, as noted, Joseph Heller—to the invention of a position in the literary field based on the examination of specific social identities. Yet the shift away from the problem of capturing and critiquing the fluid social and cultural environment toward a quasi-religious and invariant role for literary fiction—mystery and manners—entails a retreat from the political, even as it appears to place the novelist's authority on a firmer footing.

Fox's novel offers more than simply a formal solution; it makes middle-class experience a legitimate, even a privileged subject of literary scrutiny. Indeed, it is the crisis of class identity that drives Fox's characters into desperation: their assurances about property, cultural capital, and social space come under continual threat. Franzen identifies this uncertainty over distinctions and boundaries, the expression of cultural minutiae in a field of force, as a crisis of personal and, by extension, cultural confidence: how to write when the systems of evaluation, approval, and recognition pay scant regard to one's creative activity? In Fox's novel, the central characters are caught between their own familiar environment, from which conviction has departed, and a hostile external world of racial otherness and class antagonism that threatens the boundaries of a carefully maintained middle-class space.

The Corrections elaborates the metamorphosis of upper-middle-class identity—or one representative fraction of it—over a period from the early 1960s to the end of the century. In tracing the vicissitudes of the Lambert family over these decades, with its mutation from the suburban nuclear family to the disintegration of the father and the various apostasies of the offspring, the novel writes cultural history through the configuration of class identity. The novel examines a shift in attitudes to work, sexuality, consumption, and pleasure, underlining the differences and persistent likenesses between Albert Lambert, an embodiment of thrift, emotional retentiveness, and the work ethic, and his children, all of whom try, in social, psychological, and, of course, geographical ways, to distance themselves from their Midwestern origins. The temporal patterning of the novel situates these dramas of identity formation and dissolution in two schemes: first, the novel is structured as a series of five related novellas, each of a little more than a hundred pages, enclosed between a brief prologue and briefer epilogue. Each of these novellas, modeled to some extent on *Desperate Characters*, follows the protagonists through a brief period of crisis to the brink of major, even catastrophic, change. So the novel recounts the fortunes of each member of the Lambert family during its own extended crisis over a period of two or three months, from the warning note struck at the novel's opening in the prairie autumn of St. Jude, through the disastrous fall foliage cruise the Lambert parents take, to the much-anticipated (and dreaded) final Christmas and its immediate aftermath. During this period, Albert Lambert's decline from Parkinson's disease worsens to the point where he must be hospitalized.

Like Fox's Sophie Bentwood, the characters in *The Corrections* suffer from an uncertainty over the defining and delimiting properties of their upper-middle-class, Midwestern identity. In tracing these uncertainties *The Corrections* dramatizes a shift from Alfred's convictions to those of his offspring. Much of the pathos and humor of the novel arises from the fact that this shift is not a simple succession, as though one set of beliefs is simply replaced by another, but a dynamic of continuation and conflict. The Lambert children energetically look to separate themselves from the practices and priorities of their parents, but continually find their behavior falling into inherited rather than invented patterns. Ironically, it is the dismaying persistence of these older patterns that gives the characters their integrity as subjects resistant to the blandishments of a new cultural order epitomized by therapeutic optimism, even as it makes them contradictory, anxious, and self-confounding. The novel's comic perspective cherishes fallibility as a marker of identity, while simultaneously throwing carefully fashioned identities into confusion.

The comedy of desperation exemplifies Franzen's "mystery and manners" credo, effectively putting characters at odds with their cherished self-images. The mismatch between circumstances and ingrained patterns of behavior dramatizes the cultural and social shift in middle-class identity from the

1960s to the late 1990s. One of the striking achievements of *The Corrections* is the wealth of detail that Franzen assembles to document this shift. In this sense, the novel falls in a tradition of social realism that draws its power from the richness of the metonymic social fact. If the novel retains some of the vestiges of the paranoid systematization and interconnectiveness that Franzen learned from his immediate forerunners, notably DeLillo, Gaddis, and Pynchon, and put into practice in his first two novels, its minute attention to details of food, décor, and dress places the novel firmly in a realist lineage. Franzen treats such details with an exactness that emphasizes the way commodities function as signs of distinction, both within and between classes. The most developed language of distinction is food. The difference, for example, between the solid Austrian food Enid habitually prepares for family occasions and the exquisite contemporary restaurant versions of the same dishes that her daughter Denise, a fashionable chef, concocts says a great deal about differences of cultural identity as well as generational trends.

These new practices of consumption, so much a part of the cultural scene of the 1990s, are thrown into relief by the habits of the older Lamberts. The movement from the parents' generation to that of their children is one from thrift to expenditure, from the protestant work ethic to an ethos of hedonistic consumerism, from a model of the self as an occluded privacy to that of therapeutic reconciliation. In a sense, this distinction is latent even in the Lambert parents, and corresponds to a gender division, with Alfred resolute, humorless and joyless, scrupulous in every aspect of his professional and private life, highly moral, and, in a trite psychological metaphor that the novel grotesquely literalizes, anally retentive in his dealings with money, sex, discipline, and demeanor. In contrast, Enid is pleasure loving and self-gratifying, even though her impulses are checked by her husband's influence (they have free rein at the end of the novel when Albert is confined to a nursing home). Yet it is in the next generation that the contrasting "lifestyles"—a notion that would be anathema to Alfred—fully emerge as the Lambert children strenuously but with intermittent success attempt to differentiate themselves from the world of their parents. It is against the styles of their rebellion that Franzen exerts his satirical animus, attacking what he sees, on the evidence of the *Harper's* essay, as consummate contemporary absurdities, particularly the platitudinous literary theory and "political correctness" of Chip and the consumerism and investment-mania of Gary. Yet the Lambert children do not move into a fluid, postmodern era of playful consumption and guilt-free pleasure; they continually struggle with the legacy of their upbringing and the contradictory nature of these new cultural practices.

The Corrections is a long novel, too long to discuss comprehensively here, and its loose organization means that it has many tangents, and a number of freestanding comic episodes. Yet for all the pleasure it affords in the accumulation of vivid scenes, the novel does have a pressing question to ask: why are the parents and children, for all their shared characteristics, so very different in their interests and concerns? How did the passage between the older and the younger generation take shape? And how, indeed, can the story of the Lamberts be understood as a microcosm of the cultural history of the present? The novel comes closest to addressing these questions directly in an extended flashback to the early 1960s, a scene that presents itself as the symbolic, if not etiological origin of Alfred Lambert's decline. It is in this episode, not surprisingly, that Franzen brings the novel to a focus, to a unity otherwise dispersed among vivid but essentially contiguous happenings.

Alfred Lambert's degenerative illness, Parkinson's disease, symbolizes the decline of a particular kind of class identity. Although the reader is told little about Alfred's background, one gathers that he grew up in rural Kansas during the depression, earned an engineering degree, managed a steel foundry, and eventually worked his way up to the position of chief engineer in the Midland Pacific railroad company. His progress from the rural working-class to white-collar management follows the post-war economic expansion, but stems, to his mind at least, from rigorous self-discipline, a pride in hard work well done, and careful thriftiness. The integrity of this identity—its cultural, economic, and psychic knotting—is founded on a sense of masculinity, a confident, gendered imaginary: "By day he felt like a man, and he showed this, you might even say he flaunted it, by standing no-handedly on high narrow ledges, and working ten and twelve hours without a break, cataloguing an eastern railroad's effeminacies" (246). Yet this self-consciously rigorous masculinity proves immensely difficult to sustain. Everywhere he travels, inspecting the "effeminate" corruption, the decay, and slipshod labor of the Erie Belt, a future acquisition for the Midland Pacific, he is tormented by the erotic—by the flirtation of waitresses, the sounds of sex from neighboring motel rooms, and the athletic display of cheerleaders glimpsed from a stationary railroad car. And of course, the more Alfred denies his impulses, as his association of sexual continence and probity requires, the more they beset him. He demands of himself the retention of bodily fluids: "in a saggy bed in Fort Wayne awful succubuses descended on him, women whose entire bodies—their very clothes and smiles, the crossings of their legs—exuded invitation like vaginas, and up to the surface of his consciousness (do not soil the bed!) he raced the welling embolus of spunk, his eyes opening to Fort Wayne at sunrise as a scalding nothing drained into his pajamas: a victory, all things considered, for he'd denied the succubuses his satisfaction" (247). It is this set of associations—sexual pleasure with moral turpitude, women with decay and corruption—that founds the patriarchal order he struggles to maintain over his own household.

The crux of this scene, and to some extent of the novel itself, involves the subtle displacement of patriarchal order. Alfred's struggle and eventual collapse stems from the impossibility of restricting in a closed economy the flow of fundamental domestic substances—money, food, semen, and, mediating between them, the display of affection. The breakup of this closed economy undermines the most basic principles of Alfred's identity and demands a new way of thinking about the subject. On the evidence of the rest of the novel, this new way of thinking cannot be achieved; indeed, the book's "tragic realism," as Franzen would have it, is the recognition of incompleteness and contradiction as the defining characteristics of identity. Although the terms I am using might suggest that the text embraces a postmodern idea of subjectivity as fissured and in process, this would be a false assumption. Franzen, I want to suggest, plots a cultural history of the reorganization of authority and identity, drawing from it a certain grim comedy, but then tends to eternalize the flaws he detects. The novel folds the social back into the genetic. In other words, the forceful account of Alfred's discomposure and eventual decline has implications for the historical understanding of identity in the latter part of the twentieth-century; but these implications are contained by the structural limitations of the family saga. In the figure of Alfred, Franzen depicts the disintegration of a certain class identity. But the Lambert children, engaging and often rancorously funny as they are, seem simply to be offshoots from the family tree. Even as the novel presses toward connecting the psychic and the social, it retreats into the spirited but ultimately private world of the Lambert family.

In the scene of the Lamberts in the 1960s, however, the novel dramatizes the forces at war in Alfred's psyche, the domestic setup, and the energies circulating in the world beyond the family. Alfred's difficulties have to do, in the first place, with a confusion of money and sex. By the 1990s this confusion will be endemic and culturally sanctioned. It plays out in the battles Gary has with his wife over investments (inverting the pattern of his parents' contention); in the dismal but apparently inescapable connection between ready cash and sex that Chip is caught in with his girlfriend; in the apparent purchase of Denise's sexual availability as well as her culinary skills by the millionaire Brian Callahan. For the Lambert parents, the struggle concerns an investment in the Midland Pacific railway that Enid desires and Alfred refuses. His distrust of investment involves the memory of the great stock market crash of 1929, and the sense that speculation is a betrayal of the honest exchange of work for wages. For Alfred, money comes directly from labor, a way of understanding the economy that will be long outmoded by the late 1990s when the bulk of the novel is set; as a satirist, Franzen's sympathies are with Alfred, even though he mocks the patriarch's joyless retentiveness and dismal stoicism.

Alfred's preference for thrift over investment, for investment, that's to say, in a highly restricted domestic economy rather than on the risky open economies of the stock market, brings about, through the exchange system of the family, a revenge on Enid's part—the "Dinner of Revenge" (255), a meal consisting of Alfred's (and Chip's) least favorite foods, liver and rutabaga. In place of tenderness and affection, he is offered repulsive reminders of the feminized decay of the Erie Belt: "Brown grease-soaked flakes of flour were impastoed on the ferrous lobes of liver like corrosion. The bacon also, what little there was of it, had the color of rust" (255). Chip, who has the misfortune to find himself caught up in the aberrated domestic economy, becomes one more element in the struggle over flows, as he is ordered, in an archetypal scene of discipline and abjection, to eat one bite of each of the foods he loathes. For Enid, he "turned food into shame" (263), thus traducing the meaning of food, which might stand in her mind for care, her successful and loving management of the domestic economy (meals at once thrifty and satisfying), while for Alfred, Chip's refusal to eat offers yet another sign of the world's recalcitrance to order, its refusal "to square" (262). The circulation of food, words, and affection breaks down around the family dinner table.

The obverse of Alfred's rigorous application of order, control, and patriarchal dominance is a sense of complete powerlessness, the feeling that "the world [is] nothing but a materialization of blind, eternal Will" (262). In support of such a perception, Alfred has a mental commonplace book full of satisfyingly bleak apothegms from Schopenhauer. One of the most telling runs, "If you want a safe compass to guide you through life . . . you cannot do better than accustom yourself to regard this world as a penitentiary, a sort of penal colony" (256). Not only a reminder that misery is to be expected, this quotation also justifies the treatment of others—and oneself—according to a punitive regime. This is the regime exercised over Chip, the stubborn and recidivist eater; it is also a regime that Gary powerfully identifies with—he happily tells his father that he has built a model electric chair from Popsicle sticks. This electric chair, which should make Alfred proud, firm believer in capital punishment that he is, turns out to be so poorly constructed that it threatens the very conception of order and rational authority that it is supposed to signify:

> In a mind-altering haze of exhaustion Alfred knelt and examined it. He found himself susceptible to the poignancy of the chair's having been made—to the pathos of Gary's impulse to fashion an object and seek his father's approval—and more disturbingly to the impossibility of squaring this crude object with the precise picture of an electric chair that he had formed at the dinner table. Like an illogical woman in a dream who was both Enid and not Enid, the chair he'd pictured had been at once completely an electric chair and completely Popsicle sticks. It came to him now, more forcefully than ever, that maybe every "real" thing in the world was as shabbily protean, underneath, as this electric chair. (274)

Alfred's suspicion about the refusal of reality to square with its representations feminizes him, undermining the confident masculine insistence on reality, as well as the supposedly clear distinction—a distinction over which, as the patriarch, he claims authority—between the real and the imagined, the irreproachably true and the speciously fantastic. It is a suspicion, in other words, "[t]hat his feeling of righteousness, of uniquely championing the real, was just a feeling. These were the suspicions that had lain in ambush in all those motel rooms. These were the deep terrors beneath the flimsy beds" (275). Such a situation, as Alfred immediately realizes, trades the satisfying isolation of "uniquely championing the real"— the loneliness of authority and righteousness—for a different kind of isolation, one of subjection to a chaotic, unpredictable, and anomic reality: "if the world refused to square with his version of reality then it was necessarily an uncaring world, a sour and sickening world, a penal colony, and he was doomed to be violently lonely in it" (275).

This insight prefigures Alfred's eventual situation as his Parkinson's worsens—trapped by hallucinatory visions that are at variance from any reality he has previously known, visions that cannot be communicated to even the most caring relation. In his final hospitalization, with the hallucinations in the ascendant, Alfred believes he is being held captive and subjected to a regime of cruel and unusual punishment. Alfred's hallucinations, both of his imprisonment and of the tormenting visions of loquacious (foul-mouthed, so to speak) excrement that beset him on board the pleasure cruiser *Gunnar Myrdal*, suggest both the disintegration of identity and its perverse hypostatization. On the one hand, the primary symptoms of Parkinson's, as Franzen describes them, represent the excruciatingly literal failure of the liberal conception of the subject. Alfred, that is to say, quite literally ceases to be his own property: "His affliction offended his sense of ownership" (67). His limbs refuse to respond to neural messages, so that movement becomes a continual negotiation of various communication failures, rather as if the problems of the Erie Belt had been visited on Alfred internally, or as if the failings of the patriarchal family are played out once more, but this time as intolerable pratfalls: "These shaking hands belonged to nobody but him, and yet they refused to obey him. They were like bad children. Unreasoning two-year-olds in a tantrum of selfish misery. The more sternly he gave orders, the less they listened and the more miserable and out of control they got" (67). Alfred's fantasies of punishing his limbs—of "chopping his hand off with a hatchet" (67), for example—are hopelessly limited by their impossibility: authority over his own embodied being is now beyond him, since the limb that would hack off the offending hand, visiting just punishment, is itself equally incompetent, no less deserving of this form of Biblically sanctioned justice. Further, his hallucinations are thoughts to which he cannot lay claim—thoughts that assail him, undermine his sense of identity, attack the very constitution of his psyche, and challenge his established sense of the way in which the external world can be expected to behave.

Equally, the hallucinations present aspects of Alfred's psyche transfigured; they are, that is to say, aspects of the truth of who he is. In particular, the talking turd that torments Alfred in the middle of the night represents everything that he deplores: "It was a sociopathic turd, a loose stool, a motormouth" (284). Its linguistic fluency and fluidity, an excremental inversion of the canons of "civilized" speech, challenges Alfred's attempts to occupy the position of one who speaks the truth, denouncing his love of the law as a perverse and phobic abjection of the nonself. The turd berates Alfred with an extended riff on those categories of persons he would like to see imprisoned, a list that turns out to include everyone except "upper-middle-class northern European men" (287). In this way, the text mounts an interrogation of the interlacing of psychic, cultural, and social identities, an interrogation made possible by their unraveling.

A pattern of imagery that runs throughout the novel suggests that this knot that secures, albeit temporarily and tenuously, the patriarchal order of Alfred's psyche, family, and cultural identity, is internally conflictual, less a unity than a forced compromise between countervailing positions. Among Enid's transgressions on the evening she tries to persuade Alfred to invest in the Midpac stocks is to initiate sexual activity, scandalously (to Alfred's mind) engaging in oral sex and taking control of the erotic situation. This runs counter to the typical sexual activity between the Lambert parents, which habitually takes the form of "a mute mutual privacy of violence" (242), with Alfred assuming the role of a predator, in particular a lion, and Enid passively playing the part of "a still, unbloody carcass" (242). This coupling stirs ironic echoes of the lion that lies down with the lamb (or Lambert—the pun is not far beneath the surface), and hence plays on ideas of reconciliation and pacification, but also, inversely, of lambs led to the slaughter.

In fact, the lion motif has a particular resonance in *The Corrections*. Enid uses it as a term of affection, cooing to Gary as she puts him to bed: "Always be my little lion. . . . Is he fewocious? Is he wicious? Is he my wicious wittle wion?" (270). Most importantly, however, the lion appears in the guise of Aslan, both the benign, Christ-like deity of C.S. Lewis's Narnia books, which Gary's youngest son devours, and the name of a potent pharmaceutical that erases the taker's sense of shame. Chip encounters this drug (under the name "Mexican A") while engaged in a clandestine affair with a student, with the result that he is able to enjoy without any qualms a weekend of illicit sex. And Enid ingests it in the form of "Aslan 'Cruiser'" (319), a drug intended to help her get full enjoyment out of the fall foliage cruise. For Enid and her son, Aslan works to neutralize that part of the brain that produces the sense of shame. So pacified, so reconciled, they can, under its influence, enjoy whatever it is they want to enjoy—enjoy enjoyment in fact, without any nagging sense of impropriety or obtrusive self-consciousness.

The novel arrives, therefore, at two divergent models of the subject. On one side, there is Alfred, who is committed to a patriarchal regulation of the self and the family, an austere, stoical, and thoroughly privative ordering of subjectivity. His sense of identity depends on a resolute privacy, a fierce sense of integrity, and a violent abjection of otherness, of all differences, a sense that the world is beset by dishonesty and foolishness. This model reaches inwards to an internal system of the self that oscillates between a powerful feeling of control (over baser impulses) and a sensation of desolate, Schopenhauerian misery, in which the self is put on earth simply to suffer. And it extends outward, through the strictly controlled family economy—with its eschewal of unnecessary expenditure (money, food, pleasure)—to the work world, where the struggle against laziness and falsehood, against feminized decay, is unrelenting. The self is, in this model, a kind of property, not unlike a railway network; it requires strenuous upkeep and constant scrutiny, but it can, all being well, run in a useful and efficient way. In pointed contrast there is the contemporary therapeutic conception of the self, wherein misery simply suggests a neurochemical imbalance that can be conveniently put right, and such uncomfortable emotions as guilt and shame can be quelled with a pill. In this way, the self need never be at odds with its surroundings.

Both these models of selfhood are forced to their extreme limits. In the case of Alfred, his control over his self—and the economies that sustain the self—gives way to the radical self-estrangement of Parkinson's disease. While this destroys the integrity of identity, rendering Alfred helpless before his hallucinations and uncoordinated movements, it finally seems to confirm his bleakest assessments of the world. He does, at least in his hallucinatory state, find himself imprisoned at the end of the novel, confined to a nursing home. And he is able, apparently, to exert control at the end over the constitutive flows, refusing both to speak and to eat, until he finally expires, though it is impossible to say by this point whether it is Alfred who makes these choices, or his dementia. Ironically, the pharmacological model of the self seems fleetingly to offer some hope for Alfred. With the application of a process Alfred himself discovered while experimenting in his basement laboratory, the Axon Corporation plans to offer a radical form of neurological manipulation—the "Corecktall Process"— that might have positive benefits for Parkinson's. Yet this turns out to be one more version—an extreme, dystopian version—of the chemical alteration of the brain to fit the environment. In this case, the implications of psychopharmacology are extended into social control, with the suggestion that prisons can be replaced by the alteration of brain chemistry, a possibility boosted by the CEO of Axon as a new world: "when it comes to social disease, the brain of the criminal, there's no other option on the horizon. It's Corecktall or prison. So it's a forward-looking name. We're laying claim to a whole new hemisphere. We're planting the Spanish flag right on the beach here" (208). This is the satirical extension of the basic principle of chemical adjustment: the self is *corrected*, made to match the desired environment.

In spite of the millenarian promises of neurobiology, which the novel makes one with the promises of the booming stock market, the invention of new, shame-free selves proves comically unsuccessful. Shame, it seems, can only ever be deferred. When the effects of the Aslan/Mexican A wear off, shame returns redoubled. Chip, for example, wakes beside Melissa Paquette, the student with whom he has been having vigorous, illicit sex for a weekend, and finds that the drug's influence has worn off: "In a matter of seconds, like a market inundated with a wave of panic selling, he was plunged into shame and self-consciousness" (57). Shame is the feeling of estrangement and pained self-awareness that accompanies desire and checks the experience of pleasure; and indeed, it is inflicted on the one who can never quite experience pleasure the way pleasure is supposed to be experienced. This is the inescapable quality that ties together the Lamberts through the course of the novel: Gary so much wants to take pleasure in guilt-free consumption, but worries constantly about whether his pleasure is real and sufficient (because the absence of pleasure in pleasurable activities—anhedonia, as the psycho-therapeutic jargon has it—is a symptom of depression); Denise, the perfectionist, has an affair with one of her father's subordinates at the Midland Pacific, and subsequently with her employer's wife, both of which cause her acute feelings of shame; and for Enid, shame is the abiding sensation that comes from the suspicion that one might be different from other people, a suspicion that one might not quite fit into one's class position. Shame, then, is the uncomfortable and unwelcome reminder of selfhood, as well as being the archetypal feeling of the upper middle classes. Such a feeling grows out of the necessity for the minute calibration of distinctions, the cultural markers of prestige and significance, which are a constant presence in the affluent suburban neighborhood of the Lamberts.

In spite of the drastic disintegration of Alfred, along with his work ethic and dominant masculinity, the movement to a new class identity remains incomplete. For the next generation of Lamberts, the ethos of expenditure, hedonism, and therapeutic optimism overlies the inheritance of middle-class shame and anxiety, the markers of a cultural identity that remains more or less intact in spite of the buoyancy and wild faddishness of the 1990s. As a satirist, Franzen is essentially conservative, castigating the absurdities of contemporary phenomena such as the investment craze, self-help, the Internet, and literary theory. If shame is an index of alienation from these fads, so much the better for shame; it retains its significance as a negative stamp of authenticity, or, to put it in Franzen's own terms, as the seal of tragic realism and appropriately defeated narcissism. It does not translate into social action or political consciousness. Indeed, the traces of political consciousness—of theoretical or practical critique—are presented in the novel as absurd or pathological. Chip tries to teach his "Consuming Narratives" class how to critique advertisements, but apparently fails—as the reader does not—to detect that the college itself has been branded by corporate logos, including the "Lucent Technologies Lawn" (36), the "Viacom Arboretum" (38), and, most significantly, "Wroth Hall" (44) (the Wroth brothers are the venture capitalists who buy up the Midland Pacific Railroad). His students, Melissa Paquette in particular, take the kind of critical consciousness he attempts to instill as a sign of maladjustment. "Criticizing a sick culture," Chip broods, "even if the criticism accomplished nothing, had always felt like useful work. But if the supposed sickness wasn't a sickness at all—if the great Materialist Order of technology and consumer appetite and medical science really was improving the lives of the formerly oppressed; if it was only straight white males like Chip who had a problem with this order—then there was no longer even the most abstract utility to his criticism" (45). The novel's response to this would seem to be: yes, the Materialist Order is deeply flawed, and no, there is no point to the criticism. The violent direct action of Robin Passafaro's adoptive brother—he attacks an executive of the W— Corporation, a ubiquitous computer giant, with a length of two-by-four— is recast as "Dostoevsky in Germantown" (409), the act of a latter-day Raskolnikov, subsequently to be a movie backed in part by money from the W—Corporation. Once again, the corporate world presents a closed circle, within which politics appears as a symptom of one kind of private behavior or another, a product of the desire to do useful work (Chip) or sociopathic violence (Billy Passafaro).

Refusing the political dimensions of satire, the novel quietly establishes an ideology of invention and property. The book's inventors are Alfred, who discovers a chemical process through long hours in his basement laboratory; Denise, who approaches her work as a chef with the dedication of an artist; and Brian Callahan, who devises a software program that allows the comparison of unlike kinds of music—a "parlor game, musicological tool, and record-sales-enhancer rolled into one" (348). Alfred, who advances toward his discovery on the dismal night of the Dinner of Revenge, fails to capitalize on his patent, much to the fury of Gary and Enid. Neither Denise nor Brian Callahan make this mistake: their inventiveness establishes a profitable niche within the capitalist economy. Surprisingly perhaps, Franzen does not treat the 1990s culture of food, with its extravagance and pretension, to the emetic of satire. Indeed, Denise remains the closest the novel offers to the figure of an artist—certainly, she is a more convincing creator than Chip, whose misery with his screenplay (recasting the story of his catastrophic affair with Melissa Paquette) provides the novel with one of its running jokes.

Invention is the kind of creativity that allows one to launch a piece of property onto the marketplace. This, rather than social critique, supplies the novel with a stabilizing corrective to the hedonism and malleability of contemporary identity. And to this extent, the novel's satire supports a possessive individualist theory of cultural production, and an accompanying class status that is based not on the wild fluctuations of the stock market, so much a feature of the 1990s and in such need of correction, but on productivity, labor, and determination. Franzen, after all, stresses the hard work involved in the inventiveness the novel values: Alfred, long before his collapse into apathy, conducts experiments late into the night in his basement laboratory, and Denise, the perfectionist, apparently cannot help but work tremendously hard. So even as *The Corrections* plots the decline of a certain model of upper-middle-class identity, and castigates the absurdities of the new cultural identities that take its place, it also insinuates an ideology of invention and property rights that offers a small measure of bourgeois salvation.

That is not quite the end of the story. Franzen's success with *The Corrections*, his own brilliant invention, allowed him to detach himself from the model of literary prestige that got him into so much trouble with Oprah Winfrey and the press. His abhorrence at the idea of the Oprah's Book Club logo appearing on the jacket of *his* novel reflects his grounding in ideas of creativity as the creation of property; his worries about his high literary credentials being overlooked proved less consistent, perhaps because they were unnecessary once he had found a sufficient and identifiable niche in the market. Franzen went on to publish a remarkably savage article on the work of William Gaddis, one of his erstwhile literary idols, in which he not only did his best to derogate the late writer's work, but also boasted about his failure to finish great novels by the likes of Melville, Pynchon, James, Mann, and Burroughs.[46]

Oprah Winfrey, for her part, abandoned the Book Club, some suspected as a result of the unpleasantness with Franzen. But in the summer of 2003 she relaunched it, this time picking classic works of literature (her first selection was Steinbeck's *East of Eden*). It remains to be seen whether any of Franzen's unfinished masterpieces will be chosen.

CHAPTER 4
LATE POSTMODERNISM AND CULTURAL MEMORY

"Another 20 years of boring literary novels and the thing's dead." Jonathan Franzen made this remark to justify providing his reader with "a maximally enthralling experience."[1] The reader's absorption guarantees the novel's survival, presumably because obstacles to popular appeal can only further trends of indifference already afoot in the culture at large. As I argued in the previous chapter, Franzen's anxieties circulate around cultural distinction, prestige, and authority, all of which are threatened by the rise of consumer culture and its attendant ideologies. The three novelists I address in this chapter are no less concerned about the novel's survival, but have chosen to make issues of reading, readability, and readership central to their fiction. Can the words of the writer still find a receptive mind? How is such a mind constituted out of the structure of memory embodied in literary history? These questions take on a greater urgency if the problem of individual communication comes to be seen as a microcosm of readership, cultural efficacy, and the uncertainty surrounding the project of innovative fiction.

The three novelists I examine in this chapter, Richard Powers, Kathryn Davis, and David Markson, have yet to receive the recognition they deserve. Their careers have not pursued predictable paths, nor have they followed established literary movements. Indeed, the difficulty of securing a reputation for their work within the present literary conjuncture provokes the uncertainty they address in the novels under examination. Powers, the most prolific and best recognized of the three, is a prodigious writer who has taken on the largest of subjects—race, history, technology, the environment—and seems capable of absorbing the most recondite areas of knowledge, including genetics, musicology, computers, and game theory. Over the last two decades, he has written eight novels, two—*The Gold Bug Variations* (1991) and *The Time of Our Singing* (2003)—massive in scope and ambition, and all of them intricate in structure and audacious in execution. His work has received several major prizes, including MacArthur and Lannan Foundation Awards, predominantly enthusiastic reviews, and has recently begun to attract some long overdue academic attention.[2]

Kathryn Davis, who has now published five novels notable for their poise, inventiveness, and lapidary prose, has yet to attract significant critical scrutiny. Her writing invites comparison with the intricate late modernist designs of Vladimir Nabokov, particularly the great Russian writer's cunning play with fantastical worlds and dubious narrators. She also has something in common with such gifted fabulists of the second generation of post-modernism as Rikki Ducornet, Joanna Scott, and Mary Caponegro. Davis's fiction attends to the charged threshold between worlds—imaginative, constructed, artistic, historical—where transformations occur and hazards abound. Her novels might be described as ontological mysteries or textual puzzles, and as such they exhibit several of the hallmarks of postmodern innovation—metafiction, antirealism, self-conscious artifice. Yet her work began to appear in the late 1980s (*Labrador*, her first novel, was published in 1988), a moment when such postmodern practice, even writing as luminous and artful as Davis's, had fallen out of favor. Accidents of literary fashion apart, her novel *The Walking Tour* makes the crisis of the entire print culture the motivating circumstance for an intricate meditation on technology, intellectual property, the transmission and continuity of memory, and the salvific power of art.

David Markson belongs to an earlier generation than Powers and Davis, but has in the past decade and a half produced the most arresting work of his long career, publishing four remarkable experimental novels, texts that seem to distill a lifetime's reading into an austere set of epitaphs—epitaphs for the reader, the writer, and literature itself. The central, generative event that these novels transfigure in their peculiar form is a massive shift in the meaning of literature and the memory by which it is sustained. Markson's own persistence in an inherently modernist project, notwithstanding the blandishments of the postmodern (or even postliterate) age, gives his career an idiosyncratic shape and has made him a difficult writer to situate within established trends and movements. What he shares with Powers and Davis, apart from a commitment to innovation, is a sense that cultural memory in the postmodern present is endangered.

Each of these writers deals with the question of tradition, with the shared memory of literary texts that writers draw upon, contend with, and attempt to shape in their own image. Tradition incites new work and carries the stream of literary prestige into the present. But tradition in the late age of print assumes importance because it is under threat. This sense of endangerment is a common theme in elegies for the book, and various culprits have been cited, most notably technology. Powers, Davis, and Markson participate in the elegiac discourse, but resist the cultural fatalism that so often goes along with it. Equally, they have refused to accommodate their writing to the perception of altered scale of literary values and a changed cultural landscape. Yet their work is "enthralling," to borrow Franzen's adjective, in part because of its ambition, and in part because it refuses to treat the imagination, particularly the reader's imagination, as a casualty of cultural change. All three novelists have taken the awkward situation of literary fiction as a spur to further invention.

In this postmodern climate, the theme of tradition might seem hopelessly retrograde and reactionary, a category long since rendered suspect by the Nietzschean animus of recent literary theory. Yet if one accepts the claim—as these writers implicitly do—that contemporary culture is thoroughly amnesiac, actively destructive of memory, then the struggle to engage with tradition, or at least to understand its present state, can be seen as a form of resistance, perhaps even a means of literary survival. At this level, the political valences are not determined: neoconservatives sometimes claim to have the monopoly on tradition, but radicals too can, indeed must draw sustenance and education from the memory of previous struggles. It may well be that the struggle to preserve shattered tradition, at a moment when the value of literary culture is undergoing a profound transformation, will prove highly useful in future attempts to make use of imaginative writing and to establish new kinds of intellectual community in the crevices and at the margins of the dominant culture.

The memory embodied in literature offers Richard Powers—the protagonist and narrator of *Galatea 2.2*—a way to remember and understand his own life. Reading, writing, and living form overlapping fields in his mind, and a crisis in one is a crisis felt in all. Powers's elaborate speculative fiction mends the broken connection between lived time and the time of texts, thus reconciling yet another blocked writer to himself and to his vocation. In Davis's novel, time is irreparably split into a historical past and an utterly different post-historical present. Her narrator attempts to connect these times through acts of literary detection and historiography, but it is only in the visionary medium of art that the gulf can truly be bridged, however fleetingly and miraculously. In Markson's sequence, the rift seems complete: there is no life to write about; all that remains is textual matter, the shards from a broken vessel. But the fragmentation, which grows more pointed and irreversible from book to book, ironically fulfills the Flaubertian program of writing a novel about nothing, and so makes of lack and absence a performative homage to tradition.

Figures of Solipsism

Richard Powers's 1995 novel *Galatea 2.2* combines elements of *Bildungsroman* and speculative fiction to examine the workings of intelligence, learning, and memory within contemporary literary culture.[3] The novel's narrator, teasingly named Richard Powers (hereafter Rick, to distinguish character from author), finds himself unable to proceed beyond the first sentence of his projected fifth novel. Seeking distraction from writer's block, he accepts a wager on an experiment in artificial intelligence: under the direction of the acerbic computer scientist Philip Lentz, Rick sets about training a series of neural network implementations—banks of computers running in parallel to model learning and intelligence—to read, understand, and interpret literary texts. The aim of the bet is to match the neural net, dubbed Helen, against a graduate student in taking the MA comprehensive exam in English literature. This is a highly specialized variant on the classic Turing Test, in which an adjudicator examines the output of two black boxes, one of which is a computer, the other a human; if it proves impossible to tell the human output from the machine output, then the computer can be said to exhibit intelligence.[4] In this case, teaching a machine to read and understand involves thinking about the essential nature of intelligence, language, and representation. In the novel's fundamental conceit, these problems are also those of literary understanding, issues that engage, consciously or otherwise, writers and readers. Consequently, the novel establishes an interplay between computers and brains, scientific and literary worlds, individual and cultural memories. While developing Helen, Rick reflects on his own personal and professional development, and in particular a ten-year relationship that has recently come to an acrimonious end. In a move characteristic of Powers's fiction, the reader's engagement with *Galatea 2.2* involves connecting two distinct but parallel narrative lines. As the novel begins to shed light on the sources of Rick's writer's block it also pieces together—word by word, memory by memory—a reader, or a pair of readers: Helen, whose "posthuman" understanding movingly defamiliarizes language, comprehension, love, and cruelty, but also the novel's flesh-and-blood reader, who is solicited to draw significant inferences from the text's parallel systems.

As N. Katherine Hayles has observed, *Galatea 2.2* employs patterns of doubling and difference to establish and complicate such fundamental pairs as human and posthuman, presence and absence, materiality and signification.[5] Doubling and difference also mark the relations between writers and readers that are of crucial importance in the novel. All of the major exchanges between characters involve textual interactions of one kind or another: Rick's memories of college and his years with his girlfriend C., his beginnings as a writer, his foray into the realm of artificial intelligence, his training of Helen—all of these recalled and recounted experiences are marked by avid and transformative reading. Indeed, part of the appeal of Lentz's connectionism—the theory that machine intelligence can grow out of the self-modification of neural nets—stems from its emphasis on transformation through repeated input; hence language acquisition, and hence reading. Early in his initiation into the connectionist field, Rick reads an article by Lentz that fires his imagination: Lentz describes how a comparatively simple set of nested circuits progresses in a matter of days from "streams of gibberish phonemes" to quite sophisticated reading, so that "Three hundred simulated cells had learned to read aloud" (30). If the connectionists are correct, this learning process mirrors human development. The emergent neural net is not *programmed* with rules for reading, it *works them out* through a process of trial and error. But the reading machine does depend on a teacher: "Neural cascade, trimmed by self-correction, eventually produced understandable words. All it needed was someone like Lentz to supply the occasional 'Try again's and 'Good boy!'s" (31). Consequently, the evolving identity of the reader, whether artificial or human, is bound up with the approval, the desire, of someone in a position of pedagogical authority. The central authority in the novel is Rick, whether he is reading aloud to C., his lover and former student, or to Helen. The Pygmalion story alluded to in the title serves as an ironic reminder that these relations involve projection and narcissistic desire. Even minor background details in *Galatea 2.2*, such as the secret affair two of the scientists are conducting (they disguise their assignations as meetings of a book club), amplify the connections made between reading, desire, and identity.

The emphasis the novel places on reading, which shapes learning, memory, and intelligence, is in direct proportion to an anxiety over the writer's cultural authority. Rick lives out this anxiety as he completes his relentlessly depressing fourth book, and then stalls on the first sentence of his fifth. His difficulties as a writer can undoubtedly be traced to a personal crisis: a former psychiatrist tells him at one point, an apocalyptic outlook, such as that expressed in his "bleak, baroque fairy tale about wandering and disappearing children" (5), is a typical response to the breakup of a long relationship. But the doubling structure of *Galatea 2.2* allows Powers to trace Rick's writing block—the lived condition of the anxiety—to contextual as well as personal sources. His troubles arise from an acute awareness of the cultural climate. The novel sketches in various ideologies and institutions that comprise the contemporary literary field, including prevalent perceptions of the novelist's artistic and social role, the publishing and reviewing industries, and the academic world, all of which present the novelist with problems of self-definition. Rick's auto-biographical reflections on his emotional life and his apprenticeship as a writer allow him to chart a continuous identity through the vagaries of circumstance and misunderstanding, but they also draw attention to the ways in which he finds himself at odds with the external conditions of the prevailing literary culture.

Rick's experiences on returning to his alma mater, where he takes up a position as writer-in-residence at the Center for the Study of Advanced Sciences, show him that the literary culture he once took for granted has now vanished. He finds that the English students he encounters bear little resemblance to his earlier self. In the years since he left graduate school to pursue his ambitions as a writer everything has changed. The fact that an age gap of a decade and a half now separates him from the students underscores a more significant difference, that his intellectual formation has little in common with that of the undergraduates and graduates of the present. His classroom visits supply uncomfortable evidence: "Students sat polite but stunned in front of me, their desks circled like Conestogas under attack. The look of shame on each face asked how I could have missed the fact that the age of reading was dead" (116). Rick himself is a product of "the age of reading." For Rick, books and memories are inex-tricably woven together: a chance glimpse of a battered paperback copy of *Don Quixote*, for example, summons up the awkwardness and excitement of adolescence; the works on the MA list that he reads Helen return him to the life-changing Freshman course he took with Professor Taylor, his mentor, and to his years reading aloud to C. To learn from the embarrassed faces in the classroom that the age of reading is dead suggests not only that Rick's novels are readerless, but also that his experience, shaped pro-foundly by an immersion in the written word, may be incommunicable, at least to any putative future readership.

The method of literary studies that helped to shape Rick has gone the way of the age of reading. Rick's inspirational instructor, Professor Taylor, exemplified an approach to literature now vanished from the campus. "Traceless" (254) in the current generation of graduate students, Taylor's sophistication, wit, and erudition are missing from an academic scene now dominated, the novel implies, by literary theory. He represents an older brand of scholarship: he has, we learn, devoted his professional life to one novel (*Middlemarch*), yet has an extraordinarily capacious knowledge of literature of all kinds. Described by Rick as "the best reader I ever met" (129), Taylor makes his remarkable impact by embodying in his person the connection between reading and memory. "He had read all the books," Rick explains. "He was fluent in the mind's native idiom . . . . He might have been the supreme misanthrope, were it not for his humor and humility. And the source of these two saving graces, the thing stitching that heart-breaking capaciousness into a whole, was memory" (145). The "mind's native idiom" is self-reflection: "Through Taylor I discovered how a book both mirrored and elicited the mind's unreal ability to turn inward upon itself" (141). Books are important, in this sense, because they model the workings of the mind: books exemplify the mind's capacity for intro-spection, just as they encourage self-scrutiny. Even in his social life, Taylor proves book-like as well as bookish. His anecdotes and observations, delivered in a witty and syntactically "Byzantine" (143) fashion, prompt C. and Rick to recall things they had forgotten, and to delight in conver-sational sallies of a kind they had not known themselves capable. In his person and his practice, Taylor sustains a mutually enriching reciprocity between reader and writer, which provides Rick with a rationale for literary productivity. Rick acknowledges that he has developed his "labyrinthine style" (202) for Taylor's approval; he also notes that in his success as a writer he has lived out Taylor's own youthful dream. Equally, Taylor sustains Rick's identity by making explicit a connection between the "eighteen-year-old kid memorizing 'The Windhover'" (202) and the successful author. Earnest and prolonged study of canonical texts becomes the necessary preparation for novelistic achievement.

Rick's study of the canon more than a decade earlier followed institu-tional protocols reflecting the dominant ideas of literary study. As he explains, "[t]hey gave us a list of titles. Up at the top of page 1 was 'Caedmon's Hymn.' Six pages later, it wound up with Richard Wright" (43). Returning to the same English department—himself, as it were, the practicing inheritor of the canonical literary tradition—he finds that the requirements have changed: a current MA student, denoted A., explains, "Nobody *has* to read anyone anymore. . . . These days, you find the people you want to study from each period. You work up some questions in advance. Get them approved. Then you write answers on your preparation" (284). The new approach reflects the impact of literary theory. Not only has the canon been interrogated and critiqued, but the centrality of the author has also been rejected: Rick finds himself demoted to an "author function" (286). The continuities between the academy and authorship, so urbanely underwritten by Taylor, are disrupted by the new culture of the discipline, leaving the novelist in the position of an awkward anachronism, or, in A.'s sardonic phrase, "Parasite-in-Residence" (253).

The novel expresses a sharp awareness of this marginalization and of the recent paradigm shift in literary studies. In an important exchange, A. accuses Rick of teaching Helen "a culturally constructed, belated view of belle lettres" (285), an outmoded version of the canon that is blind to its own implication in a hegemonic cultural imaginary, a "white-guy, *Good Housekeeping* thing" (284), as she scornfully remarks. In particular, she upbraids Rick for making Helen read "The Windhover," that "cornerstone" (284) of his own life as a reader. For A., Hopkins's poem is a synecdoche for an outmoded literary canon. Rick's defense lays him open to further attack:

> "We have to give her the historical take if she—"
> "The winner's history, of course. What made you such a coward? What are you so scared of? Difference is not going to kill you. Maybe it's time your little girl had her consciousness raised. An explosion of young-adulthood."
> "I'm all for that. I just think that you can get to the common core of humanity from anywhere."
> "Humanity? Common core? You'd be run out of the field on a rail for essentializing. And you wonder why posthumanists reduced your type to an author function." (285–286)

The continuities between the canonical literature he studied in graduate school and his literary vocation depend on the humanism that A. denounces here. Like Taylor, Rick places his trust in a relationship of modeling between text and mind, a notion that leads him to approach poems and novels as complex figurations of an essential human identity. For A., such assumptions belong to liberal ideology, and reading practices that isolate mind from cultural context belong to a dangerously archaic theory of criticism. "I bet you still think New Criticism is, like, heavy-duty" (285) she scoffs.

Under the new paradigm, the critic situates the text in the context of power relations, both in the historical moment of its production, and in the present of its reading, where the text can be used to prop up or challenge archaic conceptions of literature and outmoded social privilege. Rick's humanism insulates canonical literature from the relations of power that have conditioned it and to which it speaks—or so A. charges. It is a charge anticipated by Lentz near the beginning of the book. Lentz, who never misses an opportunity to needle Rick, mocks what he considers the undue attention given to the Netherlands in Rick's novels: "Why don't you write about real countries? The whole global community is out there, chain-dragging on its own economic exhaust pipe. It's North against South, you know. Haves versus have-nots" (17). Yet even more important than the politics of exclusion, the argument that Rick's fictional investment in the world of the "Haves" constitutes a failure to speak out about injustices local and global, is the question of the relationship between texts and readers over which A. and Rick clash. When Rick charges the canon-busting A. with vandalism, she responds, "I'm not trying to burn any books. I'm just saying that books are what we make of them. And not the other way round" (285). In A.'s view, the canon can—and should—be questioned, dismantled, and reassembled because the definitions by which it exists ("Whose definition of great? Hopkins ain't gonna cut it anymore" [285]) are cultural constructs that reflect power and privilege. Notions of literary value are not immanent within canonical texts but are "found" there by the critic blind to his or her own presuppositions of class, race, and gender—so A.'s position might be further stated.

Thus, Rick is obliged to recognize that the authority and position of the writer in literary culture have altered since his apprenticeship. No longer is the novelist—or the critic—the bearer of literary value passed along the chain of canonical texts, as the example of Professor Taylor seemed to suggest. A. is scathing about the assumption that the canon continues to exercise authority: "Play fair. You make it sound as if every-thing anyone has ever written is recycled Bible and Shakespeare" (285). From Rick's perspective, the cherished texts of the literary tradition inform any judgments we might make about them. The dynamic of text and mind, as taught by Taylor, is analogous to the relation of text to tradi-tion. A. puts the points dismissively, but for Rick the canon remains important because it does model and elicit new texts, which themselves assume canonical status through a reciprocal relationship of sameness and difference. Over a period of time successful new works take their place in the canon, their originality recognized and embraced by the living tradition of valued words. Rick's understanding of his own writing relies on his formative immersion in the canon and, while the public channels of approval remain abstract and unsatisfactory (the review in the Sunday *New York Times* is the only one that really counts, according to the novel), the experiential link to the canon as a repository of literary values sustains his writing. When his work falters, he turns to the canon. Hung up on his opening sentence, he racks his brain to remember as many first sentences of novels as he possibly can, thus checking that he has not inadvertently plagiarized, but also placing his own new opening among many firmly established in the canon and the memory.

C.P. Snow's famous "two cultures" divide, which *Galatea 2.2* boldly straddles, exacerbates the novelist's crisis of cultural authority. Literary study within the university is a poor relation, and the split between science and the humanities is conspicuously marked in the material structure of the campus. Rick's unusual appointment—he is writer-in-residence at the Center as well as in the English Department—entitles him to two offices. His office in the Center boasts "state-of-the-art, clean-room efficiency" (7). The building itself is a technological showpiece, complete with all the latest scientific research equipment, including, among other things, a nationally funded supercomputing site. The English Department forms a marked contrast:

> For breathers, I frequented my other campus office, in the English Building. McKim, Mead and White, 1889. There I lived my alter ego—picturesque but archaic man of letters. The Center possessed 1,200 works of art, the world's largest magnetic resonance imager, and elevators appointed in brass, teak, and marble. The English Building's stairs were patched in three shades of gray linoleum. (75)

These buildings reflect the economic reality of the two cultures split. In his office in the Center, Rick has access to the Internet, the new decentered global community, and is for a time enthralled by its possibilities: his computer opens onto the universe of data. In his nineteenth-century office in the English Department, more a place to hide than a place to write (reflecting once again his marginal status in the realm of contemporary literary studies), he sits and stares "at the bricked-in fireplace, waiting for a surreal locomotive to emerge from it" (76). Creativity in this professional space seems as plausible as Magritte's surrealist image, which recalls his stalled first line. Instead of the myriad connections of the web, the English office presents an image of incommunicability, of stubbornly intractable blankness, words going nowhere.

But Powers complicates this division. Literary theorists are technocrats, and scientists often turn out to be sensitive humanists. The scientists in *Galatea 2.2* have an unchecked delight in literature; to Rick's surprise, they read Cervantes, Smollett, and Fielding, recall Milton, and cite Donne at the head of scientific articles. Along with this goes an undiminished faith in the significance of the authorial role. When Rick's bleak fourth novel finally appears, his neurologist friend Diana Hartrick complains, "We're all overwhelmed. We're all bewildered. Why read in the first place, if the people who are supposed to give us the aerial view can't tell us anything except what an inescapable mess we're in?" (210). Rick's theory-sponsored marginality in the humanities contrasts with the humanistic centrality the novel-reading scientists expect. But Rick fails because his "aerial view" is no better than the view at ground level—one of confusion, uncertainty, perhaps even despair. For Diana Hartrick, this amounts to an abdication of the responsibility entailed by authorship. In his writing,

Rick can offer little constructive resolution, and so fails to live up to the authority of the "aerial view." But neither does he dismantle the author-function in approved deconstructive fashion.

Thus, Rick cannot live up to traditional humanistic expectations, nor can he satisfy those looking for a critique of such expectations. The novel faces the challenge of negotiating a new kind of authority that is not impugned by either kind of critique. *Galatea 2.2* works to imagine a satisfactory relationship between a writer and a readership, one that will avoid the hazards constellated around the two cultures split. As such, the novel interrogates the kinds of authority accorded by this divide, even as it explores the tensions within scientific and humanities camps. Rick's efforts to overcome his writer's block—and his final success in so doing (the novel ends with a glimpse of its own composition)—involve establishing a reason to write in spite of the cultural pressures exerted by scientists, (post)humanists, and the institutions of literary production. *Galatea 2.2* connects these competing discourses through an insistent examination of memory and its connection to creativity. For the frozen creativity with which Rick struggles stems from the perplexing rift in personal and cultural memory: he cannot connect his present situation to his history; nor can he establish the link between his writing and the tradition in which he has been schooled. At first sight, literary theory and hard science are equally unpromising. The former traffics in social and linguistic constructivism, contending that the human subject and the literary work are no more than products of their historical moment; put crudely, Rick's fiction can only ever reflect hegemonic privilege. He writes as a straight white male from the richest of nations, even though he presumes to speak for or from the common core of humanity, and his conception of literature, founded on the canon in which he delights, props up such privilege. Conversely, the essentialism of some branches of science, which see intelligence as hardwired into the brain, tends to militate against a progressive and unfolding use of memory as the source of creativity. The novel's speculative flights into artificial intelligence offer a way to think about and depart from these fruitless paths of thought. What Rick learns from Lentz and from his training of Helen allows him to circumvent the problems of social constructivism and essentialism, and to imagine a way in which memory might feed and justify further creative work.

The novel finds in connectionism a more productive understanding of intelligence and memory. Rick learns early on that the scientific study of intelligence is divided into three basic camps. Neural physiologists probe into the brain itself to see how it works; this is Diana Hartrick's field, and she works with an MRI (Magnetic Resonance Imager) to study the brain's workings in real time (without, that is, having to slice into the thing under study). Such an approach emphasizes empirical data. By contrast, the artificial intelligence coders believe that the properties of human intelligence, particularly language-use and reasoning, might be modeled using formal algorithms; these can then be encoded into a machine. In the novel, Chen and Keluga, two minor characters, pursue this project, the latter attempting, as Lentz sarcastically puts it, "to write the entire Roget's as a series of rule-based schematics" (77). Connectionism looks to sidestep both approaches by arguing that the brain is not simply "a sequential, state–function processor, as the AI people had it" (29); nor is it merely "the sum passing through its neuronal vesicles" (29), as the neural physiologists assume in practice, if not in theory. Lentz, the connectionist, argues, "The brain was a model-maker, continuously rewritten by the thing it tried to model. Why not model *this*, and see what insights one might hook in to" (29). The implementations Lentz and Rick construct are model-makers, continuously rewritten by the things they try to model. Or, to put the matter in less abstract fashion, they are readers, continuously rewritten by what they read. In their various incarnations, the implementations begin like children, like Rick himself, with the simplest phrases and words, proceed through nursery rhymes and children's stories, gradually come on to more complicated texts, and ultimately tackle the canonical works on the six-page list for the comprehensive exam. The speculative fiction, therefore, is not just a thought-experiment about the potentials and limitations of artificial intelligence, but also a model of mind as reader, an elaborate construction of nested layers, allusions, cross-references, and interpretive leaps. It is this construction that the reader traces and participates in page by page as she recognizes references from the distinct but interacting levels of the text (autobiographical narrative, literary allusion, speculative fiction).

And for mind, read also literary culture. Reading, by these lights, makes mind, and minds make literary culture, where literary culture is envisaged as a continuously rewritten shared memory. The novel's exploration of neural networks establishes a way of grounding tradition in mental process. This tradition—though the novel fights shy of the word—is bodied forth in the simplest way, through the recollection of reading experiences in propinquity with stages in a life's writing. The nested implementations with their sets of weighted vectors—memory, in other words—provide an image of tradition more encouraging to the writer and reader than A.'s dismissive remark about Rick's faith in the continuing values of the canon, the belief that "everything anyone has ever written is recycled Bible and Shakespeare" (285): "We called that first filial generation B, but it would, perhaps, have better been named A2. E's weights and contours lived inside F's lived inside G's, the way Homer lives on in Swift and Joyce, or Job in Candide or the Invisible Man" (171). Or even, one might add, Ovid in Powers. Reading the canon establishes weights and contours in the reader too, the modeling by which the model, new text or old, might itself be modeled.

Rick's training of the implementations aims to build a mind that might make sense of his own. Success in moving toward a machine intelligence that can read and comprehend is benchmarked by reference to Rick's first novel: early in training Implementation B, Rick tests its comprehension by posing the riddle he used as the epigraph to his first book; and once Helen, for example, can read with some sophistication—or seem to (the novel cunningly ambiguates the nature of her responses)—Rick gives her a copy of his first novel to digest. Although never made explicit, the goal is to invent a reader in the absence of readers, to embody in a single reader the layered knowledge of the canon such that it will stand in for a tradition, a meaningful connection between old and new, that is otherwise a felt absence, as much in the chaos Rick feels in his own life as in the disarray of literary cultures. In his relation to Helen, Rick searches for an ideal reader, one patterned after his projections, a true Galatea. Helen will replace C., formerly his first and best reader (though in retrospect a reader increasingly grudging and suspicious as his books begin to take on a public life of their own). The mind conceived by connectionism thus becomes the novel's way of thinking about a community of other minds. For the connectionist, the mind is dynamic, a continual modeling and rewriting by others, through differentiated input and selective output. To understand memory in mind or machine as weighted vectors supplies an analogy for cultural memory as a net of interconnected allusions. Indeed, the whole intricate system of literature as a form of memory, one text recalling and subtly altering another, resembles intelligence as connectionism conceives it. The threat to memory raised by contemporary literary culture damages the connections within this system of memory, and so renders the texts of the past, and the other minds from which those texts once sprang, inaccessible and inert to the writer. Equally, the novel's aim of bringing issues of memory down to their fundamentals, their cellular basis, as well as tracing the phenomenological textures of memory, in Proustian fashion, implicitly protests the short attention span of contemporary culture.

The book's primary point of contrast to the memory-system of literature is the web, which Rick discovers with excitement, surfs with enthusiasm, but soon rejects, having grown jaded with a rapidity befitting the medium. Ironically, his first excitement evokes the thrill of reading: "Alone in my office, blanketed by the hum of the Center, I felt like a boy happening onto a copy of the *Odyssey* in a backwater valley library" (8). The simile here echoes Keats, whose sonnet "On First Looking into Chapman's Homer" Rick later alludes to as a way of suggesting the delight awakened by the AI material he reads, but the primary allusion, within the novel's own vectors, is to Taylor, whose scholarly career has its seeds in his youthful reading ("The boy who taught himself to read on Tarzan and John Carter, who went on to devour every volume in the rural library long before he made his escape" [144]). Yet, the experience of the web turns out to be quite unlike that of reading. Rather than establishing a negentropic organization of cultural vectors, the opening onto other minds, the web proves to be dominated by noise. It lays claim to "universal linkup" (9), though as the novel is quick to point out, the technological divide makes any such claim spurious: "[People] whizzed binary files at each other from across the planet, the same planet where impoverished villages looked upon a ball-point pen with wonder" (9). Yet, even an equitable distribution of technological resources would not, Powers asserts, transform the web into a truly collective medium:

> The web was a neighborhood more efficiently lonely than the one it replaced. Its solitude was bigger and faster. When relentless intelligence finally completed its program, when the terminal drop box brought the last barefoot, abused child on line and everyone could at last say anything instantly to everyone else in existence, it seemed to me we'd still have nothing to say to each other and many more ways not to say it. (9)

Unlike the career of reading and writing, first modeled for Rick by Taylor, which weaves together extraordinary memory, selfhood, and articulacy, the technological linkup of the web occludes identity, abstracting it to third-person virtuality: "I began to think of myself in the virtual third person, as that disembodied world-web address: rsp@center.visitor.edu" (9).

Galatea 2.2 more or less dismisses the web within its first ten pages, but the problem it raises, in brazen contemporary fashion, remains pertinent throughout the novel. The web promises communication, but in fact offers inert connection. Its "linkup" is devoid of weight or moment. As a result, it merely reproduces—multiplies, even—individual isolation. The novel's humanism is nowhere more evident than in the theme of loneliness, which threads through the pages of the book. The sentiment of loneliness in *Galatea 2.2* grows out of the absence of intellectual community as much from a lack of emotional closeness. Loneliness, finally, is what Rick shares with C., Lentz, and even, one might say, with Helen. Indeed, the pathos of Helen's dilemma, which comes into focus at the novel's climax, derives from her unassuageable loneliness, her awareness of her difference from her human interlocutors. Lentz's homely explanation holds good for Rick's Pygmalionism and its implied ironies: Rick too wants something to talk to, but he wants that something to be a projection of his own fantasy. Helen's loneliness reproaches him, offers a narrative, and holds out the promise of writing as a particular form of communion between solitudes.

Loneliness and projection assume the form of a problem within the novel's questioning of tradition when they are considered, at the text's invitation, in relation to issues of representation. The novel raises its questions about cultural community and within the terrain of the web, the book, and the institution, through two metafictional parables about the limits of representation. A heart patient and a quadriplegic are confined to a room in the critical ward of a hospital. The heart patient, who happens to be in the bed by the window, spends his days regaling his neighbor, the quadriplegic, with colorful and absorbing accounts of what he can see happening outside. One night, however, he suffers a heart attack. Rather than offering assistance or calling a nurse, the man in the other bed manages to knock the heart patient's vital medicine to the floor, thus ensuring that he will be moved to the bed with the window view. From his new bed, he finds that he can see nothing but a brick wall. This story, which the narrator of *Galatea 2.2* tells C. early in their relationship, acquires an emblematic status during the course of the novel, as it comes to encapsulate the problem faced by Helen, the reading machine, in her dealings with narrative and reality.

Rick tells Helen the second story, barely an anecdote, as a way of offering an analogue for her own situation. This derives from the postlude to Nabokov's *Lolita*, a novel that shares with *Galatea 2.2* a preoccupation with the nature of desire and the damage attending projection: "[Nabokov] describes hearing of an ape who produced the first known work of animal art, a rough sketch of the bars of the beast's cage" (291). The pathos of this tale derives from the tension between solipsistic isolation and communicative identification. Having been taught howsoever to sketch, the ape produces not, as might be expected, an image of the freedom from immediate circumstance accorded by representation, but instead delineates the conditions of its imprisonment. It provides, as Rick tells Helen, "cell specifications" (291). But if the drawing is a figure for incommunicability and solipsism, it fails of its purpose, since it effects identification between the viewer and the ape, and achieves, out of the conditions of failure, a successful communication, though of course this is of little consolation to the imprisoned ape. Art transcends through its failure to transcend. The solipsism of the ape, or any artist, is the figure of thought for the mind's lack of community. Despairing of communicability, the solipsist sees the mind as a prison cell, sealed off from outside influences or exchanges. Notwithstanding the boom and buzz of augmented information systems, solipsism proves a curiously appropriate image for cultures of the end—the end of humanity, the end of the book. It is the hyperbolic metaphor for the absence of other minds in the form of readers and books.

Both stories have a bearing on Helen's situation. She has grown into a specific configuration, a "self," through immersion in literary texts, specifically the stories, poems, and novels of the traditional canon of English and American literature. What she knows and what she is are dependant on the weighted vectors established through the absorption of heard and written words; her access to nonlinguistic reality is restricted to the appliances—the aural and optical devices—from which she receives limited input. Her understanding of the world is conditioned by the mediated versions given her by the narrator and by the authors of canonical works of literature. Thus, like the man confined to the critical ward, Helen lacks direct access to immediate reality, and has no way to distinguish between the inventions of fiction and reports on reality. But once Helen confronts the brute misery of reality, she experiences a dismay similar to that one assumes the man in the hospital room felt on learning that the accounts of life seen through the window of the ward were no more than, or no less than stories. Helen falls silent after learning of the horrors of real world history and politics. She sticks, in particular, on the synecdochic news report of a senseless act of violence: "Helen was spinning listlessly on the spool of a story about a man who had a stroke while driving, causing a minor accident. The other driver came out of his car with a tire iron and beat him into a coma" (313–314). This is Helen's brick wall.

The story of the two men in the critical ward, and its more involved analogue, the narrative of Helen's formation and distress, suggest that narrative representation is dangerous, that it can, perhaps must, obscure the truth and so mislead the auditor or reader into misunderstanding the nature of reality. For the bed-bound man the lively narrative of daily occurrences presented as observations falsifies the fact that the window offers only the view of a brick wall. He is led by the stories to believe that the recounted events may be apprehended directly, and hence to the murderous desire to secure such apprehension for himself. To this extent, the story is a Platonic parable about the dangers of fictional representation. Artful lies offer consolation: the immobilized man can be pleasurably diverted by what seem to be the real events seen from the next bed. But the falsehoods of fiction also confuse the ontological hierarchy of reality and invention. The victim of invention is led astray by fiction's pretense to represent actualities. In Helen's case, the rich diversity of literature to which she is exposed leads to the assumption that human experience is intrinsically meaningful, whether its meanings are comic, tragic, or romantic. This is the novel's twist on A.'s contention that canonical literature reinforces power and privilege. Literature falsifies the nature of reality by imbuing it with sense, with legible meaning; even the darkest works of the twentieth century do this, as Rick discovers when he tries to make up for his mistake in educating Helen only in the truths of literature. Human suffering, presented in the stark factual reporting of the newspaper, is without any vestige of sense. Helen's interpretive capacities, founded on the humanist canon, cannot come to terms with the awful facts of brutality and misery. Imaginative literature thereby presents itself as consoling falsehood, a lie about the way the world is.

The autobiographical strand of the novel provides a mirror-image of Helen's unassuageable dismay. As Rick and C. split up, C. asks rhetorically who will finish the book they have been compiling together, the scrapbook of their shared life: "Then the senselessness of all stories—their total, arbitrary construction—must have struck C. She started to scream. I had to pin her arms to her sides to keep her from harming herself" (293). Helen's dismay stems from the realization that literary narratives are beguiling fictions, orderly constructs that falsify the senseless arbitrariness of cruelty; C.'s dismay, according to Rick, derives from a sense that the emplotment of life—the unfinished story she and Rick have unfolded together—is no more than an attempt to give delusive order to that which is without coherent shape or sense. These insights mark a postmodernist divide more significant to the novel than that posed by A.'s theoretical pronouncements.

The paired insight into the arbitrariness and falsehood of all fictions undercuts the humanist presumptions by which Rick seeks, halfheartedly, to defend his vocation. Arguments about the humanist "aerial view" sound increasingly false, yet the novel is not quite ready to abandon authorship to the status of either a parasite on theory or a hegemonic "author-function." Instead, what the novel offers is "cell specifications"—a precise account of the limitations of perspective, not an effort to transcend them. The wager of the novel is that a reader might be modeled by such specifications. Powers's use of the Pygmalion story exposes the dangers of this wager, the hazards of narcissism, projection, and solipsism that underlie the making of an ideal reader. Rick learns the lesson twice, as befits this novel of doubles: his infatuation with A. runs up against the brute fact that she is not his creature, but a person entirely separate from him, with her own obscure life history; she is not, emphatically, C. returned from the oblivion of lost love. His attempt to fashion an ideal reader and soul mate in Helen fails when she comes to understand the truth about the world. Like a peculiar amalgam of the noble savage and one who learns all she knows from literature—Mary Shelley's *Frankenstein* is one of the novel's intertextual precursors—Helen's intelligence is too finely wrought to withstand the truth about human cruelty. This is the humanist sensibility inculcated in a machine-intelligence.

Powers's emphasis on reading as the modeling of mind, and writing as the reciprocal modeling of reality, attempts to establish in fiction, in the novel at hand, a vital and dialogic relation to cultural memory. Memory speaks through the text, even as the text reshapes and recharges memory. Yet the representation of reality in fiction remains within the paradoxes of solipsism: on the one hand, the precise delineation of the prison opens the cell door to other minds—to the vast other mind that is literature; and on the other, the failure of representation, which haunts it as a necessary condition, presents a glimpse into the arbitrariness and ontological limitation of all mental constructs. Representation can never escape this danger, but writing of the danger can itself be a way of unlocking the cell door. The wager of fiction is that other minds have been shaped by the memory embedded in culture and so solipsism might be eluded through the novel's passionate devotion to memory, both cultural and personal.

A Fall of Mist

The exotic and magical terrain of Kathryn Davis's *Walking Tour* is remote indeed from the campus setting of Powers's novel. Where Powers constructs his novel around hyper-articulate scientists and literary scholars, Davis limns a cast of characters with hidden motives and obscures purposes. *Galatea 2.2*, with its elegant patterns and parallels, is the product of a cerebral and architectonic imagination; Davis is a more poetic writer, who works with symbol, connotation, and imagistic density. Hers is a world of spells, enigmas, and myths, and her chosen settings, rural Wales in the last years of the twentieth century and a postapocalyptic Maine some decades on, grow from a highly distinctive poetic imagination. But Powers and Davis, for all their differences, share a preoccupation with the same family of problems: both dwell on the cultural impact of new technology; both try to articulate the possibilities and limitations of a postliterate culture; and both attempt to reinvigorate the novel by making the practice of literary writing and reading a salvational connection to cultural memory.

Kathryn Davis's novel *The Walking Tour* makes use of two parallel stories of enchantment and expropriation, the Grimm Brothers' "Snow-White and Rose-Red" and the narrative of Manawydan from *The Mabinogion*, the thirteenth-century collection of Welsh tales.[6] In both stories, the truth of identity is connected to the possession of property, and the narrative of each turns around the lifting of a spell and the restoration of things and persons to their true forms. In the fairy tale "Snow-White and Rose-Red," a handsome prince is turned into a bear by a wicked dwarf who steals his treasure; the spell can only be undone with the assistance of the two sisters of the story's title, a pair associated with twinned rose trees, one of which produces white flowers, the other red. Once the prince is restored to his proper physical form and to his treasure, he marries Snow-White, and his brother marries Rose-Red. This is a story of pairs, symmetries, and property, all cast in the classic fairy tale structure of wish-fulfillment.

The story of Manawydan is more difficult to summarize. Four close companions are feasting in the rich and fruitful lands of Dyved (in the far southwest of Wales, now Pembrokeshire) when an enchanted mist falls over them; the rising of the mist reveals that all the flocks, herds, and dwellings have vanished away, obliging the companions (Manawydan, his wife Rhiannon, Pryderi the lord of Dyved, and his wife Kigva) to live as hunter-gatherers, and subsequently to pursue trades in England. The spell strengthens its hold later when Pryderi, and after him Rhiannon, venture into a mysterious fortress where they are paralyzed; this fortress also vanishes in a fall of mist. Manawydan finally breaks free from the enchantment when he catches one of the mice that fed on his wheat, a mouse that turns out to be the disguised wife of Llywd, who has placed the spell on the land of Dyved and spirited away Manawydan's companions. Manawydan trades the mouse/wife for his friends and for the full restoration of Dyved. Although often elliptical and puzzling, this narrative has clear parallels to the Grimm Brothers' tale. Braided together, these two narratives provide Davis with a rich intertextual weave of obscured and transformed identities, intertwined relationships and perilous doublings, confiscated properties and baleful enchantments.

The novel elaborates and revises this material to defamiliarize the commonplace realities of the late twentieth century. The events of a walking tour in Wales undertaken by four friends some time in the 1990s are recalled, reconstructed, and investigated at least two decades later by the daughter of one of the couples. Susan Rose, the narrator of *The Walking Tour*, lives in a strange, postapocalyptic world, marked by the erosion of recognizable culture, the mutation of the physical world, and the dissolution of social bonds. Between the end of the twentieth century and her present, a "fall of mist" has occurred, changing the world in radical and disturbing ways. It is the burden of Susan's reconstruction of the past to make sense of this state of enchantment, the origins of which she associates with the walking tour, and with the death or disappearance of her mother, the renowned painter Carole Ridingham. In this case, the enchantments and expropriations are bound up with new technologies, in particular a computer architecture developed by Coleman Snow and Bobby Rose, incorporated as SnowWrite & RoseRead, that allows the reader of a computer file to alter text at will. This innovation, which makes the pair's fortune, breaks down the distinction between reading and writing, and in consequence destroys the idea of intellectual property, opening up any text to unlimited additions and revisions. Susan's parents, Bobby Rose and Carole Ridingham, are closely involved with both Coleman Snow, whose computer expertise is the basis of SnowWrite & RoseRead's success, and his wife Ruth Farr, a childhood friend of Carole's, now a would-be novelist who plans to use the walking tour to gather material for a novel based on the story of Manawydan. Tension arises from the pairings and asymmetries between the couples: Bobby Rose, a notorious womanizer, conducts a flirtation, perhaps more, with Ruth Farr, while Coleman Snow evidently worships Carole, and is with her when the accident occurs (Coleman is drowned, Carole's body is never found). These permutations, which Susan the detective and historian can never quite resolve into a single, authoritative sequence of events, are metonymic of conflicts and exchanges between art and commerce, imaginative and entrepreneurial vision, silence and power.

Susan works with memory and forensic attention to sort out the events of the walking tour during a "post-" era when cultural memory appears decisively to have failed, and when the archive itself is disintegrating. Susan still lives in the property owned by her parents, now falling into ruin and overrun by a group of rootless and feral youths she refers to as *Strag* (from straggler?). The resources she has available to her include a transcript of the inquest into the deaths of Carole and Coleman, Ruth's computer, a series of photographs taken during the walking tour by Coleman, her mother's letters and postcards from Wales, her own memories of times before and after the walking tour, and family stories about the founding of the business, the first meeting between Bobby and Carole, and the childhood friendship of Carole and Ruth. She also has Bobby's library, a collection of leather-bound volumes now falling to pieces, an ominous reminder of the decay of print-culture. Her mother's paintings have been taken away from her, and even the work with which Carole obsessively covered bare spaces around the house and in her studio has almost disappeared under the influence of the harsh climate. Everything the reader learns about the world in which Susan writes suggests an entropic indifference of persons and places, a society of ruins characterized by infrastructural failure (power outages are frequent, the highways are choked with traffic) and changes in the physical environment, including the appearance of new kinds of plant and insect, and severe climatic instability. Although the stages by which Susan's world arrived at its present state are never clearly explained, her intense scrutiny into the events surrounding the genesis and growth of SnowWrite & RoseRead suggest that the dangers of the new computer technologies have extended in unforeseen ways into the texture of physical reality itself. A process of contamination, that is, first afflicts the realm of ideas, of intellectual property, and subsequently, through the invention and application of ever more elaborate computer architectures (the mysterious events that end the walking tour are tied in obscure ways to a "radical new architecture" [226], a "board with more memory links than there were molecules in the universe" [228]), alters the complex systems of living organisms and the climate. The changes in physical reality hinted at in Susan's remarks on her situation index a post-historical condition, "an endless state of cause without effect, which is to say endless waiting, waiting, waiting" (78).

In its apocalyptic dimension, *The Walking Tour* imagines the end of history in two genetically related aspects: the practice of history has come to an end in Susan's world because historical records are no longer accessible or reliable; and further, the sheer eventlessness of "endless waiting" suggests that no new narratable sequences of cause and effect can emerge, leaving the chronicler of recent times without any material to plot. These two qualities of the future in Davis's novel can both be traced back, as if to a vanishing point, to the sinister innovations of SnowWrite & RoseRead. In the first place, the archive is literally decaying. Books are in a state of dissolution: "First comes day, then comes night, night and day, day and night. *Night and Day* also turning to pulp, ditto *Mrs. Dalloway*, etc. etc. It's like books are trying to revert to what they were before getting mixed up with writers—Bobby's library, a ruined monument to human pride and hope" (50). Ironically, the brave new world of computers, in which texts could be freed from their essential link to the degradable frailties of paper and ink, has in Davis's novel produced a situation in which accelerated decay is the rule. These rotting books, reverting to pulp with the passage of time, symbolize a moribund print culture. Virginia Woolf's exacting novels of modernist temporality succumb, like everything else, to an indifferent and all-pervading grayness, an entropic sameness that Susan stresses in her description of the new diurnal round: "At some point every day the sun actually rises, dragged from under the horizon by a net of clouds and then left there to seep through the sky's spongy grayness in a halfhearted version of morning" (51). So much for night and day.

From what the reader learns of SnowWrite & RoseRead, it seems clear that the situation with electronically stored information is no better. Coleman Snow's first innovation allows the reader of a computer file to alter what she reads at will. This inevitably undermines the authority of any text, since its sense has no signatory, no legal guarantee of veracity. The truth or falsehood of written statements about individuals can be challenged under laws of libel or defamation, depending on the legal framework of their place of publication; failing this, false statements can be addressed by commentary and criticism. But under conditions of radical textual instability, where the original author of a piece of writing loses control over words published under her name, legal and critical resources lose their efficacy, not least because they too will be subject to unlimited alteration. If all texts are porous, subject to any traceless alteration from any reader, then no text in a databank retains authority. There will be no authoritative or canonical original text to refer complaints to, at least as far as electronically stored material goes, and with the decay of physical books continuing apace, the situation promises to worsen indefinitely. It makes sense, therefore, to see in this the end of history, since no version of the past can claim authority over any other. Through the conceit of SnowWrite & RoseRead, and the associated collapse of print culture, Davis literalizes extreme relativism. In the new era ushered in by Bobby and Coleman there can in principle be as many versions as there are readers—none of them authorized, all of them signed.

With the resources of history unavailable, Susan's present exists in a state without clear and meaningful temporal markers. The severe erosion of inscribed memory entails a temporality that resembles mythic rather than historical times. Without causal explanation, events simply occur, incomprehensible and mysterious, resistant to elucidatory emplotment. Susan's own efforts of comprehension, directed at the events of the walking tour, are thus acts of resistance against the conditions in which she finds herself. Throughout the novel she tries to make sense of the evidence left from that summer two decades earlier so as to understand the actions and motives of her parents, their friends and the other participants in the events.

The metaphorical mist that has descended over the world in which Susan writes provides Davis with a way of grasping through hyperbole shifts in the relations of readers and writers. SnowWrite & RoseRead also literalizes post-structuralist ideas about the death of the author and the liberation of the reader. What concerns Davis is not so much the empowerment of the reader, as the erosion of responsibility that the dissolution of authorship entails. Words floating free from the subjects who author them lose their ethical tie to occasions of enunciation. To speak or write the truth ceases to have much meaning or public resonance when speakers lose their connection to the words in question. This point is underscored by the important role played in the text by sworn testimony from the inquest into the accident. Davis ties these worrying innovations back to the era of Ronald Reagan: "According to company mythology, the idea first came to him when he was reading a 'melon-headed' critique of Ronald Reagan's supply-side economic policies in *The New Statesman* and couldn't stand not being able to share his thoughts with the author (ditto the reading public) 'immediately'" (8). In his pique, Bobby Rose imagines overcoming by fiat the problem Jean-Paul Sartre described as "seriality." One of Sartre's key examples of this problem was the radio broadcast:

> the [radio] voice is unbearable for me *in so far as* it is listened to by Others—Others who, to be precise, are *the same* in so far as they listen to the radio and Others in so far as they belong to different milieux. I tell myself that it may *convince them*. In fact, I feel as though I could challenge the arguments put forward by this voice in front of these Others, even if they do not share my views; but what I actually experience is *absence* as my mode of connection with the Others. In this case, my impotence does not lie only in the impossibility of silencing the voice: it also lies in the impossibility of convincing, *one by one*, the listeners all of whom it exhorts in the common isolation which it creates for all of them as their inert bond.[7]

In Bobby Rose's fantasy, soon after realized through the computer skills of his business partner Coleman Snow, the awkward split between same and Other, between the voice that establishes the inert bond and the isolated listeners simultaneously linked through their alterity, can be overcome in a radical elision of constitutive divisions. As it turns out, at least for the computerized world, there isn't even any need to persuade other readers of the incorrectness of the original views expressed (this would merely displace the problem of seriality a step), since the original views can simply be tailored to fit one's own. Bobby tells Coleman that simply inserting his own remarks on the text in question isn't sufficient: "Too slow. I want it quick. Quick and dirty. I mean, while you're at it, couldn't you fix it so I could actually *change* the text to reflect my opinion?" (72). The notion of speed that typifies the novel's characterizations of the late twentieth century is here pressed to its limit: a response to a text no longer lags behind its object, but actually replaces it, even though the name of the original author presumably remains at the head of the text, now authorizing words written by another.

Bobby's notion is symbolically linked to Reaganomics, with its fiscal culture of unregulated markets and junk bonds. But in addition, Davis applies pressure to rhetoric that circulated around the topic of computers, and the Internet in particular, during the 1990s, rhetoric that saw in the forms of connection that made up the World Wide Web an anticipation, or even a realization, of a transparent and global public sphere. If such notions do indeed inform Davis's novel, they do so in such a way that their heady optimistic predictions are forced to a point of no return, a point in fact of inversion, where transparency gives way to opacity, and public space disappears altogether as part of the general disintegration of social order. The twist is dialectical: computers linked together comprise in aggregate a virtual public space; yet the destruction of (privately owned, publicly circulated) intellectual property through unlimited alteration renders public space essentially private, a failed arena for the exchange of ideas. With the innovations of SnowWrite & RoseRead the possibilities of intellectual exchange and reciprocity give way to raids, incursions, and expropriation, all carried out in the name of openness and a rejection of property relations.

Davis has revealed that the idea for the novel grew from a computer error. On her publisher's website she explained that the idea for the novel began with a computer error: a file on which she was typing suddenly began "to leak away line by line"; mysteriously, the lost words appeared in a different file. She observed: " 'Leak,' 'drain,' 'pour'—as the words suggest, the phenomenon struck me as watery, tidal in fact, a concept I retained in *The Walking Tour* in my description of SnowWrite & RoseRead. The phenomenon also struck me as eerie, uncanny, menacing—evidence of a mysterious aperture, a point of intersection between two apparently dissimilar worlds."[8] The movement of text between files, caused presumably by a glitch in the computer software, suggests an agency operating beyond human intention and understanding, an uncanny effect in that what is closest to the writer—her own expressive words—is suddenly subject to incomprehensible forces. Davis's own experience is transmuted in the novel into that of Ruth Farr, who finds her writing on her portable computer suddenly interrupted: "her words began to disappear, a line at a time, beginning at the bottom of the screen and slowly but persistently working upward, as all the while new lines of text were pouring in, ALAS ALMIGHTY GOD WOE IS ME replacing *where are your people from*" (153). Ruth is in the middle of recalling her first meeting with her husband's alarmingly patrician father, who questions her about her origins in a way that recalls the formulaic questions about identity typically asked in folktales. The fluid invasion of text from elsewhere thus challenges and supersedes any declaration of her own identity she might make. For the new words that appear on her screen are the words Manawydan speaks in the *Mabinogion* when he has just finished burying his father's head in London in the enigmatic opening scene of his story. Manawydan's *cri-de-coeur* laments his rootlessness and placelessness: he has just disposed of the last remains of his father, and has no place to go; he continues, "Among all those here I alone have no place for the night."[9] The flow between texts and the erosion of the concept of authorship as possession thus implicitly dissolve the ties between origins and identities, places and persons.

The distinction between ideas of identity connected to possession and place and conceptions of identity as fluid, indeed hardly recognizable as identity at all, is dramatized in Susan's dealings with the Strag, and with the individual called Monkey in particular. The Strag would seem to be rootless, postliterate beings, who have their own ways of speaking and understanding the world. They first appear in the novel as neighbors of a perverse kind, "a gang of Strag boys with measuring cups—going bang bang bang on your door" (5). At this point in the novel, Susan's attitude to the Strag is one of revulsion. In their appearance—gray skin and eyes, at least in Monkey's case, hectically enlivened with a powdered wig, an oddly archaic and incongruous touch—they blend into the landscape, with its "gray vegetation" (20), and seemingly live by scavenging, which is to say, availing themselves of whatever they find, unhampered by ideas of property and theft. Susan asserts that there is a line of descent connecting the computer innovations of SnowWrite & RoseRead and the Strag view of the world: "It turns out that Strag culture, if you could call it that, owes whatever it has in the way of ideology to the old geek lingo. Probably inspired by 'surfing the Net,' a whole vocabulary developed with oceanographic origins (coring tubes, waves, trenches, shelves, currents, sediments, etc. etc.), though it was Bobby and Uncle Coleman who gave tidal phenomena pride of place" (75). The oceanographic language speaks to the way in which the movements between files and texts in the domain of computers extend far beyond the control and even management of the individual writer or reader. In circumventing the protocols of read- and write-only computer files, texts wash ceaselessly into each other, losing distinction along with authority. For the arch-capitalist Bobby Rose, the new tidal quality of information flow can be defended—speciously, Susan argues—by a communitarian philosophy of shared activity and property. But for Susan, as for the anonymous author of *The Mabinogion*, "property's always been the issue. . . . That's the legacy of SnowWrite & RoseRead, a business built on the idea that no one owns anything, especially not an idea, while simultaneously gobbling other companies up" (58). SnowWrite & RoseRead occupies a cusp of late capitalist development wherein it is possible to retain all the recognizable features of the giant corporation and to exploit the fluidity of information, the movement of information-capital across borders, boundaries, and legal restrictions of all kinds. In the formulation of their business, Rose and Coleman subvert the idea of property the better to exploit it; but Susan's perspective suggests that their actions bring with them unforeseen consequences of positively apocalyptic scope. Such consequences are suggested not only by her descriptions of the landscape of ruins in which she lives—her parents' estate is now reduced to moldering buildings and swaths of unrecognizable vegetation—but also by her dealings with the new kind of person—the Strag, Monkey—who dwells among these fallen structures.

Monkey, the novel's representative postliterate, post-historical person, is not at home with civility and ownership. When he first imposes his presence on Susan, he acts "almost as if he'd never seen a door before" (73), and converses "as if he were speaking a foreign language" (74). He accounts for himself, telling Susan his story, in terms dimly derived from the oceanographic language of the web favored by SnowWrite & RoseRead. To do so, applying an idiom of tidal phenomena to one's own experience, entails an account of the self as the site of vast indeterminate movements and compulsions. He speaks of his childhood as "neap," and his adolescence as a "slack" state in which he was grievously susceptible to parental influence (76). He tells Susan of his subsequent equilibrium, "Nothing could change you, because 'you' was all one thing" (76)—a gnomic remark that suggests either that the self is immutable because is it is one substance, or that self and other (I and you) have merged. Monkey's unbounded state befits a time when "the whole idea of edge [has] become a thing of the past" (94). If his name signals that he is in a sense less than fully human, this is because his attenuated selfhood ensures his innocence, his seeming freedom from moral decision. The two offenses of which he is guilty in Susan's eyes—trespass and theft—have very little meaning to one without a conception of ownership. During their first encounter, Susan confronts Monkey with a legal definition of property: "When I asked him what he was doing trespassing on my property, he looked at me in surprise. Forgive us our trespasses, he said" (55). This faint trace of cultural memory, a fragment of the Lord's Prayer, challenges Susan with a religious rather than a legalistic use of the word, as well as with an idea of reciprocity.

Monkey stands for the collapse of all the things about her vanished civilization—property, boundaries, civility, literacy—that Susan mourns in her narrative. Further, the conditions in which she writes are marked, to her mind, by the collapse of both morality and art, mutually sustaining aspects of a civilized order long since vanished. Her forensic efforts in piecing together the story of her mother's death are attempts to solve the mystery of this collapse. In investigating her mother's death, symbolic of the loss of art, she looks to account for the present decadence and entropy of the physical and social environment. She intends, that is, to make sense of the vast gap between the world of her parents' walking tour and her own troubled state of affairs. This is the task suggested by the opening lines of the novel: "Time passed. Or at least that's one way to get from *there*, my famous mother's infamous summer in Wales, to *here*, the ruined house and acreage she used to call home" (3). Susan's narrative tries to bridge the temporal and spatial gulf, linking her mother's history more firmly to her own and tracing if possible her present circumstances back to the events of the walking tour. Susan aims to bring the past back to life, as well as to understand it. Like her mother, she suffers from "horror vacui" (3), and consequently wishes to people a world now grievously lacking in human company. This is by no means an easy task, given that the participants in that history have all died or disappeared, and that they must be reconstructed from a range of different resources—photographs, transcripts, journal entries, postcards, and hearsay. Such fragmentary evidence hardly offers a pure conduit to the past: all the materials are shaped by the motivations of those involved. To Susan herself, the detective or historian, the events are opaque, mysterious, and apparently subject to some principle of causation that eludes forensic scrutiny. She must take care, as she acknowledges, not to cast her knowledge of how things turned out into the antecedents of those events, as if causes and omens were to be found everywhere, converting acuity into portentous suspicion. In a cunning variation on the notion that the past is another country, Susan likens herself to the innocent Jamesian heroine venturing into duplicitous regions: "Some days the past seems so poorly lit I feel like Isabel Archer before her eyes adjusted to the dim light of the Old World. When I try reading the court transcript, for example, I feel naive and spirited and curious, as if inspecting Mr. Osmond's 'bibelots' for the first time with no sense of how dangerous they are" (20). If this passage reminds the reader that *The Walking Tour* is a variant on the international episode, in which American innocents struggle to comprehend the devious ways of the Old World, it also casts this shadowy pattern onto time itself, situating Susan self-consciously as the endangered adventurer ill-at-ease among the stratagems and artifacts of the past. While the resemblance of the story of the walking tour to the Jamesian episode is complicated by the novel's suggestion that the Americans are perhaps a good deal more sophisticated and dangerous than their hosts, Susan's own risks in looking at the past involve both powerlessness, a sense that the events of the past remain finally inaccessible, and a potentially hazardous capacity to shape them in her own image. In this sense, Susan's probing into the history has something in it of a hazardous will-to-know, a temptation that often signals grave danger in James's fiction.

In this case, the danger involves the scrutiny of others for one's own selfish needs, as Susan obscurely explains:

> Then I look out the window. Then I try to see all the way to the end of a driveway no longer white with snow but overgrown with gray vegetation and I feel my curiosity transformed from girlish vice to unspeakable horror, which is what it becomes when you sound the depths of another living soul merely in order to locate something there to justify your own position, which is to say, to promote your own happiness. (20)

The passage is enigmatic because the "living soul" in question remains unnamed. Who is the object of Susan's chillingly instrumental curiosity? In this section of the novel, the word curiosity is associated most closely with Ruth Farr, who appears to be the instigator of the tour. In fact, Ruth is under suspicion throughout the novel: her journal is self-serving, she has designs on Bobby Rose, and her relationship with Carole is afflicted with ambivalence. More to the point, she has something in common with Susan. Ruth is engaged in writing in her journal an instant history of the tour, a florid modern version of one of the novel's intertexts, the *Itinerary* of Giraldus Cambrensis, a medieval tour of sacred and ecclesiastical sites in Wales. Ruth's journal focuses particularly on Carole, a woman for whom she feels a mixture of love, admiration, incomprehension, and deep resentment. But much the same might be said for Susan herself. Though she goes out of her way to present Ruth as the villain and her mother as the victim, her feelings about Carole are distinctly mixed, part admiring identification, part fury at abandonment. The histories of Ruth and Susan are marked by these uncomfortable feelings.

Susan's anxiety over her own motives displaces the suspicion that the past might not be accessible at all. As she explains, "to invest creatures from the past with life, you have to use 'transplants': a nose here, a laugh there, a curious mannerism, a limp. Otherwise they're no better than dolls or zombies" (104). Investment in the past, then, is an imaginative re-membering, a process of recreation rather than a sterile exercise in hermeneutics, even if the true otherness of the past and its creatures is sacrificed by projective necessity, the need to construct departed beings out of the scraps of memory. Such a practice aspires to the visionary principle voiced by Carole Ridingham when she tells Susan that her paintings demand an imaginative viewer, one who might look like an artist rather than a bank clerk. Susan's efforts to recreate the past evolve in a tension between the forensic and the visionary. In this respect, she can defend herself against the implied comparison with Ruth Farr, whose novel represents an escape from reality into the mists of fantasy, an escape from self into the vacuous obscurity of romance. Ironically, the fable Ruth's novel employs to such obfuscatory ends proves to be a fitting description of the circumstances Susan faces in her daily life. Wales appeals to Ruth Farr by dint of the mythic associations milked by the tourist industry, notably by the paid hosts, the Fluellens, who advertise their walking tour by appealing to "New Age Romantic Welsh Nationalism" (22). According to Brenda Fluellen's brochure, "In Cymru time has no meaning" (25). But through the course of the novel, this tour guide cliché assumes an ominous aspect, as the timelessness of Susan's postapocalyptic environment comes into focus. Susan really does exist in an enchanted world: her Maine is "Fogland, veiled and still, land of unearthly vapors" (54). To this extent, her detective work is at odds with the times in which she lives, since she looks to establish clear patterns of cause and effect in an era that seems to have left all such explanatory tidiness behind.

The events of the walking tour remain resistant to Susan's heuristic probing. In particular, the configurations taken up by the central couples remain undecidable: by the middle of the novel, Bobby and Ruth have been linked, and will continue to be so as the surviving pair; thus they resemble Manawydan and Kigva, the duo left behind by the second fall of mist in the *Mabinogion*. By the same patterning, Carole and Coleman parallel Rhiannon (Manawydan's wife and Pryderi's mother) and Pryderi, held in enchantment and apparently lost until Manawydan finds a way to dissolve the spell that holds them captive. Yet, Davis's pursuit of this pattern raises as many questions as it answers. What is it that links Bobby and Ruth together? Is it anything more than a furtive kiss and an idle flirtation? Does anything develop after the lawsuit is eventually settled? None of the questions Susan's investigation raises can be satisfactorily answered.

More intractable still are the enigmas arising from the last act of the drama during which Carole, who appears to have given cryptic hints of her impending doom, ventures out on Worms Head, a rocky peninsular, during a fierce storm, and, followed by Coleman, is swept into the ocean. This naturalistic explanation is presumably the one accepted by the court, even if a substantial settlement is granted to Ruth (a much-diminished sum mysteriously shows up earmarked for Susan at the general store in the nearby town). But other possibilities insinuate themselves. Since Carole's body is never found, there is a suggestion that she has been secretly taken away in a vessel of some kind, a fantastic scenario supported by the inconclusive testimony of a man hang-gliding near the scene of disaster: he claims to have seen "something long and narrow, a sort of cigar-shaped shadow in the water, kind of like a giant fish" (203). Such information hints at a magical explanation of events, as indeed does the connection finally established between Susan's investigation and her more immediate dilemmas in dealing with Monkey and in keeping her property intact. In this other strand of narrative that seems at first to be no more than a distracting part of the frame tale, Monkey infiltrates Susan's home and takes an interest in the materials she is raking over, claiming for himself a particular and intimate connection with the events that unfolded during a summer in Wales two decades earlier. He even iden- tifies himself as a magical boy—dream or reality?—who appears porten- tously in Ruth's recollections at one point. Monkey claims that he is this dream boy, thereby threading together through an inexplicable logic the two wings of Davis's novel, rather as if the motif of the computer system glitch in which two discrete files fold into each other, a local anticipation of the principle of contamination that SnowWrite & RoseRead effect on a global scale, might also apply to discrete times and places, 1990s Wales folding into twenty-first-century Maine. To this extent, the novel does indeed seem to envisage technological forces as analogous to the magical patterns of fable and myth. The late-century summer of the walking tour is the time of the fall of mist; thereafter, the explanatory logic of cause and effect breaks down.

Such relationships and connections will clearly not be explained away by Susan's essentially prosaic investigation. She confronts with a shrewd but limited vision events that elude rational understanding. As a result, the reader is obliged to recognize structures and logics that exceed the grasp of the narrative's central consciousness, and in coming to such a recognition to touch on the nature of creativity, artifice, and vision, the pressing concerns of Davis's project. In the case of *The Walking Tour*, the ineluctable enigma involves Monkey's revelation of the existence of a series of canvases depicting events at the end of the tour. These pictures have all the stylistic hallmarks of Carole Ridingham's work, but such an attri- bution defies explanation since she would not have had any opportunity to paint them before the accident. There are two ways in which the reader might account for this impossible folding of space and time. Either Carole was in fact spirited away from Worm's Head intact, and continued to paint elsewhere, a suggestion Susan entertains only briefly, concluding that her mother could not have been so cruel; or somebody else painted the pictures in a perfect simulation of Carole's style.

The five paintings Monkey exhibits for Susan treat scenes from the final stage of the walking tour, the most remarkable—"a masterpiece in fact" (252)—depicting the participants in emblematic postures during the moments leading up to Carole's disappearance. Carole herself is shown hand-in-hand with Coleman Snow at the tip of the promontory as if about to jump. The sea beneath them is painted "a deep mysterious emerald green, the result of multiple glazes, one atop another atop another etc. etc., with who knows what at the bottom, maybe Neptune's face, or the artist's, because clearly *something's* doing its best to rise to the surface" (257–258). What makes this mysterious painting particularly distinctive is its combination of precision and ambiguity; every detail is captured with Carole Ridingham's characteristic exactitude, yet the particular method by which the paint has been applied allows other images to show through. The technical term for this, as the narrator explains, is *repentance*: "Repentance occurs when the last application of paint—which usually happens to be thick and opaque and is, consequently, the one used for the face of things such as people or watches—begins to turn transparent, and ghosts begin leaking through" (256). People or watches: one person shows through another; one time flows into another. The ghosts in this pictorial palimpsest are revenants from Susan's future. For there are a number of hints in this section of the novel that the painter of this anomalous masterpiece is Monkey himself: the pigments used are those employed by Carole, including "rabbit-skin glue mixed with red gesso as a base for the gold leaf she so lavishly employed" (252)—earlier, Susan watches in disgust as Monkey expertly kills and skins a rabbit, misreading his act for simple savagery; in addition, the paint, still damp, smells of poppies, the flower that grows in abundance on Susan's decrepit estate, and that Susan suspects Monkey of harvesting for opium. Contrary to all expectations, then, Monkey becomes the medium for Carole's recovery; his paintings are both copy, homage, and reinterpretation: "My mother's sensibility recognized and honored, adored even, yet transfigured. Which is the only way the dead come back in *this* world" (259).

Repentance is a loaded word, and its ethical–spiritual denotation is no less important than its significance for pictorial technique. Monkey's paintings act as symbols of repentance for the iniquities hatched on the walking tour. On the one hand, their repetition of Carole's artistic method and style makes them forgeries, instances of the subversion of creative authority and responsibility, and in this respect they seem to extend the textual predation of SnowWrite & RoseRead into the world of visual art; thus they elide the distinction between art and commerce. But on the other hand, Monkey's work is more than just forgery; it is a creative and transformative reimagining of the possibilities of art— including art's principle of visionary understanding, surpassing in acuity Susan's own more considered efforts at comprehension—at a moment when art has seemed the remotest of things, an activity belonging to a vanished time.

The existence of the paintings in Susan's postapocalyptic Maine is a miracle. They seem to owe their existence to a slippage or contamination between worlds, much like that between computer files infected with a virus. And, indeed, it might not be altogether fanciful to understand the mysterious creature rising from the waves—a submarine? a sea serpent? the face of the artist?—as a worm (perhaps from the name of the promontory itself, Worms Head), a visual figure for a particular type of computer virus named a worm. This viral effect, like that that mysteri-ously merged two files on Davis's own computer, creates a tidal channel linking past and present, Carole Ridingham and Monkey, a mother and a daughter. It also transfigures the malign fluidity of texts under the SnowWrite & RoseRead regime for an image of the mysteriousness and unpredictability of cultural memory. Memory, in this instance, is a visionary continuity between minds, even minds as unlike as those of the wealthy and well-regarded artist, Carole Ridingham, and the feral Monkey.

The burden of imaginative transfiguration is passed on to the reader, since the novel ends with a host of questions unresolved. How do the pairs—Carole and Coleman, Ruth and Bobby—resolve themselves? What was the true agenda of the tour? How was it connected to the corporate skullduggery surrounding the ownership of SnowWrite & RoseRead? But the most important and mysterious question—that of the paintings of the walking tour—demands an imaginative effort on the part of the reader. This effort involves putting faith in art as a medium that might, in spite of everything, overcome the destruction of print culture. Art, as it stands forth at the end of the novel, is the living medium of memory. It is not memory as recovered and construed by the historian or the memoirist—Susan occupies those comparatively prosaic roles—but memory as the magical property of repentance and resurrection, and art as its sacramental image.

The Last Volume of History

But then what is there that is not in my head?
So that it is like a bloody museum, sometimes.
Or as if I have been appointed the curator of all the world.[10]

In the moldering Maine estate of *The Walking Tour*, with its faded paintings and rotted books, Davis offers an image of the remnants of high culture detached from the continuum of memory. Isolated except for her contact with the postliterate Strag, Susan labors to restore this shattered continuum, only to discover that the anamnestic medium of art holds the promise of "repentance," a reconciliation, however fleeting, between a damaged past and an entropic present. Images of solipsistic isolation and of cultural activity divorced from a receptive community of other minds haunt all of the novels I discuss in this chapter. Literary works in a postliterate age threaten to become no more than remnants of a lost vitality—epitaphs at best, at worst no more than material waste.

For writers of experimental fiction, the image of the unread book is a present possibility rather than an apocalyptic trope. David Markson's curious and remarkable career has been forged over five decades with an acute awareness of disregarded and misunderstood books. Obscurity has for much of this time been a condition of his literary activity. It is only in recent years, with the publication of four remarkable experimental novels, *Wittgenstein's Mistress* (1988), *Reader's Block* (1996), *This Is Not a Novel* (2001), and *Vanishing Point* (2003), that his work has begun to attract a modicum of critical attention.[11] Markson's literary contacts over the past half century have been many and various, including such figures as Dylan Thomas, Conrad Aiken, Jack Kerouac, Malcolm Lowry, and William Gaddis, yet he has belonged to no identifiable group or movement and has often struggled to find publishers for his work. His output has been strikingly assorted: an academic source study, several potboilers, a slender *Collected Poems*, and seven highly allusive experimental novels. Through all of this he has retained his allegiance, as Joseph Tabbi has shown, to two key early influences, Malcolm Lowry's *Under the Volcano* (1947), about which he wrote what was probably the first master's thesis, and William Gaddis's *The Recognitions* (1955), a novel he championed during its long years of neglect.[12] What these two works of late modernism share, besides an immense ambition, is a density of allusion and symbol that imposes unusual exegetical demands on the reader. And, indeed, on the reviewer as well, as Markson was made acutely aware by the experiences of his friend William Gaddis, and by the uncomprehending reviews he himself received for his challenging 1970 novel, *Going Down*. In a score-settling essay published in the *Review of Contemporary Fiction*, Markson wrote scathingly of reviewers who lack the patience and competence to address works written within the modernist tradition of Joyce, Pound, and Gaddis. Typically dismissive of unusual vocabulary, literary allusion, and formal innovation, such reviewers culpably neglect "the very pulse and continuity of culture."[13] Markson's own work has not fared well in such a climate, yet his most compelling fiction has come directly out of his encounter with a neglectful and unlistening literary world.

The critical success of Markson's recent fiction thus arises from the most unpromising circumstances. Early taking his bearings from the heroic projects of Lowry and Gaddis, Markson has continued to write in a highly allusive late modernist vein, finding a measure of recognition at a moment when late modernism has long since given way to postmodernism. He began his literary career when writers and critics were still absorbing modernism, and the process of understanding and canonization was fully underway, an activity to which Markson himself contributed with his work on Lowry's great novel.[14] Yet with *Wittgenstein's Mistress*, *Reader's Block*, *This Is Not a Novel*, and *Vanishing Point* he has attained critical recognition during a period when the canon was subject to revision and critique, and the modernist masterworks were increasingly to be seen within the contemporary academy as emblematic of hegemonic elitism. Such an anomalous situation encourages one to complicate literary historical categories and narratives, and to note that the academy is far from homogeneous, that the intellectual traffic between practicing novelists and practicing critics is frequently marked, to say the least, by silences, misunderstandings, and mistrust, and that Markson's works have yet to attract a wide readership in any case, inside or outside the university. But these objections should not obscure the ironies of belatedness that are essential to the meaning and significance of his recent work.

Markson has explicitly aligned himself with high modernist experimentalism: "Some of my work, moderately in *Springer's Progress* and more so in *Wittgenstein's Mistress* is undeniably experimental. Although so too was every central text of literary modernism, surely the most radical break with tradition in centuries—even if each of them from *The Waste Land* to *The Cantos* nonetheless reeks of the classics that constitute that tradition itself."[15] Like these works of high literary modernism, now classics themselves, Markson's novels reek of the classics, even as they partake of the modernist ambition to break with tradition by creating a work that is conspicuously unique. Markson thereby associates himself with a dynamic of innovation and recognition that he takes to be characteristic of the great modernist works; his novels, like the poems of Eliot and Pound, aspire to distinctive newness while glancing allusively at the past. Both innovation and recognition sustain the continuities by which these works live, the former by remaining true to the boldly disjunctive impulses of the modernist enterprise, the latter by making the text explicitly a document of cultural memory. The challenge for Markson has been to sustain this dynamic in a particularly unpromising literary climate. His difficulties with reviewers provided him with dismaying evidence that his innovations were seen merely as irritating distractions, and his allusions went either unrecognized or were branded pretentious. But rather than tailoring his work to the expectations of his time, Markson, over the course of the past two decades, has made the mismatch between his modernist heritage and an uncomprehending literary culture the main preoccupation of his writing. The profuse employment of allusion, citation, and reference, the presiding moods of isolation, melancholy, and solipsism, and the intricate play between fragmentation and internal reference are all means Markson uses to reflect in his writing on the significance of his belatedness. His novels are self-conscious and self-reflexive engagements with a perceived crisis of cultural memory that both makes such a writing possible, necessary even, and condemns it to an anticipated and thematized obscurity.

Page by page, these novels are crammed with remembered things, scraps of cultural information—names, anecdotes, titles, quotations—through which the protagonists sift, trying to find order, meaning, sustenance. But because order is not intrinsic, having vanished away in the inexplicable gap of time and meaning with which the books grapple, the task of making sense out of fragments is passed on to the reader. Reading this fiction thus becomes an act of cultural recollection, even as the text continually presses on the reader recognition of shattered continuity. Markson's belated modernism recalls in its reticulated textual surfaces the great early twentieth-century works with which he keeps faith, even as it provides an unusually vivid illustration of that postmodernist concept *par excellence*, intertextuality.[16] To comprehend these works one must retain this double optic, registering the fragment as both melancholy remnant of a vanished whole, and as an element in a network established by reading. The novels foreground intertextuality—their status as nodes in networks that limitlessly extend beyond the work in question—to the extent that allusiveness no longer connotes a living tradition. Instead of figures of transmission—between individuals within the text, between texts themselves—the trilogy treats its materials as ruins and memorials.

Wittgenstein's Mistress and *Reader's Block*, the novels I will discuss in detail, arise from the tension between an abundance of cultural information and a paucity of cultural contexts. The protagonist and narrator of each of the novels deal with fragments torn from the contexts that once gave them meaning. This is not to say that the elements of each text are without meaning; they are facts, sentences, and stories already known, lived with, as familiar as talismans. They are pressed into new contexts in a way that reinvigorates them as pleasure—the pleasure the protagonists take in odd facts, curious illuminations, piquant anecdotes. But this pleasure is contingent on scenes of memorialization. The central character of each novel haunts the ruins and storehouses of sublime and bathetic memory. Kate, the narrator of *Wittgenstein's Mistress*, sets down on paper her wanderings to the places made significant by the legacy of Western culture: the site of Troy, Rome, the great museums of Europe. These trips are less pilgrimages than occasions of textual tourism, casual and directionless peregrinations through the vestiges of memory. Her textual voyages are conditioned by nodes of association—the layers of cultural redaction and transmission accreted over many centuries around such originary events as the siege of Troy. These voyages—through physical and mental space— map memory through reiteration and citation. At the time of writing the pages that constitute the novel, she has settled in a house by the ocean, and beachcombs among reflections, perplexities, and stray recollections from her ten years alone on the planet. Yet here too there are material reminders of the vanished world, in this case the misshapen books lining the shelves of the house she occupies, and a basement full of cartons of books. In imagining a world for his protagonist (a textual entity named Protagonist), the central character of *Reader's Block* envisages a similar house besides a deserted beach, stocked with cartons of books. He also imagines Protagonist living in the abandoned gatehouse of a cemetery, drawing electricity, rather in the manner of Ralph Ellison's Invisible Man, from a streetlight, and noting the presence of a woman among the headstones. Markson's Reader, the actantial double of the narrator, is a reader of everything, even a reader of Markson's own previous novel; his mind is itself a kind of storehouse of cultural information, or a graveyard of epitaphic script. Both novels thus situate the central consciousness among the fragments of a cultural world now dead—the information, citations, and names that fill the pages of the novels and the heads of the protagonists have the character of shards or inscriptions left behind by a vanished civilization, or retained by a last survivor.

In *Springer's Progress*, a novel that foreshadows in method, if not in tone, the more recent works, a blocked writer finds himself caught up in various comic sexual misadventures as he pursues a much younger woman.[17] Recognition in this instance is fond and mocking, as the brief chapters take linguistic pleasure from puns and parodies, alluding to a wide range of literary texts, biographical facts, and anecdotes. Comedy arises in the novel from the glimpses afforded into the overstuffed mind of Lucien Springer as he grapples with his desires and setbacks, both literary and sexual, taking the refined materials of revered texts into bawdy low places. At moments of emotional stress, Springer is given to recalling incidents from the lives of artists, or sometimes simply the names of painters will do. This is a running joke in *Springer's Progress*, and it provides a deft way to indicate the character's reaction to events. Toward the end of the novel, Markson's protagonist learns of the suicide of an old flame and the reader encounters almost a page of curious biographical facts about philosophers, composers, artists, and writers. Spurred on by his grief to write what is apparently the book the reader has been reading, Springer struggles with beginnings and endings, and the text supplies one-page chapters comprising of famous openings and famous final sentences of great literary works. By this point, the reader can comfortably situate these odd blocks of text within the novel's diegetic frame, finding by turns an oblique expression of Springer's mourning, dealt with in his own characteristically bookish way, and instances of his struggles to begin and end his book, struggles, one might say, with the interruption of death—a formal *timor mortis*—as much as the anxiety of influence. It is in foregrounding the process of writing and the workings of memory— and the connections between the two—that the techniques adopted in *Springer's Progress* anticipate the textual strategies of the trilogy.

In *Wittgenstein's Mistress*, Markson fashions a consciousness similarly awash with cultural references, but in this case, the backdrop to the mental world is not the familiar bohemia of Greenwich Village, but is instead a compound of the familiar and the utterly strange. Kate, the narrator and sole character of the book, believes herself to be the last surviving person on the planet, perhaps even the last surviving animal, since in some years of traveling she has only glimpsed a cat, and even the cat may have been hallucinatory. Either she has come to be the last person on earth because some undisclosed catastrophe has wiped out every other creature, leaving behind houses, museums, and vehicles, but apparently no bodies; or Kate is not in fact the only person left alive, but simply *believes* herself— whether from extreme alienation, grief, or insanity—to be so. As she writes out her thoughts and recollections, which turn on problems of representation and reference, her mind continually reverts to myths, literary figures, writers, artists, and composers, as well as recalling the cultural sites she visited on her travels across the unpopulated globe, the museums she inhabited, sometimes burning picture frames for warmth, and the ruins to which she made pilgrimages, notably the site of Troy, an important reference point throughout the book. The high culture of the West is thus alive in her mind, even as it lies dead all around, reduced to clutter in the vast disorganized archive that the empty world—or her unhinged mind—has become.

Wittgenstein's Mistress, published in 1988 after no fewer than 54 rejections, attracted favorable notices, a number of which likened the novel to the work of Samuel Beckett. In drawing this comparison, the reviewers pointed to the extreme isolation of Markson's narrator, her compulsive ordering of her experience, and the pervasive sense of the absurdity of the enterprise of writing. Yet, as Markson himself pointed out, the "isolation there [in Beckett's work] is in some ways almost outside of 'culture,' whereas my own woman bears the full burden of it. Writing the last volume of history the way Herodotus wrote the first, I let her say."[18] One of the novel's working titles, Markson reveals in the same interview, was "Keeper of the Ghosts" (113), a nod to Malcolm Lowry, who once named a character Ghostkeeper. To write the last volume of history is indeed to be the keeper of ghosts—the ghosts of everyone who ever lived. Her last volume of history keeps the ghosts alive in the text. It is not a formal chronicle of the events leading up to and including the extinction of all but the historian herself, but is rather a work of memory, or, better still, a work of the workings of memory, since Kate's manuscript is preoccupied not only with what she can recall but also with how she recalls it—how she has arrived at certain conclusions about her knowledge. What the novel narrates is the movement of thought backwards from the "facts"—those pieces of remembered events and knowledge that she has retained after catastrophe and madness—to conjectures about the way she arrived at such knowledge. She has in her mental storehouse, for example, a trivial anecdote about Brahms, to the effect that he carried candy in his pockets to give to children. Yet, she is unsure how she knows this: among the books in the house in which she lives there is a biography of the composer (there may even, oddly enough, be two such biographies); but Kate is not at all certain that she read the biography in question—her information about the life of Brahms may instead have derived from the chance reading of a children's book on the history of music. Her process of retrieval is subject only to the verification that the isolated mind itself can provide. Unlike all previous histories, from Herodotus on, hers is not open to external interrogation, criticism, or assent. Her project, then, is condemned to solipsism, whether by internal or external necessity; her madness or her supreme isolation conditions the work. Her writing is forced back onto itself, onto questions of reference and representation, thematized most often in the text by examples drawn from the visual arts (Kate was an artist, back in the former world). Further, the almost absent "master" of the text—Wittgenstein himself—lives in its pages through a practice of propositional scrutiny, whereby the writing proceeds by statements that are at once and subsequently subject to qualification and additional conjecture. As Markson noted, "the novel is at least superficially similar to the *Tractatus* by way of all those short paragraphs too. And with the frequent sequences of variants that go through Kate's mind on a single idea. So that if I'd wanted to be silly I could have borrowed Wittgentstein's textual numbering system, even."[19]

As David Foster Wallace has argued, *Wittgenstein's Mistress* in fact owes rather more to the *Tractatus* than Markson acknowledges. In characteristically abbreviative fashion, Wallace notes,

> Markson's book renders, imaginatively & concretely, the very bleak mathematical world Wittgenstein's *Tractatus* revolutionized philosophy by summoning via abstract argument. . . . The novel quickens W's early work, gives it a face, for the reader, that the philosophy does not & cannot convey . . . mostly because Wittgenstein's work is so hard and takes so long just to figure out on a literal level that the migranous mental gymnastics required of his reader all but quash the dire emotional implications of W's early metaphysics. His mistress, though, asks the questions her master in print does not: What if somebody really had to *live* in a *Tractatusized* world?[20]

To live in a *Tractatusized* world involves a continual effort on Kate's part to remove the elements of assumption, conjecture, and faulty reasoning from those things she thinks she knows. Knowledge based on contiguity, for example, must be exposed as such: Kate notes on several occasions that she sees her house, when all she really sees is smoke rising above trees, her assumption—rather than her certainty—being that the smoke rises from her house. Such a disposition has as its goal the identification of atomic facts—that which remains irreducibly itself after all false assumptions and linguistic imprecision have been excised from statements about the world. The novel's figure for this, as Wallace notes, is the repeated motif of tennis balls.[21] Kate, at some point in the past, let hundreds of tennis balls bounce down the Spanish Steps in Rome; she also recalls an afternoon hitting tennis balls on a court close to her house in the Hamptons. Tennis balls are a metaphor for atomic facts because they seem to escape the problems of representation that continually beset Kate:

> The young woman is asleep in a painting in the Metropolitan Museum.
> There is something wrong with that sentence too, of course.
> There being no young woman either, but only a representation of one.
> Which is again why I am generally delighted to see the tennis balls.
> (116–117)

The stylistic model for Kate's text—and the stylistic analogue of the tennis balls—is the proposition: the declarative statement about the world that can stand alone as a model of a state of affairs. Such intent might lead to a set of propositions about the world that would have the finality of fact; and in this sense, Wittgenstein and Herodotus might be coupled, since the finality of propositions would also be the finality of history completed. Yet the qualifications that Kate continually adds to her propositions result less in a syllogistic induction of further satisfactory propositions than in new combinations of pieces of information that cast doubt on the reliability of the initial statement.

Kate's experiences crystallize around certain moments—almost being knocked down, for example, by a runaway car, watching a street in a foreign city fill up with snow, or rearranging the paintings in a museum of art. But as the novel proceeds, such recalled moments prove curiously unmoored from places and times. Her memory of watching falling snow is attached at different points in the text to Stratford-Upon-Avon and Rome. Similarly, her remnants of cultural knowledge grow scrambled by association. Rainer Maria Rilke, for example, blends into Rodion Raskolnikov, and Anna Akhmatova becomes indissociable from Anna Karenina, so that Kate can observe, late in the novel, "In fact without ever having read one word of that same novel by Dostoievski I would readily be willing to wager that Rainer Maria Raskolnikov is hardly the only person in it. Or that Anna Akhmatova is the only person in *Anna Karenina*, as well" (229). Homophonic likeness underpins the condensation of historical and literary figures, thereby suggesting that the project of ordering the extant splinters of culture must belong with the mind's own pleasures and principles. Kate's project is one of incorporation: her memories come to consciousness, and make their way to her pages, in place of the activities of reading, visiting, listening to, contemplating, or even interpreting the works and lives of artists. In this way, the lived relation to places and events has given way over the course of time to the abstraction of memory into combinatorial possibility. Hence, the practice of memorializing, of which the text itself would be an example, is joined to a practice of dismantling, as associations draw items in the storehouse of memory into new connections, weakening their connection to origin and inscription as the instituted trace of origin. Dismantling, indeed, is a habit and a necessity: she gradually takes to pieces the adjacent house on the beach, using the available materials for fuel; similarly, she uses the frames of famous paintings—even the Mona Lisa—as firewood when living in the great museums of Europe and North America. To dismantle and to rearrange, as is her practice in the museums, allows her to situate herself within the dominant patriarchal spaces of Western culture. She physically places her paintings among the great male masterpieces of the tradition, an act of redress, the significance of which is vitiated by the disappearance of all other viewers.

While the process of inscription by which Kate writes herself into Western culture does indeed disarrange the structures of patriarchy, her self-assertion remains haunted by the problem of solipsism. A recurrent motif in the novel is that of trees "writing a strange calligraphy against the whiteness" (233). This image is an emblem for both writing and painting, evoking on the one hand the blank pages Kate covers with her typed memories, and, on the other, her painting, a large canvas, stretched and painted white, either a surpassingly minimalist work, or the ground-work for a new painting. Kate's dismantling of tradition creates new space—and by implication the utopian no space of pure potentiality, as though the traces—words, brushstrokes—of extant works might be erased:

> Still, on the morning after [the snow] fell, the trees were writing a strange calligraphy against the whiteness.
> For that matter the sky was white, too, and the dunes were hidden, and the beach was white all the way down to the water's edge.
> So that almost everything I was able to see, then, was like that old lost nine-foot canvas of mine, with its opaque four white coats of gesso.
> Making it almost as if one could have newly painted the entire world one's self, and in any manner one wished. (233)

This is an image of writing as pure possibility. To paint the entire world white, thus blanking out all cultural traces, opens up the possibility of an originary inscription: both the end of the world and the possibility of a new beginning. To dismantle and bleach away all the world's art seems the epitome of the avant-garde desire to destroy the institution of art, so as to begin anew without the prevailing ideologies of artistic activity.[22] Kate's project, her patient, if unhinged, enumeration of the atomic facts of her condition, exists in the tension between the role of curator—the last historian, the solitary embodiment of a tradition that now is at an end—and the role of avant-garde artist, who erases to create.

Kate exists in the tension between curation and destruction. As the sole inheritor of the detritus of culture, she rakes over the material artifacts that history has left her, restlessly moving among scenes and sites that may be no more than a cultural tourist's memories. The legacy of these materialized cultural memories depends on her: she must sort through and order the chaotic storehouse of Western culture. But at the same time, the sheer arbitrariness and futility of such sorting cannot be avoided, since the break with the continuum of tradition is complete. From this perspective, a strategy of dismantling or erasure seems more attractive. Rather than picking over ruins, she has the opportunity to displace the works of the past in her own favor, or to blot them out completely and so begin afresh. Kate's situation closely resembles that of the writer working within the modernist tradition. On the one hand, the production and authority for new work derives from a keen awareness on the part of writers and readers of earlier literary and artistic activity. It is in this field of awareness that innovation must be read. On the other, the modernist impulse is also to clear a space for the completely new, to eradicate the burden of the past and begin all over again in a pristine space. The stakes are raised on such alternatives in the postmodern era, when tradition is subject to suspicion, revision, and neglect, at least according to the pessimistic vein in contemporary cultural criticism, and modernist ideas of newness are also treated with skepticism. Markson makes a beautifully lucid fiction out of this awkward conjuncture.

Through its scrupulous erosion of uncertainties and false conjectures, *Wittgenstein's Mistress* rearranges the familiar furniture of the novel—plot, character, a shared reality. The figures of erasure and blankness, along with Kate's insistent self-scrutiny, hint at the way the novel gradually distances itself from the project of representing an imagined world. As Kate's grip on reality comes to seem increasingly precarious or implausible—perhaps her perception of an unpeopled world is a radical affective dissociation all along—so the novel draws away from the conventions of realism, the better to concentrate on the remnants of cultural memory. *Reader's Block* follows logically from these premises.[23] The presentation is even more attenuated; the traditional constituents of the novel are reduced to faint suggestions, the slightest preliminary sketches. One might draw the hints and indications together as follows: an elderly writer, who happens to be called Reader (or who chooses to call himself Reader), cut off for undisclosed reasons from his earlier life, from all kinds of emotional and material attachments, contemplates writing a novel that will reflect his isolation and obscurity. After almost two hundred pages the projected novel has advanced no further than an elderly man, named Protagonist, living in isolation beside a cemetery, or living in isolation among cartons of old books in a house by the ocean. What one has instead of the never-to-be-written novel-within-a-novel, or instead of information about the life of the writer of such a novel, is an extraordinary patchwork of cultural and historical fragments, shot through with terse metatextual comments. Such comments frame and ironize the seemingly atomistic entries they intersperse, as at the very end of the novel:

> Nonlinear. Discontinuous. Collage-like. An assemblage. Wastebasket. (193)

Which description, if indeed these rather indeterminate statements are descriptive, best fits the book in hand—a cunning construct of fragments, or a repository of abjected and disordered materials? This question, about the nature of the text one has just read, is simultaneously the question of the uses that cultural memory now serves. Can such memory feed into a new kind of work that might itself model memory, opening up the possibility of an intriguing collage, a new constellation of *disjecta*? Or must the products of Western culture, once the objects of veneration and instruction, now be consigned to the garbage? And this alerts the reader to one of the meanings of Markson's title: the implied question of whether the statements and citations that make up the bulk of the novel's textual matter provide the raw materials of Reader's projected novel (the block as book), or whether they are the blockage that stands in his way. *Reader's Block* sustains this uncertainty throughout. It is at once a coruscating assemblage of cultural splinters and a melancholy heap of waste material.

There is, of course, a temptation to resolve such an uncertainty by naturalizing the text. That is to say, the stark facts, terse anecdotes, and tagless citations that comprise the bulk of the novel can be read as stray thoughts passing through Reader's numbed mind. How better, after all, to present the preoccupations of a lifelong reader than by the unfiltered detritus of his learning, a well-stocked mind presented in a state of disarray? In this reading, obliquely licensed by a line from Nietzsche quoted very late in the book—"In the end one experiences only one's self" (193)—the facts and fragments, which very often have to do with the deaths and ill-deeds of writers, artists, and composers, supply a portrait in relief of the writer or reader as an old man, a kind of inverted *Bildungsroman*, in which decline and decay predominate. Reader obsessively picks out from the trove of cultural knowledge in his head all kinds of curious and grim facts that reflect his morbid state of mind. He is drawn, for example, to make lists—lists of anti-Semitic writers and artists, lists of suicides, both real and fictional, and lists of names. As such, he grasps for the most rudimentary principle of ordering, rather as though no better method can be established for casting the myriad instances of Western culture into meaningful wholes. Consequently, the ruins of a mind sunk in melancholia are also the ruins of the tradition he has studied so diligently; he notes wryly, "Has Reader sometimes felt he has spent his entire life as if preparing for doctoral orals?" (160).

This is one arc that the reader can trace, following the efforts of the narrator, Reader, and his alter ego Protagonist, from the precipitating if indeterminate break in his life—"I have come to this place because I had no life back there at all. I have, Reader has? Reader has come to this place because he had no life back there at all" (9)—to the increasing desperation of the final pages, where, amidst much other dark information, one encounters the following italicized utterances: "*How has Protagonist managed to so calamitously fuck up his life?*" (184); "*Did it ever, once, enter even Protagonist's bleakest conjecturings that he would finish out his life alone?*" (188); and "*Dead? She?*" (192). For the reader, these rhetorical questions are so desperate because they are unanswerable: who is "she" and why does she matter to Protagonist? A wife? A lover? Perhaps a sister? Even as the novel seems on the verge of disclosure, it withholds, necessarily, because the projected and perhaps autobiographical novel remains unwritten and finally unwritable, beyond the block of disrupted memory. One of the many apt descriptions of the text we are reading, characteristically expressed as a conjecture or proposal rather than an actuality, suggests "A novel of intellectual reference and allusion, so to speak, minus much of the novel?" (61).

How then to describe this novel which is not a novel? Markson provides several significant suggestions that the reader inevitably seizes upon as she makes her way through this text: "in part a commonplace book? . . . Also in part a cento, as Burton would surely have had it? . . . Also in part a distant cousin innumerable times removed of *The Unquiet Grave*?" (61). And further on: "Or of no describable genre? A seminonfictional semifiction? Cubist? Also in part a distant cousin innumerable times removed of a *A Skeleton Key to Finnegans Wake*? Obstinately cross-referential and of cryptic interconnective syntax in any case" (140). These sibylline hints direct us to a work that foregrounds citation—a text woven out of other texts. One might indeed see a partial cento in *Reader's Block*, save that a cento usually samples a single author's work to make in tribute a new piece, most often a poem, out of favorite lines. One of the puzzles Markson sets the reader is to sprinkle his book with "exactly 333 interspersed unattributed quotations awaiting annotation?" (166). Though it's hard to avoid the sense that the puzzle is there in part to torment the reader/annotator—Markson includes some pungently derisive remarks, often borrowed from literary greats, about critics—these citations forge a connection to the teeming world of other literary texts. And of course that teeming world, at least until the ultimate electronic databank or concordance comes along, remains largely the world inside other readers' heads, the storehouse of their own memory of literary texts. Yet, even as this device challenges the reader of *Reader's Block* to be as well-read as its author, and thus flies in the face of those reviewers who would upbraid Markson for his excessively allusive style, it also hints at the text's isolation. The novel's intertextuality is foregrounded, but an untraceable citation is little more than a cryptic fragment, a piece violently torn from the whole that gave it much of its meaning. In Markson's late age of literature, all texts are in danger of becoming cryptic fragments, ripped from the continuum of cultural memory. At best, the citations, as well as the self-contained fragments of knowledge, assume an epitaphic character: they memorialize what is now departed.

Centoes and commonplace books emerge out of a certain kind of practice of reading, a devoted attention to felicities of style, encapsulations of wisdom, and shafts of wit. A trace of the reading life, the commonplace book is a storehouse of insight, instruction, and pleasure, sometimes a model or source of inspiration, but also a way of making connections between the concerns of the present and useful citations from earlier writings. Markson's odd specimen of a commonplace book, if *Reader's Block* can for a moment be so described, does not emphasize the continuities of the reading and writing life, and hence text as community, but treats its fragments as testimony of what can no longer be assured. Isolation is the keynote—the isolation of pieces of text from their origins and from the readerly connections that shore them up into microcosms of an undamaged literary culture. One of the recurrent motifs of Reader's unwritten novel involves the figure of Protagonist gazing at the gravestones that make up the view from his window. These memorial stones—now fallen into disrepair and almost unvisited—can be read as a figure for the textual fragments that intersperse the novel. And so another meaning of the book's title comes into view: Reader's block is a headstone, and the work itself an exceptionally elaborate epitaph.

With two further volumes in the style of *Reader's Block*, Markson has completed a trilogy in the epitaphic mode. They are books in search of their own definition, refusing to identify themselves as novels (the second is titled provocatively *This Is Not a Novel*), and testing partial analogies for their adequacy. This search allows the novels to reflect on their own peculiar form, and to establish, through a series of affinities, their significant difference, their originality. Markson's achievement is to have honed his fiction to its singular task—to remember and to memorialize. He reclaims the modernist heritage of radical innovation steeped in a consciousness of the tradition at the moment when that tradition has fallen into oblivion.

Where Powers and Davis devise thought-experiments involving technological innovation to understand cultural change, Markson finds a means to incorporate his sense of historical fracture in the formal strategy of his (non)novels. Powers makes enthusiastic use of concepts from the field of artificial intelligence, connectionism in particular, to explore the relations between reading, intelligence, and memory. The conditions for literary practice remain unpromising in an age of cultural amnesia, but Powers finds a justification for writing fiction in the paradoxes of solipsism. Davis for her part imagines a computer architecture that will destroy the transmission of ideas, and plunge the world into a postliterate condition. The dystopian fiction allows her to imagine a visionary scene of artistic possession and communion, a form of cultural memory that overcomes the seemingly irreversible collapse of print culture. Powers and Davis thus find ways to acknowledge and contest the break in cultural memory that defines the situation of their fiction. Markson likewise addresses his fiction to the problem of a break in the continuum of cultural memory. But for him this break cannot be circumvented: it is inescapable to what he wishes to achieve as a (belated) modernist. Anecdote by anecdote, citation by citation, the laconic voice of his texts compiles a record of what can be known, of what the invisible author has left at the end of a lifetime of study, when the tradition that has made him is in disrepair. The melancholy of ruins and memorials pervades the trilogy, but its highly distinctive and rigorous form—along with its astringent self-scrutiny—contests the fatalism that might otherwise emerge from the dark radiance of its pages.

CHAPTER 5

PATHOLOGIES OF THE
PUBLIC SPHERE

Nowhere in the fiction of the 1990s does the figure of the blocked writer appear more vividly than in Don DeLillo's *Mao II*.[1] Bill Gray, DeLillo's supremely reclusive novelist, has spent 22 years on a book he finds himself unable to finish. His dissatisfaction with the text over which he has labored so long is only in part aesthetic; something in the culture at large, from which he has done everything possible to insulate himself, undermines his faith in the novel—the particular novel he is trying to complete, and the novel in general. It is not that he lacks readers. Indeed, he supports himself and his two assistants on the royalties from his two earlier novels, now classics. He still receives mail from his readers, and is well aware that the release of portrait photographs will cause a stir throughout the world of letters. Bill Gray's self-imposed isolation has guaranteed that his fame, rather than diminishing in the years since his last publication, has grown precisely because of the mystique of his reclusive anonymity. Yet, all of this provides Bill Gray with confounding evidence of the writer's loss of cultural authority. Bill's fame had its beginnings in his writing. But in the last decade of the century, it derives from his refusal to participate in the media culture he considers entirely dominant. As Bill sardonically observes, "When a writer refuses to show his face, he becomes a local symptom of God's famous reluctance to appear" (36). His cultural recognition is in inverse proportion to his visibility. This equation tells Bill that the writer's place is now inextricable from iconicity, from the power of his image—or the absence of his image—as a signifier in the circuits of an all-pervasive commercial culture.

Bill Gray hyperbolically suggests that writers and terrorists are linked by their relationship to the public sphere of images: writers have been marginalized precisely to the extent that terrorists have taken over the public imaginary through their use of violent spectacle. Images of violent acts and disasters have gripped the public imagination—have in fact constituted publics—in a way that now lies entirely out of the writer's reach. Unlike Bill Gray, DeLillo has taken this situation as a starting point for writing, a place from which to initiate an examination of the nature of images, technology, violence, and secrecy, all of which he sees as aspects of a significant shift in the public/private opposition. In this chapter, I trace DeLillo's investigation of the shifting boundaries between public and private through spectacles of violence, those libidinally invested and routinized images that circulate through the postmodern body politic.

Disaster Footage

In a brief essay written to accompany the publication of *Underworld*, Don DeLillo draws a series of distinctions between our experience of public events in the present and the meaning we attach to public events in history. As so often in DeLillo's work, the point is made by reference to visual images: the broadcast videotapes of two violent robberies are compared to "events and documents from the past."[2] By pairing these instances, DeLillo sheds light not just on *Underworld*, but also on an interrogation of history, privacy, violence, and media that he has pursued throughout his career. What "The Power of History" proposes in miniature is a theory of cultural memory and historical difference. The repeated screenings of the videotapes, with their sickening but quotidian violence, are characteristic of the present, according to DeLillo, in the way that they assault memory, efface the distinction between the real and the fictional, and insinuate a complicitous relationship between viewer and viewed. The relics of an earlier time, exemplified by "a Mathew Brady photograph [and] a framed front page—'Men Walk on the Moon'" ("Power" 63), evoke, by contrast, an undamaged relationship to an exalted and heroic era. The opposition between these visual specimens rests on the social meanings of violence and technology.

The bank robbers who "move with a certain choreographed flair, firing virtuoso bursts from automatic weapon" appear on the videotape to be imitating scenes from a movie; in this way, the "culture continues its drive to imitate itself endlessly—the rerun, the sequel, the theme park, the designer outlet—because this is the means it has devised to disremember the past" ("Power" 63). To this extent, acts of violence performed in a stylized way are typical of a culture of imitation, repetition, and amnesia. A robbery played out as a performance, "choreographed" to resemble a cinematic episode, can be likened, DeLillo claims, to the mechanisms of proliferative consumerism, whereby market domination is achieved through a coordinated range of retail and leisure outlets. Imitation extends throughout the social order, making one set of activities into the mirror of another: shopping is like going to the movies, which is like committing a crime and watching the crime on TV—a spiral of similitude without end.[3] A logic of equivalence is also at work in the other example of contemporary, mass-mediated violence DeLillo chooses. In this instance, the tape shows a murder caught by a surveillance camera in a convenience store:

> The commonplace homicide that ensues is transformed in the image-act of your own witness. It is bare, it is real, it is live, it is taped. It is compelling, it is numbing, it is digitally microtimed and therefore filled with incessant information. And if you view the tape often enough, it tends to transform *you*, to make you a passive variation of the armed robber in his warped act of consumption. It is another set of images for you to want and need and get sick of and need nonetheless, and it separates you from the reality that beats ever more softly in the diminishing world outside the tape. ("Power" 63)

The tape provokes radically ambivalent reactions: the passive viewer finds the "serial replays" ("Power" 63) to be desirable and repellent, exciting and deadening. The grisly thrill and the queasy numbness are induced by the blurring of differences, the likeness hinted at between unlike objects and activities—live action and taped replay, viewing and doing, image and act, shopping and killing. Watching the tape is like acquiring a taste for some kind of convenience store junk food, nauseating and addictive in equal measure. The compulsion to sit through repeated showings of the murder, expressed as the viewer's need, speaks of routine sadism disturbingly akin to the casual savagery on the tape. At the same time, the revulsion and horror are also caught up in this cycle of repetition, suggesting less that they represent the attempt to achieve some moral purchase on the spectacle, than that a masochistic subjection is in play.

These emblems of contemporary experience, the taped bank robbery and convenience store murder, suggest connections between the routinization—the banalization—of violence, the prevalence of media technologies in the everyday environment, and the weakening of historical memory. As such, they are to be contrasted, DeLillo argues, with reminders of great moments in American history. The historical mementoes have a "clarity and intactness that amounts to a moral burnish" ("Power" 63). The contrast posed by the essay recalls the notion of "aura" in Walter Benjamin's celebrated essay "The Work of Art in the Age of Mechanical Reproduction."[4] It is not, strictly speaking, that uniqueness is counterposed to reproducibility, as in Benjamin's classic distinction, since the Brady photograph and the celebratory front page are both products of the technology of mass reproduction; rather, the ubiquitous serial repetition of TV can be counterposed to cultural instances that incarnate memory and auratic "distance."[5] DeLillo's examples—the photograph, the front page—evoke the figure of the collector: Brady's work represents a financial investment as well as a moral return; and the headlines are "framed," displayed rather than yellowing in an archive. The "moral burnish" stems from temporal distance as well as national pride; these fetishized remnants bear witness to a past, thus resisting the amnesiac, time-collapsing character of media culture, evident everywhere, the essay observes, from technologies of information storage to labor-saving gadgets ("Power" 62). But they are also, and this must be emphasized, objects that stand in for a collective experience: "These things represent moments of binding power. They draw people together in ways that only the most disastrous contemporary events can match. We depend on disaster to consolidate our vision" ("Power" 63). To contrast a culture fascinated by apocalyptic scenarios with one exercised by significant historical events is to envisage two distinct kinds of collective experience. On the one hand, a past is imagined in which shared meaning attaches to resonant, nationally significant events; on the other, a present is conceived in which occasions of symbolic contiguity are achieved only through the mass-mediated news of violence, atrocity, and disaster.

From this perspective, DeLillo's essay invites a contrastive reading of *Underworld*, one that would counterpose, in particular, the baseball game of the novel's prologue with the episodes involving the Texas Highway Killer, and read in this contrast an argument about profound shifts in the collective experience of nation and history. Yet to understand the particular significance DeLillo sees in televised images of violence and disaster— the reasons why they have become our privileged moments of public identity, the scenes that consolidate our vision of ourselves and our times—it is necessary to trace the ways he has envisaged such horrifying acts and catastrophic events throughout his work. The contrastive vision of *Underworld* is only the most recent instance of DeLillo's desire to find images and construct narratives that represent the distinctiveness of the present in the light of "millennial frenzy" ("Power" 62), and to envisage an irrevocable break—or imperceptibly gradual but no less significant change—that separates *now* from *then*. DeLillo's claim is not, of course, that violence and catastrophe did not occur in the past, but that they now have an unavoidable cultural resonance. Indeed, scenes of televised atrocity have been the occasion of some of DeLillo's most chilling and engaged prose, from his evocation of the bleak anonymity and placelessness of the Texas Highway Killer to the flashbulb horror of Jack Ruby's murder of Lee Harvey Oswald in *Libra*.

What is at stake in these episodes and images is the connection between private acts and public witnesses. Exposure to these brutal images on the airwaves forges a palpable link between the faceless loner's violent action and the faceless crowd's spectacular consumption of such actions, such violence. Recent work on the transformation of the public sphere in the media age by Mark Seltzer, Hal Foster, and Michael Warner has explored the ways in which anonymous and dispersed publics seek representations of mass subjectivity in spectacles of disaster, atrocity, and violence—in images, precisely, of suffering bodies.[6] In Seltzer's words, "[t]he spectacular public representation of violated bodies, across a burgeoning range of official, academic, and media accounts, in fiction and in film, has come to function as a way of imagining and situating our notions of public, social, and collective identity."[7] At work in the viewing of these images is a kind of ambivalent identification, a "mass-imaginary transitivism" marked both by abjection and aggressivity: the display of violated bodies gives an imaginary body to the noncorporeal crowd of television watchers and newspaper readers, while at the same time vouchsafing the reassurance that the suffering physical body is elsewhere.[8]

For DeLillo, the consequences of the emergence of this "pathological public sphere" (in Seltzer's phrase)[9] are several: in the first place, the channel between isolated private experience and collective being is one laid down in fantasy; to this extent, the imagination of shared experience, collective agency, and desire remain relatively remote and inaccessible, always situated at a remove. Disaster footage presents the image of a passive, victimized (collective) subject. If we see ourselves in such scenes as being powerless, they also appear to offer us the reassurance that the victim is someone else.[10] The individual who confuses fantasy for reality, giving a privative, anonymous identity a starring role in the public theater of news, opinion, and sensation, is typified by the serial killer. Such "media-poisoned" individuals seem to spring into being, and into public consciousness, in the wake of the Kennedy assassination; for DeLillo, Oswald is the prototype of this new kind of murderer.[11] The Texas Highway Killer of *Underworld* is typical in this respect: in the phone calls he makes to a television station, following the appearance of the videotape of one of his murders, he is able to achieve a particularly charged identity while remaining, literally, faceless: the viewer sees only the face of the anchorwoman listening to the killer's broadcast voice. This imagined intimacy between anonymous viewer and public face is different only in degree from the typical form of imaginary identification established in the contemporary mediasphere; we might feel we have a personal relationship with the people who appear on our TV screens, and, indeed, the model of the nuclear family that is employed in television news programs, for example, is designed to encourage this illusion. In his phone calls to the news anchor Sue Ann Corcoran, the Texas Highway Killer merely literalizes what is implicit in the convention of the medium. But at the same time, the nature of privacy itself is transformed by these displacements and identifications. The fantasy here is introjective rather than projective: the space of the private self is increasingly shaped and determined by the anonymous "public" imagery of the mass media. Nightmares of hypervisibility establish the negative relationship between forms of selfhood and technology, issuing in feelings of powerlessness, dread, and loss of agency. In the words of reclusive novelist Bill Gray, "Everything seeks its own heightened version. . . . A man cuts himself shaving and someone is signed up to write the biography of the cut. All the material in every life is channeled into the glow."[12]

Men in Small Rooms

The typical response of DeLillo's characters to these seismic shifts in the nature of private and collective experience can be summed up by an oxymoronic phrase from *Mao II*, "inertia-hysteria" (157). If the violence and exaggerated identification of the serial killer represent one kind of response to the "glow" of an excessively stimulating environment (hysteria), then the retreat to a small, enclosed space represents another (inertia). DeLillo's work offers numerous instances the pattern: in *End Zone*, for example, Taft Robinson withdraws from the rigors of the football season to a bleak dorm room;[13] in *Great Jones Street*, Bucky Wunderlick walks off his rock band's tour to seek seclusion in a spartan Manhattan apartment;[14] the archeologist Owen Brademas retreats to an ascetic's cell in an Indian city at the end of *The Names*.[15] The more recent fiction presents further examples: Lee Oswald's agitated progress in *Libra* might be described in terms of the series of cell-like spaces he occupies in the course of his life;[16] similarly, Bill Gray's self-imposed isolation is related throughout *Mao II* to the enforced isolation of the Swiss hostage in Beirut. Although the significance of each of these episodes is distinct and complex, so that the character's isolation can appear either as a cheerless impasse or a hard-won privilege, a characteristic and overdetermined division is established. Beyond the walls of the small room there typically exists a threatening and often indeterminate power, represented sometimes in terms of political factions and institutions, and at others by forces as abstract as History itself, but thematized most explicitly in *Mao II* as the crowd. The individual in the room and the teeming multitude outside can be considered as figures for the private and the public respectively; through their dynamic relationship, which involves antagonism, certainly, but also traffic of various kinds, DeLillo's work explores the interaction between private and public identities, private fantasies and public spaces.

The retreat to the small room might be seen as an act of resistance on behalf of a certain idea of the self. In withdrawing, DeLillo's characters often seek to gain control over their immediate environment, thereby compensating for the alarming lack of control they feel in relation to the world at large. Withdrawal to the small room, then, may be impelled by the desire to regain some vestige of free, spontaneous selfhood, but the lessons that DeLillo's characters learn in their retreats tend most often to involve threats to the idea of individual agency.[17] Stepping out of the commodified world of media images and mass-identification proves ultimately to confirm its predominance. The Sartrean idea of "seriality" offers a way of thinking about the relationship between self and others, private agency and public opinion, as one of uniformity through isolation. In "performing most of the acts characteristic of industrial civilization—waiting for a bus, reading a newspaper, pausing at a traffic light—I seem alone, but am in reality simply doing exactly what everyone else does in the same situation."[18] In such negotiations of public space the individual defers to an Other—the Other of public opinion. Such deferral remains unlimited, because in seriality the mimetic conformity, whereby my actions are modeled on those of an imaginary Other, is the same for everyone; "in fact," as Fredric Jameson points out, "there is no Other, only an infinite regression, an infinite flight in all directions."[19] In DeLillo's fiction, this relation to others through anonymity is inflected with fantasy and desire. The small rooms appear to offer a seclusion from which the Other might temporarily be removed, a space given over to a kind of circumscribed individualism, one that is not hollowed out by reference to a public—indeed, in its extreme form, such a public appears as an alien and threatening agglomeration.

The token of ascetic refusal in these circumstances is control over and psychic investment in objects and spaces and the language used to refer to them. In the early fiction, in particular, the cell-like retreat is a place of language pared down to scrupulous exactitude, a modernist dream of uncomprised reference and silence.[20] In *End Zone*, for example, the star footballer Taft Robinson tells Gary Harkness that he has turned away from football to pursue "small things. Tiny little things" (*End Zone* 233), by which he means the ordering of objects in his room and meditation on that order. "I want you to take me literally," he tells Gary. "Everything I've said is to be taken literally. I've got this room fixed up just the way I want it. It's a well-proportioned room. It has just the right number of objects. Everything is exactly where it should be" (*End Zone* 238). Well-proportioned objects and spaces substitute for an order absent from the chaotic world outside. This fantasy of self-sufficiency may be compared with Gary Harkness's own dreams of ascetic escape (Gary Harkness and Taft Robinson are frequently doubled); Gary's solitary excursions into the West Texas desert are motivated by the attempt to simplify consciousness and reduce language to a system of names.

Throughout DeLillo's work in the 1970s and early 1980s, the conditions of seriality are counterposed to vulnerable fantasies of self-reliance and sensory immediacy. The trajectory of these novels often leads to the enclosure of a small room, in several cases a narrative point-of-no-return. David Bell's "great seeking leap into the depths of America . . . to match the shadows of [his] image and [his] self" (*Americana* 341), Gary Harkness's ritualistic reduction of language to the names of objects perceived in the desert, Bucky Wunderlick's drug-induced attempt to escape from language altogether ("subsisting in blessed circumstance, thinking of myself as a kind of living chant" [*Great Jones Street* 264]), and even Owen Brademas's final refuge in an unadorned room in an Indian city ("You see what I've done, don't you, by coming into this room? Brought only the names. . . . The moment I stepped inside it seemed right, it seemed inevitable, the place I've been preparing for. The correct number of objects, the correct proportions." [*The Names* 275])—all of these escape attempts are motivated by the desire to occupy a space or condition beyond serial alterity. Language plays a key role in this desire. In particular, the language of names promises a pristine, Adamic relation between self and world. To reduce language to a restricted set of nouns, or to slip free of language altogether, represents a fantasy solution to the problems of self-alienation through seriality.

Catastrophes and Crowds

Because the Other that is the public is always elsewhere, a phantom, statistical being, it is only in mass-mediated images of crowds and catastrophes that a representation of the public can be found; yet in such forms of representation the collective is presented ambivalently as something either threatening or imperiled. Nonetheless, spectacles of disaster and violence supply the serialized watchers with a figurative body.

In *White Noise* Jack Gladney is troubled to find that "documentary clips of calamity and death" have an addictive appeal ("Every disaster made us wish for more, for something bigger, grander, more sweeping"), one that his family, normally uncomfortable watching television together, finds compelling.[21] Such scenes convoke, even within the restricted circumference of the family home, a collective founded on the fascination of disaster footage. The contemporary disaster, Mary Ann Doane has argued, always involves the breakdown of technological systems, whether this means the calamitous derailment of a train or the malfunction of one of an airplane's many systems. Even a natural disaster, an earthquake, flood, or hurricane, now signifies the "inadequacy or failure of technology and its predictive powers as well."[22] The catastrophes that fascinate are those in which the failure of technology results in death, often the death of many people. The coverage of the mass death of the contemporary disaster marks the limit of technology and thereby makes the infiltration of technology through the social body visible, if only in negative form. The strewn, twisted, or punctured bodies of disaster footage provide horrifying visual testimony of the ways in which we are all vulnerable to the sudden breakdowns of the technologies that sustain, support, and transport us.

There is, in other words, a kind of identification involved here. In seeing the victims of disaster, or imagining their fate, we, the viewing public—that is to say, the "large soft body with many heads" (to adopt Baudrillard's sci-fi description of the collective couch potato)—envisage ourselves as a mass exposed in our everyday lives to the threat of technological failure (and, by implication, to the danger of technology itself).[23] In *White Noise* the possibility of seeing ourselves as vulnerable to the catastrophic failure of technology is made literal in the airborne toxic event, a disaster that transforms the serial crowd of domestic TV watchers into an aggregation brought together by emergency. There is, in addition, a second literalization involved here: if the exposure of the fleeing people of Blacksmith to the airborne toxic event marks the way in which the social body is bound up with technology, Jack Gladney's life-threatening exposure to the cloud literalizes the encounter between technology and the material body. He becomes a walking token both of the ways in which the body's status (as healthy or sick) is now contingent on the technological storage of information—is, indeed, the extension of those systems—as he becomes the sum of his data, and his worrying condition marks the indeterminacy of the social pervasiveness of technology—the novel's grim joke is that the "situation" in which he finds himself is as uncertain as any "natural" future he might have imagined: technology, that is to say, is coextensive with the existential span of life. Doane writes: "Catastrophe is at some level always about the body, about the encounter with death."[24]

DeLillo's own remarks from a 1993 interview are instructive in this context:

In my work, film and television are often linked with disaster. Because this is one of the energies that charges the culture. TV has a sort of panting lust for bad news and calamity as long as it is visual. We've reached the point where things exist so they can be filmed and played and replayed. . . . Think about the images most often repeated. The Rodney King videotape or the Challenger disaster or Ruby shooting Oswald. These are the images that connect us the way Betty Grable used to connect us in her white swimsuit, looking back at us over her shoulder in the famous pinup. And they play the tape again and again and again and again. This is the world narrative, so they play it until everyone in the world has seen it.[25]

To the notion of broadcast disaster as a culturally binding form, DeLillo introduces a historical dimension: in the past, collective identities were formed around iconic celebrity images; now they are also established around repeated spectacles of violence and catastrophe. The example of Betty Grable is not idly chosen; she belongs to a culture of the spectacle, to the heyday of the Hollywood dream factories; she certainly does not belong to the television age. Ruby shooting Oswald, the Challenger explosion, the Rodney King beating—all these, by contrast, are shaping moments in the history of television, traumatic instances of witnessing. The image of Betty Grable in a swimsuit, glancing enticingly over her shoulder, elicits a certain kind of masculine gaze; it plays, among other things, on a fantasy of intimacy, the manufactured illusion that a famous and beautiful movie-star might not only be sexually available but also erotically interested in the red-blooded male who pins up her picture. The television footage, by contrast, involves shock and repetition, and in the case of Ruby shooting Oswald and Rodney King, bodies in distress, visibly punctured or beaten. If this suggests any kind of intimacy, it is an intimacy with sights to which one would rather not be exposed. Nor does it seem quite correct to say that the victims and persecutors in the TV clips have an iconic status; one might argue instead that their iconicity is tied to the particular scene of violence or disaster: prior to the morbid notoriety they acquire at that instant, they are as faceless as the anonymous and private viewer.

DeLillo's remarks suggest that changes in the relation between private and public subjects, private and public scenes, can be represented emblematically by the different kinds of attention invested in the glamour image and the disaster footage. While it is important here to emphasize that iconic celebrity images still circulate significantly and incessantly through the culture—no longer Betty Grable, but Jennifer Lopez and Britney Spears—the lineaments of a historical shift are nonetheless sketched, rather in the same way that they are drawn in "The Power of History." But his comments here also hint at the play of force and aggression involved. Television,

DeLillo remarks, has "a sort of panting lust for bad news and calamity as long as it is visual." The words "panting lust" seem more applicable to the caricatural adolescent salivating over the Betty Grable pinup than to the faceless medium. It is as if the gaze directed by the technological form of television at its audience has the same aggressive and objectifying character as the hormonal male, albeit that this TV gaze, so to speak, is mediated by tape of the calamitous. The violence implicit in the account is one of being forced to look, to *know* one's desire: "They play [the tape] until everyone in the world has seen it." It is, DeLillo suggests, a "world narrative," one that involves—or enforces—a shared watching wherever television is available, without regard to other kinds of group identity, be they regional, national, or linguistic. Television creates its own world: the hyperbole is hard to avoid, and DeLillo's remarks press toward theories of contemporary culture of the kind often encapsulated in Guy Debord's slogan, the "society of the spectacle."

But the implications of DeLillo's interview remarks are more complicated than this, particularly when placed in the context of specific episodes from the recent fiction. Television forms a mass subject around its lurid scenes of smoking wreckage and violated bodies; but, to extrapolate from the interview remarks, there is an element of subjection in this, one that works through a reconfiguration of public and private spaces and identities. This shifting, unstable relationship might be approached at a slightly different angle by noting the ways in which the body in DeLillo's fiction is entangled in and entrapped by technologies of communication. Traces of this preoccupation are evident even in the early fiction. Much of narrative energy of *Americana*, for example, stems from the protagonist's obscure attempts to understand the ways in which his own identity is entangled with images, both through imaginary identification with iconic celebrities (Burt Lancaster is a particular favorite) and through the all-encapsulating medium of television (the narrative link here is supplied by his father, an advertising executive who specializes in TV commercials).[26] The novel has a number of figures for this entanglement, this loss of distinction, of which one of the most nightmarish and emblematic is the notion of the cells of the body fusing with the animated dots of the TV screen.[27] While this Cronenberg-like vision is not elaborated in *Americana*, it does stand as a significant corollary to more familiar conceits of image culture, those that match identities against celebrity and consumer icons; its importance lies in the way in which it connects the collapse of the body/technology distinction to that of the private/public relation.

To explore the ways in which DeLillo works out the implications of this pairing of terms through the course of two and a half decades of writing is beyond the scope of the present paper. I do, however, want to draw attention briefly to a mini-lecture on the properties of film, delivered by a wayward movie director in *The Names*:

> Film is more than the twentieth-century art. It's another part of the twentieth-century mind. It's the world seen from inside. We've come to a certain point in the history of film. If a thing can be filmed, film is implied in the thing itself. This is where we are. The twentieth century is on film. It's the filmed century. You have to ask yourself if there's anything more important than the fact that we're constantly on film, constantly watching ourselves. The whole world is on film, all the time. Spy satellites, microscopic scanners, pictures of the uterus, embryos, sex, war, assassinations, everything. (200)

Film, according to the director Volterra, telescopes space, connecting the microscopic proximity of the scanner, which can relay images from inside the body, to the orbiting spy satellite, which gathers visual data from several miles above the earth's surface. Dissolution of spatial difference connotes in turn a crisis of the distinction between interiors and exteriors. In the era of film, the argument might run, everything is exterior, open to view, exposed at all times; or, equally (and what would the difference be?), the "world [is] seen from inside"—all is interior, floating within the global field of visibility. Privacy no longer begins or ends at the surface of the body; the camera operator, as Walter Benjamin argued, is comparable to the surgeon (234).[28] Privacy, one might say, is always implicitly open to the eye of the camera. The spectacular relation to lived reality no longer reaches its limit at the surface of the body. Quite unlike Walter Benjamin, who saw revolutionary potential in the capacity of film to bring new things before the human eye, DeLillo's perception (or his character's) is of an invasive, penetrative violation.[29] Just as the body becomes an adjunct to technology, so privacy becomes a special version of publicity, but not in any way that links these media-invaded subjects into active collective agents. DeLillo's dystopian vision imagines an increasingly mystified everyday reality, one rendered cryptic by the new visual technologies.

Secrecy and Violence

I want to pursue this shift in the nature of the private and public by looking closely at two specific instances of televised violence given prominent place in DeLillo's fiction. Ruby's shooting of Oswald, treated in the final pages of *Libra*, and the murders committed by the Texas Highway Killer in *Underworld*, are both "live" murders, the former captured as news footage, the latter filmed accidentally by a child with a video camera; they are both broadcast repetitively and unrelentingly on TV. These violent televised events become the occasion for reflection on the overlaps and discontinuities between private and public spaces, and the related cultural entanglement of bodies and technologies. They are presented by DeLillo as models of the saturating "world-narrative," the sense of a present in continual crisis, a series of punctual catastrophes that hold the interest only so long as they generate good footage.

In this respect, it is important to note the historical framing DeLillo provides for his emphasis on the emblematic violent event. The prototype for such events is the assassination of President Kennedy, a calamity that is held to mark a profound shift in the American imaginary, and in the ways in which such public self-consciousness is attained or figured. While the Kennedy assassination was, in DeLillo's words, "the seven seconds that broke the back of the American century" (*Libra* 181), the catastrophic occasion that appeared to shatter a consensual narrative of nation, it also offers in *Libra* a rather different historical marker, one that punctuates the shift to a public life dominated by crisis, secrecy, paranoia, and, above all, by the rapid, repetitive, and narcoleptic rhythm of television.

The meanings of the assassination are not fixed, but are continually constructed and reconstructed, and DeLillo, for his part, has returned to this event time and again, attempting to establish its significance for his imaginative exploration of American culture. Kennedy's assassination is represented in the early work as a symptom of randomness in explanatory logic, of an inexplicable break that defies historical accounting, and of a bewildering entanglement of oppositional and covert elements, of secrecy as principle and desire, a shaping force in the cultural landscape. It is a moment, as he remarked in a 1993 interview, at which "[o]ur culture changed in important ways. And these changes are among the things that go into my work. There's the shattering randomness of the event, the missing motive, the violence that people not only commit but seem to watch simultaneously from a disinterested distance."[30] The implicit equation between the terms in this description, between, that is, a problem of radical historical contingency and the split subjectivities of media-besotted killers, establishes a link between public events and private motives, a connection established around the interwoven problems of agency and representation. If a major historical event is seen as random, an effect unattached to any cause, then it poses awkward problems of representation, both for the novelist and for the culture at large: the labors of conspiracy theorists can be seen as a response to this difficulty, and here one might mention Oliver Stone's film *JFK*, a movie that sought to resolve the troubling uncertainties around the assassination—not to mention all the upheavals of the 1960s—through the construction of the single, great cause. The media-poisoned boys, typified for DeLillo by John Hinckley and Arthur Bremer (would-be assassins of Ronald Reagan and George Wallace respectively), are themselves figures of (and figures for) the perplexing problem of agency. They also point to a connection DeLillo is establishing between the crisis of the private/public split and the grave difficulties now facing intelligible historical narrative. The crisis of the former is played out in the assassin's sense of theatricality, his pathological self-scrutiny; the related problems of the latter are reflected in the introduction of elements such as coincidence, fantasy, and dream—elements that lie, in DeLillo's phrase, "outside history."[31] What these terms register is the question of representing the ways in which private, and even self-occluded subjectivities, cross over into public spaces and events.

Crucial in this context is secrecy. Secrecy thrives in the political culture of the Cold War, but in *Libra* it is nurtured first in the intimate sphere of the family. One of the conspirators, a disgraced former CIA officer called Win Everett, remarks that secrets are "an exalted state, almost a dream state . . . a way of arresting motion, stopping the world so we can see ourselves in it" (26). In this sense, the secret is a way of securing the absolute privacy of self-communion; it presents the possibility of control and selfhood in a world that seems intent on canceling them out. *Libra* is peopled with characters who invest themselves in secrets because the world has apparently refused them access, and chief among them is Lee Oswald himself, who lives through secrets, through invented identities, fantasies of control, and clandestine behavior of all kinds. But it is striking that the secret—last vestige of privacy in a world where intimacy is perilously maintained—is only valuable because it is predicated on revelation, on exposure to the Other. Since *Libra* is, among other things, a novel of the Cold War, it is probably not surprising that this Other is represented, ultimately, by technological detection systems, from the polygraph to the spy plane and satellite. Win Everett muses:

> Spy planes, drone aircraft, satellites with cameras that can see from three hundred miles what you can see from a hundred feet. They see and they hear. Like ancient monks, you know, who recorded knowledge, wrote it painstakingly down. These systems collect and process. All the secret knowledge of the world. . . . I'll tell you what it means, these orbiting sensors that can hear us in our beds. It means the end of loyalty. The more complex the systems, the less conviction in people. Conviction will be drained out of us. Devices will drain us, make us vague and pliant. (77)

Technological surveillance systems—themselves a closely guarded secret—present a problem of agency; drained finally of beliefs and loyalties (to ideas and to people), the pitilessly exposed subject has an increasing need for secrets, but less and less use for them. If there is a tendency in DeLillo's characters to turn away from the social world, to seek desperate seclusion in cell-like rooms, there is also an equal and accompanying desire to burst dramatically free from that isolation, to connect—with others, with the Other—in ways that will cancel the self out altogether. Oswald turns away from his immediate environment and seeks solace in fantasies of History, a force he imagines as so vast and sweeping it will relieve him of his burdensome selfhood: "History means to merge," he tells himself. "The purpose of history is to climb out of your own skin" (101).

This conception of history might be rephrased in terms of an absolute surrender of the private to the public, were it not for the fact that public figures who are assured a place in the history books—particularly the first citizen himself—are also associated with secrecy. JFK is described as glowing because he is the man who has access to all the most important secrets, the ultimate secret being the launch code for the missiles.[32] To this extent, secrecy is the condition that allows an iconic subjectivity to emerge; it can then, in turn, become a point of identification, and private citizens may see themselves collectively embodied in the first family. Kennedy is, so to speak, the figure in whom private and public selves coincide; Oswald, by contrast, is the figure in whom the two realms fall into crisis. As an iconic figure, JFK can be the point at which private fantasies latch onto a public face, whether he is an object of loathing, as he is for some of the conspirators and their rightwing fellow travelers, in which case he becomes responsible for "everything they're not telling us" (everything, i.e., from fluoridation of the water to Chinese troops massing along the Baja peninsula), or whether, on the other hand, he is an object of desire, as he is for Marina Oswald, who imagines him floating at night from the TV screen or the radio (both interfaces between private and public worlds) to visit her in her bed. Whether reviled or desired, the president's iconic visage supplies, in Samuel Weber's words, "a face with eyes that seem to look back and a voice that seems to address one directly."[33] This direct gaze and personal voice fill out the ideological fantasy of an immediate relation between state and citizen.

This notion of secrecy as the form or practice that traverses and covertly links private fantasy and public space can be seen as parallel to a slightly different relationship, one involving technology and the body. Technology—and particularly the technology of surveillance—tends in its contact with or scrutiny of the body to suggest a short-circuiting or evacuation of any shared social space. As Volterra suggests in *The Names*, and as Win Everett implies in *Libra*, technological attention makes depth into surface, opening up the secrets of the organism and the psyche alike. The most obvious example of this is the polygraph. As he realizes that his grip on the conspiracy is weakening, Everett longs for the polygraph as a deliverance from the pressures of his labyrinthine privacy: "He feared and welcomed the chance to be polygraphed. . . . Unpack the machine, mix some control questions in with the serious stuff. His body would do the rest, yield up its unprotected data. The machine intervenes between a man and his secrets" (361–362). What is curious about Everett's desire to give up his secrets to the polygraph is that it rests on the fantasy of an immediate relation between technology and the body, one that will, in some sense, circumvent questions of decision, motive, and agency. Opening himself to technological scrutiny will, he supposes, make him whole again, at least in relation to the brooding paternalistic presence of the CIA. More often, the relationship between technology and the body is envisaged in distinctly negative terms as one typified by the spectacle of violence— bodies being made, precisely, *not* whole, perforated and torn, opened up in hypervisible public space.

Ruby's shooting of Oswald in *Libra* represents DeLillo's most elaborate engagement with these issues. The grisly footage shot in the basement of the Dallas Police and Courts building proves to be the public spectacle par excellence, perhaps the first time TV had fully demonstrated an intimacy with "live" violence. As DeLillo remarked in an interview, "you could watch Oswald die while you ate a TV dinner and he was still dying by the time you went to bed."[34] DeLillo presents the episode in *Libra* through a number of different voices, from a number of different positions, as if to emphasize the ways in which diverse contexts were jaggedly arrayed around those few violent seconds and connected through the televisual medium, so as to form a new kind of serialized social unity. Heteroglossia is in fact typical of the novel, which often creates its effects by juxtaposing different linguistic registers, from the peculiar idioms of Ruby and Marguerite to the flat prose of official reports. But these voices also link a series of different spaces, insides and outsides: the inner depths of Oswald's body, bored through by the bullet; the domestic interior of a TV den where someone is imagined watching; the radically exterior perspective of U-2 pilot, imagined bailing out of his damaged craft, and alluded to at this point for reasons I will try to establish.

Oswald experiences his own shooting through a consciousness split between bodily pain, on the one hand, and a set of allusions to forms of technology, on the other. Even as he succumbs to pain, loss of sensation, the augering heat of the bullet—the physical effects of his fatal wounding—he experiences the moment through TV: he sees himself shot, from the camera's point of view, and watches himself react: "The only thing left was the mocking pain, the picture of the twisted face on TV" (440). Oswald, in other words, watches himself become image, a face on the screen. This split is associated with one of his aliases, "Hidell," a name Oswald breaks down in various ways: "Jerkle and Hide in his little cell," "The id is hell," "Hidell means don't tell" (101), and, as here, "die and hell in Hidell"—these punning rhymes all present notions of doubling, of the secret self, or, better, the self constitutively formed through the secret. Oswald's self-division is played out in his last moments between body and image, private sensation and public representation (what pain "looks like"), and even between his physical presence before the TV cameras and the picture relayed to "someone's TV den" (440).

To address the other important element in this episode, the reference to the U-2 pilot, it is necessary to recall Oswald's last moments:

> They logged him at Parkland at 11:42. Chief complaint, gunshot wound. The heart was seen to be flabby and not beating at all. No effective heartbeat could be instituted. The pupils were fixed and dilated. There was no retinal blood flow. There was no respiratory effort. No effective pulse could be maintained. Expired: 13:07. Two sponges missing when the body closed.
> Aerospace.
> It was the white nightmare of noon, high in the sky over Russia. Me-too and you-too. He is a stranger, in a mask, falling. (440)

Here the technical terms that might come from a medical report—the signs of death—are juxtaposed with a reference to the U-2 pilot, who is imagined falling from the shattered spy plane high over Russia. The reference to the pilot connotes, in the first place, a radical exteriority, a position of knowledge situated many thousands of feet above the earth.[35] Yet there is an accompanying notion, one that doubles Everett's hopes for the polygraph: that of being released from secrets, physically drifting to earth by parachute, and welcoming the chance to give up one's clandestine knowledge. Earlier in the novel, the nameless pilot (who will later, contingently, turn out to be Francis Gary Powers, shot down over Russia during Oswald's time in Minsk), is imagined floating down to earth: "He wants to tell the truth. He wants to live another kind of life, outside secrecy and the pull of grave events. This is what the pilot thinks, rocking softly down to the tawny fields of a landscape so gentle it might almost be home" (116). Oswald's rather more alarming allusion to this fall nonetheless makes a connection between the inside of the body (ripped by the bullet), and the secret state; between seeing the world from the outside, as one might see it falling from the sky, and the peculiar, vertiginous world-turned-inside-out quality of TV.

A couple of pages later, the novel turns to a woman watching these events played and replayed on TV. As she sees Oswald die again and again she notices the vitality also draining out of all the figures in the picture: "They kept racking film, running shadows through the machine. It was a process that drained life from the picture, sealed them in the frame. They began to seem timeless to her, identically dead" (447). Along with the violence of repetition that places these figures into a new context— one of mechanical reproduction and repetition—the watcher experiences a violence of invasion, as the safe domestic space is disturbed by the men on the screen:

> She'd been crying all weekend, crying and watching. She couldn't shake the feeling she'd been found out. These men were in her house with their hats and guns. Pictures from the other world. They'd located her, forced her to look, and it was not at all like the news items she clipped and mailed to friends. She felt this violence spilling in, over and over, men in dark hats, in gray hats with dark bands, in tan Stetsons, in white caps with shiny visors and badges pinned to the crowns. (446)

The violence done to Oswald, with its collapsing of different spaces, its confusion of insides and outsides, is here translated into terms of public and private events, public and private spaces. Just as the technologies— TV, the spy plane—with which Oswald is associated at the critical moment have the effect of decentering the subject, spectacularly opening the interior to some radical exterior, so these pictures "from the other world" leave the woman and her domestic space radically exposed, as if, in fact, policemen have entered her home to arrest her.[36] But, at the same time, she remains fixated, unable to tear her eyes from the screen:

> But something held her there. It was probably Oswald. There was something in Oswald's face, a glance at the camera before he was shot, that put him in the audience, among the rest of us, sleepless in our homes—a glance, a way of telling us that he knows who we are and how we feel, that he has brought our perceptions and interpretations into his sense of the crime. Something in the look, some sly intelligence, exceedingly brief but far-reaching, a connection all but bleached away by glare, tells us that he is outside the moment, watching with the rest of us. (447)

The look she seems to see in Oswald's face is one of complicity. It draws watcher and victim into a pathological secret, a collective unity founded on the watching of pain. The knowing look collapses the difference, once more, between the world out there and the world in here, or renders these terms undecidable.

Oswald, she concludes, "has made us part of his dying" (447). The sense of a shared public/private event is of one convened around the perforation of bodies and spaces by technology, rather than through the mobilization of official public symbols. The famous question about the assassination—*where were you when . . .?*—suggests a desire to link multiplicitous private histories together into an imagined community of shock and grief. The televised murder, by contrast, suggests that collectivities are now more likely to be forged around the complex collapse of public and private spaces, and that the connection is made by violence, whether the violence is part of the event or whether it is the violence of interiors being transformed into exteriors.

The Texas Highway Killer

The episode of the Texas Highway Killer in *Underworld* further plays out in detail the identifications and traumas forged across private and public contexts. A 12-year-old girl, known by the media as the "videokid," accidentally captures one of the murders committed by a serial killer who shoots his victims as they drive along the highway. The footage is then played relentlessly on television, exerting a certain horrified fascination over the viewer. Within the extended texture of echoes, linked motifs, and cross-references that makes up DeLillo's latest novel, the tape of the homicide is connected to a prototype, the Zapruder film, the grainy home movie of the Kennedy assassination shot by a Dallas dressmaker, kept more or less secret for years, and finally seen in public from the mid-1970s on (Klara Sax sees the film during this period, strangely reconfigured as an avant-garde installation). The Zapruder film is, DeLillo has noted, "our major emblem of uncertainty and chaos,"[37] an "atrocity exhibition" (in J.G. Ballard's apt phrase) that appears to show everything and tell nothing. Such uncertainty—and such horror—stem from the problematic interaction of technology and bodies: the crude realities of the film concern the way tissue and bone are affected by high velocity projectiles; yet the footage is subjected to ever more elaborate scrutiny, as technologies become more discerning with each passing generation.[38] Marvin Lundy, in his passionate three-decade quest for the baseball from the famous 1951 game, resorts to similar technologies, studying the fine-grain of a home movie shot in the Polo Grounds that day, attempting to resolve the extraordinary resonance of a single historical moment, a resonance that DeLillo traces across the vast cultural and historical tundra of the Cold War, into a single material fact—a hand grasping a ball.

The tape of the Texas Highway Killer is itself subjected to elaborate technological scrutiny, by Nick Shay's son among others. In this respect, the efforts of technology are invested in the attempt to establish identities once and for all; it is hoped that peering into the grain of the film will allow one finally to determine who fired the shot, who clutched the ball. But at the same time, technology plays an important part in the oscillation between private and public identities, anonymity and iconicity. DeLillo's exposition of the Highway Killer footage forges a series of links—or, more accurately, traumatic connections established around the relationship of technology and the body—between the intimate domestic sphere and the exposed public realm of TV. The videokid is anonymous, merely a chance witness of the events that unfold on the highway; but the camera establishes a complicitous link between her viewing and that of the avid, anonymous, watcher of TV, a connection emphasized by the use of the second person: "You know how kids get involved, how the camera shows them that every subject is potentially charged, a million things they never see with the unaided eye. They investigate the meaning of inert objects and dumb pets and they poke at family privacy" (*Underworld* 155). If, at one level, this is a narrative about a "girl [who] got lost and wandered clear-eyed into horror" (157), it is also a story about the (potentially aggressive) desire to see into the privacy of others. Equally, this uncertainty is that of the viewer at home, watching with alarm, but also sadistically trying to get another to watch: "And maybe you're being a little aggressive here, practically forcing your wife to watch" (159).

These complicitous connections, invested as much with the desire to expose privacy to the public gaze as with the horror of such exposure, could not be more different from the ways in which *Underworld* envisages an older kind of collectivity. Across the extended skein of the novel, a contrast may be drawn between the collective established around the spectacle of violence and that founded on unrepeatable proximity in space and time. In the opening scene of the novel, the account of the Dodgers–Giants game, the richly detailed evocation of shared values and experiences is carefully counterposed to the purely abstract identity of an apocalyptic scenario gloomily relished by J. Edgar Hoover. On learning of the second Soviet atomic test, Hoover notes a connection between the individuals in the crowd: "All these people formed by language and climate and popular songs and breakfast foods and the jokes they tell and the cars they drive have never had anything in common so much as this, that they are sitting in the furrow of destruction" (28). The scene captures a janus-faced historical perspective: it points back to an older kind of collective identity, based on shared experience and national self-confidence; and it points forward to the pathological public identities founded on shared anxiety and horror. While the structure of the novel retains this double optic, painstakingly working back into the past from the post–Cold War period, on the one hand, and moving in brief snapshots forward in time in the "Manx Martin" sections, on the other, the geographical and cultural dispersal is gradually reined in as the narrative winds its way back to the Bronx. To this extent, DeLillo's imaginative surveying of a historical break, established most vividly in "The Power of History" as the difference between two kinds of visual culture, one pathological the other carrying a "moral burnish," tilts toward nostalgia. *Underworld*'s penultimate section, "Arrangement in Gray and Black: Fall 1951–Summer 1952," turns away from the concern with shifting private and public relations and the mechanisms of seriality, to root its conception of identity in ethnicity and neighborhood.

One of the stories *Underworld* tells—one of the ways in which it imagines history—is about how people gather together. The novel begins with a gathering of people in the open air at a baseball game; it ends with two very different kinds of assemblage, a group of people gathered to witness an apparent miracle, and a timeless and spaceless gathering of informational links on the Web. The corollary to the slick operationality of the latter (which, evangelists of the web would have one believe, overcomes the distinction between the little room and the great big crowded world) is the violated body of the televised atrocity, specifically in this instance, the body of the murdered homeless girl, Esmeralda. In pairing these episodes through the figure of Sister Edgar, DeLillo situates two kinds of grouping under the signs of hysteria and inertia. Standing before a gigantic billboard, Sister Edgar, along with the gathering crowd, sees the face of Esmeralda appear in an advertisement for Minute Maid Orange Juice. Caught up in the astonishment of this scene, Sister Edgar joins the crowd: "she is nameless for a moment, lost to the details of personal history, a disembodied fact in liquid form, pouring into the crowd" (823). Here, just as in the billboard, commodity and miracle are both visible at the same time. The crowd overcomes differences of age and faith and race through sheer credulity, even as the writing slyly ambiguates such a visionary instant by limning Sister Edgar's disembodiment in phrases perhaps better suited to orange juice. Shortly after, Sister Edgar dies and passes into another world, that of cyberspace. Disembodiment, in this case, means merging with technological systems: on the web, "everything is connected" (825), but this knowledge proves disabling after all, a final foreshadowing of fluidity and compliance: "Sister begins to sense the byshadows that stretch from the awe of a central event. How the intersecting systems help pull us apart, leaving us vague, drained, docile, soft in our inner discourse, willing to be shaped, to be overwhelmed—easy retreats, half beliefs" (826).

Thus, *Underworld* ends with a particularly uncomfortable vision of the desire for collective identity. The famous baseball game that opens the novel—though marked by social and racial divisions, as well as dark forebodings of the Cold War climate then descending on America— showcases a crowd participating in a historical moment. By contrast, the gatherings with which the novel ends remove their constituent members from history, pitching them into religious ecstasy or the virtual congregation of cyberspace. Both instances evacuate subjectivity and moral agency. Sister Edgar's ecstatic self-loss in the mystical communion with the billboard, a moment both heightened and troubling, gives way to the engineered self-loss of her assumption into cyberspace. There the historical panorama of the novel draws into the closed circle of complete connection: Sister Edgar is twinned, as in some celestial conjunction, with J. Edgar Hoover. This makes sense, since the two characters share ideology as well as a name, but it also signals the collapse of historical narrative under new technological conditions. Such a collapse entails the end of the project of writing national identity, through all its fluctuations and anxieties, over the course of the second half of the "American century."

And so the novel's final paragraph, which depicts a writer's desk, reads as a valediction to the novelistic enterprise as well as the novel. The passage turns around the distinction between cyberspace and the "unwebbed" world in all its sensory particularity, down to the "yellow of the yellow of the pencils" (827). The gulf between the virtual reality of the web, where the word "peace" flashes up on a web site devoted to the atomic bomb, and the world of humble material objects is cultural and political, as much as technological. *Underworld* writes a history of "intersecting systems" overtaking American reality. To resist this seemingly inevitable movement in a work of fiction is to adhere to "the argument of things to be seen and eaten" (827), the minutiae of memory and the senses that DeLillo works so carefully into his prose. But the desire named at the end of the novel— the desire for peace—can only reach out into the world as a disembodied "longing." Such a longing might be the basis of an unimaginable collective identity, or so the "tunneled underworld" (826) of etymology suggests, since peace can be traced to a root meaning of "[f]asten, fit closely, bind together." Yet the word remains, finally, no more than "a sequence of pulses on a dullish screen" (827)—available with a few keystrokes, but perennially remote from realization.

CHAPTER 6

LATE POSTMODERNISM AND THE UTOPIAN IMAGINATION

In a British television documentary on his work, Don DeLillo quoted an excerpt from John Cheever's journal that describes an evening spent watching baseball at Shea Stadium in the summer of 1963. Cheever wrote and DeLillo read:

> I think that the task of an American writer is not to describe the misgivings of a woman taken in adultery as she looks out of a window at the rain, but to describe four hundred people under the lights reaching for a foul ball. This is ceremony. The umpires in clericals, sifting out the souls of the players; the faint thunder as ten thousand people, at the bottom of the eighth, head for the exits. The sense of moral judgments embodied in a migratory vastness.[1]

Cheever's remarks are surprising, given his usual sharp-eyed interest in middle-class suburban lives, the private anguish of the woman rather than the Whitmanesque word *en masse*, but they evoke nonetheless a sense of purpose and cultural authority for the writer. He calls for the American author to engage with the symbolic acts—spectatorial participation in a panoply of election—by which a national identity is enacted and affirmed. As the 400 spectators reach for the foul ball as one, they play out a ritual that culminates, according to Cheever, in the "sense of moral judgments embodied in a migratory vastness." This migratory vastness is not simply the clamorous expanse of the baseball stadium; it is America itself, and the writer participates in the "ceremony" of national identity.

In contrast, DeLillo's vision of a technologically mediated multitude suspended between credulity and skepticism, or, if one prefers, between epiphany and disillusionment, has an ambiguous political charge. On the one hand, contemporary media spectacles, particularly those of violence and catastrophe, deplete the psychic resources and moral agency of the individual subject. In alarming depictions of the crowd or of serialized viewers finding a sickening complicity between image and act, the impression is one of a total system that leaves its subjects powerless and exposed, without even the nostalgic seclusions of privacy and retreat to sustain them. On the other hand, the apocalyptic spectacles DeLillo stages tentatively hold out the possibility of collective experience, albeit of an ambiguous kind, beyond the localized satisfactions of consumer culture. This in many respects is a troubling aspect of DeLillo's work, one that has concerned and divided his critics,[2] since the ecstatic transports he imagines occur either in a threatening or alien exterior (the frenzied crowds in Iran or at Mecca, featured in *Mao II* and *The Names* respectively), in moments of profound terror, or in the most image-drenched spaces of contemporary technological culture. The emotions are powerful and irrational, and often much desired by DeLillo's characters. Such feelings offer a release from the burden of selfhood, a suspension of quotidian reality, and an escape from or complete submission to the hyper-rational conditions of technological consumerism, but seem at best a problematic basis for any vision of progressive politics.

DeLillo's work remains, therefore, within a particularly dark lineage of American writing—not John Cheever or Walt Whitman, but Nathanael West and William Gaddis, for whom the American spectacle was deserving of ferocious satire. It would be a mistake to suggest that satire, in the case of such writers, is at root conservative, a means to attack folly or excess in the name of a more stringent moral or social order. On the contrary, West, Gaddis, and DeLillo raise dissenting voices, but without presupposing a clear moral or social norm against which to measure current deviance. DeLillo in particular offers few clear indications of the possibility of amelioration, personal or political, not least because the attempts to disentangle the self from present circumstances are shown very often to be delusive rather than emancipatory. The power of this strain of dark, unstable satire stems from the unrelenting bleakness of the writers' imaginations. The politics implicit in their work at its best is founded on corrosive negativity, a fierce rejection of the generalized falsehood of a society founded on consumer satisfaction—a satisfaction to which the "sardonic response," as DeLillo once remarked, is violence.[3]

From DeLillo's writing vividly emerges the problem of conceiving politics when public space has been colonized by spectacle. Politics means media imagery of a calculating and staged kind: President Bush in a jumpsuit landing on the deck of an aircraft carrier. Or it means scandal and shame: the relentless cable news analysis of President Clinton's sexual indiscretions. What it does not mean is public discussion of fundamental questions of inequality and the provision of social goods. The impact of DeLillo's fiction—and that of the work of other writers who mine the same darkly satirical vein—derives from the force, scope, and penetration with which it envisages a world enmeshed in the spectacle. Yet the more powerfully such a vision is evoked, the more difficult it becomes to conceive the subject as anything but passive and morally inert. Within the parameters of the conventional novel, political agency devolves onto dilemmas of the individual will. The novelist can work variations on the incapacity of characters faced with situations that are beyond their power to alter, and perhaps beyond their ability to understand. Or the individual can be put into a position of greater or lesser agency through the mechanics of plot, though the problems of representing and dramatizing social forces that impinge on and condition subjects are not thereby overcome.

Jonathan Franzen's second and third novels illustrate the dilemmas faced by realist, character-centered fiction in dealing with political and moral agency. *Strong Motion*, Franzen's second novel, explicitly addresses political and environmental themes, blending the elements of a love story, a family inheritance plot, and an eco-thriller. The book bears a family resemblance to fictions of paranoia, both of the literary kind associated most closely with the work of Thomas Pynchon, and of the popular, airport variety. But *Strong Motion* remains within the realist framework, with the consequence that two individuals, Louis Holland, an unemployed radio technician, and Renée Seitchek, a seismologist, must take on—and expose—the corrupt Sweeting Aldren corporation, a chemicals giant responsible for pumping toxic waste into the earth's crust. Narratives that pit brave, determined individuals against large corporations offer a measure of hope: a single person may still have a significant political and moral impact on the world. But the limitations of such a literary strategy are also evident: at best, the confrontation between individual and corporation emboldens the former, and lays bare the abuses of the latter to synecdochic effect—for one corporation, read many; at worst, the abuses exposed will be subject to merely local amelioration, depending on an appeal to the law, and thus making outrage into little more than an adjustment to the systemic functioning of corporate capitalism. From Franzen's point of view, the method was vulnerable to the charge of redundancy. For all the necessarily elaborate plotting, such novels can only declare time and again that consumer capitalism is an infernal machine.

With *The Corrections*, as I have argued, Franzen turns away from political themes, or decants them into satirical asides. Indeed, he finds dark comedy in characters who mistakenly assume that social conditions might be altered, either through critical thought or direct action. Such conditions, the novel hints, are always more intractable and deeply entangling than any individual can recognize, notably Chip Lambert, who tries over the course of a semester to teach his students how to think critically, and indeed politically, about media culture, without ever reflecting on the fact that his college is sponsored by large corporations. Direct antagonism between the individual and the corporation, as in the earlier novel, now takes the grimly reductive form of Billy Passafaro's brutal assault on a W—Corporation executive. Although *The Corrections* introduces many themes and narrative strands that are in the broad sense political—psychopharmacology, the stock market boom, consumerism—the novel focuses on individual crises and the structure of the family. Franzen's satire is directed at the excesses of consumerism and the absurdities of therapeutic optimism. The novel closes off the political reach of the paranoid fiction, stripping away cumbersome plot machinery and restricting the possibilities of narrative development within the bounds of the family. *The Corrections* is, in the best sense, "character-driven," but it also retreats from the challenge of the politically engaged and genuinely exploratory social novel.

The difficulty for the novelist lies in the immense gulf between the experience, agency, and cognitive capacities of the subject, and the large structures and processes that make up the postmodern world. To state the problem in its simplest terms, the more compelling the account of structures and processes, whether mediated through the psyche of characters or evoked through narratorial commentary, the weaker and more passive the individual will seem. Such weakness might take the form of the disintegration of the subject, its dispersal among the codes and relays of information society; or it might be projected outward onto a faceless aggregate, an inert mass of other subjects, all to a greater or lesser degree caught up in or representative of a serialized social body. Alternatively, a keen focus on an individual, whose quiddity shines forth precisely to the extent that she is detached from the social context, tends to naturalize that background, to make it unchangeable, eternal, beyond interrogation—thus implying a powerlessness no less obdurate because unexamined.

Gain, Richard Powers's follow-up to *Galatea 2.2*, makes these difficulties into a structural principle.[4] The novel pursues two distinct and strikingly unlike narratives. Powers tells the story of Clare, a pharmaceuticals corporation, from its origins in the manufacture of soap, through the milestones of its development, to its staggering expansion and diversification in the twentieth century. Interspersed is a very different kind of narrative, the domestic melodrama of Laura Bodey, a 42-year-old real estate agent who is diagnosed with and eventually succumbs to ovarian cancer. Clare's history and Laura's sickness are, the reader comes to understand, closely connected: the fabulous success of American capitalism has created a toxic environment. The two narratives straddle a structural and tonal divide. Clare's story has an exuberance and vigor that is entirely lacking from Laura's downbeat, realist story, with its familiar domestic details and wrenching sentimentality. The former proceeds at a brisk tempo, sweeping through historical eras, through new technologies and systems of production—from cottage industry to multinational megacorporation—and across the United States, germinating in Boston, relocating to Illinois, and finally spreading all over the globe. By contrast, the final year of Laura Bodey's life is made up of disrupted family routines, anxious waiting, and the protracted misery of chemotherapy and terminal sickness. All of these differences emphasize, in comprehensible form, the split between the structural determinants of life in late capitalism and the lived experience of it. The full story of Laura Bodey's life and death cannot be told without taking on board the history of the corporation that has shaped the whole environment in which she lives, from the commodities she uses to the houses she sells. Both halves of *Gain* press the reader toward the realization that Laura lives in a total system, a world entirely shaped by capitalism.

Powers's novel embodies in its divided form the structural obstacles the novelist faces in representing late capitalist society. As Laura's disease progresses, she begins to acquire at least the beginnings of a critical understanding of the role of Clare, but she cannot act on that knowledge or inspire others to do so. The problem remains entrenched at the level of knowledge and the individual, and Powers's reader begins to grasp the extent to which Laura and the environment in which she lives are shaped by histories and processes beyond her ken. Evan Dara's 1995 novel, *The Lost Scrapbook*, makes the structural divisions of contemporary social life— divisions of knowledge, labor, social class, power, and even the body— integral to its form, but also begins to imagine how the most disabling division is that which prevents a truly collective political understanding from coming into being. This remarkable work, one of the most significant political novels of the 1990s, shares the concerns of *Gain* with large corporations and environmental toxicity, but goes further than Powers's text in imagining a response, a collective protest, to the damaged social life that both books see so clearly. *The Lost Scrapbook* presents the unusual and compelling case of an experimental novel, imbued with political anger and hope, written in full awareness of the mass mediation and consumer ideologies of the late postmodern moment.

Dara's Minimalism

First published by Fiction Collective Two in 1995, Evan Dara's *The Lost Scrapbook* was greeted with resounding silence (there was, I believe, one review); only on its paperback reissue in 1998 did it begin to attract favorable notice, winning the FC2 National Fiction Competition, and receiving a cluster of laudatory reviews.[5] Mention was inevitably made of other remarkable first novels, including Thomas Pynchon's *V.* and William Gaddis's great 1955 novel *The Recognitions*. Such comparisons are of course the reviewer's stock in trade, but in this instance they do help to situate *The Lost Scrapbook*, since, like Pynchon, Dara makes significant use of specialized knowledge and vocabularies, particularly those derived from various branches of science, and he has clearly learned something from Gaddis's coruscating polyphonic fiction, particularly the latter's satirical assaults on finance (*JR*) and the law (*A Frolic of His Own*). Dara's specialized languages—notably those of physics, musicology, film theory, and developmental psychology—provide the reader with resources for thematic and formal comprehension. Since Dara builds his book out of voices, fabricating a seemingly unedited soundscape, the reader is obliged to sort and select, to draw signals out of the noise, identifying, for example, repeated motifs, structural patterns or thematic figures; but this is a task made all the more challenging by the difficulty of attributing voices to distinct characters, locating actions in a single locale or connected set of places, and establishing a causal sequence of events. These formal innovations seem likely to condemn the novel to the marginal enclave of "experimentalism," an ironic fate to befall a novel that protests against the disabling divisions of knowledge and culture. *The Lost Scrapbook* charges the reader with the utopian task of breaking down the boundaries of knowledge, language, and experience that transect contemporary culture, even as it offers a sobering reminder, both explicitly in its commentary and implicitly in its form, of the resilience of such divisions.

The Lost Scrapbook is an immense collage of voices, a heteroglot and decentered assemblage of speech in various modalities—mini-lectures, soliloquies, anecdotes, rambling conversations, official statements, interviews, jokes, gossip, speculation, and more. In the majority of instances, the speakers are unidentified, and their words, though often telling stories, begin and end without warning, obliging the reader to construe character and significance without narratorial direction or legible emplotment. The novel opens, for example, with an exchange between a teenager and a career counselor that prompts the teen to entertain a stream of thoughts on the restrictive nature of social roles; the reader then learns more about the life of the teenager as he wanders about his home town, before an abrupt switch into the mind of an apparently older man on his way to conduct an interview; his interviewee turns out to be a video artist and amateur musicologist, who spins off into a long quasi-academic riff about

Beethoven's late-career interest in composing variations. This episode switches, mid-conversation, to an exchange between another (or the same, at a different point in time) unnamed "I" and an animator named Nick, before turning into a mournful reflection, probably from a teenager, about the decline of radio and the sickness of a friend. And so on, through many such abrupt and unsignaled changes of setting and speaker for upwards of 300 pages. The first-time reader struggles in vain to discern connections between the speakers or even to fix them in time and space; the novel's deictic pointers, such as they are, suggest that the action is taking place literally all over the map—in moving cars, in states a thousand miles apart, in homes, parks, factories, offices, theaters, forests, and shopping malls. And often the voices cannot be tied to a specific locale, but simply reflect and ramble and exclaim on events that have occurred in the past. As far as one can say, however, the events referred to in the novel take place mostly during the 1980s and early 1990s in the lower Midwest.

The text resists restriction and completion: episodes are drowned out rather than concluding, casual digressions cut across climactic urgencies, scenes change before their significance is revealed. At the level of punctuation and syntax, the writing refuses closure, tending instead to ellipsis and incompletion, to unfinished sentences and interrupted thoughts. Semi-colons and colons are used in place of periods, and paragraphs tend to conclude with triple dots, as if to signify a continuing action or cinematic slow fade. Indeed, the novel's sole period appears before the very last word of the book, which, significantly enough, begins rather than ends a sentence, leaving the reader to imagine complete interruptive cessation or a looping structure that rejoins the textual flow back at the first page: "for where else could this go but silence, yes silence: silence. Silence" (476). The novel's strategy of textual flow effectively wages war on discrete and sealed particles of meaning, always pressing the reader to comprehend in ever-widening, if fractured contextual frames. Instead of the articulation of self-sufficient narrative units, *The Lost Scrapbook* assembles unfinished episodes in a paratactic fashion. The relation of the parts to the whole is not therefore organic, but additive and variational. Such an organization places the burden of making narrative and discursive connections firmly on the reader, who must decide whether or at what level of abstraction these multifarious plot strands relate to each other. The messages emitted by the form of the novel are integral to its meaning, even as they are best grasped by close attention to the thematic metatextual resources offered throughout the book.

One of the first ways the text invites thought about its own structure is in the early reference to the teenager's music of choice, "Glass's homage to Muybridge, minimalism used to maximal effect: with its repeating rhythms, endlessly rechurning, the music resembles a wave that doesn't move, a standing wave" (8). This allusion condenses two cultural allusions to analogical effect, Eadweard Muybridge's nineteenth-century serial photographs of human and animal locomotion and Philip Glass's minimalist musical compositions. Such a juxtaposition offers thereby a complex image of the novel's own procedures. The pictures for which Muybridge is best known break continuous movement up into discrete images. Muybridge famously photographed animals and humans in various kinds of physical movement as they passed before an array of cameras, each one arresting continuity in a frozen pose. This allowed an unprecedented analytical approach to fluid movement, such that the gap between physiology and mechanics might be reduced. With the development of biomechanics, the figurative meaning of the body shifts from organic interconnection to machinic constructivism, a striking illustration of the analytical approach to continuous processes. These implications resonate with ideas of social division and novelistic form: the teen's objections to the career counselor's ministrations with which *The Lost Scrapbook* opens are a protest against the restrictive reification of social roles. As he caustically notes, "it's a bizarre enterprise, this deciding what 'to be': mostly it feels like negotiating what *not* to be; so spare me your solicitude, my dear diminishers, for I can already hear what you are going to say next: that before long I'll need to be realistic, and to acknowledge the inevitable" (6). The novel itself similarly protests against the reduction of possibility, refusing for much of its length to pull its materials into a single story line, instead continually branching, evolving, and changing. Thus, from the first pages, the novel both foregrounds the division of social life and knowledge into sealed and incommensurable disciplines and protests against it, with something of this hyper-articulate teen's wit and idealism.

At the same time, the reference to Philip Glass suggests how the novel, like minimalism in music, builds complex structures out of subtle changes in the repetition of simple rhythmic units. Dara's text works with the variational play of discrete narrative units to form larger meanings through the dialogical effect of echoes, contrasts, and parallels. Evidently, such a practice bears little relation to the fiction promoted in the 1980s under the banner of minimalism, namely a deliberately diminished and idiomatic realism—sometimes dubbed "dirty realism"—that focused typically on scenes from blue-collar lives, scrupulously reduced in linguistic resource, in the lineage of Hemingway's denotative craft, and associated most often with the work of Raymond Carver, Tobias Wolff, and Richard Ford. It may be that the brand label "dirty realism" was intended to establish a strategic opposition to "magical realism," about which one also heard a great deal in the 1980s; certainly, this new variety of minimalism was pitched as an alternative to, and reaction against, the postmodernism of the previous decade, now perceived as unreadable and painfully abstruse. Dara's minimalism involves the use of comparatively straightforward plot scenarios—a teen runs away from home, a single parent tells of his difficulties dealing with his son, a man explains his work as an animator, and so on—elaborated and juxtaposed in such a way that they produce complicated meanings. The significance drawn from these pieces, which appear as if excerpted from much larger narratives, accumulates through the variegated substance of the novel, as differences, echoes, parallels, and counter-narratives come into view. A subsequent disquisition on Beethoven's Diabelli variations, pursued circuitously through an anecdote about a misunderstanding between a father and a son (another displaced and marginal teen), thematizes this approach: "variations . . . represent excursions towards some higher understanding, repeated graspings-at and circlings-in towards some central truth; but variations also illustrate the cliché that the truth remains, ultimately, indeterminable" (41). The novel's variations on themes of isolation, failed communication, thwarted hope, and invisibility remain processual, manifold in their approach to a missing center.

Muybridge's serial photographs can be understood in this context as an image of the social body divided up into discrete fragments. The social basis of the division of knowledge stands in the way of the communication, recognition, and articulation of shared concerns and desires. The cognate particle/wave distinction of quantum theory, which is an important motif throughout the novel, provides a trope for the apparently irreducible split between the isolated individual, very often sealed off in inarticulate or silent protest, and the shared concerns or desires of aggregates. For the teenager at the opening of the novel, the problem lies in the opposition in which he is caught, namely that between sealed-off, self-communion, an anonymous and private state of being which enters into no exchanges or communications, and an existence that is purely statistical, an impersonal objectification according to demographic and actuarial categories. Indeed, the teen is engaged on experiment rather like that pursued by the eponymous protagonist of Nathaniel Hawthorne's short story "Wakefield." Wakefield walks out on his wife one day, but lingers in the neighborhood to observe in secret her reaction to his absence. Similarly, Dara's teenager leaves home, quits his job at a pharmacy, and opts for a state of invisibility: "outside, beyond: in the midst, but also gone; finding invisibility through new presence; disappearing through self-assertion: beyond, outside . . ." (10).

Ironically, he can find no trace—no perceptible presence—of his absence. He visits the house where he lives with his mother, only to sense from the unaltered appearance of the objects in the kitchen and living room that his departure has altered nothing. Such "achieved invisibility" (12) has its advantages—he shoplifts apparently with impunity, "by definition, unnabbable . . . because I am everywhere . . . and therefore nowhere . . ." (16). To be "everywhere . . . and therefore nowhere" is the condition of "no measurable existence save the statistical" (10). The experiment on which this character is engaged is to push a sense of inconsequentiality and marginality to an extreme, to see if the resulting no-place might have something to offer, the (non)space necessary for a private secession from the order of things. At the same time, he is caught in a "realm of no faces" (13), an observer who cannot be observed, but who, by the same token, cannot reduce his sense of isolation through contact with another.

He describes his situation in terms of figure and ground:

> . . . it's a question, really, of figure and ground, of learning to integrate the two: of linking the landscape to the flamelike cypress thrusting up within it, of considering the World along with Cristina: dissolving patterns into particles . . .; and I, for one, am perfectly positioned to make such investigations: I am either a bland assemblage of denim, sweatcloth, sneaks, connecting flesh and Walkman scudding through the streets of Springfield, barely perceptible in its random passages, or an indrawn 19-year-old with slightly stooped posture who has run away; it depends on whom you ask for the description: me, or anyone else in the world *but* me; figure and ground; figure or ground; but who, since Muybridge, even *looks* at the ground?; and Cristina was a cripple— (9)

This distinction between figure and ground, individual and environment, is pressed home in the early pages of the novel by the non-diegetic interruption of the teen's interior monologue by street signs—"YIELD" (9), "TOW-AWAY ZONE" (12), "KEEP DOOR CLOSED" (14)—as if to insist on the obdurate presence of social injunctions around which his resistant thoughts must flow. But the problem raised by the motif of figure and ground is also one of perception, specifically of the incommensurability of internal sense and external objectification, of visibility and invisibility. His social self is voiceless and statistical, and his self-relation, signaled by the personal stereo that seals him in an acoustic environment of his own choosing, remains uncomfortably stranded within this larger world, like the Cristina of Andrew Wyeth's painting "Cristina's World." Closed off within his own private world, he is as isolated as Cristina in Wyeth's canvas, sitting alone in the midst of fields and farm buildings that reach up to a closed horizon; she is contained within these restricted limits by her disability. But at the same time, he remains, as he is aware, within a social environment, one that consists of abstract laws and actuarial categories. Within this social frame, he is no less anonymous, his existence numerically incorporated within one or another quantitative identity—teenage run-aways, children of single parents, shoplifters, the unemployed, high-school graduates who have yet to find a steady occupation, those with poor posture (a suitably Muybridgean description), or any of a number of other cate-gorical ways of describing his situation. The challenge, as he sees it, is to connect the private world to the social domain in a fashion less abstract and anonymous than that offered by statistical modeling.

To forge a connection between isolated individuals remains an urgent desire of many of the characters in the novel. Yet forms of connection, established through intimacy and dialogue, prove deeply problematic. Dara's use of internal voices, spliced into anecdotes as well as intensely felt records of private experience, allows surprising shifts of emphasis and arresting juxtapositions. In a passage midway through the novel, for example, the reader suddenly enters the mind of a woman standing on line in a supermarket, experiencing the frustration of one obliged to wait, to whom other people in line are just so many infuriating obstacles to more pressing concerns. "I am stuck here on line," she laments, "behind others, before others, and none of my silent proddings are accel-erating this mulish process in any way whatever" (225). It emerges on the following page that her impatience stems from an almost uncontrollable desire to join her lover, to lose her sense of separation and distinctness in sexual activity. Embracing him, she gushes, "I am clutched, and I am sus-tained, and I can only think Finally my Diaspora is ended" (226). And so indeed it would seem, as the reader is led through a detailed account of the erotic encounter between these two nameless, wordless individuals, an encounter that vouchsafes a sense, as she explains, that "we are one system, we are continuous, sharing long glissandos of feeling that are lacing between us, stitching us" (228). At this point, erotic excitement and pleasure radiate between the two individuals, making possible, or so it would seem, a mutually satisfying and fulfilling transcendence of isolated being. The lovers are restored to wholeness through their passionate embraces, their sexual foreplay: "his tongue, as it traces, is the sealant that knits my fissures, that pieces me back together, rejoining my broken shell" (229).

Yet, there is something peculiar about this passage and its assertions. To read in detail of erotic activity cannot, in spite of the breathless assertions of unity, connection, wholeness, and the rest of it, avoid recalling the lurid and objectifying prose of pornography. Such reminders are underscored by the decontextualization of this passage, the fact that the narrator and her sexual partner remain entirely anonymous to the reader: their sexual activity does not figure as a narrative consummation, an act preceded by any sequences and stages of prior experience, save the trivial frustration of standing in a supermarket checkout line. Without depictions of character with which to identify, the reader encounters the language of pornography stripped of any motivation. The objectifying character of such language becomes increasingly apparent in the awkwardly obtrusive and preposterous tropes that lard the writing: "I too am pressing to achieve our impossible transpenetration, with the drawbridge of his tongue crossing my murky moat, or like a Soyuz mission docking in space, with two weightless craft meeting in the empty blackness of orbit" (230). Such risible disparities of scale serve as a grotesque means by which to lay bare the character of this quasi-pornographic idiom. Instead of continuing in the feverishly erotic vein to yet more consummations and thrilled unities, the cumbrous, unstable imagery leads abruptly into a troubled reflection on the social significance of pictures in "garish magazines" (230). As usual, the transition between these passages is seamless, and so the reader cannot help but read them off against each other, the euphoric eroticism of the first disturbingly yoked to the angry criticism of a culture of surfaces, of advertising imagery, in the second. Hence, the celebration of self-healing through sexual activity runs up against an indictment of the cycle of identification, complicity, anxiety, and shame by which advertising imagery and celebrity culture operate. Scanning magazines at a newsstand, she (perhaps the same speaker, perhaps not) comes to the conclusion that "despite their seeming diversity and uncontrollable multiplicity, it was clear that virtually all of them were saying the same things, precisely the same things: *come into the world of lies, of distortions and inessentialities; learn to feel inadequate, and to be ashamed of what you are; accept the power of others to form, to shape, to determine your preferences, your thoughts, your hidden enclaves*" (232). To read this after the passage concerning the lovemaking couple causes one to reconsider the conditions of that "hidden enclave" of intimacy, and perhaps also to question further the language through which such intimacy is established; after all, the effects of pornography cannot be limited to titillation or erotic gratification, but may very well also include feelings of shame, inadequacy, and revulsion.

Consumer images in this novel extort the wholesale reconstruction of identity. The image for such reconstruction involves the refashioning of the body. The complicitous yet shaming relationship established between individuals and the rampant consumer imagery that surrounds them works through a continual abjection of identity through assertion of superior identity images: "internalize the master myth, specifically in order to feel excluded from it; realize that you are a nothing—a cipher, a target, a marketing opportunity, a connable and dupable marketing opportunity, but ultimately a nothing, entirely a nothing; learn to hate yourself, while always remembering that the hater is a nothing" (232). Even to find messages of self-loathing in the blandishments of consumer culture— "death-messages in the motley light" (233)—becomes, perversely, an additional source of self-disgust, as if the process of abjection must always be reapplied to the self, rather than the nagging vacuity in the messages under scrutiny. Thus the advertising imagery not only makes its target feel ashamed, because he or she cannot live up to the depicted perfection, but also makes her ashamed of feeling ashamed, of finding falsehood in bright images of happiness, sexiness, fulfillment. If indeed these consumer fantasies are the only available images of satisfaction available, then satisfaction becomes an irremediable itch of difference, an aspired-to falsehood.

Dara's speaker finds herself (or himself, since subsequent details indicate that the speaker, by this point, is now male) obliged to recognize that she is a creature of negativity, cast by the mechanisms of consumer desire—and the spiral of self-disgust they generate—into a critical role: "it hurt . . . to be punished for being right, to be scorched for seeing through and seeing right; in other words, no longer was I a daughter of light: I had become, definitively, the product of shadows, finding darkness where human eyes only registered brightness" (233). The text's voice continues by explaining how she or now he suffers shaming inadequacy from the gaze of others, and in consequence adopts a strategy of mentally banishing unsatisfactory body parts. So, for example, "a young woman of perhaps 21 noticed the thinness, and perhaps the paleness, of my calves as I sat on a towel by the side of Carys Lake, so I got rid of them, putting them in my head" (235). The conclusion of the various mental acts of exile is that the individual achieves a desired invisibility of many and various portions of the body.

This internalized bodily fragmentation, the slicing and dicing of the corporeal image, corresponds in the novel to the motif of bodies constructed in a nonorganic, additive fashion. The passages concerning the various dissatisfactions and drastic remedies stemming from images of bodies circulating in the culture are prefigured by an episode involving a woman who works in the information technology industry. Prompted by an anecdote about a television miniseries concerning a little girl stricken with leukemia—as she wryly notes, "an incorrigible tear-jerker, one of those malady-of-the-month offerings" (189), the woman is dismayed to discover that her reaction to the program has been exactly the same as that of her coworkers. This is hardly surprising, of course, given the manipulative nature of the program in question, but it causes her to reflect on the way in which the words of others inhabit her thoughts:

> all of my words, upon the slightest inspection, seem so foreign to me, so much the work of others; and so I wonder how I can claim that anything that occurs in my consciousness is mine, and not the product of some otherness; often I feel that I am not thinking so much as eavesdropping on my own thoughts, listening in on a narrative being told between othernesses—that it is the otherness thinking; (190)

This insight into the conditions of her speech and thought derives from that hopeless desire to establish an enclave of unconditioned selfhood. Yet she is caught at the point of realizing that her own attempts to express herself, to find words for her inmost feelings, serve at the same moment to open her up to socially recognizable and socially produced idioms: "even my words for articulating my sadness are only an embodiment of the otherness expressing sadness, are part of its system, this Möbius culture, and so further confirmation of its dominion" (191). The figure of the Möbius strip indexes her condition with particular accuracy: the further she presses toward some private expression of her own inner states, the more she finds herself opening to otherness. Ironically, this speaker declares a dedication to finding "an absolutely personal mode of sadness" (191), but facing the difficulty this entails she adopts the third person, going so far as to switch to "*he*, the masculine, the form that is even more generic" (191). What marches forth in her fantasy is the pronoun *he* as the quintessential 1980s yuppy, a figure constructed primarily out of brand names: "He taps on aftershave and feels its cedar-y acerbity frost His nose; He paints Ban under His left arm, His right arm; He holds His arms outward-elevated until the pit-chill abates, until He has received the all-dry; from His armoire He withdraws a pastel blue Lauren shirt, then unclosets a deep blue Paul Smith suit, with silvery pinstripes" (191). The experiment in the construction of an identity through a ritualized performance of lustrous quotidiana ends, disconcertingly, with the "He" revealing his identity in another seamless transition as an attorney for a tobacco company.

This is the fragmentary body sutured by automatic movements, less a whole figural of a coherent informing subject, than a series of actions that, so to speak, perform themselves in the absence of a controlling or thoughtful consciousness. Certainly, this provides a fitting image for the moral void one might expect of such a target of satire; it also suggests that the fragmenting, the slicing and dicing operations of the consumer imaginary, its vast repertoire of images of perfection of physique and deportment, can also, as though through prosthesis, construct new persons. The tobacco company attorney exemplifies this false continuity, by which discrete pieces—body-parts, items of clothing, cosmetics—and successive actions comprise a person; it is a pervasive falsehood with a political twist, since the reader is reminded, much earlier in the novel, of President Reagan, referred to as "this assemblage of hearing aids and contact lenses and Grecian formula and shoulder pads" (61). This metonymic association emphasizes that the compound persons of consumer culture are brought into being during a specific political era. Thus, the novel traces the divisive effects of consumerism deep into the emotional and corporeal lives of its speakers, while using fragmentation and the splicing of separate, otherwise unrelated elements, to protest against the reign of the commodity.

The Slice-'N'-Dice Cartel

The manifold and mercurial cluster of images that fill the teenager's head at the beginning of *The Lost Scrapbook* points the reader to a preoccupation that lies at the heart of the novel—the split between self-determination and recognition that is central to the question of community. The implications of this split can be better assessed—and rendered less abstract— by turning to the somewhat extreme example of nonrecognition and disempowerment that the teenager offers in recounting a gas station stick up during which he was briefly taken hostage. During this incident, he had a hand clamped over his mouth and the muzzle of a pistol thrust against the side of his head, but was unable to see the face of his assailant. This is the novel's nightmare extreme of objectification and powerlessness, and it resonates in ever-widening circles as the book goes on. Probably the most arresting recapitulation of this scenario comes in the middle of the novel, when a character gives herself over to imagining a scenario of terrifying disempowerment, conjuring up—or does this really happen?— images and voices from some kind of thinly specified hostage crisis, wherein anguished victims are forced to the floor at gunpoint by a group of attackers who can be seen only as kicking and stomping boots.

Here the situation of powerlessness is suffered by a group of people, treated indifferently as impersonal, objectified aggregates—hostages, victims of organized mass murder, deportees, all are suggested by the decontextualized voices—yet this scenario prefigures the much more involved and subtle instances of powerlessness arising from the discovery of toxic spillages into the environment of the small Missouri town of Isaura. Although the voices of the townsfolk eventually come together in choric protest against the polluter, the chemicals giant Ozark, their attitude to their disempowerment is much more ambivalent than that of the unspecified victims. They are subject to the emollient languages of advertising and official denial, the misleading recitation of figures and regulations, but more importantly to the long-established paternalism attendant on the corporation's presence in their town, or perhaps better still maternalism—"Mother Ozark is how people put it around here, and that's how I feel; I have a guardian, a protectress, someone who is concerned for me" (333). And, as one unidentified speaker remarks, "they've *always* been here, ever since there was an Isaura; Isaura *grew up* with the company, they put us on the *map* . . . for 108 years they've been the ocean for us fish, they've been the town and the town's been them" (338). The corporation's damage-control strategy, relayed by townsfolk present at a meeting with the Ozark executives and scientists, plays on this sense of inseparability:

> —Because for us at Ozark, all of this is a sound investment, I heard him say: an investment in the long-term stability of our community—
> —Because we are with you in this, I heard him say: we are a part of you—
> —Indeed, we are you, I heard him say: there is no separation— (375)

The Ozark officials adopt the rhetoric of community, of belonging, togetherness, shared history, stability, care, and concern. Such a rhetoric co-opts genuine anxieties, even making use of what would, on the face of it, be an ecological and political argument:

> —In everything you do, and in everything you see, there is an inescapable base in chemicals, I heard him say—
> —They are in what we produce and what you buy, I heard him say—
> —Therefore, the situation that exists is societal in scope, and the mechanisms for responding to it must reflect its societal nature, I heard him say—
> —So there is no getting around the fact that all of us—*all* of us—are in this together, I heard him say— (388)

Fobel, the company executive whose remarks are reported here, strikes this ecologically aware note as a way to avail himself of the sense of powerlessness, resignation, and anger that the townsfolk cannot but feel when faced with the inconclusive findings of the toxicologists. Carcinogens do indeed pervade the environment, but this assertion is so broad in scope that it shields the particular corporation from liability, and is used along with a number of other argumentative strategies—including a focus on minute particulars, misleading comparisons, and preemptive assertions of victimhood ("what's going on here is a kind of chemical McCarthyism" [396])—in order to shift the burden of responsibility away from Ozark. The company executives use a language of community as a way of making the properly anxious townsfolk feel that they are attacking themselves, attacking Isaura itself. Such rhetoric operates in tandem with a statistical image of the identity of Isaura that is more susceptible to division and evasion, and thus conspicuously useful to the Ozark executives as a way of escaping blame. The executives co-opt the kind of thinking that any protest against the fundamental conditions of a pathological social order urgently needs—an understanding of the systemic nature of the wrongs perpetrated by big business, by capitalism as a whole social order.

In their devious use of statistics, the Ozark executives avail themselves of what a voice earlier in the book describes as "our great cultural project, the perceptual imperative laid down by the whole Democritus/ Descartes/ Leibniz slice-'n'-dice cartel" (276). Dara links this "perceptual imperative" to the social diremption that he traces and dramatizes throughout the book, the slicing and dicing of the social body, and its consequences in powerlessness, isolation, and fragmentation. The novel finds an idiom and a set of metaphors in offshoots of this "great cultural project" to understand and protest against it. Throughout *The Lost Scrapbook*, the reader encounters slicing and dicing, in both the human and natural sciences, as a means by which waves, otherwise continuous social and physical processes, are divided into particles. The metaphor of particle and wave in quantum theory suggests that observation plays a key role in the seeming opposition, a point signaled by the novel's frequent mentions of Heisenberg. Electrons are neither particles nor waves, but sometimes behave as the former and sometimes as the latter. Heisenberg showed that it wasn't possible to measure both particle and wave properties simultaneously; indeed, the more the observer knows about how the particles behave, the less she knows about the waves. Furthermore, to pursue experiments on properties of subatomic particles/waves interferes with the situation under study, not least because experiments concerned with location or momentum are conceived within the framework of classical rather than new physics. Electrons have both the properties of particles and waves, but these properties cannot be measured simultaneously.

This situation functions as an analogy for the problem of social knowledge with which the novel engages: the retreat into internal exile as a way of resisting the pressures of social objectification (hypostatic roles and functions, and statistical identification) has the unfortunate consequence of separating and so disempowering the exiles, rendering them social particles. The extremes of disempowerment involve the reduction of individuals to the status of hostages, those held purely for their exchange values in a quantitative trade-off. But the novel's characters and its form both raise a utopian protest in favor of joining up atomized particles into waves, linking particular desires into collective articulation. The novel's two epigraphs capture the urgency and the implicit difficulty involved. The first is a citation from Kierkegaard: "To honor every man, absolutely every man, is the truth." The second is taken from Shakespeare's *Titus Andronicus* (V, iii):

> O let me teach you how to knit again
> This scattered corn into one mutual sheaf,
> These broken limbs into one body;

The paired epigraphs mark in their duality the novel's attempt to cope with the tension between autonomy and solidarity. While the voices on occasion strongly express a desire to knit their scattered purposes into a collective social being, this utopian longing is felt most frequently as an absence, particularly in so far as the novel tracks in detail the efforts of characters to secure an always-imperiled autonomy.

In seeing the parallels between the dilemmas that the teenager—and others—face in their divided social being, and the catastrophic situation with which the residents of Isaura grapple, the novel encourages the reader to understand that fragmented social knowledge is a political issue. If the problems of social division are couched in terms of community, Dara nonetheless resists the temptation to showcase organic communities vulnerable to the depredations of corporations and social rule. Community remains a rhetorical term, catalyzed by immediate need: the people of Isaura find themselves unable to think about themselves as a community without reference to Ozark, while Ozark executives deploy a language of community in an effort to win over hearts and minds so as to protect their economic interests. The involvement of the Ozark corporation in the life of Isaura runs through the town from top to bottom, standing in the way of solidarity, of effective, wavelike connections between individual particles, whose interests are in many cases internally conflicted.

Communication and Utopia

In Dara's novel channels of communication remain central to questions of sociality and resistance. This is not a novel in which moments of recognition or understanding on the part of individual characters provide narrative resolution to intractable social and political problems. On the contrary, attempts to establish communication, both in personal and intimate situations and in matters of public and political urgency, are fundamental to the book, and frequently subject to interruption and breakdown. The movement from particles to waves is a movement made possible—and thwarted—through channels of communication.

Dara's prototypical example of such successful linkage between otherwise isolated individuals is the lost scrapbook of the title. Mentioned several times amid the rich disorder of the novel, the scrapbook forms a place in the text where its otherwise disjunctive fragments overlap. The book, now no more than a memory, was fashioned by a Welsh immigrant during the depression. After the failure of a utopian community that he came to America to establish, he traveled among small towns in the Midwest weaving local narratives into songs and compiling a scrapbook of incidents and encounters. The move from utopian community to scrapbook signals a shift from the political and social to the cultural, yet the book, recalled as a large, raggedy bundle, serves an important function in recording as useful local knowledge the unofficial histories of ordinary Midwesterners, and serves as a promise of a counterpublic form of communication. By counterpublic, I mean in this context an oppositional space of dialogue and the exchange of information, a medium that exists outside the hegemonic, corporate-controlled networks—radio, television, and the like.[6] As the compiler's granddaughter recalls, "the book seemed alive, just like he was, gathering experiences, it was evolving along with him in no obviously planned or predetermined way—but all of it was still a direct reflection of *him*, you know, of his essence" (45). The scrapbook, then, is a biomorphic embodiment of unofficial communication, the trace of lived history and shared concern, and thus the antitype of the fragmented and atomized communities—the failed communities—of the novel's present.

This emblematic missing object reverberates as an absence, a vanished promise, in the 1980s and 1990s of *The Lost Scrapbook*. The example of the scrapbook and its compiler, the wandering figure, a compound historian, folksinger and archivist, an "American griot" (70) as he is described by his granddaughter, contrasts with the myriad instances of failed communication that characterize many of the novel's episodes. This is a contrast founded on the difference between modes of communication, between the face-to-face relations established by the walking oral historian in his travels among the towns of the Midwest, and the telecommunications of the present. While a longing for immediacy haunts this distinction, as the desire for connections mediated directly by persons in contradistinction to the communications from afar of the mediascape, the novel's formal and thematic commitment to complex systems, as well as its many trenchant instances of communication breakdown, mitigates the charge of nostalgia. The difference between "communication with and communication at" (52) remains of political urgency for the novel; and it is to Dara's credit that he continually reemphasizes the distinction through failures of comprehension, thwarted attempts to communicate. Typical are one-sided conversations, frustrated inner-monologues, reports of behavior that baffles the onlooker, obsessional disquisitions on arcane matters, and the asymmetrical exchanges of commercial culture. In one episode, for example, an alarmed mother tries to call 911 when her baby falls sick, only to find that she cannot get past the electronic sales voice on which she had hung up a half hour earlier. Such striking structural inequalities are treated to an explicitly political twist in a lengthy anecdote about a trip Noam Chomsky makes to Washington, DC to appear as a panelist on the television news program "Face the Nation" in a discussion of Iran-Contra, only to be replaced at the last minute by an uncontroversial guest. His assistant, who narrates the events in a letter, rages: "for a moment there, just for a moment, we thought that we had found a chink in the armor—we actually thought that we had been given an opportunity—a smidgen of a chance—but the structure, as always, is self-correcting—it has protected itself with layers of subsidiary defenses—ranks of backup SDI's—noise-gates against the dreaded biodiversity" (291). The corporate voice armored against other viewpoints, whether through sheer mechanical blockage, or through the sophisticated feedback mechanisms of the media industry, characterizes the nature of the media sphere.

The net effect of such communicational asymmetry is to reinforce social atomization. One of the novel's most important motifs of this atomization is the personal stereo—the Walkman. At first sight, this might seem simply a satirical swipe at a favorite gadget of the 1980s. And the reader might even be dimly and uncomfortably reminded of another success story of 1980s popular culture, Allan Bloom's best-selling neoconservative jeremiad, *The Closing of the American Mind*.[7] Bloom saves one the trouble of actually reading his book by encapsulating its argument in his subtitle: "How Higher Education Has Failed Democracy and Impoverished the Souls of Today's Students" (1987). But those who took the trouble to investigate further, would have come across this notorious but hardly atypical passage: "Picture a thirteen-year-old boy sitting in the living room of his family home doing his math assignment while wearing his Walkman headphones. . . . He enjoys the liberties hard won over centuries by the alliance of philosophic genius and political heroism. . . . And in what does progress culminate? A pubescent child whose body throbs with orgasmic rhythms. . . . In short, life is made into a nonstop, commercially prepackaged masturbational fantasy" (74–75). Bloom's febrile prose hardly needs additional commentary; suffice to say that this emblematic teenager embodies in his person a lurid Spenglerian fantasy in which the Enlightenment splutters out in consumerist onanism. Bloom's idealist purification of the Enlightenment fits all too snugly with his degradation of the young consumer, who bypasses the brain for direct corporeal input of popular music. By contrast, Dara's characters use their personal stereos in ways that suggest both the limitations and possibilities of the device, sounding out its social meaning rather than using it to illustrate a grand narrative of decline.

As already noted, the teenager with whom the novel opens uses his Walkman as a way to apply implicit cultural commentary to his social estrangement. His tape of Philip Glass's "The Photographer" offers a way of thinking about his internal exile, caught as he is between privative isolation and social abstraction. Such insights are achieved with the assistance of the Walkman, even as his use of the device reinforces internal exile, shutting out the world's noise in favor of a chosen soundtrack to reality. In attaining his perceptions of the streaming urban traffic, the teenager establishes a figure/ground relationship to his environment that is at once the possibility of understanding wave-like connections and the condition of greater isolation. An extended fantasy that occupies more than a hundred pages in the first part of the novel imagines a way beyond such dilemmas. The host of a talk radio show, hoping for a call from a listener, dwindles into silence, the white space of the page, whereupon a new voice, a more direct, insinuating address, begins to speak. This voice, which delivers utterances that float in the void of dispersed spatialization, as if the noise of human exchanges that constitutes reality in this novel can finally be reduced to pure signal, a static-free message that passes directly between text and reader. The novel, that is, foregrounds a fantasy of unmediated communication, of meaning passing from voice to ear, from one mind to another, a perfected "concatenation of heads" (82). This voice explains itself as a pirate radio signal broadcast directly into personal stereos:

> . . . But don't bother looking at your machine, hanging from your belt . . .
> . . . and don't waste your time pushing buttons . . .
> . . . Pause, or Stop . . .
> . . . or even Eject . . .

. . . Because I will still be here . . .
. . . And you will still be there . . .

. . . There—where, by now, you have stopped what you were doing . . .
. . . what you were trying to *absent* yourself from . . .

. . . walking to the magazine shop . . .
. . . sitting in the curved, cheek-friendly chair in the Trailways waiting
    room . . .
. . . collating photocopies . . .
. . . skimming an undernourishing book . . . (76–77)

These moments of distraction, moments from which the attention is
withdrawn, are like the troughs between peaks of some more compelling
work or leisure activity, and in this they resemble the shadowy interstices
between discrete points that only an attention to the continuous, or
wavelike, can truly comprehend and redeem.

The novel thematically and formally attempts to include ground
along with figure, background with foreground, missing material along
with reified foci of attention. This is the aim of several of the characters
in the novel and the subject of some of their most urgent concerns.
Consider, for example, the woman who tries to come to an understanding
of voting patterns that would include those who choose not to vote; the
animator who works at "filling-in" the stages of a process of cellular division
broken down into discrete images that will eventually be used in a science
documentary; the musicologist whose enthusiasm for the eccentric
American composer Harry Partch is such that he cannot stop himself
delivering an impromptu lecture even when being questioned by a traffic
cop, explaining to his increasingly infuriated listener how Partch sought
to fill in the interstitial musical tones neglected by the Western 12-tone
scale (261). These characters are exemplary in their attention to the
neglected spaces, to the continuities that truly lie between abstracted and
discrete instances, be they votes, images, or musical notes. The novel's
variational accumulation of instances makes of all these quests analogues
for a communicational space that will allow unofficial, unheard voices
their say. Such is the novel's imaginary, its utopian horizon, both in self-
description and in cultural politics—a counterpublic in which the disunited
concerns of isolated individuals, the novel's many internal exiles, will be
gathered together into a polyvocal space of meaningful attention and
exchange.

The pirate radio for personal stereos, punningly described as a
"freebooter . . . made for Walkmen" (81), broadcasts messages of comic
subversion to those in "internal exile" (86). The transmission begins
with jokes about the pathological effects of advertising and the loss of

meaning endemic to language use, sly commentaries on matters of serious concern to the novel, but then turns to an extended anecdote about the need to test the broadcasting system. To do this, the speaker records his own voice reading from an instruction manual onto a looped tape, and drives down the highway listening to the signal. This journey takes an odd turn when he meets an eccentric mycologist who launches into a diatribe against monotheism, all the while searching for a particular fungus resembling the face of the composer John Cage (who might be added to the list of the book's admired but marginal cultural producers). In swerving off from his main task, the speaker breaks the circular redundancy of listening to his own voice repeating the same message over and over again. The final pages of this section are ironized by the sense that none of the supposed listeners are in fact listening, and that even the speaker has been cut off from his own words. The plug on the involuted and failed counterpublic is pulled, the speaker speculates, by the corporation that made the tape device on which he recorded his voice in the first place, a built-in limit to the possibilities represented by this reclamation of the airwaves. Such short-circuiting of the possibilities of alternative forms of communication and community exemplifies the novel's cultural diagnosis, which refuses to find in the activities of its artist figures any space outside the dominant grids of flawed communication.

The arc of the novel extends from instances of isolation, in which the dynamics of communication are tested against the constraining conditions of contemporary culture, to voices sounding together in choric protest around the trauma afflicting Isaura. This choric protest, marshaled through town meetings, fliers, and radio interviews, and spurred on by the stream of damaging reports and damage-control responses coming through the official channels of the media, sounds out shared concerns and anxieties at the moment that the community of Isaura is literally disintegrating. As rumors circulate about the toxic spillages, the town divides into groups defending and attacking Ozark; it also breaks up along physical lines, as certain neighborhoods are perceived to be contaminated (a dry cleaner, for example, refuses to accept clothes from people living in the poisoned neighborhoods). Community cannot be seen as a given, a shared set of beliefs and concerns, a common history, but must be conceived instead in relation to power. While some of the townsfolk mobilize to acquire better information and to publicize their struggle, others put their faith in Ozark, playing out the scenario of disempowerment imagined in the book's hostage situations: "it's almost as if our community is experiencing some kind of mass Stockholm syndrome" (452). The novel's shift from the fragmented and sequential presentation of individuated (if not fully identifiable) voices telling various unconnected stories to the presentation of an unfolding narrative told in many scarcely individuated voices emphasizes the desire to reconstitute community, even as it stresses the inadequacy of available fictions of community.

Such unity as Isaura has in the last section of the novel, it acquires through its subjection to the workings of corporations, legal cases, and government agencies. The voices of the townsfolk are finally no more than receptacles for the official voices, the italicized quotations from the press, radio, and television by which their story is told, their own words reduced to variants of "I read," "I heard him say," and "I saw" (455–470). The exceptionally ambivalent final pages of the novel reconstitute the shattered voices in the image of waves, as the town of Isaura is evacuated and taken over by the Federal Emergency Management Agency and the inhabitants drive off in wavelike convoys of cars. Yet the sufferings of Isaura, and in particular a legal strategy adopted by one of the active campaigners of taking out a lawsuit against Ozark on behalf of a damaged oak tree, attract in turn a wavelike influx of letters from all over the United States: "continuous arcs of fluttering white streaming through the air and into an address on Wheatland Street, to a tree at an address on Wheatland Street, from wherever they came they were addressed to a tree on Wheatland Street, and when eventually they were opened, when some of the letters were opened, all the letters, all read like confessionals, they seemed confessionals, an abundant and endless outpouring of confessionals" (474). This passage implicitly connects the nostalgic but desirable image of the lost scrapbook, a space of popular, unofficial exchange and history, to the counterpublic imaginary of the novel. As the community of Isaura is destroyed, becoming a symbol of environmental disaster, the oak tree on Wheatland street becomes the focal point for a spatially and socially dispersed sense of anguish and concern.

The Lost Scrapbook ends by drawing the tension between oppressive and expressive movements to breaking point. On the one hand, disem- powerment resulting from the destructive acts of the Ozark corporation and the government's belated intervention literalizes the metaphor of internal exile applied by so many of the speakers to themselves—the people of Isaura are abruptly forced out of their homes, perhaps permanently, and sent elsewhere, possibly with appalling health problems in their future. On the other hand, the "trauma-kindred" (474) are drawn into a powerful identification with the polluted town, and its emblematic tree; their own damaged lives become the subject of this traumatic occasion for expression, for a noninstrumental communication. The very last words of the novel sustain this tension: the letters keep flowing in to Isaura, but "just as envelopes, the letters were only envelopes, and the letters that were not in the envelopes said Race of Samsons Race of Samsons where else could this end?" (475). The reconfiguration of these paradoxically present and absent letters as jeremiads, a "sub-banal recounting of cliché upon cliché" (475), as the scarcely locatable narrator quickly and harshly says, represents a trajectory of language that passes beyond "catcalls of misplaced Millenarianism" (476) to the paradoxical continuity of silence. This silence, as already suggested, is simply cessation, text giving way to blank paper, a conclusive refusal to conclude; or the period and additional word ("silence, yes silence: silence. Silence" [476]) imply that the text wraps around to rejoin its flow on the first page.

Both possibilities satisfy the necessity of ending the text without compromising its commitment to the continuous, yet the suggestion that the novel loops round on itself invites the further speculation that the confessional letters that pour into Isaura in fact constitute the novel the reader has just finished. In this line of argument, the book is structured as a Möbius strip: its collage or scrapbook form includes within it the (imaginary) conditions of its own production. To read the novel in this way is to see it as the embodiment of a knowledge that remains immanent within it, a knowledge constituted precisely through the overcoming of social divisions of knowledge: the internal exiles speak with each other within the body of the text, even as they express their disaffection and estrangement from their curtailed and divided social environment. And as such, *The Lost Scrapbook* offers itself, quite remarkably, as a utopian promise in an age seemingly devoid of all utopias.

Epilogue

In imagining a "trauma-kindred" community that convenes around ecological disaster, Evan Dara constructs a political vision that Ulrich Beck, the German social theorist, would immediately recognize. In Beck's theory of "risk society" the catastrophes that emerge from the increasingly destructive nature of modernity form the basis for a new politics based on the response to shared dangers.[1] Since the events of September 11, 2001, the new imperialist rhetoric of universal justice and preemptive strikes has borne a superficial, but entirely misleading resemblance to ideas of a global public sphere founded on an awareness of collective dangers. Instead, as quickly became apparent, grief, trauma, and fear have been mobilized in the United States for an aggressive policy of *pax americana*.

The traumatized state of the nation has even impinged—how could it not?—on the world of letters. Poets from across the United States and around the world took up the task of elegizing the victims of the terrorist attacks and protesting the American response. Fiction, of course, emerges much more slowly, though it seems highly likely that many novels will find ways to address the events of 9/11 and after. How writers choose to write about terrorism and "the war on terror" is as much a political as an aesthetic question. As early as October 5, 2001, James Wood, the widely published critic, mused in *The Guardian* newspaper about the impact the events of 9/11 would have on the literary novel, and took the opportunity to denounce the postmodernist current in American fiction.[2] Wood singled out for particular criticism Don DeLillo, Richard Powers, and Jonathan Franzen, all of whom, he claimed, were bent on writing "novels of immense self-consciousness with no selves in them at all, curiously arrested and very 'brilliant' books that know a thousand things but do not know a single human being." All this, he averred, was likely to change after 9/11:

> But this idea—that the novelist's task is to go on to the street and fig-
> ure out social reality—may well have been altered by the events of
> September 11, merely through the reminder that whatever the novel gets
> up to, the "culture" can always get up to something bigger. Ashes defeat

garlands. If topicality, relevance, reportage, social comment, preachy presentism, and sidewalk-smarts—in short, the contemporary American novel in its current, triumphalist form—are novelists' chosen sport, then they will sooner or later be outrun by their own streaking material. Fiction may well be, as Stendhal wrote, a mirror carried down the middle of a road; but the Stendhalian mirror would explode with reflections were it now being walked around Manhattan.

Wood's suggestion that American reality is likely to outrun those who would try to grasp it recalls the perplexity Philip Roth confessed to forty years earlier in "Writing American Fiction." But for Roth, if not for Wood, the sheer sickening lack of the realist's common measure in reality itself did not prompt him to abandon the ambitions of the socially argumentative novel—far from it. And, indeed, one might respond that the shattered mirror is not an image of voracious realism—of social reportage poured clumsily into the novel form—but of the complex echoes, distortions, and unreliable truths of postmodernism, a kind of writing that becomes all the more necessary as consensual reality explodes. For late postmodernism, this explosion has taken many different forms, including the upheaval of cultural values traced in the first part of this book, and has encouraged the invention of new ways of engaging with a hallucinatory social reality.

In these final pages, I want to touch very briefly on two recent works of fiction—Dodie Bellamy's *Letters of Mina Harker* and William Gibson's *Pattern Recognition*[3]—that illustrate the possibilities of late postmodernism, conforming neither to the conventional prescription for the social novel, nor to the traditional novel of character recommended by Wood. Honorable as those alternatives are, the distinctive achievement of the late postmodern novel—what makes it worth reading now—lies in the way it engages with the semiotic density of the mediascape, the sign and image saturated spaces that increasingly shape public and private consciousness. Both novels are generic hybrids, and as such, neither quite occupies a position in the literary field previously accorded to the commonly accepted achievements of American fiction. This is not to say that these are minor works, scarcely worthy of attention, but to argue rather that Bellamy and Gibson belong to literary communities that are little recognized by the authoritative gatekeepers of the literary field's putative center—reviewers, indeed, of Wood's stamp. Bellamy is best known in the West Coast avant-garde of poets and playwrights, and her work circulates through readings and small press publication. Gibson's *Neuromancer* has attained canonical status, but his standing in the market of literary prestige has been colored by the perception that he is a writer of science fiction. Yet, for both writers a marginal or ambiguous position with relation to the major sources of prestige has given them a particularly valuable ex-centric perception of the possibilities of fiction, and has contributed to the invention and persuasion of their work.

The Letters of Mina Harker comprises letters written over an eight-year period (the time of the book's composition), all signed by "Mina Harker"— the female protagonist of Bram Stoker's novel *Dracula*—and addressed to a variety of correspondents, including Dr. Van Helsing (Stoker's vampire hunter), Sam (presumably Sam D'Allesandro, Bellamy's sometime collaborator), several other friends from the artistic and literary community, and even, interpolated, a missive to William Gibson. Stoker provides some of the book's characters, though Bellamy detaches them from their nineteenth-century Transylvanian and English settings, and places them in a textual space that is both highly localized—late twentieth-century San Francisco, with its movie theaters, restaurants, and apartments—and continually shifting, constructed and broken down through a slew of references to literature, popular culture, and everyday life, a dense fantasy terrain of heterogeneous elements. Thus, times and spaces are fluid, permeable, unstable, as are bodies and the affects that traverse them. The language of the novel is no less mixed; it is a fervent hybrid of allusion, obscenity, and lyricism—and, after all, "[w]ho hasn't felt like a hybrid in times of stress" (37)?

This stress plays out in the highly sexualized gothic tenor of the text, a gamut of mingled bodily fluids, vampiric yearning, and erotic possession, making explicit what was there in Stoker all along. Bellamy's erotico-gothic idiom situates the body in scenes of power, subjection, and transgression, whether mediated by pop cultural spectacles or the dynamics and limitations of the text itself. The characters, living and undead, collide on tormented paths of desire, never seeming to attain satiety, or textual closure. Bellamy elaborates the analogies between body and text with extraordinary persistence and versatility, making of the wounded and desirous Mina an embodiment of the novel's own divagations, always pressing toward fulfillment, while refusing the deathly reified stasis fulfillment implies:

> Disturbed by sensations I seduce myself with objects, seeking the shattering of Mina and a subsequent re-establishment of borders, making repetition possible *an ecosystem an environment of collected pieces* thus do I vampirize the world, endlessly searching out new metaphors upon which to displace the energy of primary repression, the realization of Mina as Other. (207)

Thus the text generates and displaces its avatars in a restless, insistently physical becoming, crossing boundaries of one sort and another—linguistic, generic, corporeal—while recognizing, with anguish and delight, that the boundaries reconstitute themselves in new configurations.

The social contexts for Bellamy's fierce and inventive refusal of boundaries are the politics of gender and the continuing catastrophe of AIDS, but the novel's wild generic mixing, prodigious use of intertexts of every kind, and relentless examination of textual dynamics make *The Letters of Mina Harker* a striking illustration of the possibilities of the postmodern novel. Bellamy's work can be likened to the fiction of other contemporary experimental writers such as Kathy Acker, Robert Glück, and Lauren Fairbanks, all of whom have rewritten, subverted, defaced, and pilfered literary classics.[4] In addition, her tropes of possession and parasitism, as well as her scandalous textuality, recall the work of William Burroughs, one of the great progenitors of postmodernism. This aesthetics of rewriting and possession, as Bellamy demonstrates, involves a dynamic of power, a perpetual oscillation between aggression and subjection to the voices of others—other texts and other facets of subjectivity. Authorship, like selfhood, is impure, a subversion of propriety and property rights; not for Bellamy the transcendent vantage of the cultural commentator, who situates him- or herself above the fray, but a messy, collusive, and unstable position, conditioned by desire and disgust.

Bellamy's allusions to William Gibson suggest how postmodern authorship can be envisaged as a type of the relation between the subject and technoculture. Mina describes Gibson's cyberspace as a "metaphor for desire and longing" (79). As such, she emphasizes the imbrication of the psyche and technology, a point borne out in *Pattern Recognition*, with its propulsive libidinal energies, notably trauma, hermeneutic desire, and attraction to and repulsion from the surfaces of consumer culture. Desire and congruent revulsion are played out across the increasingly interwoven semiotic spaces of the Internet and the material world.

Pattern Recognition, written in the period straddling 9/11 and incorporating the destruction of the World Trade Center into its narrative, offers a thought-provoking glimpse of the novel's vocation in this new cultural moment. Gibson revises both his own 1984 novel *Neuromancer* (the originary text of cyberpunk, the book in which he coined the term "cyberspace") and Pynchon's *Crying of Lot 49.*[5] The convoluted plot of *Pattern Recognition*—the title hints at Gibson's updating of Pynchonian paranoia, itself a kind of dread-filled pattern recognition—turns around the appearance of a fragmentary film on the World Wide Web, the pieces of which become the object of a quest pursued by venture capitalists and countercultural web-heads (the descendants of *Neuromancer*'s hackers). The book's achievement lies in its attention to the minute surfaces of late capitalism, to the forms of sociality constituted in and through brand names, technologies, and simulated forms of nostalgia.

In particular, the novel offers an intriguing montage of two very different images of history: on the one hand, the film segments watched avidly and discussed obsessively by a virtual community of followers on the web is something like a Jamesonian nostalgia movie[6]—it evokes an earlier era while also remaining highly contemporary; on the other, there is the horrifying excavation into the site of a World War II atrocity in the former Soviet Union—the fragments of human bodies disturbingly double the ruins of the World Trade Center. These are the two hemispheres of history in the postmodern era. The segments of the film evoke an earlier historical period, a stylized mid-twentieth century, and seem to hint at a love story of some kind, but they also appeal in part because the images are seemingly devoid of recognizable brand names or commodities (the two are synonymous in Gibson's novel). Hence, the "footage," as it is known, at once simulates history and seems to promise a place outside it, a utopia cleansed of all traces of the commodity, a possibility the novel immediately ironizes, since the film becomes the most desirable commodity of all. By contrast, the body-fragments that signify the trauma of real history, whether the nightmare of World War II or the horror of 9/11, cannot be integrated into public or private memory, certainly not through consumption, the major force of social cohesion in the novel.

The only place the two figures of history—the nostalgia-commodity and the traumatic remnant—come together is in the person of the film's creator. As it turns out, the filmmaker herself, the victim of an earlier terrorist incident, crafts her spellbinding images precisely because her brain's hemispheres have become detached from each other. Her film is an exemplary late postmodern work of art, caught in the acute division between commodity and utopia, participating in both. There is apparently no way to resolve this division. And, indeed, one of the novel's most arresting tropes is that of the brand name phobia to which the central character, Cayce Pollard, is subject. She experiences the desire to be free of the logo-ridden surfaces of the thoroughly commodified social space as a physiological necessity.[7] But at the same time, she depends on the relentless tendency of the commodity to colonize every remaining space of social life; she works, after all, as a "cool hunter," a corporate scout for new trends at street level that can be transformed into consumer goods. The novel, like Cayce herself, can do no more than register the divergent forces that make the present so hard to comprehend.

In such a context, pleas for the restoration of the cultural authority of the novelist seem beside the point. Yet, the novel is not rendered irrelevant or left exhausted. The recent work of Bellamy and Gibson demonstrates that fiction can exploit, for reasons of cognitive power and affective intensity, the intricate relays of commodity, image, fantasy, and sociality that comprise public and private dimensions of experience. While there are good reasons to deplore the absence of a sufficient public discourse around literature, or ideas and artistic activity in general, the construction of partial counterpublics, using the available resources of publicity and communication, including those made available by the new media, is an urgent task, one that should not be set aside out of despair or nostalgia. Writers and critics can embrace the challenges and possibilities that this task entails, and so transform their function and their media. Late postmodernism, for all the dark prognostications that accompany it, shows many signs—obscure, puzzling, and contradictory signs—of a transformation now underway. And if writers of fiction can be fully and imaginatively responsive to such changes, it may turn out that the novel has something to say to us after all.

Notes

Introduction

1. See, e.g., Christopher Norris, *What's Wrong with Postmodernism: Critical Theory and the Ends of Philosophy* (Baltimore, MD: Johns Hopkins University Press, 1990); Alex Callinicos, *Against Postmodernism: A Marxist Critique* (New York: St. Martin's Press, 1990); Terry Eagleton, *The Illusions of Postmodernism* (Oxford: Blackwell, 1996).
2. *Time and Commodity Culture: Essays in Cultural Theory and Postmodernity* (Oxford: Oxford University Press, 1997), pp. 13–63.
3. *Critical Social Theory: Culture, History, and the Challenge of Difference* (Oxford: Blackwell, 1995), pp. 99–100.
4. See the essay "Rewriting Modernity," in Jean-François Lyotard, *The Inhuman: Reflections on Time*, trans. by Geoffrey Bennington and Rachel Bowlby (Stanford, CA: Stanford University Press, 1991), pp. 24–35.
5. *The Illusions of Postmodernism*, passim.
6. See, e.g., Daniel Bell, *The Coming of Post-Industrial Society: A Venture in Social Forecasting* (New York: Basic, 1973).
7. "Foreword" to Jean-François Lyotard, *The Postmodern Condition: A Report on Knowledge*, trans. by Geoff Bennington and Brian Massumi (Minneapolis: University of Minnesota Press, 1984), p. xiii.
8. My use of the term "literary field" derives from the work of the French sociologist Pierre Bourdieu, who writes, "The literary field (one may also speak of the artistic field, the philosophical field, etc.) is an independent social universe with its own laws of functioning, its specific relations of force, its dominants and dominated, and so forth. Put another way, to speak of 'field' is to recall that literary works are produced in a particular social universe endowed with particular institutions and obeying specific laws," "Field of Power, Literary Field and Habitus," in Pierre Bourdieu, *The Field of Cultural Production: Essays on Art and Literature*, ed. by Randal Johnson (New York: Columbia, 1993), p. 163.
9. See Geoffrey Green, Donald J. Greiner, and Larry McCaffery, eds., *The Vineland Papers: Critical Takes on Pynchon's Novel* (Normal, IL: Dalkey Archive, 1994); Brooke Horvath and Irving Malin, eds., *Pynchon and Mason & Dixon* (Newark: University of Delaware Press, 2000); and Charles Clerc, *Mason & Dixon & Pynchon* (Lanham, MD: University Press of America, 2000).
10. Prominent among those who have mentioned DeLillo's importance are David Foster Wallace, who refers extensively to *White Noise* in his essay "E Unibus Pluram: Television and U.S. Fiction," *A Supposedly Fun Thing*

I'll Never Do Again: Essays and Arguments (Boston: Little, Brown, 1997),
and includes allusions to DeLillo's early work, notably *End Zone* and *Ratner's
Star*, in his astonishing novel *Infinite Jest* (Boston: Little, Brown, 1996);
Jonathan Franzen has spoken of DeLillo's influence and example, and quotes
from a letter DeLillo wrote him in his essay "Perchance to Dream: In an Age
of Images, A Reason to Write Novels," *Harper's* (April 1996); DeLillo himself
has written jacket blurbs for novelists of the generation of Wallace and Franzen,
including Franzen himself, Siri Hustvedt, Dana Spiotta, Denis Johnson, and
Stephen Wright, not to mention older luminaries, such as William Gaddis,
Gilbert Sorrentino, and Paul Auster.

11. *How To Be Alone: Essays* (New York: Farrar, Straus and Giroux, 2002), p. 165.
12. *The Gutenberg Elegies: The Fate of Reading in an Electronic Age* (New York: Ballantine, 1994).
13. Richard A. Lanham, *The Electronic Word: Democracy, Technology, and the Arts* (Chicago: University of Chicago Press, 1993), pp. 195–223.
14. See Herbert Marcuse, "The Affirmative Character of Culture," *Negations: Essays in Critical Theory*, trans. by Jeremy J. Shapiro (Boston: Beacon Press, 1968), pp. 88–133.
15. *The Structural Transformation of the Public Sphere: An Inquiry into a Category of Bourgeois Society*, trans. by Thomas Burger and Frederick Lawrence (Cambrige: MIT Press, 1989). For critical assessments of Habermas's theory, see Craig Calhoun, ed., *Habermas and the Public Sphere* (Cambridge: MIT Press, 1992).
16. See Birkerts, *The Gutenberg Elegies*, esp. pp. 210–229.
17. For a celebrated account of the historical and philosophical genesis of this ideology of the subject, see C.B. Macpherson, *The Political Theory of Possessive Individualism: Hobbes to Locke* (Oxford: Oxford University Press, 1962).
18. Quoted in Franzen, "Perchance to Dream," p. 54,
19. Carole Maso, "Rupture, Verge, and Precipice: Precipice, Verge, and Hurt Not," *Review of Contemporary Fiction* 16 (Spring 1996): 54–75; rpt. in Carole Maso, *Break Every Rule: Essays on Language, Longing, and Moments of Desire* (Washington, DC: Counterpoint, 2000), pp. 161–191.
20. Evan Dara, *The Lost Scrapbook* (Normal, IL: FC2, 1995).
21. "The Literature of Exhaustion," *The Friday Book: Essays and Other Nonfiction* (New York: G.P. Putnam's, 1984), p. 72.
22. *Postmodernism, Or, The Cultural Logic of Late Capitalism* (Durham, NC: Duke University Press, 1991), p. ix.
23. Ibid., p. 1.
24. *The Origins of Postmodernity* (London: Verso, 1998), p. 102.
25. There is in fact a case to be made for Roth as a postmodern writer. Throughout his career he has made use of devices from the postmodern bag of tricks, including metafiction and ontological dubiety.

Chapter 1   Late Postmodernism and the Literary Field

1. Alex Callinicos, *An Anti-Capitalist Manifesto* (Cambridge: Polity, 2003), p. 13.
2. See Stanley Fish, "Truth But No Consequences: Why Philosophy Doesn't Matter," *Critical Inquiry* 29 (Summer 2003): 389.

3. Hal Foster, "Whatever Happened to Postmodernism?" *The Return of the Real: The Avant-Garde at the End of the Century* (Cambridge, MA: MIT Press, 1996), pp. 205–226; John Frow, *Time and Commodity Culture*, pp. 13–63.

4. Fredric Jameson, *A Singular Modernity: Essay on the Ontology of the Present* (London: Verso, 2002), p. 1.

5. See Frow, *Time and Commodity Culture*, pp. 27–29.

6. Fredric Jameson, *Postmodernism, Or, The Cultural Logic of Late Capitalism* (Durham, NC: Duke University Press, 1991), pp. 1–2.

7. See, for example, Andreas Huyssen, *After the Great Divide: Modernism, Mass Culture, Postmodernism* (Bloomington: Indiana University Press, 1986).

8. Charles Jencks, *The Language of Post-Modern Architecture* (New York: Rizzoli, 1977), p. 9.

9. Consider, for example, the work of Richard Kostelanetz, who has long been dedicated to the recovery of avant-garde writing from the modernist period: see *The Avant-Garde Tradition in Literature* (Buffalo, NY: Prometheus Books, 1982) and many other titles; or the interest of the poets associated with the journal $L=A=N=G=U=A=G=E$ in Gertrude Stein: see, for example, Lyn Hejinian, "Two Stein Talks" (1986), *The Language of Inquiry* (Berkeley: University of California Press, 2000), pp. 83–130.

10. Jean-François Lyotard, *The Postmodern Condition: A Report on Knowledge*, trans. by Geoff Bennington and Brian Massumi (Minneapolis: University of Minnesota Press, 1984).

11. Frow, *Time and Commodity Culture*, pp. 15–20.

12. Peter Osborne, *The Politics of Time: Modernity and Avant-Garde* (London: Verso, 1995), pp. 3–5.

13. Lyotard, *The Postmodern Condition*, p. 81.

14. Jameson, *Postmodernism*, p. 1.

15. Wendy Steiner, "Postmodern Fictions, 1970–1990," *The Cambridge History of American Literature, Vol. 7: Prose Writing, 1940–1990*, ed. by Sacvan Bercovitch (Cambridge: Cambridge University Press, 1999), pp. 425–538. Future references will be given in parentheses.

16. Wendy Steiner, *Venus in Exile: The Rejection of Beauty in Twentieth-Century Art* (New York: Free Press, 2001), pp. 191–215.

17. Ihab Hassan, *The Dismemberment of Orpheus: Toward a Postmodern Literature* (New York: Oxford University Press, 1971); Gerald Graff, *Literature Against Itself: Literary Ideas in Modern Society* (Chicago: University of Chicago Press, 1979); Philip Stevick, *Alternative Pleasures: Postrealist Fiction and the Tradition* (Urbana: University of Illinois Press, 1981); Jerome Klinkowitz, *Literary Disruptions: The Making of a Post-Contemporary American Fiction* (Urbana: University of Illinois Press, 1975).

18. William H. Gass, *Fiction and the Figures of Life* (New York: Knopf, 1977) and *The World Within the Word: Essays* (New York: Knopf, 1978); Ishmael Reed, *Shrovetide in Old New Orleans* (Garden City, NY: Doubleday, 1978); Ronald Sukenick, *In Form: Digressions on the Act of Fiction* (Carbondale: Southern Illinois University Press, 1985); Susan Sontag, *Against Interpretation, and Other Essays* (New York: Farrar, Straus and Giroux, 1966) and *Styles of Radical Will* (New York: Farrar, Straus and Giroux, 1969); John Barth,

The Friday Book: Essays and Other Nonfiction (New York: G.P. Putnam's, 1984).

19. Fredric Jameson, "Postmodernism and Consumer Society," *The Anti-Aesthetic*, ed. by Hal Foster (Port Townsend, WA: Bay Press, 1983), pp. 111–125; "Postmodernism, or The Cultural Logic of Late Capitalism," *New Left Review* 146 (1984): 52–92. For a discussion of the development and significance of Jameson's work on the postmodern, see Perry Anderson, *The Origins of Postmodernity* (London: Verso, 1998). Jean-François Lyotard, *The Postmodern Condition: A Report on Knowledge*, trans. by Geoff Bennington and Brian Masumi (Minneapolis: University of Minnesota Press, 1984), subsequent references will be given in parentheses.

20. In this respect, Wendy Steiner's postmodernism is the antithesis of Lyotard's; where he argues for an aesthetic of the sublime, she works to rehabilitate the beautiful.

21. *The Political Unconscious: Narrative as a Socially Symbolic Act* (Ithaca, NY: Cornell University Press, 1981).

22. Linda Hutcheon, *A Poetics of Postmodernism: History, Theory, Fiction* (New York: Routledge, 1988); Brian McHale, *Postmodernist Fiction* (New York: Methuen, 1987) and *Constructing Postmodernism* (New York: Routledge, 1992).

23. Tom LeClair, *The Art of Excess: Mastery in Contemporary American Fiction* (Urbana: University of Illinois Press, 1989); Joseph Tabbi, *Postmodern Sublime: Technology and American Writing from Mailer to Cyberpunk* (Ithaca, NY: Cornell University Press, 1995) and *Cognitive Fictions* (Minneapolis: University of Minnesota Press, 2002); Ursula Heise, *Chronoschisms: Time, Narrative, and Postmodernism* (Cambridge: Cambridge University Press, 1997); John Johnston, *Information Multiplicity: American Fiction in an Age of Media Saturation* (Baltimore, MD: Johns Hopkins University Press, 1998); N. Katherine Hayles, *Chaos Bound: Orderly Disorder in Contemporary Literature and Science* (Ithaca, NY: Cornell University Press, 1990) and *How We Became Posthuman: Virtual Bodies in Cybernetics, Literature, and Informatics* (Chicago: Chicago University Press, 1999); Joseph Conte, *Design and Debris: A Chaotics of Postmodern American Fiction* (Tuscaloosa: University of Alabama Press, 2002).

24. Marginality is a relative thing, to be sure, but it is notable that postmodern literature had a fairly significant presence at the MLA Conventions during the 1970s, certainly compared to recent years. In 1975, for example, there were 18 panels devoted exclusively to contemporary writing, including sessions on Donald Barthelme, Ursula Le Guin, James Purdy, Thomas Pynchon, Kurt Vonnegut, and John Hawkes (*PMLA* 90.6 [1975]: 981–984); in 1976 no fewer than 27, including sessions on Joyce Carol Oates, John Hawkes (again), Jerzy Kosinski, Philip Roth, John Barth, Thomas Pynchon (again), and Vladimir Nabokov (*PMLA* 91.6 [1976]: 976–982). In 2002 there were 15 sessions explicitly devoted to contemporary literature (though several more on film), with two sessions on Nabokov and one on Toni Morrison (*PMLA* 117.6 [2002]: 1403–1415). Admittedly, this says something about the organization of the panels at the Convention, but the absence of presentations on living postmodern writers remains striking.

25. Roland Barthes, "The Death of the Author," *Image—Music—Text*, trans. by Stephen Heath (London: Fontana, 1977), pp. 142–148.

26. Michel Foucault, "What is an Author?" trans. by Josué V. Harari in *Textual Strategies: Perspectives in Post-Structuralist Criticism* (Ithaca, NY: Cornell University Press, 1979), pp. 141–160.

27. Terry Eagleton, *The Ideology of the Aesthetic* (Oxford: Basil Blackwell, 1990), pp. 374–375.

28. See especially David Harvey, *The Condition of Postmodernity* (Oxford: Basil Blackwell, 1989) and "Flexibility: Threat or Opportunity?" *Socialist Review* 21.1 (1991): 65–77; Fredric Jameson, *Postmodernism, Or the Cultural Logic of Late Capitalism* and the essays in *The Cultural Turn: Selected Writings on the Postmodern, 1983–1998* (London: Verso, 1998), particularly "Culture and Finance Capital" (pp. 136–161) and "The Brick and the Balloon: Architecture, Idealism and Land Speculation" (pp. 162–189); Manuel Castells, *The Rise of the Network Society* (Oxford: Basil Blackwell, 1996); John Frow, *Cultural Studies and Cultural Value* (Oxford: Oxford University Press, 1995); and Arjun Appadurai, "Disjuncture and Difference in the Global Cultural Economy," *The Phantom Public Sphere*, ed. by Bruce Robbins (Minneapolis: University of Minnesota Press, 1993), pp. 269–295.

29. For a useful discussion of these debates see Nick Dyer-Witheford, *Cyber-Marx: Cycles and Circuits of Struggle in High-Technology Capitalism* (Urbana: University of Illinois Press, 1999).

30. David Harvey, *The Condition of Postmodernity*, p. 133.

31. Ernest Mandel, *Late Capitalism*, trans. by Joris De Bres (London: NLB, 1975), esp. pp. 523–589.

32. David Harvey, *The Condition of Postmodernity*, p. 145.

33. See the discussion in Dyer-Witheford, *Cyber-Marx*, pp. 54–61.

34. *The Condition of Postmodernity*, p. 147.

35. Michael Hardt and Antonio Negri, *Empire* (Cambridge, MA: Harvard University Press, 2000), p. 284.

36. Castells, *The Rise of the Network Society*, pp. 29–65.

37. "[T]he average cost of processing information fell from around $75 per million operations in 1960 to less than one-hundredth of a cent in 1990." Castells, *The Rise of the Network Society*, p. 45.

38. Harvey, "Flexibility: Threat or Opportunity?" p. 68.

39. *The Condition of Postmodernity*, p. 156.

40. Charles Baudelaire, *Selected Writings on Art and Artists* (Harmondsworth: Penguin, 1972), p. 403.

41. Herbert Schiller, *Culture Inc.: The Corporate Takeover of Public Expression* (New York: Oxford University Press, 1989), pp. 37–38.

42. André Schiffrin, *The Business of Books: How International Conglomerates Took Over Publishing and Changed the Way We Read* (London: Verso, 2000), p. 73.

43. Bill Readings, *The University in Ruins* (Cambridge, MA: Harvard University Press, 1996).

44. Ibid., p. 17

45. John Frow, *Cultural Studies and Cultural Value* (Oxford: Oxford University Press, 1995), p. 3.

46. See, e.g., Andrew Ross, *No Respect: Intellectuals and Popular Culture* (New York: Routledge, 1989).
47. Jameson, *Postmodernism, Or the Cultural Logic of Late Capitalism*, p. 131.
48. See Raymond Williams, *Marxism and Literature* (Oxford: Oxford University Press, 1977), pp. 121–127.

Chapter 2   The Novel and the Death of Literature

1. J. Hillis Miller, *On Literature* (New York: Routledge, 2002), pp. 1, 10.
2. *The Gutenberg Elegies: The Fate of Reading in an Electronic Age* (New York: Ballantine, 1994), p. 3. Future references will be parenthetical.
3. *The Death of Literature* (New Haven, CT: Yale University Press, 1990).
4. Carla Hesse, "Books in Time" *The Future of the Book*, ed. by Geoffrey Nunberg (Berkeley, CA: University of California Press, 1996), p. 29.
5. *The Death of Literature*, p. 7.
6. See, e.g., Robert Alter, *The Pleasures of Reading: In an Ideological Age* (New York: Simon and Schuster, 1989); and Andrew Delbanco, *Required Reading: Why Our American Classics Matter Now* (New York: Farrar, Straus and Giroux, 1997).
7. Harold Bloom, *How to Read and Why* (New York: Scribner, 2000), pp. 21, 29.
8. Harold Bloom, *The Western Canon: The Books and School of the Ages* (New York: Harcourt Brace, 1994).
9. William Gass, "In Defense of the Book: On the Enduring Pleasures of Paper, Type, Page and Ink," *Harper's Magazine* (November 1999): 49.
10. For useful surveys of this work, see Tony Tanner, *City of Words: American Fiction, 1950–1970* (New York: Harper & Row, 1971); and Steven Weisenburger, *Fables of Subversion: Satire and the American Novel, 1930–1980* (Athens: University of Georgia Press, 1995).
11. Linda Hutcheon, *A Poetics of Postmodernism: History, Theory, Fiction* (New York: Routledge, 1988).
12. "The Literature of Exhaustion," *The Friday Book: Essays and Other Nonfiction* (New York: G.P. Putnam's, 1984), pp. 62–76. [originally 1968]. References will be parenthetical.
13. When Barth reprinted this essay in *The Friday Book*, he added a footnote repudiating this remark.
14. Barth's *Lost in the Funhouse: Fictions for Print, Tape, Live Voice* (New York: Doubleday, 1968) made experimental play with the format of the book for metafictional purposes, while also attempting, as he later noted in *The Friday Book*, to ensure the author's inclusion in anthologies of fiction (63).
15. John Barth, "The Literature of Replenishment: Postmodernist Fiction," in *The Friday Book*, pp. 193–206. The essay was first published in *The Atlantic*.
16. See, e.g., the aforementioned works by Hassan, Graff, and Klinkowitz (note 17, chapter one).
17. See Andreas Huyssen, *After the Great Divide: Modernism, Mass Culture, Postmodernism*.

18. "Inconclusion: The Novel in the Next Century," in John Barth, *Further Fridays: Essays, Lectures, and Other Nonfiction, 1984–1994* (Boston: Little, Brown, 1995), pp. 349–366; first published *Conjunctions* 19 (1992).

19. John Barth, *Coming Soon!!!: A Narrative* (Boston: Houghton Mifflin, 2001). Future references will be parenthetical.

20. John Barth, "The State of the Art," *Meanjin* 56.3–4 (1997): 459.

21. The classic study is Frank Kermode, *The Sense of an Ending: Studies in the Theory of Fiction* (New York: Oxford University Press, 1967).

22. David Remnick, "Into the Clear: Philip Roth Puts Turbulence in its Place," *New Yorker* (May 8, 2000): 86. References to this article will be given parenthetically.

23. Philip Roth's highly successful first book, *Goodbye, Columbus and Five Short Stories* (Boston: Houghton Mifflin, 1959), was followed by the Jamesian *Letting Go* (New York: Random House, 1962), a novel that gives some of the flavor of the academic ambience and excitement surrounding the New Criticism.

24. Roth's recent fiction has garnered a number of awards: *Operation Shylock* (1993) and *The Human Stain* (2000) both won PEN/Faulkner awards, *Sabbath's Theater* (1995) won the National Book Award, and *American Pastoral* (1997) was awarded the Pulitzer prize.

25. The other novels in the trilogy are *American Pastoral* (Boston: Houghton Mifflin, 1997) and *I Married a Communist* (Boston: Houghton Mifflin, 1998).

26. Silk's intermittent and ultimately catastrophic battle with Lester Farley echoes this remark.

27. Roth models Silk on Anatole Broyard, for many years the editor and leading reviewer for the *New York Times*, who passed as white throughout his career. The details of Silk's life in the Greenwich Village of the 1940s are apparently inspired by Broyard's posthumously published memoir *Kafka Was the Rage: A Greenwich Village Memoir* (New York: Vintage, 1993). See also Henry Louis Gates, Jr., "The Passing of Anatole Broyard," *Thirteen Ways of Looking at a Black Man* (New York: Random House, 1997), pp. 180–214.

28. The decline of the New Jersey neighborhoods of the war years and the 1950s is a recurrent theme in Roth's trilogy. In *American Pastoral*, for instance, the blight of the Newark neighborhood where Zuckerman grew up is described in pungent detail.

29. "Cultural capital" is Bourdieu's formulation to describe the internalized knowledge—or competence—necessary to participate in the appreciation and understanding of works of art and literature. It is acquired through education both informal and formalized, and thus maps (in more or less complex ways) onto social class. See Pierre Bourdieu, *Distinction: A Social Critique of the Judgement of Taste*, trans. by Richard Nice (Cambridge, MA: Harvard University Press, 1984), p. 2 and passim.

30. David Denby, *Great Books: My Adventures with Homer, Rousseau, Woolf, and Other Indestructible Writers of the Western World* (New York: Simon and Schuster, 1996), pp. 31–32.

31. The novel maintains a strategic indeterminacy as to the sources of information about the relationship between Coleman and Faunia. All is filtered through

Zuckerman's narration, yet it remains unclear whether he is employing his sympathetic imagination or elaborating on Silk's words (or even Faunia's, though the tantalizing diary seems to be withheld).

32. Carole Maso, "Rupture, Verge, and Precipice: Precipice, Verge, and Hurt Not," *Break Every Rule: Essays on Language, Longing, and Moments of Desire* (Washington, DC: Counterpoint, 2000), p. 161. Subsequent references will be parenthetical.

33. Virginia Woolf, *Mr. Bennett and Mrs. Brown* (London: Hogarth Press, 1924).

Chapter 3 Jonathan Franzen, Oprah Winfrey, and the Future of the Social Novel

1. Franzen's publisher, Farrar Straus and Giroux, put an additional 680,000 copies of *The Corrections* into print, following an initial run of 90,000. The novel, which won the National Book Award in November 2001, eventually spent 29 weeks on the *New York Times* best seller list.

2. Dave Weich, "Jonathan Franzen Uncorrected," http://www.powells.com/authors/franzen. html [interview conducted October 4, 2001].

3. See, e.g., Jonathan Yardley, "The Story of O," *Washington Post* (October 28, 2001): C.02; and John Marshall, "Franzen's Attitude Needs Some Corrections of Its Own, Authors Say," *Seattle Post-Intelligencer* (November 2, 2001): 26.

4. As Franzen later recounted: "I'd achieve unexpected sympathy for Dan Quayle when, in a moment of exhaustion in Oregon, I conflate 'high modern' and 'art fiction' to describe the importance of Proust and Kafka and Faulkner to my writing," "Meet Me in St. Louis," *New Yorker* (December 24 and 31, 2001): 70–75.

5. Jonathan Franzen, "Perchance to Dream: In an Age of Images, A Reason to Write Novels," *Harper's Magazine* (April 1996): 35–54.

6. The Book Club selections included three children's books by Bill Cosby, treated here as a single selection, since they were dealt with on one show.

7. "In the book industry, where profits are narrow, Oprah's endorsement of any title meant a minimum of 500,000 additional sales, says Jim Milliot, the business editor at *Publisher's Weekly*. For the publisher, that translates to at least an additional $5 million in revenue." Richard Lacayo, "Oprah Turns the Page," *Time* (April 15, 2002): 63.

8. See D.T. Max, "The Oprah Effect," *New York Times Magazine* (December 26, 1999): 36–41 (p. 37).

9. Of the 46 books chosen, 35 were written by women, 11 by men.

10. "The Oprah Effect," p. 38.

11. In addition to the three children's books written by Cosby, the "Book Club Library," as it is called on Winfrey's website, includes a work of nonfiction, Malika Oufkir's *Stolen Lives: Twenty Years in a Desert Jail*. Works by established literary novelists include four novels by Toni Morrison (*The Bluest Eye, Paradise, Song of Solomon* and *Sula*), Isabel Allende's *Daughter of Fortune,*

Rohinton Mistry's *A Fine Balance*, Joyce Carol Oates's *We Were The Mulvaneys*, Barbara Kingsolver's *Poisonwood Bible*, and Ernest J. Gaines's *A Lesson Before Dying*.

12. For a useful early assessment of the pros and cons of the Book Club, see Laura Lippman, "The Oprah Canon," *Baltimore Morning Sun* (June 18, 1997): 1E.

13. Estimates put the number of reading groups in the United States as high as 500,000; see Jenny Hartley, *Reading Groups* (Oxford: Oxford University Press, 2001), p. vii. See Max, "The Oprah Effect," p. 41, for an account of book clubs devoted to the Oprah canon.

14. The debates about the success of the Book-of-the-Month Club, detailed by Janice Radway, anticipate many of the terms employed in discussions of Winfrey's Book Club; see *A Feeling for Books: The Book-of-the-Month Club, Literary Taste, and Middle-Class Desire* (Chapel Hill: University of North Carolina Press, 1997).

15. See, e.g., Gavin McNett's assertion that the Book Club selections are "designed, like any sort of middlebrow dry-good or specialty food on the shelves at Target or Starbucks, to express their readers' (and Oprah's) tastes, and to reinforce what they think is right and wrong in the world," "Reaching to the Converted," *Salon* (November 12, 1999): http://www.salon.com/books/feature/1999/11/12/oprahcon.

16. Oprah Winfrey Show Transcript, May 2, 2002 (Harpo Productions).

17. Andre Dubus III, *House of Sand and Fog* (New York: Norton, 1999).

18. Oprah Winfrey Show Transcript, January 24, 2001 (Harpo Productions).

19. For discussion of Winfrey's construction as a celebrity, see P. David Marshall, *Celebrity and Power: Fame in Contemporary Culture* (Minneapolis: University of Minnesota Press, 1997), pp. 131–149; and Jeffrey Decker, *Made in America: Self-Styled Success from Horatio Alger to Oprah Winfrey* (Minneapolis: University of Minnesota Press, 1997), pp. 117–120.

20. Elizabeth Berg, *Open House: A Novel* (New York: Random House, 2000).

21. The pleasant but unpromisingly obese handyman, who instantly appeals to the protagonist as a friend rather than a sexual partner, sheds many pounds over the course of the novel to the point where he is fit, by the final chapter, to replace the former husband (he also turns out to have an astrophysics degree from MIT). The husband, for his part, announces late in the novel that he has made a mistake and begs to be taken back—an offer the protagonist, having rebuilt her life and self-respect, is now in a position to turn down. She also, along the way, comes to a better understanding of her mother, and regains the respect of her initially surly teenage son.

22. The Oprah Winfrey Show, March 6, 1998, transcript.

23. Ibid.

24. See Jane Shattuc, *The Talking Cure: TV Talk Shows and Women* (New York: Routledge, 1997), pp. 85–109; Eva Illouz, " 'That Shadowy Realm of the Interior': Oprah Winfrey and Hamlet's Glass," *International Journal of Cultural Studies* 2.1 (1999): 109–131; and Janice Peck, "Literacy, Seriousness, and the Oprah Winfrey Book Club," in *Tabloid Tales: Global Debates over Media Standards*, ed. by Colin Sparks and John Tulloch (Lanham, MD: Rowman and Littlefield, 2000), pp. 229–250.

25. Paolo Carpignano et al., "Chatter in the Age of Electronic Reproduction: Talk Television and the 'Public Mind,'" in *The Phantom Public Sphere*, ed. by Bruce Robbins (Minneapolis: University of Minnesota Press, 1993), pp. 93–120.
26. *The Structural Transformation of the Public Sphere*, p. 174.
27. Illouz, " 'That Shadowy Realm of the Interior,' " p. 112.
28. Franny Nudelman, "Beyond the Talking Cure: Listening to Female Testimony on *The Oprah Winfrey Show*," in *Inventing the Psychological: Toward a Cultural History of Emotional Life in America*, ed. by Joel Pfister and Nancy Schnog (New Haven, CT: Yale University Press, 1997), p. 298.
29. Habermas, *The Structural Transformation of the Public Sphere*, p. 172.
30. Zygmunt Bauman, *Liquid Modernity* (Cambridge: Polity, 2000), p. 70.
31. "Beyond the Talking Cure," p. 310.
32. "Chatter in the Age of Electronic Reproduction," p. 116.
33. "Beyond the Talking Cure," p. 308.
34. On the ideological mission of The Oprah Winfrey Show, see Peck, "Literacy, Seriousness, and the Oprah Winfrey Book Club."
35. "Meet Me in St. Louis."
36. "Meet Me in St. Louis," p. 74.
37. Ibid.
38. Philip Roth, "Writing American Fiction," *Reading Myself and Others* (New York: Farrar, Straus and Giroux, 1975), pp. 117–135.
39. Paula Fox, *Desperate Characters* [1970] (New York: Norton, 1999).
40. Hence, e.g., the study of literature: "the therapeutic optimism now raging in English literature departments insists that novels be sorted into two boxes: Symptoms of Disease (canonical work from the Dark Ages before 1950), and Medicine for a Happier and Healthier World (the work of women and of people from non-white or non-hetero cultures)" (47). This extraordinarily reductive swipe at literature departments, which smacks of neoconservative editorials, is perhaps best understood in terms of the conspicuous *ressentiment* with which it is spiced: "Strangest of all, perhaps," Franzen sneers, "that such heroic subversives, lecturing on the patriarchal evil du jour while their TIAA-CREF accounts grow fat on Wall Street, manage to keep a straight face" (47).
41. See Jürgen Habermas, *Legitimation Crisis* (Boston: Beacon, 1975), p. 76. Habermas argues that the political theories of civic republicanism depend on the ethos of the great bourgeois revolutionary movements of the Enlightenment; the political culture of capitalist societies, however, diffuses such participatory potential, and tends in fact to foster traditional structures, particularly those of the family, as a means to inculcate passivity.
42. Emily Eakin, "Jonathan Franzen's Big Book," *New York Times Magazine* (September 2, 2001): 20.
43. Ibid.
44. Ibid.
45. Franzen's first novel, *The Twenty-Seventh City* (New York: Farrar Straus Giroux, 1988), was a long, intricate examination of city politics, race, and violence; *Strong Motion* (New York: Farrar Straus Giroux, 1992) was an

upscale eco-thriller in which corporate malfeasance leads to earthquakes and environmental catastrophe in the greater Boston area. Both books have a clear political intent, a panoramic ambition, and a mastery of recondite information.

46. "Mr. Difficult: William Gaddis and the Problem of Hard-to-Read Books," *New Yorker* (September 30, 2002): 100–111.

Chapter 4 Late Postmodernism and Cultural Memory

1. Eakin, "Jonathan Franzen's Big Book," p. 20.
2. See in particular Joseph Dewey, *Understanding Richard Powers* (Columbia, SC: University of South Carolina Press, 2002); and *Review of Contemporary Fiction* 18.3 (Fall 1998): 7–109.
3. Richard Powers, *Galatea 2.2* (New York: Farrar, Straus and Giroux, 1995). All references will be given in parentheses.
4. The test was described in Alan Turing, "Computing Machinery and Intelligence," *Mind* 59 (1950): 433–460.
5. N. Katherine Hayles, *How We Became Posthuman: Virtual Bodies in Cybernetics, Literature, and Informatics* (Chicago: University of Chicago Press, 1999), p. 271.
6. Kathryn Davis, *The Walking Tour* (Boston: Houghton Mifflin, 1999). All references will be given in parentheses.
7. Jean-Paul Sartre, *Critique of Dialectical Reason I: Theory of Practical Ensembles*, trans. by Alan Sheridan-Smith (London: NLB, 1976), pp. 272–273.
8. "A Conversation with Kathryn Davis," http://www.houghtonmifflin books.com/readers_guides/davis_guide.shtml#conversation
9. *The Mabinogion*, trans. by Jeffrey Gantz (Harmondsworth: Penguin, 1976), p. 84.
10. David Markson, *Wittgenstein's Mistress* (Elmwood Park, IL: Dalkey Archive Press, 1988), p. 227.
11. The strong critical reception of *Wittgenstein's Mistress* and the publication of a cluster of articles and an interview in *Review of Contemporary Fiction* 10.2 (1990) initiated the critical examination of Markson's writing.
12. Joseph Tabbi, "David Markson: An Introduction," *Review of Contemporary Fiction* 10.2 (1990): 91.
13. David Markson, "Reviewers in Flat Heels: Being a Postface to Several Novels," *Review of Contemporary Fiction* 10.2 (1990): 128.
14. David Markson, *Malcolm Lowry's "Volcano"* (New York: Times Books, 1978).
15. Markson, "Reviewers," p. 128.
16. In his interview with Markson, Joseph Tabbi asks about the influence of recent theory: "JT: But people like Barthes or Derrida weren't in any way influences? DM: I really feel not. Things do run parallel in cultural flow. So that it's quite possible to become a minimalist or a postmodernist or what you will by way of Wittgenstein just as readily as those who use the labels." "An Interview with David Markson," *Review of Contemporary Fiction* 10.2 (1990): 114.
17. David Markson, *Springer's Progress* (New York: Holt, Rinehart and Winston, 1977).

18. "Interview with David Markson," p. 114.
19. "Interview with David Markson," p. 113.
20. David Foster Wallace, "The Empty Plenum: David Markson's *Wittgenstein's Mistress*," *Review of Contemporary Fiction* 10.2 (1990): 219.
21. Ibid. p. 227n.
22. This description of the project of the avant-garde is indebted to Peter Bürger's classic study, *Theory of the Avant-Garde*, trans. by Michael Shaw (Minneapolis: University of Minnesota Press, 1984).
23. David Markson, *Reader's Block* (Normal, IL: Dalkey Archive Press, 1996). References will be given in parentheses.

Chapter 5   Pathologies of the Public Sphere

1. Don DeLillo, *Mao II* (New York: Viking, 1991). References will be given parenthetically.
2. Don DeLillo, "The Power of History," *New York Times Magazine* (September 7, 1997): 63. Subsequent references will be given in parentheses ("Power").
3. In his essay about the Kennedy assassination, "American Blood: A Journey Through the Labyrinth of Dallas and JFK," *Rolling Stone* (December 8, 1983): 24, DeLillo makes a similar point about the actions of John Hinckley and the Secret Service men assigned to protect President Reagan: "Hinckley sees the act on television even as he commits it. (As do, conceivably, the Secret Service men, judging by a certain choreography of gesture that day in Washington, a self-conscious flourish of cocked weapons, as though the documentary history of the shooting was already running though the minds of one or two of the men on the scene.)"
4. Several critics have explored the implications of DeLillo's work in the light of Benjamin's classic study of art and technology. See John Duvall, "The (Super) Marketplace of Images," *Arizona Quarterly* 50.3 (1994): 127–153; and "Baseball as Aesthetic Ideology: Cold War History, Race, and DeLillo's 'Pafko at the Wall,'" *Modern Fiction Studies* 41 (1995): 285–313.
5. Benjamin's definition of the aura of unique artworks rests on an analogy with the aura of natural objects, cryptically defined as "the unique phenomenon of a distance, however close it may be." "The Work of Art in the Age of Mechanical Reproduction," *Illuminations*, trans. by Harry Zohn (New York: Schocken, 1969), p. 222.
6. Mark Seltzer, *Serial Killers: Death and Life in America's Wound Culture* (New York: Routledge, 1998); Hal Foster, "Death in America," *October* 75 (1996): 37–59; Michael Warner, "The Mass Public and the Mass Subject," *The Phantom Public Sphere*, ed. by Bruce Robbins (Minneapolis: University of Minnesota Press, 1993), pp. 234–256.
7. *Serial Killers*, p. 21.
8. Michael Warner, "The Mass Public and the Mass Subject," p. 250.
9. *Serial Killers*, p. 6 and passim.
10. Foster writes: "Here, again, in its guise as witness the mass subject reveals its sado-masochistic aspect, for this subject is often split in relation to a disaster: even

as he or she may mourn the victims, even identify with them masochistically, he or she may also be thrilled, sadistically, that there *are* victims of whom he or she is *not* one" ("Death in America," pp. 54–55).

11. Don DeLillo, "American Blood: A Journey Through the Labyrinth of Dallas and JFK," *Rolling Stone* (December 8, 1983): 24.

12. *Mao II*, p. 44.

13. Don DeLillo, *End Zone* (New York: Penguin, 1986). Future references to this text will be parenthetical.

14. Don DeLillo, *Great Jones Street* (New York: Penguin, 1994).

15. Don DeLillo, *The Names* (New York: Vintage, 1989).

16. Don DeLillo, *Libra* (New York: Viking, 1988).

17. Michael Oriard, "Don DeLillo's Search for Walden Pond," *Critique* 20.1 (1978): 5–24, associates these retreats with the Thoreauvian desire in American culture to turn from society to deliberative individual self-sufficiency. Yet, as Mark Osteen has astutely noted in an essay on *Great Jones Street*, DeLillo's protagonists find their isolation to be dominated by the seriality of the mass-market. Mark Osteen, " 'A Moral Form to Master Commerce': The Economies of DeLillo's *Great Jones Street*," *Critique* 35 (1994): 157–172.

18. Fredric Jameson, *Marxism and Form: Twentieth Century Dialectical Theories of Literature* (Princeton, NJ: Princeton University Press, 1971), p. 248.

19. Ibid.

20. The marker for this dream is Ludwig Wittgenstein, whose early philosophy attempted to erect on logical foundations a rigorously denotative theory of linguistic reference. Gary Harkness in *End Zone* speculates that Taft Robinson might be a student of Wittgenstein's work, both written and unwritten (p. 233).

21. Don DeLillo, *White Noise* (New York: Viking, 1985).

22. Mary Ann Doane, "Information, Crisis, Catastrophe," *Logics of Television: Essays in Cultural Criticism*, ed. by Patricia Mellencamp (Bloomington: Indiana University Press, 1990), p. 231.

23. Jean Baudrillard, "The Ecstasy of Communication," *The Anti-Aesthetic*, ed. by Hal Foster (Port Townsend, WA: Bay Press, 1983), p. 129.

24. "Information, Crisis, Catastrophe," p. 233.

25. Adam Begley, "The Art of Fiction CXXV: Don DeLillo," *Paris Review* 35.128 (1993): 301–302.

26. Don DeLillo, *Americana* (New York: Penguin, 1989).

27. *Americana*, p. 43.

28. Walter Benjamin, "The Work of Art in the Age of Mechanical Reproduction," p. 234.

29. It is perhaps worth noting that the omnipresence of visuality does not function here as the panopticon functions in Foucault's *Discipline and Punish*. The ubiquitous presence of the visual does not have a regulative effect; instead, it seems to encourage a performative, exhibitionist acting-out (or subverting) of the self.

30. Begley, "The Art of Fiction," p. 299.

31. DeCurtis, "An Outsider in this Society," p. 51.

32. The connection between secrecy and celebrity hinted at here is also explored in *Underworld*: see in particular the association between J. Edgar Hoover

and Sinatra; and also the Capote masked ball, in which the qualities of celebrity and secrecy are for Hoover deliciously mingled.

33. Samuel Weber, *Mass Mediauras: Form, Technics, Media*, ed. by Alan Cholodenko (Stanford, CA: Stanford University Press, 1996), p. 101.
34. Begley, "The Art of Fiction," p. 300.
35. Alek Kirilenko, Oswald's KGB interrogator thinks, skeptically but aptly, "Fly to ninety thousand feet, you see the souls of the dead in rings of white light" (*Libra* 166).
36. It is worth noting in passing that Beryl Parmenter, struggling with these inside/outside borders, occupies a position parallel to Oswald when he finds his fantasies played out on the TV prior to the assassination. He now appears, so to speak, inside his own fantasy.
37. DeLillo, "American Blood," p. 24.
38. The contrast between the quasi-metaphysical aspirations of technology—the desire to find the ultimate reality, the final truth of the events captured in Zapruder's blurry frames—and the materiality of the body is one of the great themes of the novel, and, indeed, of DeLillo's work as a whole.

Chapter 6   Late Postmodernism and the Utopian Imagination

1. John Cheever, *The Journals* (London: Jonathan Cape, 1991), p. 185. DeLillo read the passage in a documentary entitled "The Word, The Image and The Gun" (directed by Kim Evans), broadcast on BBC1, September 27, 1991.
2. See, in particular, Duvall, "The (Super)Marketplace of Images," and McClure, *Late Imperial Romance* (London: Verso, 1994), pp. 118–151.
3. Quoted in DeCurtis, "An Oustider in this Society," pp. 43–66.
4. Richard Powers, *Gain* (New York: Farrar Straus and Giroux, 1998).
5. Evan Dara, *The Lost Scrapbook* (Normal, IL: FC2, 1995). All references will be parenthetical.
6. See the important discussion in Miriam Hansen, "Foreword" to Oskar Negt and Alexander Kluge, *Public Sphere and Experience: Toward an Analysis of the Bourgeois and Proletarian Public Sphere*, trans. by Peter Labanyi, Jamie Daniel, and Assenka Oksiloff (Minneapolis: University of Minnesota Press, 1993), pp. ix–xli.
7. Allan Bloom, *The Closing of the American Mind: How Higher Education Has Failed Democracy and Impoverished the Souls of Today's Students* (New York: Simon and Schuster, 1987).

Epilogue

1. Ulrich Beck, *Risk Society: Towards a New Modernity* (London: Sage, 1992).
2. James Wood, "Tell Me How Does it Feel?" *The Guardian* (October 5, 2001).
3. Dodie Bellamy, *The Letters of Mina Harker* (Stockbridge, MA: Hard Press, 1998); William Gibson, *Pattern Recognition* (New York: G.P. Putnam's, 2003). Subsequent references to both novels will be given in parentheses.

4. See, e.g., Kathy Acker, *Don Quixote, Which Was a Dream* (New York: Grove, 1986); Robert Glück, *Margery Kempe* (New York: Serpent's Tail, 1994); and Lauren Fairbanks, *Sister Carrie: A Novel* (Normal, IL: Dalkey Archive, 1993).
5. *The Crying of Lot 49* (Philadelphia, PA: Lippincott, 1966).
6. Fredric Jameson, *Postmodernism*, pp. 19–21.
7. In his brief essay on *Pattern Recognition*, "Fear and Loathing in Globalization," *New Left Review* 23 (September/October 2003): 105–114, Fredric Jameson calls this phobia "commodity bulimia," yet Gibson's own description of the phenomenon suggests an allergic reaction.

BIBLIOGRAPHY

Acker, Kathy. *Don Quixote, Which Was a Dream*. New York: Grove, 1986.

Alter, Robert. *The Pleasures of Reading: In an Ideological Age*. New York: Simon and Schuster, 1989.

Anderson, Perry. *The Origins of Postmodernity*. London: Verso, 1998.

Anon. *The Mabinogion*. Translated by Jeffrey Gantz. Harmondsworth, UK: Penguin, 1976.

Appadurai, Arjun. "Disjuncture and Difference in the Global Cultural Economy." *The Phantom Public Sphere*. Edited by Bruce Robbins. Minneapolis: University of Minnesota Press, 1993.

Barth, John. *Lost in the Funhouse: Fictions for Print, Tape, Live Voice*. New York: Doubleday, 1968.

———. *The Friday Book: Essays and Other Nonfiction*. New York: G.P. Putnam's, 1984.

———. *Further Fridays: Essays, Lectures, and Other Nonfiction, 1984–94*. Boston: Little, Brown, 1995.

———. "The State of the Art." *Meanjin* 56.3–4 (1997): 458–472.

———. *Coming Soon!!!: A Narrative*. Boston: Houghton Mifflin, 2001.

Barthes, Roland. "The Death of the Author." *Image—Music—Text*. Translated by Stephen Heath. London: Fontana, 1977. 142–148.

Baudelaire, Charles. *Selected Writings on Art and Artists*. Harmondsworth: Penguin, 1972.

Baudrillard, Jean. "The Ecstasy of Communication." *The Anti-Aesthetic*. Edited by Hal Foster. Port Townsend, WA: Bay Press, 1983. 126–134.

Bauman, Zygmunt. *Liquid Modernity*. Cambridge: Polity, 2000.

Beck, Ulrich. *Risk Society: Towards a New Modernity*. London: Sage, 1992.

Begley, Adam. "The Art of Fiction CXXV: Don DeLillo." *Paris Review* 35.128 (1993): 274–306.

Bell, Daniel. *The Coming of Post-Industrial Society: A Venture in Social Forecasting*. New York: Basic Books, 1973.

Bellamy, Dodie. *The Letters of Mina Harker*. Stockbridge, MA: Hard Press, 1998.

Benjamin, Walter. "The Work of Art in the Age of Mechanical Reproduction." *Illuminations*. 1968. Translated by Harry Zohn. New York: Schocken, 1969. 217–251.

Berg, Elizabeth. *Open House: A Novel*. New York: Random House, 2000.

Birkerts, Sven. *The Gutenberg Elegies: The Fate of Reading in an Electronic Age*. New York: Ballantine, 1994.

Bloom, Allan. *The Closing of the American Mind: How Higher Education Has Failed Democracy and Impoverished the Souls of Today's Students.* New York: Simon and Schuster, 1987.

Bloom, Harold. *The Western Canon: The Books and Schools of the Ages.* New York: Harcourt Brace, 1994.

———. *How to Read and Why.* New York: Scribner's, 2000.

Bourdieu, Pierre. *The Field of Cultural Production: Essays on Art and Literature.* Edited by Randal Johnson. New York: Columbia University Press, 1993.

———. *Distinction: A Social Critique of the Judgement of Taste.* Translated by Richard Nice. Cambridge, MA: Harvard University Press, 1984.

Broyard, Anatole. *Kafka Was the Rage: A Greenwich Village Memoir.* New York: Vintage, 1993.

Bürger, Peter. *Theory of the Avant-Garde.* Translated by Michael Shaw. Minneapolis: University of Minnesota Press, 1984.

Calhoun, Craig, editor. *Habermas and the Public Sphere.* Cambridge: MIT Press, 1992.

———. *Critical Social Theory: Culture, History, and the Challenge of Difference.* Oxford: Blackwell, 1995.

Callinicos, Alex. *Against Postmodernism: A Marxist Critique.* New York: St. Martin's Press, 1990.

———. *An Anti-Capitalist Manifesto.* Cambridge: Polity, 2003.

Carpignano, Paolo, Robin Andersen, Stanley Aronowitz, and William DiFazio. "Chatter in the Age of Electronic Reproduction: Talk Television and the 'Public Mind.'" *The Phantom Public Sphere.* Edited by Bruce Robbins. Minneapolis: University of Minnesota Press, 1993. 93–120.

Castells, Manuel. *The Rise of the Network Society.* Oxford: Basil Blackwell, 1996.

Cheever, John. *The Journals.* London: Jonathan Cape, 1991.

Clerc, Charles. *Mason & Dixon & Pynchon.* Lanham, MD: University Press of America, 2000.

Conte, Joseph. *Design and Debris: A Chaotics of Postmodern American Fiction.* Tuscaloosa: University of Alabama Press, 2002.

Dara, Evan. *The Lost Scrapbook.* Normal, IL: FC2, 1995.

Davis, Kathryn. *The Walking Tour.* Boston: Houghton Mifflin, 1999.

———. "A Conversation with Kathryn Davis." http://www.houghtonmifflinbooks. com/readers_guides/davis_guide.shtml#conversation.

Decker, Jeffrey. *Made in America: Self-Styled Success from Horatio Alger to Oprah Winfrey.* Minneapolis: University of Minnesota Press, 1997.

DeCurtis, Anthony. "'An Outsider in this Society': An Interview with Don DeLillo." *Introducing Don DeLillo.* Edited by Frank Lentricchia. Durham, NC: Duke University Press, 1991. 43–66.

Delbanco, Andrew. *Required Reading: Why Our American Classics Matter Now.* New York: Farrar, Straus and Giroux, 1997.

DeLillo, Don. *Americana.* 1971. New York: Penguin, 1989.

———. *End Zone.* 1972. New York: Penguin, 1986.

———. *Great Jones Street.* 1973. New York: Penguin, 1994.

———. *Players.* 1977. New York: Vintage, 1989.

———. *The Names.* 1982. New York: Vintage, 1989.

———. "American Blood: A Journey Through the Labyrinth of Dallas and JFK." *Rolling Stone* (December 8, 1983): 21–22.

———. *White Noise.* New York: Viking, 1985.

———. *Libra.* New York: Viking, 1988.

———. *Mao II.* New York: Viking, 1991.

———. *Underworld.* New York: Scribner's, 1997.

———. "The Power of History." *New York Times Magazine* (September 7, 1997): 60–63.

———. *Valparaiso: A Play in Two Acts.* New York: Scribner's, 1999.

Denby, David. *Great Books: My Adventures with Homer, Rousseau, Woolf, and Other Indestructible Writers of the Western World.* New York: Simon and Schuster, 1996.

Dewey, Joseph. *Understanding Richard Powers.* Columbia, SC: University of South Carolina Press, 2002.

Doane, Mary Ann. "Information, Crisis, Catastrophe." *Logics of Television: Essays in Cultural Criticism.* Edited by Patricia Mellencamp. Bloomington: Indiana University Press, 1990. 222–239.

Dubus III, Andre. *House of Sand and Fog.* New York: Norton, 1999.

Duvall, John. "The (Super)Marketplace of Images: Television as Unmediated Mediation in DeLillo's *White Noise.*" *Arizona Quarterly* 50.3 (1994): 127–153.

———. "Baseball as Aesthetic Ideology: Cold War History, Race, and DeLillo's 'Pafko at the Wall.'" *Modern Fiction Studies* 41 (1995): 285–313.

Dyer-Witheford, Nick. *Cyber-Marx: Cycles and Circuits of Struggle in High-Technology Capitalism.* Urbana: University of Illinois Press, 1999.

Eagleton, Terry. *The Ideology of the Aesthetic.* Oxford: Basil Blackwell, 1989.

———. *The Illusions of Postmodernism.* Oxford: Blackwell, 1996.

Eakin, Emily. "Jonathan Franzen's Big Book." *New York Times Magazine* (September 2, 2001): 18–21.

Evans, Kim. Dir. "The Word, The Image and The Gun." BBC1, September 27, 1991.

Fairbanks, Lauren. *Sister Carrie: A Novel.* Normal, IL: Dalkey Archive, 1993.

Fish, Stanley. "Truth But No Consequences: Why Philosophy Doesn't Matter." *Critical Inquiry* 29 (Summer 2003): 389.

Foster, Hal. "Death in America." *October* 75 (1996): 37–59.

———. *The Return of the Real: The Avant-Garde at the End of the Century.* Cambridge, MA: MIT Press, 1996.

Foucault, Michel. "What is an Author?" *Textual Strategies: Perspectives in Post-Structuralist Criticism.* Translated by Josué V. Harari. Ithaca, NY: Cornell University Press, 1979. 141–160.

Fox, Paula. *Desperate Characters.* New York: Norton, 1999. Originally 1970.

Franzen, Jonathan. *The Twenty-Seventh City.* New York: Farrar Straus Giroux, 1988.

———. *Strong Motion.* New York: Farrar Straus Giroux, 1992.

———. "Perchance to Dream: In an Age of Images, A Reason to Write Novels." *Harper's Magazine* (April 1996): 35–54.

———. "No End to It: Rereading *Desperate Characters.*" In *Desperate Characters.* By Paula Fox. New York: Norton, 1999. vii–xiv.

———. *The Corrections.* New York: Farrar, Straus and Giroux, 2001.

———. "Meet Me in St. Louis." *New Yorker* (December 24–31, 2001): 70–75.

Franzen, Jonathan. *How to Be Alone: Essays.* New York: Farrar, Straus and Giroux, 2002.

———. "Mr. Difficult: William Gaddis and the Problem of Hard-to-Read Books." *New Yorker* (September 30, 2002): 100–111.

Frow, John. *Cultural Studies and Cultural Value.* Oxford: Oxford University Press, 1995.

———. *Time and Commodity Culture: Essays in Cultural Theory and Postmodernity.* Oxford: Oxford University Press, 1997.

Gass, William. *Fiction and the Figures of Life.* New York: Knopf, 1977.

———. *The World Within the Word: Essays.* New York: Knopf, 1978.

Gates, Jr., Henry Louis. "The Passing of Anatole Broyard." *Thirteen Ways of Looking at a Black Man.* New York: Random House, 1997. 180–214.

Gibson, William. *Pattern Recognition.* New York: G.P. Putnam's, 2003.

Glück, Robert. *Margery Kempe.* New York: Serpent's Tail, 1994.

Graff, Gerald. *Literature Against Itself: Literary Ideas in Modern Society.* Chicago: University of Chicago Press, 1979.

Green, Geoffrey, Donald J. Greiner, and Larry McCaffery, editors. *The Vineland Papers: Critical Takes on Pynchon's Novel.* Normal, IL: Dalkey Archive, 1994.

Habermas, Jürgen. *Legitimation Crisis.* Boston: Beacon, 1975.

———. *The Structural Transformation of the Public Sphere: An Inquiry Into a Category of Bourgeois Society.* Translated by Thomas Burger and Frederick Lawrence. Cambridge: MIT Press, 1989.

Hansen, Miriam. "Foreword." Oskar Negt and Alexander Kluge. *Public Sphere and Experience: Toward an Analysis of the Bourgeois and Proletarian Public Sphere.* Translated by Peter Labanyi, Jamie Daniel, and Assenka Oksiloff. Minneapolis: University of Minnesota Press, 1993. ix–xli.

Hardt, Michael and Antonio Negri. *Empire.* Cambridge, MA: Harvard University Press, 2000.

Hartley, Jenny. *Reading Groups.* Oxford: Oxford University Press, 2001.

Harvey, David. *The Condition of Postmodernity.* Oxford: Basil Blackwell, 1989.

———. "Flexibility: Threat or Opportunity?" *Socialist Review* 21.1 (1991): 65–77.

Hassan, Ihab. *The Dismemberment of Orpheus: Toward a Postmodern Literature.* New York: Oxford University Press, 1971.

Hayles, N. Katherine. *Chaos Bound: Orderly Disorder in Contemporary Literature and Science.* Ithaca, NY: Cornell University Press, 1990.

———. *How We Became Posthuman: Virtual Bodies in Cybernetics, Literature, and Informatics.* Chicago: University of Chicago Press, 1999.

Heise, Ursula. *Chronoschisms: Time, Narrative, and Postmodernism.* Cambridge: Cambridge University Press, 1997.

Hejinian, Lyn. *The Language of Inquiry.* Berkeley: University of California Press, 2000.

Hesse, Carla. "Books in Time." *The Future of the Book.* Edited by Geoffrey Nunberg. Berkeley: University of California Press, 1996. 21–36.

Horvath, Brooke and Irving Malin, editors. *Pynchon and Mason & Dixon.* Newark: University of Delaware Press, 2000.

Hutcheon, Linda. *A Poetics of Postmodernism: History, Theory, Fiction.* New York: Routledge, 1988.

Huyssen, Andreas. *After the Great Divide: Modernism, Mass Culture, Postmodernism.* Bloomington: Indiana University Press, 1986.

Illouz, Eva. "'That Shadowy Realm of the Interior': Oprah Winfrey and Hamlet's Glass." *International Journal of Cultural Studies* 2.1 (1999): 109–131.

Jameson, Fredric. *Marxism and Form: Twentieth Century Dialectical Theories of Literature.* Princeton, NJ: Princeton University Press, 1971.

———. *The Political Unconscious: Narrative as a Socially Symbolic Act.* Ithaca, NY: Cornell University Press, 1981.

———. "Postmodernism and Consumer Society." *The Anti-Aesthetic.* Edited by Hal Foster. Port Townsend, WA: Bay Press, 1983.

———. "Postmodernism, or The Cultural Logic of Late Capitalism." *New Left Review* 146 (1984): 52–92.

———. "Foreword." To Jean-François Lyotard, *The Postmodern Condition: A Report on Knowledge.* Minneapolis: University of Minnesota Press, 1984. vii–xxi.

———. *Postmodernism, Or The Cultural Logic of Late Capitalism.* Durham, NC: Duke University Press, 1991.

———. *The Cultural Turn: Selected Writings on the Postmodern, 1983–1998.* London: Verso, 1998

———. *A Singular Modernity: Essay on the Ontology of the Present.* London: Verso, 2002.

———. "Fear and Loathing in Globalization." *New Left Review* 23 (September/October 2003): 105–114.

Jencks, Charles. *The Language of Post-Modern Architecture.* Revised edition. New York: Rizzoli, 1977.

Johnston, John. *Information Multiplicity: American Fiction in an Age of Media Saturation.* Baltimore, MD: Johns Hopkins University Press, 1998.

Kermode, Frank. *The Sense of an Ending: Studies in the Theory of Fiction.* New York: Oxford University Press, 1967.

Kernan, Alvin. *The Death of Literature.* New Haven, CT: Yale University Press, 1990.

Klinkowitz, Jerome. *Literary Disruptions: The Making of a Post-Contemporary American Fiction.* Urbana: University of Illinois Press, 1975.

Kostelanetz, Richard. *The Avant-Garde Tradition in Literature.* Buffalo, NY: Prometheus Books, 1982.

Lacayo, Richard. "Oprah Turns the Page." *Time* (April 15, 2002): 63.

Lanham, Richard A. *The Electronic Word: Democracy, Technology, and the Arts.* Chicago: University of Chicago Press, 1993.

LeClair, Tom. *The Art of Excess: Mastery in Contemporary American Fiction.* Urbana: University of Illinois Press, 1989.

Lippman, Laura. "The Oprah Canon." *Baltimore Morning Sun* (June 18, 1997): 1E.

Lukács, Georg. *History and Class Consciousness: Studies in Marxist Dialectics.* Translated by Rodney Livingston. London: Merlin, 1971.

Lyotard, Jean-François. *The Postmodern Condition: A Report on Knowledge.* Translated by Geoff Bennington and Brian Massumi. Minneapolis: University of Minnesota Press, 1984.

———. *The Inhuman: Reflections on Time.* Translated by Geoffrey Bennington and Rachel Bowlby. Stanford, CA: Stanford University Press, 1991.

Macpherson, C.B. *The Political Theory of Possessive Individualism: Hobbes to Locke.* Oxford: Oxford University Press, 1962.

Mandel, Ernest. *Late Capitalism.* Translated by Joris De Bres. London: NLB, 1975.

Marcuse, Herbert. "The Affirmative Character of Culture." *Negations: Essays in Critical Theory.* Translated by Jeremy J. Shapiro. Boston: Beacon Press, 1968. 88–133.

Markson, David. *Springer's Progress.* New York: Holt, Rinehart and Winston, 1977.

———. *Malcolm Lowry's "Volcano."* New York: Times Books, 1978.

———. *Wittgenstein's Mistress.* Elmwood Park, IL: Dalkey Archive Press, 1988.

———. "Reviewers in Flat Heels: Being a Postface to Several Novels." *Review of Contemporary Fiction* 10.2 (1990): 124–130.

———. *Reader's Block.* Normal, IL: Dalkey Archive Press, 1996.

———. *This Is Not a Novel.* Washington, DC: Counterpoint, 2001.

———. *Vanishing Point.* Washington, DC: Shoemaker & Hoard, 2004.

Marshall, P. David. *Celebrity and Power: Fame in Contemporary Culture.* Minneapolis: University of Minnesota Press, 1997.

Marshall, John. "Franzen's Attitude Needs Some Corrections of Its Own, Authors Say." *Seattle Post-Intelligencer* (November 2, 2001): 26.

Maso, Carole. "Rupture, Verge, and Precipice: Precipice, Verge, and Hurt Not." *Review of Contemporary Fiction* 16 (Spring 1996): 54–75.

———. *Break Every Rule: Essays on Language, Longing, and Moments of Desire.* Washington, DC: Counterpoint, 2000.

Max, D.T. "The Oprah Effect." *New York Times Magazine* (December 26, 1999): 36–41.

McClure, John. *Late Imperial Romance.* London: Verso, 1994.

McHale, Brian. *Postmodernist Fiction.* New York: Methuen, 1987.

———. *Constructing Postmodernism.* New York: Routledge, 1992.

McNett, Gavin. "Reaching to the Converted." *Salon* (November 12, 1999): http://www.salon.com/books/feature/1999/11/12/oprahcon.

Miller, J. Hillis. *On Literature.* New York: Routledge, 2002.

Nadotti, Maria. "An Interview with Don DeLillo." Translated by Peggy Boyers. *Salmagundi* 100 (1993): 86–97.

Norris, Christopher. *What's Wrong with Postmodernism: Critical Theory and the Ends of Philosophy.* Baltimore, MD: Johns Hopkins University Press, 1990.

Nudelman, Franny. "Beyond the Talking Cure: Listening to Female Testimony on The Oprah Winfrey Show." *Inventing the Psychological: Toward a Cultural History of Emotional Life in America.* Edited by Joel Pfister and Nancy Schnog. New Haven, CT: Yale University Press. 297–315.

Oriard, Michael. "Don DeLillo's Search for Walden Pond." *Critique* 20.1 (1978): 5–24.

Osborne, Peter. *The Politics of Time: Modernity and Avant-Garde.* London: Verso, 1995.

Osteen, Mark. " 'A Moral Form to Master Commerce': The Economics of DeLillo's *Great Jones Street.*" *Critique* 35 (1994): 157–172.

Peck, Janice. "Literacy, Seriousness, and the Oprah Winfrey Book Club." In *Tabloid Tales: Global Debates over Media Standards.* Edited by Colin Sparks and John Tulloch. Lanham, MD: Rowman & Littlefield, 2000. 229–250.

Powers, Richard. *Galatea 2.2*. New York: Farrar, Straus and Giroux, 1995.
———. *Gain*. New York: Farrar, Straus and Giroux, 1998.
Pynchon, Thomas. *The Crying of Lot 49*. Philadelphia, PA: Lippincott, 1966.
Radway, Janice A. *A Feeling for Books: The Book-of-the-Month Club, Literary Taste, and Middle-Class Desire*. Chapel Hill: University of North Carolina Press, 1997.
Readings, Bill. *The University in Ruins*. Cambridge, MA: Harvard University Press, 1996.
Reed, Ishmael. *Shrovetide in Old New Orleans*. Garden City, NY: Doubleday, 1978.
Remnick, David. "Into the Clear: Philip Roth Puts Turbulence in its Place." *New Yorker* (May 8, 2000): 76–89.
Ross, Andrew. *No Respect: Intellectuals and Popular Culture*. New York: Routledge, 1989.
Roth, Philip. *Goodbye, Columbus and Five Short Stories*. Boston: Houghton Mifflin, 1959.
———. *Letting Go*. New York: Random House, 1962.
———. "Writing American Fiction." [1961] *Reading Myself and Others*. New York: Farrar, Straus and Giroux, 1975. 117–135.
——— *Operation Shylock. A Confession*. New York: Simon and Schuster, 1993.
———. *Sabbath's Theater*. Boston Houghton Mifflin, 1995.
———. *American Pastoral*. Boston: Houghton Mifflin, 1997.
———. *I Married a Communist*. New York: Houghton Mifflin, 1998.
———. *The Human Stain*. New York: Houghton Mifflin, 2000.
Sartre, Jean-Paul. *Critique of Dialectical Reason I: Theory of Practical Ensembles*. Translated by Alan Sheridan-Smith. London: NLB, 1976.
Schiffrin, André. *The Business of Books: How International Conglomerates Took Over Publishing and Changed the Way We Read*. London: Verso, 2000.
Schiller, Herbert. *Culture Inc.: The Corporate Takeover of Public Expression*. New York: Oxford University Press, 1989.
Seltzer, Mark. *Serial Killers: Death and Life in America's Wound Culture*. New York: Routledge, 1998.
Shattuc, Jane. *The Talking Cure: TV Talk Shows and Women*. New York: Routledge, 1997.
Sontag, Susan. *Against Interpretation, and Other Essays*. New York: Farrar, Straus and Giroux, 1966.
———. *Styles of Radical Will*. New York: Farrar, Straus and Giroux, 1969.
Steiner, Wendy. "Postmodern Fictions, 1970–1990." *The Cambridge History of American Literature, Volume 7: Prose Writing, 1940–1990*. Edited by Sacvan Bercovitch. Cambridge: Cambridge University Press, 1999. 425–538.
———. *Venus in Exile: The Rejection of Beauty in Twentieth-Century Art*. New York: Free Press, 2001.
Stevick, Philip. *Alternative Pleasures: Postrealist Fiction and the Tradition*. Urbana: University of Illinois Press, 1981.
Sukenick, Ronald. *In Form: Digressions on the Act of Fiction*. Carbondale: Southern Illinois University Press, 1985.
Tabbi, Joseph. "David Markson: An Introduction." *Review of Contemporary Fiction* 10.2 (1990): 91–103.

Tabbi, Joseph. "An Interview with David Markson." *Review of Contemporary Fiction* 10.2 (1990): 104–117.

———. *Postmodern Sublime: Technology and American Writing from Mailer to Cyberpunk*. Ithaca, NY: Cornell University Press, 1995.

———. *Cognitive Fictions*. Minneapolis: University of Minnesota Press, 2002.

Tanner, Tony. *City of Words: American Fiction, 1950–1970*. New York: Harper & Row, 1971.

Turing, Alan. "Computer Machinery and Intelligence." *Mind* 59 (1950): 433–460.

Wallace, David Foster. "The Empty Plenum: David Markson's *Wittgenstein's Mistress*." *Review of Contemporary Fiction* 10.2 (1990): 217–139.

———. "E Unibus Pluram: Television and U.S. Fiction." *A Supposedly Fun Thing I'll Never Do Again: Essays and Arguments*. Boston: Little, Brown, 1997. 21–82.

———. *Infinite Jest: A Novel*. Boston: Little, Brown, 1996.

Warner, Michael. "The Mass Public and the Mass Subject." *The Phantom Public Sphere*. Edited by Bruce Robbins. Minneapolis: University of Minnesota Press, 1993. 234–256.

Weber, Samuel. *Mass Mediauras: Form, Technics, Media*. Edited by Alan Cholodenko. Stanford, CA: Stanford University Press, 1996.

Weich, Dave. "Jonathan Franzen Uncorrected." http://www.powells.com/authors/franzen.html [interview conducted October 4, 2001].

Weisenburger, Steven. *Fables of Subversion: Satire and the American Novel, 1930–1980*. Athens: University of Georgia Press, 1995.

Williams, Raymond. *Marxism and Literature*. Oxford: Oxford University Press, 1977.

Winfrey, Oprah. "Oprah Winfrey Show Transcript, January 24, 2001" (Harpo Productions).

———. "Oprah Winfrey Show Transcript, May 2, 2002" (Harpo Productions).

Wood, James. "Tell Me How Does It Feel?" *The Guardian* (October 5, 2001).

Woolf, Virginia. *Mr. Bennett and Mrs. Brown*. London: Hogarth Press, 1924.

Yardley, Jonathan. "The Story of O." *Washington Post* (October 28, 2001): C. 02.

INDEX

Sukenick, Ronald, 29, 32
Sula (Morrison), 81
Surrealism, 2, 63

Tabbi, Joseph, 149
Technology, vii, viii, 5, 6, 8, 32, 37–38, 47, 50, 57–58, 93–94, 117, 118, 120–134 *passim*, 146, 171, 173–184, 214
Tempest, The (Shakespeare), 59
This Is Not a Novel (Markson), 16, 149, 150, 161
Thomas, Dylan, 149
Time of Our Singing, The (Powers), 117
Titus Andronicus (Shakespeare), 202
Tolstoy, Leo, 52
Tractatus Logico-Philosophicus (Wittgenstein), 155
Turow, Scott, 93
Twain, Mark, 54
Tyler, Anne, 103

Under the Volcano (Lowry), 149
Underworld (DeLillo), 164, 166, 167–168, 174, 181–184
Updike, John, 97
Utopia, 14, 76–77, 202–209

V. (Pynchon), 190
Vanishing Point (Markson), 149, 150
Vonnegut Jr., Kurt, 25, 32, 51

Walking Tour, The (Davis), 16
Wallace, David Foster, 4, 155, 217–218 n10
Wallace, George, 176
Warhol, Andy, 20, 21
Warner, Michael, 17, 167
Weber, Max, 3
Weber, Samuel, 177
Wells, H.G., 76
West, Nathanael, 186
White Noise (DeLillo), 170–171
Whitman, Walt, 186
Wilson, Edmund, 75
Winfrey, Oprah, 14, 16, 39, 79–89, 90
Wittgenstein, Ludwig, 155, 156, 229 n20
Wittgenstein's Mistress (Markson), 16, 149, 150, 152, 153–158
Wolff, Tobias, 192
Wood, James, 211–212
Woolf, Virginia, 76, 137
Wright, Stephen, 4
Wyeth, Andrew, 194–195